Praise for Lorelei James's
All Jacked Up

"...Besides the extra steamy love scenes, ALL JACKED UP is filled with snappy dialogue and lots of tenderness and emotion. This was definitely a book to read through in one night, because it was just too good to put down."
~ *Cheryl M., Romance Junkies*

"...The characters of Keely and Jack are rich and nicely developed, the plot fast moving, the sex blistering hot...I can safely say that All Jacked Up is now my new favorite in a series filled with keeper books..."
~ *Mystical Nymph, Literary Nymphs Reviews*

"...This is one sexually explosive adventure you don't want to miss...Jack and Keely's story is another great addition to this series and one that I will continue to re-read as more of the Rough Riders books are released..."
~ *Jacquelyn W., The Romance Studio*

"...I was thoroughly entertained by their verbal sparring and witty banter. They're a well matched pair, with electric chemistry and as much as they try to fight against it, by professing to hate each other, it's not long before "hate" turns into passion in this wonderful story..."
~ *Kara, Fallen Angel Reviews*

"Ahhh....Another winner penned by Lorelei James...Jack and Keely are in for a wild ride trying to convince their families and friends that they love each other... This was another great book that you should definitely pick up!"
~ *Laura, Two Lips Reviews*

Look for these titles by
Lorelei James

All Jacked Up

Lorelei James

A Samhain Publishing, Ltd. publication.

Samhain Publishing, Ltd.
577 Mulberry Street, Suite 1520
Macon, GA 31201
www.samhainpublishing.com

Editing by Lindsey Faber
Cover by Scott Carpenter

First Samhain Publishing, Ltd. electronic publication: November 2009
First Samhain Publishing, Ltd. print publication: October 2010

Dedication

To wild child bad girls—current, former, wannabe—everywhere, and the men who want to claim them, rather than tame them...

Chapter One

Keely McKay's lucky cowgirl boots kicked up clouds of dust as she paced across the wooden plank floor.

A mouse skittered in front of her and she jumped like a scalded cat.

So much for maintaining nerves of steel.

Well, at least she hadn't shrieked like a scream queen from some cheesy slasher flick.

In the last twenty-three minutes and forty-two seconds she'd chewed her bottom lip to the point she tasted blood beneath the cherry-flavored lip gloss. Not only that, her fingers hurt from continually cracking her knuckles. Frogs jumped in her stomach and were stuck in her throat. She'd clenched her jaw hard enough to make her earlobes sting. Given her erratic physical reactions, one would believe she was facing the hangman's noose. An executioner's blade. Or a blind date.

She was meeting a man. A man she didn't know. A man she'd never spoken to. A man who held her entire future in his hands.

And that absolutely chapped her ass, sucked balls and blew donkey dick.

No man ever had that much power over Keely McKay. She'd made sure of it. Even with five older brothers, and a dozen older male cousins, she'd always been the queen bee. Using her stubbornness to get her way, not her feminine wiles.

Not that she was opposed to flashing her cleavage to get a leg up in this situation.

No need. You are a professional, qualified woman. Not a Nervous Nellie. Not a Wild Child. Buck up. Chin up. This is your time to shine.

There were a hundred reasons why good fortune should finally smile on her. She'd done everything right on the business front: secured the funding and found the building to further the cause she believed in. On the personal side: she was a loving daughter, a dedicated sister, a loyal friend, an involved aunt. A proud member of the Wyoming community she'd grown up in and hoped to grow old in. She took pride in her ability to connect with people from all walks of life. She derived great joy from helping people. Heck, she'd chosen her career because she was good at those things.

She wasn't looking for kudos or glory, just a place where she could do what she loved, help people heal close to home— close to their families.

Now that her dream of giving back to the community— filling a need for rural healthcare—was within her grasp, would this mysterious man help smooth a path to success? Or would he trip her up?

Maybe all this worry was for nothing. Maybe she'd get lucky. God knew if the decision were based on hard work, dedication, knowledge and drive, she'd be golden.

Restless, she wandered through the main floor of the century-old building, originally Moorcroft's first general store. During the course of its existence, it'd housed the post office and an attorney's office. For the last thirty years it'd sat empty.

She'd always wondered why no one had renovated the stalwart stone building—an answer she was now learning firsthand. New construction of steel frame structures was easier, cheaper, faster and more efficient. Hence, many historic buildings were lost to the blade of a bulldozer or tumbled by a wrecking ball. A sad situation for a western state with precious few architectural treasures in the first place.

So the State of Wyoming had wisened up and toughened regulations, forming the Wyoming Historical Western Preservation Committee to deal with the lax construction policies and administration of fines. The committee also gauged a structure's historical merit, determining those to be listed on the official register, as well as overseeing any structural and architectural changes of registered buildings, both on the state level and with recommendation to the National Historic Register.

Talk about a taste of bureaucracy.

After dealing with committees and subcommittees, and tracking down funding sources, Keely discovered the entire house of cards depended upon whether she could convince the certified architectural restoration specialist to oversee the project. The company representative insisted on making a personal appearance to gauge the validity of the proposed project before rendering a decision.

As if the situation wasn't convoluted enough, she'd inadvertently discovered the restoration company she'd contacted and the company that owned the Sandstone Building she lived in...were one in the same. Western Property Management Services and Full Circle Consulting shared the same PO box in Denver.

If she believed in fate, she'd take that as a good sign.

The door creaked and a shaft of sunlight seared her retinas. Keely blocked the bright ray with her hand, willing her heart to stop racing as fast as a spooked antelope. This was it. Her future. Her destiny.

Please. Just this one time. Let things go my way.

She plastered on a charming smile.

As the form sauntered closer, Keely blinked several times. No way. Had to be a trick of the light. Or a trick of the swirling dust motes. Her eyes—shit, maybe she needed glasses. The male figure with a laconic walk looked like...nah. It couldn't be him.

Could it?

All six foot four inches, two hundred odd pounds of muscle and grace pulled into sharp focus.

Keely gasped like a Victorian maiden.

Or maybe she had stumbled onto the set of a low budget horror movie.

The man was a stunning example of masculine flawlessness.

And the dead last man in the world Keely ever wanted to deal with.

Her brother's best friend.

The older brother of the guy who'd dumped her.

The jerk who'd left her high and dry at her brother's wedding reception three years ago.

11

Jack Donohue.

That bitch fate had a nasty sense of humor.

Chapter Two

Jack Donohue believed he'd adequately prepared himself for meeting Keely McKay. Boning up on his sarcasm. Practicing his disdain. Confident those reactions would prevent his instantaneous red-hot jolt of desire.

It didn't work. The damn woman had gotten under his skin like a burr. Or tick. Or a fever. Or blood poisoning.

His gaze zoomed over her pointy-toed boots, skintight denim, gaudy rhinestone belt, plaid, pearl-buttoned shirt and stopped on her arms defiantly folded across her chest.

Definitely not his type.

A square, yet decidedly feminine jaw shadowed her willowy neck. Her upper lip was a perfect cupid's bow. Her lower lip was plump in the center and drooped outward slightly, which contrasted with the upturned corners of her wide mouth, creating a permanent smirk. Jack remembered how sweet and hot her smirking mouth felt moving beneath his.

Her pert, freckled nose wrinkled. Those sapphire blue eyes blazed and his groin tightened in response.

Jesus. What kind of sick fuck got off on a woman glaring at him?

You. When the woman in question has starred in your X-rated fantasies for the last eleven years.

No doubt his intense scrutiny would raise her ire. Chances were slim the hotheaded cowgirl had mastered the art of curbing her tongue.

"You've got to be kidding me. *You* are Full Circle Consulting? And Western Property Management?"

He tried—and failed—not to look smug. "Afraid so."

"Not only are you my expert consultant, you're my landlord?"

"I thought you might be surprised."

"Surprised? Try shocked. Dismayed. Completely and utterly crushed. Talk about unreal. Could my life get any worse at this moment?" She held up her hand. "No. Please. Don't answer that. I cannot believe I pinned all my hopes on this..." Her voice broke and she turned away.

He waited, but Keely didn't toss out a barbed parting shot. She didn't do anything at all.

Damn. Why was he disappointed? He hadn't prepared for her immediate admission of defeat. He'd anticipated verbal sparring. Sad that he'd actually looked forward to going head to head with Keely. Her insults were lightning fast and usually funny as hell—even if he refused to admit that to her. "Look, surprise factor aside, can I ask you something?"

Keely offered him a bad-tempered shrug.

"Did Carter send you to me for help with this project?"

"No. Carter doesn't know I've bought this building."

He frowned. "Why not?"

"Because it's my deal, okay? I didn't want interference from my brothers. Ditto for my parents, my aunts, my uncles and two billion cousins."

"Doesn't the McKay family handbook clearly state you all have to tell each other everything?"

His attempt at humor fell short when Keely flicked him a dour look. "Go ahead and call Carter. Laugh with him about his clueless little sister. I should be used to it by now."

Her retreat into silence disturbed him. He waited for her to speak or to lash out or something.

But minutes ticked by and nothing passed through her compressed lips but angry puffs of air.

Finally, Jack said, "What's really going on here? No bullshit charm, Keely. No insults. No half-truths."

Keely sagged against the wall. "Buying this crappy old building was the first step of turning my dream into reality."

"What dream?"

She studied him to gauge his sincerity. Apparently she found something that allowed her to offer an explanation. "My dream has been to open a physical therapy clinic with enough space to eventually expand into a full-service healthcare center."

Jack was taken aback. And a little impressed. "Really?"

She nodded. "Rural healthcare sucks, especially out here where it can be a hundred miles between towns of any size. For the last four years, I've worked my ass off saving money to open my own rehab clinic. Dr. Monroe has referred her repetitive injury patients to me and she promised if I got the place up and running, she'd open a satellite office here. So, I've been moonlighting at the VA in Cheyenne for the cash and the practical experience. At some point, I realized this building was ideal. Not too big. Not too small. Centrally located. Perfect, right? Still, I knew my brothers would try to talk me out of buying it because it needs so much work, but there's just something about this forgotten place that speaks to me. That's why I didn't tell them. They wouldn't get it."

He recognized Keely's frustration at having a vision no one else saw or understood.

"I wanted something that was just mine. I wanted to do it my way, with my money, and my ideas. But this clinic would benefit everyone, not just me, so it's not about my ego but about me wanting to help people." Her eyes searched his, almost frantically. "Haven't you ever wanted to prove yourself? To be different or do something different from what people expect of you?"

"Of course."

"So I was feeling cocky that I'd pulled it off. Everything was going miraculously well. The real estate broker kept quiet. As did the banker. I thought I'd jumped through all the proper hoops. Imagine my surprise when I learned I can't change a freakin' thing on the building that I now *own* without the step-by-step approval of some damn committee."

Welcome to his world.

"Oh, and on top of that, I have to hire a qualified expert, already certified by the committee, to oversee the remodeling process. So the specialist can reassure the committee that my contractors aren't destroying the 'unique and key' elements that make it a historic building."

Jack dealt with the pros and cons of rebuilding versus restoration every damn day and it never got easier. Or clearer.

"This place was—*is*—in absolute disrepair. Know what's

asinine? The committee would let the building fall to ruin rather than allow me to make desperately needed improvements that don't meet with some—" she gestured wildly, "—obscure set of rules. Which was why I contacted Full Circle Consulting."

"Lucky me," he drawled.

"I had not a friggin' clue you owned the company or trust me, Jack, I never would've called you."

"I'm deeply hurt."

"Don't give me ideas," she warned.

"Did you try another company?"

"They turned me down. The project is too small and they're too busy. The other companies I found aren't certified in Wyoming. It could take up to a year for the official certification process, provided they actually give a damn about becoming certified in Wyoming—which most don't."

"Look. To be honest, it's not about the money. I don't have the time—"

"For a small-potatoes project like this? You could've saved yourself some of that precious time and called me rather than driving up here from Colorado. Or was the prospect of seeing my disappointment too big a temptation to resist? Did you rub your hands with glee at the thought of crushing my dreams?"

"Keely, just listen—"

"Don't you dare try and placate me, Jack Donohue."

"I'm not. What was the name of the other company you contacted?"

"BDM Incorporated. They're based out of Chicago. Anyway, it doesn't really matter now, does it? I'm screwed." She spun on the bootheel and disappeared around the corner.

Jack clenched his fist by his side. BDM. His former partner Baxter's company. Baxter's luxury of blithely turning down work, when Jack raced all over the damn country taking every job in every podunk town from Barrow, Alaska to Bangor, Maine, burned his ass.

You don't have to take every job. You don't need the money.

True, but it was a matter of pride to prove to the restoration community that his expertise was just as much in demand as Baxter's after their professional split. Jack suspected the reason Baxter's company had refused to consider Keely's restoration was because BDM was in the queue for a prestigious project in

Utah.

A select group of architectural specialists had been invited to bid on a complete restoration of two city blocks in the small burg of Milford, Utah. The Milford Historical Preservation Consortium was a privately funded organization, insistent upon hiring a company whose morals and ideals meshed with theirs.

Although Jack's professional qualifications were top-flight, his personal qualifications had disappointed the committee. No long-term relationship, no wife, no kids, no religious affiliation.

Baxter retained the advantage on the Milford project because he was married. During their partnership, Baxter's main focus had been drumming up business. Jack stayed in the trenches with the contractors and traveled extensively while Baxter remained in the Chicago office. Baxter's availability was why Jack's former girlfriend Martine was now Baxter's wife.

Martine. Beautiful. Educated. Sophisticated. Every quality Jack had required in a woman. The double whammy of Martine and Baxter's betrayal had nearly crippled him. Baxter was twenty years Martine's senior, a balding man with a big gut and a bigger mouth, but Baxter's bank account was his biggest asset.

Rather than allow the situation to explode into an ugly scandal, Jack bowed out of the partnership, licked his wounds, relocated to Colorado and hung out his shingle. Now his former partner was his main competition.

Too bad Jack couldn't conjure up a wife. Then Baxter would be out on his fat ass as far as the Milford job. Jack wanted that project and he'd do anything to get it.

Anything.

So what are you doing in Wyoming, pissing with Keely McKay? She can't help you.

But you could help her. This is a noble project. And you're a quart low on nobility since you've been chasing the gravy train the last few years.

Nudged by his conscience, Jack followed the foot-traffic pattern on the dusty floor, mentally tallying the building wreckage as he bypassed it.

Keely stood in front of a busted window, staring at the faded blacktop. She whirled around, her body stiffening at his approach.

Jack's body stiffened too—for an entirely different reason. The sweet perfume of spring lilacs wafted toward him. Pure lust grabbed him by the short hairs. That intoxicating aroma had haunted him since the night he'd filled his lungs with her scent. Breathing nothing but her. Tasting nothing but her. Swallowing her hunger and letting it feed his... He shook his head to clear the memory. It hadn't ended well. Every encounter with Keely McKay ended badly.

Whose fault is that?

His. Hers. Who the hell knew why they threw atomic sparks off each other?

"So, did you follow me just to glare at me? Or have you already formulated a nasty comment to fling at me before you leave?"

"Maybe I'm formulating an eviction notice."

Keely's lush lips parted, then flattened.

"Tell me, Miz McKay, why was I unaware you were renting the Sandstone apartment?"

"Tell me, Mr. Donohue, why was I unaware you were my landlord for the Sandstone apartment?" she lobbed back.

Jack ignored her taunt. "I hate that you pulled one over on me."

"I imagine so. But that sort of makes us even for you pulling one over on me today, doncha think?"

"Not even close."

"Besides, it's hardly *my* fault you are unaware of your individual renters. I sent references, which *your* company approved. I paid the security deposit, which *your* company still has."

"That doesn't change the fact had I known, I never would've rented to you."

Keely shifted to an aggressive posture. "Why not?"

"Because I don't like you. I don't trust you."

"Ditto, but your personal dislike is a moot point because I've never been late paying rent. It's not like I'm throwing wild parties or staging orgies."

When he quirked a questioning brow at the "orgies" comment, she cocked her head pertly. Like a trained dog. Right. Keely McKay was more pit bull than pampered poodle and he ought to brace himself for her biting sarcasm. "Being rude to

18

me is not helping your situation," Jack pointed out.

"Just how could my situation get any worse? The apartment I've lived in for two years—"

"Two years? My property management company doesn't offer two year contracts."

Her defiant chin lifted a notch. "I finished the term of Domini's lease after she married Cam. I applied the following year under my own name when the lease came up for renewal. Like I said, your company could've denied me then."

During that crazy time, not only had Jack dissolved his partnership with Baxter Ducheyne, his father had also died unexpectedly. Jack's attention to his rental properties had been nearly nonexistent. Owning properties in three states meant he couldn't remember every tenant, but Keely's name would've jumped out at him like a rabid skunk.

"As the building owner, I can terminate any lease agreement at any time, for any reason."

"Is that your way of telling me to pack my shit?"

As much as he wanted to bark out a gleeful *yes!* he hesitated. Carter McKay would be livid if Jack unceremoniously booted his beloved baby sister from the apartment, particularly when Carter discovered Jack hadn't disclosed that he owned the Sandstone Building. The same building which housed the restaurant Carter's wife managed as well as three other businesses owned by various McKay spouses.

Talk about a clusterfuck.

"Hello? Earth to Jack."

Jack refocused. Keely glared at him. Jesus. She was gorgeous when she was pissed off. Maybe especially when she was pissed off.

"You gonna answer me? Or do you have a limp tongue as well as a limp—"

"Careful what you say next, cowgirl," Jack warned. "You'd be wise not to tick off your landlord."

She snorted. "You're kicking me out anyway, so what do I have to lose?"

"I haven't decided if I'm kicking you out."

Keely's razor-sharp gaze pierced him. "Now are you going to tease me and claim you're not passing on the project?"

He shrugged, knowing his non-response would drive her

crazy.

She waited.

So did he.

"Answer me. Why are you dicking with my head, Jack?"

"Because I can. Because I get off on it."

"I'll tell you where to get off, bucko."

"Big talk. I suspect you're all talk."

"I am not all talk," she huffed.

"Then take your best shot." Jack grinned nastily. "But you'd better make it count, because what goes around, comes around."

Her eyes flicked over him from head to toe. "Such macho trash talk from coming from a guy who's dressed like he just stepped off the cover of *GQ*."

"Says the woman who's a candidate for *What Not To Wear*," he volleyed back.

"Ooh." Keely snapped her fingers in a Z shape. "You told me, girlfriend. Will your boyfriend be jealous we're tossing bitchy banter back and forth?"

Jack laughed. "*That's* your best shot? Accusing me of being gay?"

Keely snorted again. "Accusing? Dude. My gaydar goes haywire around you."

"And you're an expert in all things gay because you live in Buttfuck, Wyoming?" he said with amusement.

"Why, Jack-off... You actually have a sense of humor! You should share that playful side more often. Guys really go for it."

He laughed again. "Name one thing about me that sets off your finely honed gaydar sensors."

Her gaze dropped to the floor. "Your shoes. Straight men don't wear tasseled loafers."

"Bullshit."

"Okay. Straight men in *Wyoming* don't wear tasseled loafers. But since you're from South Dakota, maybe you missed the memo." Keely studied him helpfully. "I'll even impart a bonus reason why my gaydar goes off."

Fascinated by her twisted logic, Jack murmured, "This ought to be stellar."

"Remember what happened at Colt and India's wedding

reception? Or should I say what *didn't* happen? That proves you're not attracted to—"

"It only proved I'm not attracted to *you*, cowgirl." He was such a liar. And a sucker. The immediate hurt look in Keely's eyes almost weakened him into apologizing for being a jerk now and being an idiot back then.

But Keely rallied. "If you are so hetero, why haven't I ever seen you with a woman?"

"Because we don't exactly run in the same social circles."

"Justin let it slip you've never brought a woman home. So I'm just saying..."

Jack hadn't brought his girlfriends home due to his never-ending embarrassment about being raised on a farm. "Unlike my little brother, I don't drag every skank home to meet Mom."

Keely's jaw dropped. "Are you calling me a skank?"

"Are you denying you had a threesome with my brother and his best friend?"

"No, but if that makes me a skank then you're one too! I overheard Carter bragging to Colt about you guys having threesomes all the damn time in college!"

The woman had balls. Keely didn't apologize, justify or explain her past sexual behavior. Strange to think he would've thought less of her if she had.

Several brutal moments passed.

Finally, something clicked with her and she backed up. Way up. A look of mortification entered her eyes. "I'm sorry. God. I don't know what it is about you that pushes all my wrong buttons, Jack. Insulting you... Lord. I'm usually way more professional than that and I apologize. Profusely."

The sincerity of her regret surprised him.

She sighed and crossed her arms over her chest. "It's not your fault everything is so screwed up. It's also not your problem that I naively pinned all my hopes on Full Circle Consulting to get me back on track. I know better. I-I just wish there was something..." Her voice dropped and she bit her lip.

Oh fuck no. Was tough as nails Keely McKay about to burst into tears?

Don't fall for it.

But he found himself drawn to her anyway. "Hey. Cowgirl. Don't cry."

"I'm not." She expelled a watery laugh. "Although, you should know I was prepared to throw myself at your feet and promise I'll do anything if you'll help me."

Anything? Now we're talking.

A preposterous idea began to form. One so...crazy she might actually go for it. Maybe they could help each other out.

"Anything?" he prompted.

Keely's steely, yet teary-eyed gaze met his. "Yes. Anything."

Jack leaned forward. "Then marry me."

Chapter Three

"M-marry you?" Keely sputtered. "Is this some kind of sick joke?"

"No. I'm dead-ass serious."

"Why the fuck would I marry you? I don't even *like* you."

"Back atcha, babe, but this could solve both of our problems."

"You are my problem," she grumbled.

"Just hear me out, okay?"

"I'll listen until the guys with the straightjackets arrive, because you are certifiable."

Jack loomed over her, his vibrant green eyes blazing. "Didn't you just say you'd do *anything* to get me to oversee your project?"

"Yes. But—"

"Then shut up and listen."

Damn man. Bossing her around.

You like it. You like that he doesn't fall in line.

"Last week I was shut out of consideration for a huge restoration project because of my marital status...or lack thereof."

Keely blinked at him. "Why would it matter whether or not you were married?"

"It just does," he said testily.

"Is the remodel job in a nunnery or something?" Heaven knew Jack Donohue would tempt a nun into tasting the sins of the flesh. Repeatedly. With absolute gusto and zero repentance.

"No. But you're thinking along the right lines. The committee choosing the overseeing company for this project is very conservative, very traditional and they have the money to be choosy." He sighed. "Might seem weird, but religious organizations often select their contractors based on their religious preference."

"Really?"

He nodded. "Say the Catholic church is adding on. They have the right to consider only Catholic contractors. This group set up parameters that might seem unusual, but I've dealt with far worse constraints, believe me."

"Is it an issue of the consultant having to live in this conservative town for the duration of the project? Is the committee afraid a hot single guy will pose a threat to the unattached ladies?"

"Hot single guy?" he repeated, tacking on a bad-boy grin. "Careful, Keely, you might give me the wrong idea that you're somewhat attracted to me."

Instead of saying, *You are all that hotness and a bag of chips, baby,* Keely rolled her eyes.

"After I visited the site and met with the committee last week, I knew they were interested in my ideas. But when it came to my personal life...their enthusiasm waned."

Her brain warned, *Don't ask him if the committee thinks he's gay,* but it was no use; her mouth ignored the directive. "Are they afraid you have a male lover hiding in the closet at home?"

With that snarky comment, she'd pushed Jack too far.

He crowded her against the wall. "You looking for a firsthand demonstration of my heterosexual prowess, cowgirl? Because I'm more than up for the challenge."

Please. Your body is hot and hard and you smell so damn good and it's been ages since I've had a real man this sexy this close to me. "Umm..."

"Jesus." Jack leapt back and rubbed the squished section of skin between his dark eyebrows. "You can rile me up in no time flat."

"Which is why this marriage idea would never work. We've come to verbal blows more than a few times."

"True."

"Plus we don't even live in the same state."

"Let me think." He paced, muttering to himself. He stopped

in front of her with a triumphant gleam. "A wedding is out. How about if we announce we're engaged?"

"Engaged in what? Battle? Not a newsflash, Jack."

He scowled. "Smartass. I'm serious."

"So am I. How is an engagement any better?"

"It'd explain why we're living apart."

Keely stared at him. "You are insane. How do you propose we explain the fact we can't stand each other?"

"We'd have to change that. In public we'll have to moon around in love or some such sappy shit. Pretend we rock each other's world."

She swallowed her immediate response—*never fucking happening*—and said, "That's impossible."

Those piercing green eyes narrowed. "Why? Are you in a relationship?"

"No. What about you?"

"It's been three years since I found my girlfriend fucking my business partner and I ended up getting fucked."

Whoa. Some woman was stupid enough to cheat on Jack Donohue? Keely wanted the down and dirty details, but Jack stalked off. He jammed his hand through his hair as he stared out the dirt-caked window.

"Jack? What happened?"

"My personal and professional life went up in flames. None of that garbage matters now. But this job in Milford? It's more than a job. It's like I have a chance to get back what I lost."

His embarrassment sparked a feeling scarily close to real sympathy. And empathy. Salvaging pride was something she understood. "Look, before I scream *no fucking way* and run, spell out exactly what I gain from this devil's bargain, if I decide to do it."

"I'll personally oversee your restoration project. After I examine the renovation plans from your contractor, I'll call the head of the Wyoming Historic Preservation Committee and officially sign on as your consultant. They'll expect me to monitor compliance frequently since this will be a rush job."

Her head buzzed with a mix of excitement and fear. Maybe her life wasn't in the toilet. But she played it cool. "What would you expect from me?"

"I'll need a minimum of one month commitment from you.

During this engagement you'll travel to Milford with me and convince the committee we're madly in love."

"Didn't you tell me the committee is aware you've been single for a while?"

Jack paced again. "I didn't share specifics on my personal life. I more or less sidestepped the question. But there has to be a way we can convince them we've secretly been together for the last few months..." He snapped his fingers. "Aha! I've got it."

"Got what?"

"The reason we didn't go public with our relationship—even with families—was because of our rocky past. I saw you as my best friend's pesky little sister; you were dumped by my little brother. But we crossed paths again when you needed my help with this restoration project. It turned into something more than a working relationship. Each hour we spent together built on our past as a bridge to our future until *bam*—change of heart."

Keely began to clap.

Jack gave her that devil-may-care grin and bestowed a deep bow.

"I have no doubt the story is plausible for the Milford crowd, but you're forgetting one teensy tiny detail. We can't be selective about who we tell. We have to tell everyone. Which means we have to convince my entire family that we're a couple."

A look of horror crossed his face.

"See what I mean? No one who knows us will *ever* believe we put our differences aside. Not for an hour, not for a day and certainly not forever. Neither one of us can act that well. So thanks for stopping by personally and ruining my life." Keely ducked under his arm and started walking away.

"That's it?"

"Yep. Don't let the door hit your ass on the way out. Literally. It might fall and crush you."

His deep, sexy laugh unfurled an unwanted reaction low in her belly.

"What's so funny?"

"I thought you said you weren't all talk. I never imagined wild child Keely McKay was afraid."

Keely wheeled around. "Excuse me? What am I afraid of?"

"Me."

"For Christsake! That's ridiculous. Why would I be afraid of you?"

"Maybe you're afraid I can make you fall in love with me for real."

"*Make* me fall in love with you? Dude. The only thing you make me want to do is punch you in the face."

"See? Sarcasm is a defense mechanism to mask your fear." With each word he'd closed the distance between them. "So it's easier to slink away."

"Oh. My. God. I knew you had a big ego, but—"

Jack clamped his hands on her butt. Keely shrieked but he held tight, jerking her lower body to his. "An ego isn't the only thing that's big about me, baby. Want to ride on the Jack-hammer? Guaranteed to rev you up all night long."

Eww. Eww. Eww. "Let go!"

"There's no shame in admitting you want me." He nuzzled the skin in front of her ear and a shiver trilled down her neck.

"Is this greasy used car salesman act supposed to be turning me on? Because it ain't working, bucko."

He laughed softly. "Not trying to turn you on, just proving I can act. You really believed I'd morphed into a creepy scuzzball, huh?"

Yes, dammit. Jack won that round.

"We can do this, Keely. If you say yes, we'll both get what we want: you'll get the building remodel approval, I'll have a chance at the Milford project and we'll both have our pride. After it's over we can go back to hating each other, same as always."

Keely admitted there was a certain appeal in his off-the-wall proposal. She'd kept her family in the dark about the purchase of the building and her career plans. If she confessed the reason for her secretiveness was also due in part to her intimate relationship with her former nemesis, Jack Donohue...that would make perfect sense.

Jack whispered huskily, "I can tell you're warming to the idea."

"How?"

"You're pressing yourself into me instead of away from me."

She was? Holy crap! What was wrong with her? Keely put

her hands on his firm chest and tried to shove him. The damn solid man didn't budge. He squeezed her closer. "Now, is that any way to treat your intended?"

"I intend to scour myself with bleach when this is all over."

"Fair enough. But for now…do we have a deal?"

Say no. Scream no. It's not worth it.

"Yes. But—"

Jack held up his hand and dug out his cell phone. He dialed. Waited with a smug grin. "Henry? Jack Donohue. I just wanted to thank you for your hospitality last week. Milford is a great town and I appreciate the chance to talk with you and the committee about my ideas. Anyway, the reason I called… Did you perchance find a gold watch in your office? Oh. No, that's fine. I'm just wondering how to explain the loss of it to my fiancée, since it was a gift from her."

No going back now.

He locked his gaze to hers. "Really? I thought I'd told you about Keely. No? Well, we've kept it under wraps, but the cat is out of the bag now." Jack's teeth gleamed a victorious smile. "Of course I'd love to bring her to Milford. Sure. Call me after you talk to the committee and have a firm date."

He hung up, punching the air with a loud "Yes!" the most juvenile gesture she'd witnessed from stick-up-his-ass Jack Donohue. "It's on."

"So I gathered. What now?"

Jack looked at his watch. "As much as I don't want to drive back to Denver, I've got no choice. But I'll be back tomorrow with my stuff."

"Stuff? What stuff? Work stuff?"

"And personal stuff. I'll be working out of the apartment for a while. There's wireless Internet, right?"

"Whoa whoa whoa. Working out of the apartment? As in *my* apartment?"

"Remember who owns the building? Now it's *our* apartment," he corrected with an edge to his voice. "Not only will I be working here, I'll be living here."

"What? No! Oh, hell no. You can't just move in with me."

Cue his wolfish grin. "Oh, cowgirl, I most certainly can."

Holy shit. He could. She was so monumentally screwed.

"Have the building plans ready for me to look at day after

tomorrow."

"Don't boss me around, Jack."

"Get used to it, Keely."

Did he honestly expect her to play the part of docile little wifey-to-be when they weren't in the public eye?

Fuck that.

Before Keely voiced a protest, Jack tucked her hair behind her ear, letting his sure, yet teasing touch linger on the curve of her cheek. God. He had the most amazing hands.

"Why don't you set up dinner with your parents? So we can tell them our good news. Hopefully that'll pave the way to convincing your family we're head over heels in love."

She wrinkled her nose. Right. If Cam leveled his nasty cop stare at her, she'd spill her guts. Carter would cajole and tease her into admitting it was a sham. Colt could pin her down and tickle the truth out of her. Colby would tie her to the corral until she confessed the hard facts. Cord would just send his wife AJ to nag her. Her best friend would never believe Keely was knocking loafers with Jack, let alone letting those loafers reside under her bed permanently.

This so wasn't going to work.

Jack retreated and pointed at her. "That's exactly what I'm talking about, Keely. You'd better get used to gazing at me with adoration, not disgust."

"Yeah? Then you'd better bring me a big goddamn engagement ring as an incentive to pretend I love you."

Late the following afternoon, Jack yelled, "Honey, I'm home."

Keely gaped at him as he scaled the stairs. "Jesus, Jack, why don't you scream that a little louder so AJ, India and Domini all come barreling up here?"

An oversized duffel and an enormous suit bag hit the landing at the top of the stairs. "But their feminine squealing about your good luck landing me as your mate might be a tad embarrassing for you, buttercup."

"You are about four seconds from me knocking you off this landing, bucko."

"No big, wet, sloppy kiss for your traveling man? Fine."

Jack adjusted the backpack straps and bent down to retrieve his other bags.

She elbowed him in the gut as soon as his hands were full. "There's your kiss—Irish style, *honey*."

"Dammit, Keely. That was uncalled for."

"Probably. But it was fun."

"Payback's a bitch. Remember that."

She had a feeling it was going to be a long night.

They decided to stick to basics about the engagement. Keely had contacted Jack for his expertise on her concerns about buying the building. They met in Denver and Cheyenne, talked, one thing led to another...blah blah blah. Instant love.

Too bad she'd had to suck down two slugs of whiskey before her "love" drove them out to her folks' house.

Jack parked by the barn and faced her. "Ready?"

"No. We're forgetting something." She pinned him with a dubious look. "Crap. I don't have an engagement ring. They won't believe you can't live without me if you—"

"I bought a damn ring, Keely." He opened the glove compartment and pulled out a blue velvet jewelry box. "We should've done this earlier, so I hope it fits. May I have your hand?"

Keely closed her eyes as the cool metal slid up to her knuckle. This was not how she imagined the magic moment when the man of her dreams slipped a ring on her finger.

"You afraid to look?" he prompted.

"Uh-huh."

Jack chuckled. "Come on, cowgirl, give me some credit. I didn't dig it out of a Cracker Jack box."

Her hand felt heavy. No wonder. When she peeked at the square cut diamond set in a platinum band, she realized the stone was the size of her fingernail. Keely met Jack's gaze. "Is this for real?"

"What? The stone? Yes, it's real."

"Guess you took me seriously about the gigantic ring, huh?"

"I figured ten plus carats would get your attention."

"And the attention of anyone within a mile." Keely waggled her fingers, admiring the diamond's flash of brilliance. "This is spectacular. I don't know what to say."

"That's gotta be a first," he said dryly. "*Thank you, Jack*, would be a start."

Keely angled across the console and placed her hand on his smoothly shaven cheek. "Thank you, Jack."

His eyes were soft, a luminous green, nearly hypnotic. The moment was so intimate she almost believed it was real.

Her dad knocked on the window and barked, "You comin' in or what?" and brought a screaming halt to her momentary lapse in judgment.

Jack kissed the inside of her forearm and mouthed, "Show time."

Nerves danced in her belly. Over the years she'd stretched or circumvented the truth with her parents, but never uttered such a bald-faced lie as, "Jack and I are getting married!"

Keely's parents took the news like she'd expected: complete and utter disbelief.

Of course, her mother tried to be polite. Show some kind of enthusiasm and not accuse her only daughter of absolute insanity.

Her father wasn't so tactful. He demanded to know if she was pregnant.

Keely deflected additional questions about their impending nuptials by discussing her purchase of the Brewster Building. In minute detail. She'd droned on so long she'd even managed to bore herself in the highly embellished retelling.

"How'd you keep something this big under wraps, girlie?" her father challenged.

"The usual. Threats. Bribes." She fluttered her lashes at Jack. "Charm. When it all came together so suddenly, it seemed like..."

"Destiny," Jack finished silkily.

Oh gag.

"It's too goddamn quick, if you ask me," her dad groused.

"What? Me buying the building? Or me getting married?"

"Both. How do you know what you're getting into?"

"I didn't. That's why I contacted Jack. He's the expert."

Her dad's eyes darkened further. "Expert? Hell, how many

times have you been married, boy?"

"None," Jack answered evenly.

"Daddy, I was talking about Jack's restoration expertise, not his marriage expertise."

Carson harrumphed.

"Have you thought about a wedding date?" Carolyn asked.

Jack sent Carolyn a dazzling smile. "I'd vote for immediately, but it depends on our schedules. Keely is anxious to get the clinic up and running, so finishing the building is our first priority."

"We talking weeks or months?"

"Months, probably."

Carolyn sipped her tea and cast Carson a sly look. "You thinking what I'm thinking, dear?"

"That this engagement is a sign of the apocalypse?"

"Daddy!" She looked to her mother for support and wished she hadn't. Shit. This was not going well. Her mother's eyes held that calculating squint that never boded well for anyone.

"No. I'm thinking we can throw Keely and Jack an engagement party the likes this town has never seen. Right away."

Keely stopped stirring her mashed potatoes. "What? No. Ma. That's not necessary—"

"Of course it's necessary, sweetheart. Our only daughter is tying the knot with the man of her dreams. We want everyone— and I mean *everyone*—in four counties to rejoice with us in the news that the last McKay wild child has been tamed."

Tamed? Oh for fuck's sake.

"If that doesn't call for an enormous party with all the trimmings I don't know what does."

Don't panic. Smile. Act like this is no big deal.

"Besides, sweetie, with so many, many, *many* family members and friends here, it is the best way to make the official announcement and allow them to congratulate you in person. Don't you remember how wild and fun Colt and India's wedding reception was?"

Poor Jack looked positively green. Keely would've enjoyed his discomfort if she hadn't felt a little green herself. Still, she couldn't resist taking a shot at him. "It's something Jack and I will never forget, will we? Are you *up* for this, Jack darlin'?"

His lips curled in a half-smile. "The more the merrier, as you always say, right?" he shot right back.

Bastard.

"I'm sure Jack's mother has her own list of who she's inviting. We don't only want McKays and Wests in attendance, right? Anyway, if you'll leave me her phone number, Jack, I'll call her tomorrow. Between the two of us we'll have everything organized, so all you two lovebirds will need to do is show up at the party."

Jack's glass of milk stopped midair. "You're calling my mother to help?"

"Naturally." Carolyn set her teacup in the saucer. "Is that a problem?"

"No, not at all," Keely inserted smoothly. "It's very thoughtful of you, Ma, wanting to include Doro from the get-go. Except we haven't told Jack's mother about the engagement yet."

There was that *no bullshit* glare from her dad again. "Why the hell not? You embarrassed about marryin' my girl, Donohue?"

"No sir."

"We haven't told her because we wanted to tell you first," Keely said.

Her father's glower lingered on Jack as he passed Carolyn another packet of sugar.

"We're calling Doro tonight, right honey?" she cooed at Jack.

"Absolutely, buttercup," Jack cooed back.

"Have you told any of your brothers yet?" Carson demanded.

"No."

"AJ?"

"No."

"Chassie?"

"No."

"Ramona?"

Keely shook her head.

"Doesn't seem like you're all fired up to strap on that old ball and chain if you ain't tellin' anyone that matters to you, baby girl."

"I'm telling you and Mama, Daddy. Doesn't that count?"

When he squinted, Keely realized he knew she was up to something. The man always busted her.

"Anyway, Jack and I are thrilled you're throwing us a party," Keely said with as much false cheer as she could muster. She patted her mother's hand, making sure she got a good look at her ginormous engagement ring. "I'm putting you one hundred percent in charge of planning the engagement party you've always dreamed for me."

"With games?"

"No!" Dammit. "I mean, why waste all the good games when there are men around? I say let's save the games for the bridal shower."

Her mother's gaze turned shrewd. "Does that mean you'll wear a dress? A nice dress? Not a jean skirt and boots? Or a miniskirt and boots?"

Hell no. "Well—"

Jack leaned forward, the picture of earnestness. "I promise she'll look appropriate for the occasion even if I have to dress her myself."

"Thank you, Jack."

"My pleasure, Carolyn. Can I help you clear the dishes before Keely and I take off?"

Keely wasn't sure if her ears were playing tricks on her, or if her father actually muttered, "Suck up."

While Jack tried to charm her mother in the kitchen, her dad took two shot glasses from the china hutch. He poured Jameson whiskey in each glass and passed one to her.

"Shouldn't Mama and Jack be here if we're toasting in celebration of my upcoming marriage?"

"I ain't celebrating. This whole thing is giving me indigestion and whiskey is better than Tums. Drink up." His gaze turned crafty when Keely hesitated. "Unless you really have a bun in the oven and that's why you ain't drinkin' my good Irish?"

The cunning coot had played her good. She slammed the shot and poured another and slammed it too. "Happy now?"

"Ain't nothin' about this situation that makes me happy, punkin."

"Why not?"

The blue eyes she'd inherited pinned her in place. "Because he shoulda talked to me about marryin' you first."

For Christsake. *That's* why her dad was pissy?

"Might seem old-fashioned, but you *are* my only daughter." He knocked back a slug of whiskey. "I'm just sayin' it woulda been nice to've been asked."

Keely was strangely touched. She moved to where he sat in his favorite chair and wrapped her arms around him from behind. "If it'll make you feel better, I'll chew him out for it."

"It'd make me feel better if you weren't marryin' him at all. It's too damn quick."

"I'll remind you that you proposed to Mama the night you met her. So try again."

He harrumphed, "Smartypants. He ain't your type."

Since when wasn't tall, handsome, well-built, sarcastic and rich not her type? "Meaning what?"

"He ain't a cowboy, Keely."

"You're the first and only cowboy in my life, Daddy. I wouldn't think you'd want the competition."

"Suck up, but I'll take it." He pressed his leathery cheek to hers. "Now go on, get outta here and stop drinkin' all my damn whiskey."

Chapter Four

"An engagement party?" Jack bit off the second she shut the car door.

Keely squirmed. "What was I supposed to say?"

"*No* would've been a good place to start."

"You're an opportunist. Think of it as the ultimate occasion to convince people we're really getting married."

Jack swallowed his retort and turned up the radio.

Keely lasted about thirty-five seconds before she flipped the music off. "You actually like that noise?"

"Why would I listen to it if I didn't?"

"You probably think it makes you sound sophisticated if you tell people you listen to jazz."

"And I'd be better off listening to that goat-yodeling crap you prefer?"

"Yep. At least it's honest."

"As honest as the Nashville music executives can manipulate in a slick multimillion dollar recording studio with a marketing team in the wings."

"Testy much?"

"Your fault," he pointed out.

"How is it my fault?"

"You're in my car, ripping on my music choices." He expelled a heavy sigh. "Can you just not talk for the rest of the drive?"

"Fine."

A minute later she dragged out her iPod and sang along. Loudly. By the time Jack parked behind her building, he almost wished he hadn't asked her not to talk.

Keely appraised him coolly. "Want me to stay in the car with you while you call your mother?"

"For what? To hold my hand?"

"Fuck off, Jack. I thought Doro would want to talk to me, but you can deal with her on your own." Just as she grabbed the door handle to get out, Jack hit the automatic locks. Keely faced him again, fury in her stiff movements. "Let. Me. Out."

"Sorry. And yes, buttercup, I'd like it if you stuck around when I called her." He offered her a winsome smile. "My mother adores you. She hoped you and Justin would end up together."

Keely redirected her eyes away from his. "Yeah, well, I hope to hell she doesn't know why that one didn't work out."

"It didn't work out because you broke up with Justin."

No answer.

Her long pauses always made him nervous. "Keely?"

"You're wrong. Justin broke up with me after *you* told him to ditch me."

Jack silently repeated the numerical sequence of *pi* to the fifteenth digit before he spoke. "Are you really blaming me for my brother's stupidity?"

"Partially."

"Why?"

She spun toward him. "I don't know why Justin told you about our New Year's tryst with his friend Logan. God knows I never would've told any of my brothers about my sexcapades. I'm assuming Justin wanted to...impress you or some damn thing. All I know is Justin told me that you told him I wasn't the woman for him."

"What?"

"Justin didn't come right out and admit he was calling it quits because of the threesome, but he hinted pretty strongly that my slutty behavior—which he enjoyed immensely while we were in the moment, mind you—was why he was breaking up with me...after talking to you."

"For fuck's sake. Justin is an idiot."

"You didn't say any of that shit to him?"

"What I said was he should know you weren't the woman for him because it didn't bother him to watch his buddy fucking you. I said if Justin loved you, he should've thrown Logan out the goddamn hotel window for daring to put his hands on you."

Jack remembered being extremely pissed off because his brother had Keely McKay in his bed and wasn't man enough to keep her satisfied, nor was he man enough to call the shots.

Comprehension dawned in her eyes. "You're serious."

"Completely. That dumbass took it totally out of context and you blame me."

"Not entirely. I mostly blamed Justin."

"Good. He couldn't handle you anyway, could he?"

"Nope." She gifted him with a flirty grin that made his balls tighten. "You think he'll be upset by our engagement?"

"Probably. But he won't freak out as much as your brother."

"Which brother?"

"Carter."

Keely snorted. "Carter is a pussycat. You oughta be worried about Cam; he's always armed. Plus, he knows we had an...incident at Colt and India's wedding reception."

No wonder the guy always glared at him. "Did you tell him what happened?"

"Are you kiddin'? I haven't told anyone the embarrassing truth. All Cam knows is that I was unhappy and it was your fault."

"Fantastic." Jack jammed his hands through his hair again. "We really have to call everyone tonight, don't we?"

"Yep. And since your folks didn't reproduce like rabbits, your list is considerably smaller than mine."

"My mom and dad always wanted more kids. It'd be easier on her now if she had more family around..." Guilt popped up. Again. Followed quickly by sorrow. Again.

She smoothed her hand up his forearm. "I'm sorry about your dad, Jack. Marvin was very sweet to me the couple of times I met him."

A hollow emptiness expanded in his chest whenever his dad's name was mentioned. "Thanks."

"As long as I'm apologizing... I'm really sorry I was such a jerk two years ago at my family picnic. When I saw you moping around, I thought it was because I refused to talk to you. I had no idea it was because your dad had died. After Macie chewed my ass, I went looking for you to express my condolences, but you were already gone."

"It's okay. Maybe you can run interference for me with Macie when she finds out I own the Sandstone Building. I imagine she'll rip me a new one."

"Deal." She gestured to his phone. "Get crackin'. I'll hang out until you're done."

His mother was beside herself he'd snatched up that "fine young woman" Keely McKay for his wife. She spent more time chatting with Keely than with him. Maybe because Keely snapped a picture of her engagement ring with her cell phone and sent it to her. Maybe because Keely begged her to help Carolyn plan the engagement party. But Jack couldn't accuse Keely of pandering, because she genuinely liked his mother. He felt his first twinge of guilt about this charade; it'd hurt his mother when he and Keely called off the engagement.

A sexy trill of laughter caught Jack's attention and he watched Keely's lips curve into a smile. "Honestly, we didn't tell anyone, so your boy isn't keeping you out of the loop, Doro. I promise. Yes. I'll tell him."

"Tell me what?"

Keely clicked the off button. "Your mom says your dad would be proud of you."

More guilt.

"Who's next on your list?"

"Can't we just send everyone else a text message with that picture of your engagement ring?" Hell. That actually sounded whiny. What the fuck was happening to him?

"That's a great idea but let's take a picture of us. The light is all golden and glowy right now." She yanked on the door handle. Four times in rapid succession. "Let me out."

"Patience isn't your strong suit, is it?"

"Better learn that early on." After Jack skirted the front end of the car, Keely positioned him against the passenger side and took over. He allowed it. For now. But the cowgirl was sorely mistaken if she thought he was malleable like the men she usually dated.

"Put your hand here. No, here. Now pull me close. Angle your head into mine. Hang on. I wanna get the ring in the pic too." She settled her left hand prominently in the center of his chest. "Okay. Hold that beautiful smile on the count of three. One. Two..."

At the last second, Jack turned and kissed her cheek.

"Dammit, Jack." She jumped away from him. "That was uncalled for."

"Told you payback was a bitch. So let's see it."

"No." Keely lifted the camera out of his reach. "You don't get to—"

"Yes I do." Jack snatched the phone, clicking to the last picture. He grinned. The light reflected off Keely's glossy black hair, creating a halo effect. She smiled prettily as he lovingly smooched her cheek. He flipped it around so she could see the screen.

"It's okay, but I think—"

"Anyone looking at this will think we're happy, and that's the point, right?" He pushed a few buttons and sent the picture to everyone in her phone book with the message, *Jack Donohue and I are engaged! Love, Keely.* "There. It's a done deal. Now everyone knows."

"What?" Keely swiped the phone and scrolled down. "No, no, no, no! You sent this to everyone? Including... Omigod, Casey and Renner and Kent?"

"Who are Casey and Renner and Kent?"

"Some guys I've been—"

Jack boxed her against her the car with his body, forcing her undivided attention. "You will not fuck around on me, *ever*, understand? No calling other guys. No flirting with other guys. No kissing other guys. No touching other guys. As far as the world is concerned, we are engaged for real, and you will not embarrass me, or yourself, by acting any way other than wildly in love with me, got it?"

Her gaze slid to his mouth and she licked her lips.

Fuck. He'd spent way too many hours thinking about what he'd do if that tempting mouth of hers was ever close to his again. If he lowered his head he could taste the juicy sweetness of those full red lips as he swallowed her surprised moan...

The phone in his hand buzzed with a text message.

Dammit all to hell. "I said got it?"

"Uh-huh." She kept peering at him with those enormous midnight blue eyes.

"Nothing to say?" he prompted.

"Just one thing."

"What?"

"Possessive much?"

You don't know the half of it. Jack permitted a feral smile. "Better learn that early on." He pushed back and tucked the phone in her front shirt pocket. "Go upstairs and make your calls. I'll be right up."

Keely sauntered away.

Jack dug his cell phone out and brought up the engagement picture he'd forwarded to himself. It exemplified a couple who looked wildly in love. He reworded the text message and hit *send all.*

No going back now.

Three hours later, Jack punched his lace pillow for the millionth time. He could not get comfortable in this stupid, lumpy, midget-sized bed.

You can't get comfortable because you've got a hard-on the size of a Louisville Slugger.

He stared at the rows of stuffed animals lining the bookshelves. Creepy damn things. Then he gazed at the ceiling, wide-awake.

He'd spent the last two hours trying not to gawk at Keely's legs. Or her ass. Or her tits. Or the little slice of her belly that teased where her booty shorts gapped in the front. Or where the bottom curve of her butt cheeks peeked out in the back.

What kind of man got hard from a pair of flannel shorts?

He did, evidently. She hadn't been deliberately teasing him either. If Keely had slunk out of her bedroom in a skimpy Victoria's Secret getup, he wouldn't have reacted.

Right. Keely McKay could wear sackcloth and ashes and he'd be lusting after her.

She'd all but ignored him as she cleaned up the kitchen. Tidied up the living room. She'd handed him the remote to an older model TV. Talk about horrified—no big screen/flat screen and no cable. That'd change first thing tomorrow.

Then Keely bid him goodnight. At ten-thirty. Jack didn't know what to do with himself. He could crack open his laptop, but work didn't appeal to him. Wandering down to the local bar alone didn't sound like fun. Watching TV was out. He set up his coffeemaker. Then he'd gone to bed.

And there he lay with his dick as rigid as rebar.

Every time he thought of something nonsexual, such as his conversation with Carter—which was little more than profanity laced threats. Or his conversation with Justin—which was little more than the accusation Jack had fucked up Justin's relationship with Keely just so Jack could have her—the throbbing in his groin abated somewhat.

Somewhat.

But then Keely, the sexy, sassy, sultry, sweet-smelling cowgirl from hell would float into his mind's eye again and he'd be back to square one. Hard, horny. Hating he had no outlet.

Wrong. There's no shame in beating off. No different than any other night in your pathetic sex life.

True. So Jack closed his eyes, spread his legs and took himself in hand. He imagined Keely easing that yellow tank top up, revealing the creamy expanse of her taut belly. In his fantasy, her belly button was pierced and a little silver cowbell jangled with every twitch of her curvy hips.

He stroked his cock from root to tip.

She tossed the tank top and cupped her tits. They were on the small side, but Jack wasn't a tit man anyway. Her thumbs drew circles around the rosy nipples, brushing the tips until they puckered. She moaned and slid her palms down her belly, beneath the waistband of the flannel shorts, swinging her hips with gusto. Her long black hair whipped from side to side as she shimmied the shorts off. Her pussy was shaved except for a tiny strip of black hair. She traced the line of her slit with a slender finger, parting the delicate pink lips.

Oh fuck yeah. His hand on his cock moved faster.

The phantom image of Keely drifted forward, her come-hither stare locked on the movement of his fist as he beat off. She placed her left foot on the footboard, giving him an unobstructed view of her glistening sex. She thrust her middle finger into her cunt and moaned softly as she pumped it in and out. Showing him the wetness, biting her lip as she pleasured herself in front of him.

When she started grinding the heel of her hand into her clit and pinching her nipple, the *slap slap slap* of Jack working his cock became louder. Keely pulled her fingers from her juicy sex and sucked them into her wicked mouth.

Jack lost it, furiously pulling on his cock until his release spurted out and coated his hand.

After he'd caught his breath, he opened his eyes. Alone in his room, whacking off to an illusion again. But damn, what an illusion.

What if it weren't? Once the news of their engagement spread, everyone would assume they were sleeping together. What if he could have Keely as his sexual playmate for a little while?

Right. Keely would totally go for that. Never mind the fact they couldn't stand each other. And at least in his delusion Keely hadn't spoken and ruined it, like he was sure she would in real life.

No. It was better to have the fantasy in this case.

Mind made up, Jack finally relaxed enough to drift toward sleep.

At seven o'clock an unfamiliar screeching whir woke Keely. She jumped out of bed in her underwear and a camisole and raced into the kitchen, figuring an appliance had exploded. But the noise was from some fancy-ass coffee pot. Beans were grinding, steam billowed, water hissed and popped. A loud click and the aroma of hot, fresh coffee rolled out.

Keely's mouth watered.

"A thing of beauty, isn't it?"

Jack's deep, scratchy morning voice sent a pleasant tingle down her spine.

"It's awful damn noisy. Does it bake muffins too?"

"Doesn't need to. It makes the best coffee in the world and you'll forget all about muffins once you get a taste. If you ask me real nice I might even let you have a cup."

"If you ask me real nice, I might even let you *borrow* a cup."

"This one—" he plucked a mug from the dish rack, "—will be just fine."

She ripped her favorite cup out of his grasp. "Huh-uh. Find another one and keep your paws off this one."

"You always this cranky in the morning?"

"Yes. Get used to it."

"Maybe you should go back to bed."

"Fine." Keely spun on her heel and slammed her bedroom door. She set her favorite UWYO mug on the nightstand and threw herself on the bed.

Dammit. She did not want to share her apartment or anything in it with Jack. Not coffee. Not small talk. She would never survive this fake engagement. Never. She might as well march right back out there and give him back the ostentatious ring along with a really nasty piece of her mind.

"Keely?"

She lifted her head and glared at him. "What?"

"I was kidding about sending you back to bed. Did you want coffee?"

What the heck? Why was Jack being nice to her?

Just go with it.

Keely inhaled a slow, deep breath. "Sure. Just let me throw something on."

Jack's gaze systematically inched up her body. When their eyes met, the heat and interest she saw floored her. "No need to get dressed on my account. In fact, all you really need is your special cup, cowgirl."

"You suggesting a clothing optional coffee klatch?"

His answering smile was decidedly wicked. "Works for me."

The man was succeeding at keeping her off balance.

She detoured to the bathroom and brushed her teeth, but didn't attempt to fix her bedhead. In the kitchen area, she sat across from Jack at the small dinette set.

He poured coffee from an insulated silver carafe. "I don't think I asked you last night if you'd set up a meeting time with Chet and Remy today."

"We're meeting with them at two."

Jack frowned. "I was hoping to get it out of the way first thing this morning."

"They're working on a job outside of Aladdin and that was the earliest they could get away." Keely blew on her coffee before she took a sip. Oh. It was heavenly. Not too bitter, not too bland. She took another sip. Yep. Second one just as good as the first.

"You like it?"

"Mmm-hmm. However, I find it...interesting that of all the

items you could've brought from your place in Denver, a coffeepot topped the list."

"Not just a coffeepot, a coffeemaker," he scoffed. "The premier all-in-one brew system using the French press method. And I only buy free-trade Guatemalan coffee beans which makes the entire coffee experience nearly—"

"Orgasmic?" she supplied.

"A dirty and mean sense of humor first thing in the morning. I may learn to like you yet." He smiled when she stuck out her tongue at him. "After I call the cable company and get us hooked up to the twenty-first century, I'll head over to Spearfish and pick up a new TV before the two o'clock meeting."

"Why? I don't watch much TV."

"I do."

"How often do you plan on being here?"

"As long as it takes."

"I'm assuming the boob tube is going in your bedroom?"

"Where would I put it amidst all those stuffed animals?" Jack shook his head. "It goes in the living room."

Don't argue. He'll just remind you he owns the apartment and can put anything wherever he damn well pleases.

"Whatever. I'm hitting the shower." Maybe it was petty, but she stayed under the spray until not a drop of hot water remained. She smeared in her favorite lotion—Sky Blue Lilac Dreams—from head to toe, and ran a comb through her tangled hair, calling it good. Most days she didn't fuss with her appearance. No exception today because she did not want Jack Donohue thinking she'd duded herself up for him.

Normally she'd walk naked to her bedroom, but with Jack here... Her inner bad girl urged her to saunter buck-ass nekkid right past him. Her inner good girl primly reminded her to cover herself so not an inch of skin was visible.

Her inner good girl won for a change. She wrapped a towel around her torso before she scooted into her bedroom.

Keely had just finished dressing when she heard loud knocking on the door. Early for visitors but she knew who'd popped by unannounced. Without guilt.

AJ stood on the landing, gripping Foster's hand. "What's this pile of garbage about you marrying Jack Donohue?" AJ demanded.

"It's not garbage." Keely clapped her hands and Foster ran into her arms with a heart-melting little boy giggle. She lifted him and spun him around to more giggles. "Didja miss your Auntie, Fos?"

"Uh-huh."

She looked him over, completely smitten. With his dark hair and lanky build, Foster would be the spitting image of his father, Cord, if not for the silvery hue of his eyes, which he'd inherited from AJ.

He slapped his palms on her cheeks. "Play Legos?"

"I swear you only love me for my toys." She kissed his forehead before setting him down. She grabbed the box out of the toy closet and dumped the contents on the rug. "He's either gonna grow up to be a bricklayer or a house builder."

"You are avoiding the question. I want all the details, Keely West McKay, and I want them right now."

Keely sighed. "I know you can't have coffee in your condition, but do you want a glass of juice?"

AJ folded her arms across her chest in a belligerent posture. "Nope. Spill. Now."

"A few months back I bought a building in Moorcroft to turn into a clinic—"

"And you didn't tell me that either? Geez, K, I thought I was your best friend and now I find out—"

"You are my best friend, but this was something I couldn't talk about to anyone."

"Anyone except Jack Donohue?" AJ retorted.

How was she supposed to convince AJ, who could sniff out a lie at twenty paces, the engagement to Jack was real? In AJ's hormonal state, joking, cajoling and dodging would only annoy her. Best to go on the defensive. Keely offered a brittle smile. "Hard to believe, but I do have a life outside of Sundance and the McKay family. Since I spend half my time working at the VA in Cheyenne, you wouldn't know anything about that part of my life."

"So fill me in."

After rambling on about her need for secretiveness she sighed. "Long story short, I contacted an approved historic restoration company, only to discover that Jack owns the company. We got to talking and the more time we spent together, the more things...changed between us."

"How long since this 'change' has taken place?"

"Two months. Give or take."

"And you didn't think to mention to me or anyone else in the family that you'd fallen for the man you used to hate?"

"It's not like that—"

"It is for me. I still sorta hate him on your behalf, K..." AJ's nose wrinkled. "I cannot wrap my head around the fact you're marrying him."

"Hate is a strong word for the man who's your landlord," Keely said sardonically.

"My landlord?" Her eyes widened with understanding. "For Healing Touch Massage?"

"Yep, which means he's also Macie's landlord for Dewey's Delish Dish, and India's landlord for India's Ink, and Skylar's landlord for Sky Blue."

"You're kidding me. Jack owns the Sandstone Building?"

"Uh-huh. Jack Donohue is Western Property Management. Evidently he owns a half a dozen different rental properties across several states."

After a minute or so, AJ snapped, "So Jack's been having a big chuckle keeping that information from us?"

"You'll have to ask him." And Keely couldn't wait to witness India's reaction. Talk about ripping him a new one. That woman redefined *in your face* and she was ten times worse when she was knocked up. Heh heh.

The bathroom door creaked. Both Keely and AJ spun toward the sound. Jack strode out.

Keely clenched her jaw to prevent it from falling to the floor. Holy freakin' shit. Jack was shirtless. His upper body was a mass of defined muscles—his pecs, biceps and triceps were as perfect as the smooth bronze skin covering his immense frame. His waistline tapered into a flat abdomen and slim hips, hugged by the low-slung jeans. She'd never seen Jack wear jeans. The man who lived in suits looked...well suited to 501s.

The tips of his dark, wet hair brushed his shoulders, reinforcing his wild look. His mouth curled up in a sultry smile when his gaze connected with Keely's.

A powerful lust steamrolled her.

Jack crossed the room with panther-like grace.

Her body stiffened when he nuzzled the side of her neck and circled his big hands around her upper arms.

"You didn't leave me any hot water again, babe. I had to take a cold shower."

Oh hell. He smelled delectable. Despite his claim of cold water, his chest felt hot enough to scorch her clothes. "Sorry. Maybe you oughta sweet-talk the landlord into replacing the tiny overworked water heater."

"Your sweet-talking gets you whatever you want with me. And a cold shower was probably in my best interest this morning after last night." Jack straightened and smiled at AJ. "Mrs. McKay. Nice to see you." His gaze momentarily dropped to the swell of her abdomen. "Congrats. When are you due?"

"Four months. Take that into consideration when you're picking a wedding date. Keely does not want her matron of honor to be nine months pregnant in the wedding pictures."

"So noted," Jack murmured.

"Look!" was shouted behind them.

They turned toward Foster, who'd stacked the Legos in the shape of a house.

"That's great." Jack crouched down and admired Foster's creation. "Interesting how you used red at the bottom and yellow at the top. Very original."

Foster blinked silvery eyes at Jack.

"He's a little shy," AJ said.

"Nah. He's just thinking. You're a craftsman, aren't you? Me too. Let's see what we can come up with. I used to spend hours playing Legos. I forgot how much I loved them." Jack settled next to Foster and grabbed four long sections of white block and lined them up on the base.

Keely melted a little, seeing Jack engrossed in playtime with her nephew. She never imagined he'd be the type of guy who'd sit on the floor and play Legos.

Don't fall for his softer side. It's not real. It's part of the scam.

Wasn't it?

AJ tugged Keely into the kitchen. She whispered fiercely, "Okay. I'll admit I see his appeal. Not only is he unbelievably good looking, he's got an amazing body and he likes kids—"

"And don't forget he's loaded," Keely added.

AJ whapped her on the arm. "That is *not* how you choose a man you'll spend the rest of your life with. I imagine the sex is pretty rockin' too?"

Keely's gaze skittered away and she prayed AJ would drop it.

No such luck.

"Oh. My. God."

She couldn't look at AJ, fearing her best friend had guessed the truth about the Jack situation. "What?"

"This is the real deal for you, isn't it?"

"What makes you say that?"

"Because you're not regaling me with tales of the size of his penis, or how he screwed you in the bathroom at Coors Field, or how you went down on him on a twisty mountain road, or the wicked tricks he can perform with his long tongue."

"So?"

"So, keeping the intimate details to yourself means what happens between you two is too personal to share."

Or there aren't any down and dirty details to share.

AJ hugged her and sniffled in her ear. "I'm happy for you, K. Even if Jack isn't the man I'd choose for you."

Me neither. "Thanks."

Keely silently breathed a sigh of relief. If she'd convinced AJ about the legitimacy of the engagement, she should be home free as far as the rest of her family buying it.

"What's going on?" Jack rounded the corner with Foster, burning Keely with a pointed look.

"Girl talk. AJ has great ideas for the centerpieces for the engagement party. A bouquet of Wyoming wildflowers—"

Jack held up his hand. "You promised no party details, remember? I need the keys to your truck for my trip to Spearfish."

Keely opened her mouth to belt out, *Oh hell no, you ain't touchin' my truck* when she noticed the challenge in his eyes. "Jack, darlin', I can drive. In fact, I'd love to go with you since we've spent so little time together recently."

"See how sweet she is?" Jack said to AJ with a totally fake smile. "But I realize you have tons of stuff to do around the apartment today—cooking, cleaning, pressing my work shirts, organizing my side of the dresser before we pore over the plans with West Construction this afternoon."

"That is true." She heaved a dramatic sigh. "Swapping cars today will work out great."

Alarm danced through Jack's eyes.

She bit her cheek to stop the laughter. Jack babied his 760li Series BMW. The notion of handing her the keys would give him a nervous breakdown.

Which would serve him right.

Chapter Five

"I see some things haven't changed between you two," AJ said. "There's a fight brewing and I don't wanna be around for the making up part." She took Foster's hand. "Come on, son. Aunt Domini has a bowl of Cheerios with your name on it downstairs at Dewey's."

Foster didn't hug Keely goodbye. The only thing that interested the kid more than Legos was food.

The door slammed.

"Did you tell her the truth?" Jack demanded.

"No. She thinks because I haven't been regaling her with tales of our kinky sexual exploits that this must be *wuv, twue wuv.*"

"Quoting *The Princess Bride* will not steer my focus from the fact you are *not* driving my car today or any other day, buttercup."

"Why not? We're engaged. It is my right to drive it, especially if you're taking off in my truck."

"Where do you need to go today?"

Nowhere, but she wasn't about to admit that to him. "I have a life, Jack. I have a job. I need a car. And no, I'm not asking anyone to ferry me around town when there's a perfectly good car sitting in the parking lot. Besides, people would gossip that my fiancé doesn't trust me to touch his precious Beemer."

Jack loomed over her. "I *don't* trust you. Do you have any idea how much I paid for that car?"

"Way, way too much?" she asked sweetly.

He growled.

"Who cares? It's just a car."

"Just a car? It's a feat of German engineering—"

"Some feat! It doesn't have a trunk big enough to hold more than a French press coffeepot made in China and a bag of Guatemalan coffee beans." When he snarled, she jabbed him in the chest with her index finger. "Here's the deal. The only way I'll let you borrow my truck to pick up that all important big-screen TV is if you let me drive your car."

Jack paced to the living room. Muttered to himself and stalked back to her. "Fine. But if anything happens, and I mean a single rock chip or an itty bitty scratch, I will take it out of your hide, understand?"

"Completely. I'll treat it like it's my own."

And that's probably why Keely got a speeding ticket not two hours later.

But it'd been so damn tempting. A V-12 with 360 horses under the hood? And a long stretch of empty black road in front of her? Sheer heaven.

She'd neglected to mention her love of fast cars to her intended. Trading in her old Corvette, after the years she'd spent zipping through traffic in Denver and opening the throttle on the deserted highways of the west, had broken her heart. But when Keely moved back home for good, she knew Wyoming weather could change in a heartbeat. Making the long, lonely drive between Sundance and Cheyenne in the winter months was dangerous and necessitated a four-wheel drive truck.

So if Keely stumbled on the chance to rod the piss out of a car meant to be driven hard and fast and loose, she did so without an ounce of guilt.

Just her bad luck she'd blazed past a Crook County Sheriff's car as she'd hit the one hundred thirty miles per hour mark. When the flashing lights finally caught up with her, she hoped Sheriff Shortbull was behind the wheel. He'd let her off with a warning. He always did. She manufactured a charming but contrite smile.

Keely watched in the rearview mirror as the driver's side door of the cop car opened. Her smile dried up. Her stomach dipped. The unmistakable hulking form of her brother Cam started toward her.

Shit.

She reluctantly rolled down her window. "I can explain—"

"License and registration."

"Cam. Seriously. Just listen for a sec."

He stuck his head inside the car. "Not. Another. Word. License and registration."

Keely popped the glove box and found the vehicle registration right where it was supposed to be. She passed it and her license through the window, waiting while Cam did his cop thing. "Exit the vehicle and come with me."

Keely trudged to the passenger side of the cop car and climbed in.

"Did Jack really let you drive his car? Or did you steal it when he wasn't looking?"

"He let me have it. We traded. He needed my truck."

"Does he know you drive like an idiot?"

She glared at him.

"And what is this bullshit about you and Jack Donohue getting married anyhow?"

Big brother number four didn't beat around the bush. She allowed him time to recant his jerky statement. When he didn't, she offered him a haughty, "It's not bullshit."

Cam ripped his sunglasses off. His eyes snapped fire. "Yes, it is. I know you. I've seen the venom in your eyes when you look at him, so don't give me that 'I'm madly in love with him' crap. Come clean. Right now."

The truth was, Cam did know her to the bone and she had one chance to deflect the conversation. "Okay, smarty, if you know me so well, then what have I been working on for the last four months?"

He squinted at her with his *I can toss your smart ass in jail* stare.

Keely didn't back down. "You don't have a clue, do you?"

"Well, sweetheart, whatever you've secretly been working on, you've done a damn good job of hiding it, not only from me, but from the family. And I would know all about hiding stuff, wouldn't I? So who better than me to ferret out the truth?"

"But—"

"Uh-uh. I ain't done. What I do know, little sis, is Jack Donohue did something to you at Colt and India's wedding reception that made you cry. I've never pushed the issue, even when I wanted to castrate the son of a bitch for hurting you. And if I thought he'd physically injured you? I would've killed him on the spot. Period."

Yikes.

"So tell me the truth."

She hated to lie to her brother. Cam considered lying the ultimate sin, the biggest betrayal, but she did it anyway. "Yes, I hated Jack. No doubt we've had a rocky past. The reason I haven't told you what went down between us that night is because it's between me and Jack. You also know me well enough that if he would've hurt me, I would've sliced off his dick before you'd gotten the chance. That said, I've changed. Jack has changed. When I needed his help, he really came through for me."

The squinty-eyed stare he'd inherited from Dad appeared again. "Help with what?"

"The building I bought in Moorcroft."

"What building? Jesus, Keely, why haven't I heard about this before now?"

"Because it's none of your business." For the one-trillionth time, Keely explained. Cam wasn't any happier with the explanation than anyone else had been.

"We—me, Cord, Colby, Colt, Carter, Kade, Kane, Quinn and Ben—would've helped you check it out. We're family. You should've come to us first."

"Far as I can tell, none of you are licensed with the Wyoming Historical Society to facilitate the approval of my remodeling plans. Jack is. So all you, Cord, Colby, Colt, Carter, Kade, Kane, Quinn, and Ben could've done is tell me the building needs a shitload of work, which I already knew. To be fair, I did talk to Chet and Remy, so I rounded up all the expert help I needed on the construction front. What I need from you right now is your support in other ways."

"Such as?"

"Don't give me grief about my engagement to Jack. He's my...choice."

"Fine. I'll drop it for now. But I'm still writing you a ticket for reckless driving."

Keely would gladly take the two hundred dollar fine instead

of subjecting herself to Cam's continued scrutiny. She smiled. "Where do I sign?"

Jack pulled up behind his BMW in the parking lot of the Brewster Building and did a visual sweep for damages. Lucky for that mouthy cowgirl, everything looked fine.

He re-secured the tie-downs over the boxes in the back of the truck and grabbed his clipboard before heading up the steps.

Inside, he let the ambience of the past and the promise of the future wash over him. Sometimes when he stood in an old building, he swore the energy of previous inhabitants surrounded him. Guiding him to consider the past. This project was no different, despite the bizarre circumstances.

Jack glanced at the painted tin ceiling. Made notes. He checked the buckled walls. Every inch of the lathe and plaster had to come out. Ripping out the plumbing upstairs would fix the water damage problems. He wandered, half-listening to the banging and clanking of tools.

A long staircase spiraled up the right side, ending in a balcony. The curved banister was in decent shape, although the wooden balustrades were missing. He'd need a specific solution for those repairs on the remodel plans. Since the staircase was the architectural focal point of the room, it needed to retain as much of the original design as possible.

He'd scrawled another question about replacing the individual glass windows fronting the offices on the balcony, when Keely barreled around the corner, carrying a rotting chunk of plasterboard. She heaved it out the side door with a grunt. "Gross-ass shit."

"What was it?"

She gasped and whirled around. "Whoa. I didn't know you were here."

"I guessed that. What were you tossing out?"

"Somebody put a moldy chunk of Sheetrock in front of the old boiler access and it sealed shut, probably with the help of a gallon of mouse piss." She shuddered. "Nasty, smelly mess."

"Are Chet and Remy around?"

"Yeah." Keely whistled shrilly. "Guys! Jack is here."

Jack winced. "A warning about your deafening whistle might be in order next time."

"Where would be the fun in that?"

Two guys bounded down the stairs. Both mid-thirties. The tall, stocky man had curly light brown hair and dark eyes. The shorter, stockier man had curly dark brown hair and light eyes. Jack vaguely remembered meeting them at Carter's wedding. He thrust out his hand. "Jack Donohue. Full Circle Consulting."

The taller guy spoke first. "Chet West. West Construction."

The shorter guy inserted himself between them. "Remy West, also of West Construction. Cousin Keely here told us you own the Sandstone Building. Is that true?"

Jack nodded. "You guys did a great job on that remodel."

"Like we had a choice," Chet said. "Now I know why you were such a hardass on approving the plans. Architects as owners are construction guys' worst nightmare."

"And yet you're back for more."

Remy smiled. "We ain't dumb. You may be a pain in the butt, but you paid top dollar and gave us a good recommendation."

"How come I didn't know that?" Keely demanded of her cousins.

"Because we keep our mouths shut. No matter what." Chet's gaze moved between Keely and Jack. "So can you. Keely never once mentioned being involved with you on a personal level. She played all coy and secretive about her 'expert' help."

Jack lifted a brow at Keely. "We've been discreet, haven't we, buttercup? Now we're engaged and there's no denying I'm a lucky man." When he attempted to put his arm around her, she flinched. Damn woman could at least pretend his touch didn't repulse her. Just to be ornery, he jerked her to his side, keeping their bodies touching. "Come on, Keely, no need to act shy. We are with family." He kissed the top of her head. "It's sweet how much she really is the blushing-bride type beneath that blustering cowgirl exterior."

Keely froze, then stiffened with anger.

Jack wondered if he should've worn a cup.

Chet addressed Keely. "Aunt Caro is throwing a big bash for you guys, huh?"

"Next weekend. We'd love for you to come, but I'll warn ya, my brothers will be gunning for you."

"Why?"

"For keeping the building buying a secret from them."

"Let the McKays bring it," Remy said. "We don't back down for no one. Our word is our bond."

"Amen, bro." Chet and Remy bumped fists.

"Speaking of bond...your business paperwork is up to date. If West Construction forged a deal with Keely about specific duties, project costs, potential overruns and a timeframe for each stage, then as far as I'm concerned, we're good to go on Monday."

"I sense a but."

Jack flashed his teeth at Chet. "A couple of minor considerations that don't have to be addressed today, but I'd like clarification on next week. Deal?"

"Hell yeah it's a deal." Remy shook Jack's hand first, followed by Chet.

"Thank you. One other thing. Would you be interested in replacing the water heater in Keely's apartment? I never knew how bad it was until I started staying with her."

"Sure. You want us to do it now?"

"If you have time."

"Follow us to the building supply store. I'm pretty sure Jeb keeps an extra unit around. You've got a truck?"

Keely snorted. "Think you can fit it in the trunk of your Beemer?"

"I have Keely's truck, but the back is filled with electronic equipment."

"No problem. We'll pick up the replacement, meetcha at the apartment and help you unload." Remy lightly punched Keely in the arm. "Got yourself a good one there, K."

When they were out of earshot, Keely mumbled, "Such suckers for an open wallet."

"As soon as they're gone tonight, we *will* be having a serious discussion about a few things." Jack dangled her keys, with the rubber ducky key chain, in front of her scowling face. "Give me back my car."

"Not until you've unloaded your shit from my truck."

Back at the apartment, Chet and Remy hauled up the bulky boxes, insisting on helping Jack mount the TV after they installed the new water heater. By the time they left it was after eight.

Jack heard her settle across from him and crack the top on a bottle—on a bottle of beer he'd bought.

"You said we had to talk. So talk."

"Give me a second to enjoy my beer before you launch into an argument with me, okay?"

"I don't always argue with you."

"Yes, you do."

"No, I don't."

"See?"

Keely blew out an impatient breath. "Sorry."

He tried to get comfortable on the lopsided couch as he sipped his beer and gathered his thoughts. Better to jump in feet first than to dip a toe in the water, knowing the shark would bite either way. "Why do you flinch whenever I touch you?"

"Well, duh. I'm not used to you touching me, Jack."

"Bingo. You need to get used to it." Jack didn't break eye contact. "Come over here by me."

Her flip, "No thanks. I'm perfectly comfortable here," annoyed the shit out of him.

"Get over here. Now. Or I will pick you up and drag you." Her tiny flare of fear had him backtracking. "Just do it. Please."

Keely shrugged and plunked beside him. "Now what?"

Jack set his hand in the middle of her right thigh. She jumped and knocked his hand away. "See what I mean?"

"Dammit. I didn't think. I just reacted."

"Which means we need to condition you to change your reaction."

Skepticism filled her eyes. "I suppose you've figured out a way to 'condition' me."

"I have an idea or two."

"This oughta be fun," she grumbled.

"Oh, most definitely fun." He grinned, knew it looked unrepentant and didn't care. "Don't trust me, do you?"

"Why should I?"

"Maybe that's the basis of our problem."

"No. The basis of our problem is we don't like each other, Jack. Which makes it hard to have trust. Why don't you tell me about this conditioning method?"

"I'd rather show you." He gently placed his hand on her face and she flinched. "Relax."

"I am!" she snapped, ducking away.

Jack removed his hand, waited a beat, then caressed her cheek with the back of his knuckles.

She flinched again.

"Dammit, Keely, it's not like I'm going to hit you. Sit still."

"At least if you were hitting me I could hit you back."

His hand froze. "You'd rather I was hitting you than touching you?"

Keely held her body immobile, which didn't provide him any more encouragement than her cringing.

Great. Between Martine dumping him and the incident with Keely—which affected him far more than he'd ever admitted to himself—his sexual ego had taken a serious hit in recent years. Was he doing this all wrong?

She exhaled. "Okay. Try again."

He set his hand on her knee. "Maybe we should start here."

"See? I hardly flinched at all."

"That's heartening." Jack lightly caressed the smooth skin. She didn't object. This could work if he took baby steps.

Yeah, if you're lucky maybe the prickly woman will let you hold her hand tomorrow.

The sexual cynic inside him laughed that only a hard-up moron became excited by stroking Keely's cute kneecap.

Fuck. This was so not him. Waiting. Asking permission. He was large and in charge.

"Maybe we should start with you dousing me with tequila," Keely muttered.

Jack scowled. "You have to get drunk just to talk to me?"

"You asked."

"Can you not be contrary for one goddamn second?"

Keely opened her mouth, probably to fire off, *I'm not contrary*, but she snapped it shut.

Ah. Progress. While he waited for her to jumpstart the conversation, he lightly swept his thumb over the top of her knee.

"What should we chat about?" she intoned sweetly.

"Bring me up to speed on your family. You could talk about them all damn night."

A small smile. "True. What do you want to know?"

"I imagine you spend significant time with your nephews since you have an entire closet filled with toys."

"You noticed. Except I have nieces now too."

"Who has girls?

"I've always counted Kade's three daughters as my nieces since Kade is like my sixth brother. And Chassie has sweet little baby Sophia, but I'm talking about Cam and Domini's girls, Oxsana and Liesl."

"Huh. Carter told me they planned to adopt twins. A boy and a girl?"

"They did. Dimitri is Oxsana's twin brother. When Cam and Domini were at the orphanage in Romania, Liesl, who was five at the time, began following them around, sharing Dimitri and Oxsana's likes and dislikes."

"Liesl spoke English?"

"I guess she learned from watching TV."

He playfully bumped her with his shoulder. "See? TV's not all bad."

Keely's beautiful, wistful smile appeared again. "According to Cam, Domini would've brought every kid in the orphanage home, so it's ironic Cam was the one who pushed to adopt Liesl."

"Why?" Jack's hand inched higher on her leg.

"Cam, being nosy Cam, noticed Liesl limped, but she'd always shuffle away and hide whenever he asked her about it. When he grilled the orphanage caretakers, they told him her leg had been blown off by a land mine when she was two."

"Holy shit. Seriously?"

"Yeah. She'd wandered away from her drug-addled parents into a freakin' minefield. Then they abandoned her into state care. Luckily she got a prosthetic leg, which isn't always the case, and actually, is out of the norm."

"Why's that?"

She shrugged. "Fittings are difficult for younger kids because they grow so much. Balance is always an issue. They constantly need new prosthetics and each one is expensive. You can imagine that isn't a priority in what's basically a third world orphanage."

"Sounds like you know a lot about prosthetics," he murmured.

"I learned tons helping Cam find the right one. Anyway, Cam was heartbroken no one wanted to adopt her due to her handicap. He understands probably better than anyone what it's like to live with that embarrassment. That fear of being alone." She paused. "He fought for her. He wouldn't leave Romania without her, actually. So Liesl returned to the U.S. with them and the twins. Every day, for like three months after they brought her home, Liesl battled going to sleep at night. She was afraid she'd wake up and find her new life was all a dream."

Keely's voice broke and Jack squeezed her thigh.

"And now...I can't imagine Liesl not being part of their family. Cam's quiet life and pristine house is a thing of the past but he and Domini wouldn't have it any other way."

"Sounds like they should be canonized."

"I suspect they're not done adding to their brood. It's funny. Cam was always ambivalent about being a parent. So it's hysterical he'll probably end up with the most kids out of any of my brothers. That said, God knows all my brother's wives are in some freaky race to see who can pop out the most McKays. Jesus. They're all pregnant *again*. It's an epidemic that makes me want to stay far, far away from their overactive uteruses."

He gently stroked her soft skin, watching her closely. "They're all pregnant?"

"Yep. Channing, AJ and Macie are knocked up. So's India. And Chassie. And my cousin Quinn's wife, Libby, is on baby number two. On the West side, Blake's wife, Willow, is expecting their first. His brother Nick's wife, Holly, is expecting their second."

Jack whistled. "That's some seriously scary reproductive mojo."

"Tell me about it. That doesn't include any of my friends. Many are on baby number three. Heck, some of them are already on husband number three."

61

As stealthily as possible, Jack slipped his arm behind Keely on the back of the couch. Her hair was long enough he could twine a silky section around his index finger. "You've never been tempted to take the plunge?"

"I've had my fair share of boyfriends. Some say more than my fair share, but I've never seen myself with any of them long term."

"Why do you think that is?"

Her body tensed. "I don't know. Maybe I'm flawed. I'm sure you'd derive great joy in detailing all that is wrong with me."

"I don't know if your opinion of me bothers me worse than your opinion of yourself."

Keely snorted. "Please."

"You don't need me to tell you you're a beautiful woman, Keely. You didn't offer a glimpse of your insecurity because you were fishing for compliments."

Silence. An unhappy, uncomfortable silence.

"What did I say?"

"Stop teasing me." She attempted to squirm away.

"I'm not teasing you." *Don't snap at her.* "Why is it so damn hard for you to take a compliment from me?"

"Because you've never given me one and it's insincere," she retorted.

Jack tugged on her hair until she faced him. "If you're challenging my sincerity, then I should at least get a chance to prove it."

"I don't need proof. We're pretending to be engaged for Christsake. How much more insincere can it get?"

"We might be lying about some things, but this...pull between us is real."

Keely shivered. "That's not—"

"I can demonstrate if you like."

"I thought you were conditioning me?"

"That too," he murmured. "Take a chance, cowgirl."

"And if I say no you'll call me a chicken?"

"Yep. I'll even cluck."

She laughed softly. "You are crazy."

"I know. It's part of my charm." Jack angled his head until his nose brushed her ear. Goddamn. The woman's scent was a shot of adrenaline straight to his groin. "Close your eyes, Keely."

"Jack, I don't think—"

"Don't think. Just do it."

She muttered unintelligibly, but she complied.

Fascinating.

He dragged his fingers to the top of her thigh where her hand clenched into a fist. He brushed his mouth across the lilac scented skin below her ear. "My lips are a perfect fit for this spot, right here."

She arched into him slightly.

"I could spend an hour touching you with my mouth and my hands."

"Over my clothes?"

"To start. Then I'd unbutton your shirt, kissing each section of skin as I bared it. I'd look my fill. I'd taste my fill."

"And then?"

Jack's lips skimmed the hollow of her throat. "And then whatever you want, Keely, just name it."

"What is this proving?" she asked breathlessly.

"Nothing. I'm conditioning you to my touch, remember?"

"So this is just a game?"

"Yes." Jack let his heated breath follow the sexy curvature of her jaw. "And no. Getting you comfortable with my touch is a means to an end, but the process isn't a hardship. Not at all." Hadn't the woman noticed his cock straining against his zipper?

Keely's breath caught when he tugged on her earlobe with his teeth.

He smiled against her cheek, figuring he'd won her over. "Am I proving myself?"

"No."

"Why not?" Jarred by her response, he stilled. If he hadn't persuaded her, then why was her voice unsteady? Why was her breath choppy?

"Because you're not the type of man to take it slow or give me a play by play."

"And you know me so well?" he murmured with a trace of humor.

"Well enough to know I prefer the zero to four second response time you have, whether it's in anger or with lust.

That's honest. This calculated seduction is not." Keely extracted herself from him and stood. She reached for her beer. "Maybe it would be better if we just watched TV."

Chapter Six

That sneaky bastard.

Keely turned, blocking Jack's view as she pressed the bottle of beer to her lips and drained it.

Damn. Her entire body—blood, muscles, tissues, bones—felt as if he'd zapped her with a cattle prod. Wobbly knees, dry throat, rapid heartbeat, damp panties, haywire responses from a simple touch? Damn embarrassing. Jack had stroked, whispered and teased until she was mere seconds from mounting him.

She'd enjoyed plenty of lovers. Men who'd rocked her world in bed. But she'd never experienced such a visceral reaction to a man's heated touch and the soothing cadence of a deep voice drifting across her skin.

"Keely? You okay?"

She jumped. Damn him. She would not be a freakin' wreck of hormones in her own space. "You want another beer?"

"You having one?"

I'm having two. "Yep."

"Then I'll take one. Since I bought them."

Keely booked it to the kitchen. She took her time uncapping the beer bottles, stalling really. But she needn't have bothered; Jack was yakking on his cell phone when she returned. She sat across from him, propped her booted feet on the coffee table and studied him.

Jack Donohue was a total contradiction. Polished, yet rugged. Confident, yet not overtly cocky. Professional, yet an air of wildness surrounded him. Down to earth, as well as aloof. Smokin' hot, yet ice cold.

Who was he?

Will the real Jack Donohue please stand up?

Although Jack wasn't talking to her, she sensed his intense focus on her, totally on her. She couldn't drop her guard around him for a single second. Screw the conditioning exercises. She'd never get accustomed to the way Jack made her feel.

"I shouldn't have to handle it. Because it's not in my job description, nor is it in my contract. Yes, I'm sure. And for the record, I was against hiring them in the first place. No. This is not an 'I told you so' moment, George. What am I supposed to do about it from here? You're there, I'm not. Handle it. You're the GC. No. Because I can't right now."

Jack stopped and stared at her.

It wasn't a cool look. Oh no. The molten look in Jack's eyes was hot enough to melt cinderblocks. He wanted her. Keely knew if she stayed in this room, he'd have her the second he ended the call. His way. And she wouldn't do a damn thing to stop him.

Keely listened to her inner voice advising retreat. Keeping their gazes locked, she saluted with the bottle and backtracked into her bedroom. She leaned against the door and locked it, trying to calm her racing heart.

But over the rapid *lub-dub lub-dub lub-dub*, she swore she heard the sound of Jack...clucking.

The next morning Keely was up and out of the apartment before Jack stopped snoring in the guest bedroom.

Once again she hadn't beaten Dr. Joely Monroe into the office. The doc's door was wide open and a regular old coffeepot—not some fancy-schmancy French-Chinese hybrid—was brimming with fresh, hot, strong coffee. Keely grabbed a cup and plopped across from the doc.

"Make yourself comfy."

"I am, Doc. Thank you."

Dr. Monroe's eyes glommed onto Keely's left hand. "Nice ring. New, isn't it?"

Keely had been freelancing in the clinic as a physical and occupational therapist for more than two years. From the start

Doc Monroe had encouraged Keely's dream to own a physical therapy clinic. She'd offered advice and a recommendation to the Rural Medical Initiative about funding the venture. But Keely didn't feel comfortable talking to the doctor about her personal life.

Sometimes Keely wondered why she kept her life compartmentalized; she told AJ about her love life, Ramona about her career issues, her brothers and parents the entertaining tidbits, but no one knew all sides of her. How refreshing would it be to just be herself with one person? How bizarre would it be if that person was...Jack?

"Yes, it's brand spankin' new."

"I keep secrets for a living, McKay. We work together two, three days a week. You couldn't have given me a hint you were seriously involved with someone?"

"Umm. He's from out of town."

"What's his name?"

Satan. "Jack Donohue. In my own defense, it was sudden. And no, I'm not pregnant."

"How'd you meet?"

"He's Carter's best friend, so I've known him forever. He's also an architect specializing in restoration and his business is based out of Denver. He's supervising my building remodel."

"Mmm-hmm." The doc blew across her coffee. "I suppose that's why you've been gone so much? Hooking up with him in Denver?"

"Partially. But the VA consultant fee is three times what you pay me. Can't blame a girl for making a living." She offered an impish smile.

"I don't. I just hope you know what you're doing."

"With Jack or with the building?"

"Both. Now that you've begun the process of readying a space for a clinic, I'd hate to see you abandon your dream and move to the big city to be some hotshot architect's wife."

Keely scalded her tongue with coffee to keep from refuting the statement.

The doc asked, "Are Chet and Remy doing the remodel?"

"I wouldn't trust it to anyone else."

"Smart girl. Maybe I'll swing by and check out the progress. I've been debating whether to remodel my kitchen."

"You're never home long enough to eat a meal, let alone cook one."

Doc's gaze fell to her coffee cup. "Maybe I'm seeking changes in my life too. I'm tired of all work and no play."

"If you're looking for a man to play with, I can hook you up with one of my cousins."

"Just one?"

Keely blinked at her. "How many do you need?"

Dr. Monroe's sly smile gave her a younger, playful appearance. "Enough to keep me from getting bored." She drained her coffee. "Let's see what torturous schedule Brenda lined up for us today."

Hours later, Keely kicked the foot exerciser beneath the bench in the PT room. She glanced at the clock and handed her last client of the day a towel. "I'll see you next week, Gladys."

"But I'm feeling better, Keely. I don't need to—"

"Yes, you do. You had a hip replacement. My job is to make sure you're doing your exercises and not spending all your time watching TV."

Gladys looked petulant. "It's not like I have anything better to do."

Keely scooted forward on her rolling chair and took Gladys's hands. "I understand you miss Paul. But letting your health deteriorate... He wouldn't want that for you. I don't want that for you. You shouldn't want that for yourself."

Her eyes clouded with tears. "What am I supposed to do?"

"I'm not advocating you start kickin' up your heels at the Golden Boot, but you need to do a physical activity every day. The simple exercises I showed you are enough. Keep a log this week of what you've done, how you've felt afterward, and we'll go over it next week, okay?"

"That's fair. Thanks for not yelling at me."

"Oh pooh. I'm not exactly a drill sergeant."

"Which is why I keep coming back to you, sweetie." Gladys rubbed her thumb across Keely's engagement ring. "This is new. Pretty and shiny, like new love. What is your young man like?"

A pain in the ass.

Not a response poor Gladys would understand since she'd lost her husband of fifty years just last fall. "Jack? He's...smart."

Gladys harrumphed. "Details, girlie. What does he look like?"

Keely rattled off, "Tall, dark and handsome doesn't even begin to describe him. He's gorgeous, outrageously sexy, with this killer smile and these intense green eyes that just seem to bore into my soul." She froze. Good Lord. Had she really regurgitated that out loud? She actually sounded like a lovesick fool.

Maybe you are.

"Men like that are always good between the sheets too."

Lifting her gaze to Gladys's, she said, "No comment."

"Which tells me everything I need to know." Gladys winked and pushed to her feet.

Keely followed Gladys into the waiting room. Her PT sessions were "open door policy" meaning family members could pop in and observe the session. Her eyes narrowed on the man lounging outside the therapy room. "Jack? What are you doin' here?"

"I thought I'd surprise you. Take you out for dinner." He pressed his mouth to hers while her jaw hung half-open in shock. His lips moved to her ear. "Do you really consider me outrageously sexy, cowgirl?"

"In your dreams," she whispered back. Not that she wanted to revisit the explicit sexual dreams she'd been having damn near every night since Jack had moved in.

"Now isn't that sweet," Gladys said dreamily.

Sweet as snake oil.

"Since my intended doesn't intend to introduce us, I'll introduce myself." Jack clasped both Gladys's hands in his. "Jack Donohue."

"Gladys Johansson. You can call me Gladys. Actually, you can call me anytime."

"Need help out to your car?" Keely asked, trying to sidestep Jack.

"No, sweetie. You go on and get ready for your young man."

Jack grinned. "I'd be happy to walk you out while Keely is gussying herself up for me, Miz Gladys."

Keely snorted.

"I'd like that." Gladys waggled her fingers at Keely. "Toodles until next week."

When Jack sauntered back in, still smirking, Keely bit her tongue against lashing out at him for his presumptive behavior, not only with her, but also with her client.

"She is a sweetheart. Reminds me of a lady back home who used to serve me cookies and lemonade after I mowed her lawn. I always ended up staying and chatting with her for an hour or two."

Okay. That showed her a different side of Jack. Which seemed ironic, since earlier she'd been reflecting on those different, unknown, sides of herself.

"I'm starved. Where can we eat around here besides Dewey's?"

"I'm sure you're used to finer dining establishments than what's available in the Sundance-Moorcroft metro area."

"Glad you think so highly of me," he muttered.

"If the tasseled loafer fits..."

"Nice dig. Only took you thirty seconds. You're slacking, buttercup."

Keely shrugged. "I'm tired. My brain is sluggish. How about pizza?"

"No."

"Subway?"

"No."

"There's bar food at the Rusty Spur and the Golden Boot."

Impatiently, he said, "Just ride with me and we'll find someplace, okay?"

"I'll save you time and gas. If you're hungry there are two options. Dewey's or the Twin Pines."

"Let's go there."

"I can't. I can't step foot in the place, actually."

"Why not?"

"Umm. I've been banned from Twin Pines. For life. I think."

Jack's too-handsome face registered shock. "You've got to be kidding me."

"Nope."

"What did you do to get banned for life?"

"I was in a bar fight."

"You started a bar fight?"

"No, but I sure as hell didn't back down from one when someone else did. Stuff got broken. Bottles, tables, noses." She waved him off. "Old news."

"Not to me, but disturbing news nonetheless." Jack scowled. "Dewey's it is."

"I'll meet you. I have to close up and file my paperwork."

Keely considered changing her work clothes, but Jack would think she'd gussied herself up for him, so no dice. In Dewey's, she spotted him in the far corner booth. He stood, waiting to reseat himself until after she'd sat. Okay. That gentlemanly courtesy was impressive. And sweet. And unexpected.

Nervous, because this felt like an actual date, she flipped through the menu even when she'd memorized it ages ago. "What are you having?"

"Chicken fried steak."

"Sounds good. Been a while since I've had it."

"Careful, we're actually agreeing on something."

"Maybe it's a full moon."

His answering bad boy grin had her heart doing the two-step.

After the waitress took their order, Jack stared at her with unabashed interest. "What?" she said testily.

"I don't even know when your birthday is."

"It's not like you'll be around to shower me with expensive presents."

"We need to know some of that stuff about each other before the engagement party."

True. Especially in light of suspicions all wasn't right with said engagement. "May twenty-third. I'm twenty-seven. You?"

"April fourth. I'm thirty-four."

"You're an old timer, eh?"

A slight scowl. "I'd say experienced."

"So, Mr. Experienced, what other secrets do we need to share?"

"Start with the basic first date stuff. What's your favorite food?"

"Steak. Followed closely by bacon. Followed closely by chocolate." She picked up a straw and rolled it between her fingers. "I'll bet I can guess yours."

"No, you won't."

"Yes, I will."

There was that wicked grin again. "I dare you to try."

Keely considered him. "This is way too easy, Jack."

"So stun me with your insight, cowgirl."

"Poached salmon. Wild rice pilaf. Brussel sprouts. Plain cheesecake."

A stricken look crossed his face.

She smirked. "I totally nailed you didn't I?"

Jack angled across the table. "Not. Even. Close. But I am intrigued by the thought of you nailing me."

Oh. Hello lust. "The thought of nailing you has me equally intrigued." She offered him a coquettish look. "Are you a breast or a thigh guy?"

That caught him off guard enough his gaze actually dropped to her chest. "Ummm. What?"

"Or chicken?" she taunted softly.

His hot eyes returned to hers. "My favorite food is not chicken. It's not a nice juicy rump...roast, although I admit to being more of a butt man than a breast man."

Keely blinked. She was quickly losing control of this conversation.

"I'll give you one more chance to nail me," Jack said with a sexy rasp.

"Only one?" she cooed back.

Jack's hungry gaze zeroed in on her mouth. "Playing fast and loose will only encourage me to play the same. Be certain you're prepared for what that entails."

Yikes. "Speaking of favorite foods, I'm betting yours is some kind of wild game that fits with your personality. Boar?"

His lips lifted. "Wrong. This round goes to me. My favorite food is homemade meatloaf. Followed closely by mashed potatoes and gravy. Followed closely by corn on the cob."

"Holy crap. That's so...Midwestern of you, GQ."

"Surprised?"

"Very." Down home cooking appealed to Jack more than

haute cuisine? Man. He'd surprised her like four times today. "Your turn to guess. What's my favorite movie?"

"Easy. *The Princess Bride.*" He grinned. "What's mine?"

"*The Jerk,*" she shot back.

Jack laughed. A deep, rumbly, sexy sound and she caught herself wanting to smile and sigh at the same time.

"Try again."

"*Jackass?*" she tossed out.

More laughter.

"Okay. I give."

"*True Lies,*" he said.

"That seems appropriate."

Silence.

Keely fiddled with the straw, rolling it back and forth in the condensation.

Jack snatched her hand, stopping the fidgety movement.

Talk about big hands. Not soft, girly hands either, but rough. Manly. His fingers were long and thick, sprinkled with just enough dark hair to be masculine, not apelike. God. It'd been forever since she'd had a real man's hands stroking her bare skin. Would Jack be gentle? Teasing? Or forceful?

"Keely?"

She shifted her gaze up. The curiosity or guilt he saw in her eyes caused a spark of heat to flare in his.

Jack stretched across the table until their mouths were a kiss apart. "We're fucking kidding ourselves that we can keep this platonic for much longer."

The growly timbre of his voice destroyed any smartass comment she might've conjured. She wanted to hear that growling noise against her throat, in her ear, on her belly, on the insides of her thighs.

"Don't look at me like that," she breathed.

"Like what?"

"Like you want to—"

"Isn't this sweet, you two lovebirds holding hands and whispering naughty nothings to each other."

Keely looked up at India with murder in her eyes.

Jack recovered quickly. "India. Nice to see you looking so...round. Congratulations."

"Oh, bite me, Donohue. Babies rock but pregnancy sucks." India cocked her hip against the side of the booth. "Since you're gonna be part of the family now, I expect my rent won't go up. *Ever*. Especially in light of the fact you withheld the information about being our landlord."

Jack muttered something about false expectations.

Now this was better. Watching Jack get raked over the coals for a change.

"How are the engagement party preparations going?"

Talk about a short attention span. "Mom is doing everything. Jack's mother is coming Friday to help. We're staying out of the way."

"So how is it that you guys ended up together?" India asked.

Keely changed the subject. "You feeling okay?"

"Fine and fucking dandy. Fat as a frog. You've gotten worse at deflection, by the way, so suck it up and answer my question."

"Pregnancy has made you mean."

"*Meaner.* Start talking about how this love match came about."

"We're blaming you and Colt."

Jack went board stiff across from her.

"What did we have to do with it?" India demanded.

"Your wedding reception was the first time Jack and I acted on our attraction to each other, wasn't it, darlin'?"

He nodded and kissed her hand.

"Once we started working together...it was pointless to resist."

"It was destiny," Jack murmured.

"This sappy crap is making me want to barf," India said.

The waitress dropped off their food. "India, your order is done. I'll get it and meet you at the register."

"Thanks."

"Is it your night to cook?" Keely asked innocently.

"Ooh, you're as funny as my husband. I'm starved all the freakin' time." She shouted, "Hey, Bea, throw in like a dozen cookies too, willya?"

With that India waddled away.

"Pregnant women are so easily distracted by food."

Jack frowned at her. "Is there any place we can go in this town without running into one of your relatives?"

"Nope." Keely released his hand and reached for her steak knife, half-resentful, half-glad India had ruined the moment.

Jack wasn't surprised they finished the meal in near silence. In near record time too.

He paid the check and Keely headed upstairs to the apartment. The thought of watching her sexy ass shake as those long legs climbed the stairs made his dick hard.

Damn her relatives. She'd almost admitted she wanted him as much as he wanted her. He was to the *fuck it* point—he was fucked if he did and fucked if he didn't fuck her. Might as well grab some smokin' hot sex while he could get it.

"Keely?"

"In the living room."

She'd curled up in her favorite corner of the couch and flipped through the three channels. "When is the cable company supposed to be here?"

"Tomorrow. Between eight and noon. Will you be around?"

Keely's gaze flicked to him. "Why? Aren't you gonna be here to take care of it since it was your idea?"

Jack plopped on the couch. "Things went to shit today and I'm flying to Iowa first thing in the morning to straighten it out. I'll be back Friday night, Saturday morning at the latest."

"Whoa. Wait a second. Saturday night is our engagement party. You cannot miss that! The whole reason we're having the stupid party is for people to think we're getting married. Do you know how humiliating it'll be if you don't show up—"

"I'll be here, okay?"

"You'd better be. I mean it. So help me God, Jack Donohue, if you aren't standing beside me wearing a fake-ass smile to rival mine, I will track you down and flay off every bit of your yellow skin with a bullwhip."

Her lack of faith in him rankled. "Don't threaten me."

"It's not a threat. It's a promise."

"Big talk, tough girl."

"Just sayin'..." She turned away.

"Give me the damn remote."

"Fine." Keely threw it at him.

After ten minutes of enduring an insipid sitcom, she spoke. "Where does jetting off to Iowa leave my project this week?"

Her petulance wasn't from the interruption in the restaurant, but a business-related snit? That annoyed him even worse. "It wouldn't matter if I were here or not at this stage. I've stuck around because I was cementing our cover."

"Anxious to get back to your fast-paced lifestyle in Denver?"

"Yeah, some great lifestyle. I've been busy trying to play catch up the last couple years after everything went to hell. Living high on the hog hasn't been my number one priority." He looked at her, wondering if he sounded bitter to her. "What?"

"Which is worse? The fact she left you for him? Or losing the partnership?"

No one had ever asked that question. "Both. Everything tumbled like a house of cards."

"Did your folks meet her?"

Jack laughed. "Are you kidding? Talk about an episode of *Green Acres.*"

"So you're embarrassed about bein' raised on a farm?"

"Yes. Could we please—"

"Why? Justin wasn't embarrassed."

"Justin was a rodeo cowboy and it fed into his persona. I'm an architect and it detracts from mine. Big difference. How many guys did you bring home to meet the parents?"

"Point taken. But not bringing dates here wasn't because my rural roots mortified me. Mostly I was embarrassed about the kind of guys I'd been dating."

Her honesty shook him to his core and spurred him to follow suit. "Look. My parents didn't know anything about Martine except I dated her and we broke up. They didn't know why my partnership with Baxter hit the skids either. None of it mattered because my dad had a fatal heart attack a month later."

"Is that why Justin dropped out of the PBR tour?"

"Yeah. He's taken over running the farm, which is what he and Dad always wanted. None of us expected it'd be so soon." It infuriated Jack that his dad had worked himself into an early grave. Infuriated and saddened him. "Anyway, Justin keeps an eye on Mom."

"Do you ever help out?"

"If you mean throwing money at them out of guilt, yes. If you mean sitting in the combine or—" *going home to face my past,* "—slipping on a pair of coveralls and shoveling manure, no."

"So they don't know—"

"No. I keep my business and personal lives separate," he said curtly.

When she opened her mouth to argue, Jack silenced her with a harsh look.

"Don't presume to dissect the way I handle my family life when you handle yours awful damn close to the same way."

Keely's head fell back into the couch cushion. "We're never gonna pull this off, Jack. We can't go five minutes without sniping at each other."

"We managed more than five minutes in the restaurant."

"Pure luck. Lightning won't strike the same place twice."

"Then let's force it to strike again."

"Wow. That sounds fun. *Not.*"

Just to be obstinate, he scooted closer to her. "Your middle name is West. What's mine?"

"Jack...*Off* Donohue?"

"Funny. My middle name is Michael."

"Jack Michael. Kinda sounds like—"

"Chas Michael Michaels," they said simultaneously.

He grinned. "Maybe we do have a few things in common."

"Name one thing besides lowbrow movies."

"We both like Carter's kids."

"True."

"What about sports?"

"I like rodeo."

"That's it?"

Keely shrugged. "Yep."

"Figures. I watched VERSUS when Justin was on the PBR tour, but after he left I stopped. You don't like football or baseball?"

"Ugh. No. Men will watch anything with balls. Which is why I'm surprised about men's homophobia." She shot him a sideways glance. "If you tell me you like men's wrestling or figure skating I'll knit you a rainbow sweater, GQ."

Good God, Keely was a pain in the ass. He wanted to kiss that smart mouth so much it bordered on ridiculous.

Jack draped his arm across the back of the sofa, feeling like a teenage boy attempting to get to second base. Hah. Try again. He hadn't made it to first base with her.

Yet.

No reaction to him invading her space.

Stubborn woman. If Keely wouldn't acknowledge him, he'd goad her. "What were you about to say in the restaurant before India interrupted us?"

"I don't remember," she replied flippantly.

"That's crap."

"Seriously. I don't. I've been told I have a very short attention span."

He clucked a couple of times.

She jabbed his gut with her elbow. "I ain't skeered a nothin'."

"Prove it. Tell me."

Keely debated. Then her words tumbled out in a rush, "Why you were looking at me like that?"

"Like what?" he asked inanely, even when he knew.

"Like you wanted to devour me. You looked at me like that once before. At Colt and India's wedding reception. Remember?"

The memory broadsided him. After his life went to shit in Chicago, he'd hid out at Carter and Macie's to try and get his head on straight. At Carter's insistence, he'd tagged along to Colt and India's wedding reception. He'd ended up doing whiskey shots with Carter, Colby and Cord. Seeing the men's connections with their wives only increased his sense of displacement, of disillusionment. Of the bone-deep fear he'd never be worthy of that kind of love and devotion, let alone find it. No matter how much he drank, he felt completely sober...until he'd clapped eyes on Keely McKay. Talk about punch drunk. She was breathtaking. When their eyes met, a primal need consumed him.

Jack had crossed the floor, taken her hand and led her out of the big tent without a single word. He hadn't cared that she wore high heels. He hadn't cared she was in a long, formal bridesmaid's dress. He hadn't cared about anything but slaking his lust with her sexy, nubile body while gazing into her incredible midnight blue eyes.

Once they were finally alone, Jack couldn't voice a coherent thought, so he kissed her.

It was the single most explosive kiss he'd ever experienced. It literally knocked them both to their knees. They rolled around on the cold ground amidst the dirt, rocks and hay. Every kiss burned hotter. Every touch built his pure blinding lust for her higher. Keely's urgent whispers tickled his ear as her hands worked his belt buckle.

That's where the memory blurred. Hell, that's where it ended completely. Jack woke up alone, hours later, freezing, with his pants unzipped. His stomach hurt—probably she'd socked him in the gut after his untimely fall into drunkenness. His body had picked a bad time to succumb to the whiskey.

Although they'd never spoken of what hadn't happened, from that moment on, Keely McKay had hated the sight of him.

Not that he blamed her. He couldn't even look at her now.

"I don't know how to interpret that look any better now than I did back then," she said, subtly bringing him back to the present.

Jack twined his fingers in her hair. "How long we can continue this pretense we're not imagining balling each other's brains out?"

"Once bitten, twice shy, Jack. Flirting to cement our 'cover' is one thing. Beyond that...not happening."

He gave her credit. Keely didn't scoot away from his touch to prove her point. "So if I kissed you right now?"

"I'd enjoy it, but that's as far as it'd go."

"We can go directly to the bed twenty feet from here," he said with a silken purr. "We've got nothing but time."

Keely's eyes widened with pure comic sarcasm. "Ooh. And would you need time to snag your bottle of Viagra?"

Jack yanked on her hair. "FYI, buttercup, I don't need any fucking Viagra."

"Really?" She batted at his hold until he released her hair. "It would've been handy three years ago when my hand was on your deflating cock."

His humor vanished as his pride emerged. "You want to

know why I lost my erection that night?" Jack crowded her until they were nose to nose. "Because I imagined you fucking my little brother. I realized I didn't want sloppy seconds."

Keely shoved him and scrambled off the couch. "That's an interesting lie, Mr. Limp Dick. Keep believing it if it serves your self-deluding reputation as a stud."

"Don't believe me?"

"You just pegged my bullshit meter to an all time high. It's called 'whiskey dick' for a reason, Jack-*off*."

Silence.

Jesus. Man up. She deserves better.

As Jack started to apologize, to admit his shame about the incident and plead for another chance, Keely loomed over him, shaking with fury.

"Have an awesome fucking time in Iowa. But if you pull a no show Saturday night, I'll track you down and skin you alive—starting with your squishy dick. Not a threat, a promise." She retreated to her bedroom and slammed the door.

Not what he'd been angling for tonight. Not at all. And yet, he wasn't surprised. Turned on, but not surprised.

Viagra.

As if.

Jack adjusted his erection. He considered breaking down her damn door and dropping his pants to prove "squishy" wasn't in his goddamn realm of existence when in her company.

Right. Terrific plan. The mouthy cowgirl probably had shotguns under her bed.

Screw that. Jack wasn't backing down. However, pushing her tonight smacked of harassment.

But this was far from over.

Chapter Seven

She was going to fucking kill him.

Jack wasn't here yet.

His plane had been delayed leaving Des Moines. They'd spoken briefly once and not about the farce they were presenting to their family and friends...in less than an hour.

"Nervous, dear?"

Keely turned and smiled at Jack's mother, Dorothy "Doro" Donohue. "Yes. I've been to engagement parties before, but never mine. I tend to get nervous in new situations."

"Jack does too, if that's any consolation. But I'm sure you already knew that."

No, she hadn't a clue the infallible Jack Donohue experienced anxious moments. Who better than his mother to share his foibles? "Really? He's kept that from me. He's always so...poised."

"I'm sure he's gotten over it. We all overcome adversity." Doro fussed with the strap on Keely's dress. "My Jack is a good man. We couldn't have kept the farm after Marvin died if not for Jack's financial support."

Keely was speechless. Obviously Doro wanted to connect with her, regardless of whether Jack would be livid she'd spilled intimate details of his family's financial struggles.

"Listen to me blather on. I know I've said it a hundred times, but I'm happy he's settling down with you, Keely. Hopefully he'll take time to enjoy his life with you. You'll be good for him."

"Why?"

"I imagine you call him on his b.s."

"Doro!"

"Oh, please. Jack is a man who expects to be in charge all the time. He needs a strong woman who'll stand up to him. You knocking him down a peg or two will keep him grounded and your lives interesting, that's for sure."

Keely smiled. She genuinely adored the plump, sweet widow with the gentle disposition. Pity the only thing Jack inherited from Doro were her green eyes. "Thanks for coming to help my mom get ready for this."

She waved off Keely's thanks. "It's been a treat to be around your family. Your brothers' wives certainly are a fertile bunch."

"Ain't that the truth."

"You'll have to draw straws for the ring bearer position."

Because she was feeling ornery, Keely said, "I'm hoping the fertility blessing holds true for Jack and me. He wants a pile of kids. Right away."

Doro's entire face lit up. "Really? Well, Jack isn't exactly a pup, is he? And I would love to have grandbabies to spoil."

"Be sure and ask Jack about it when you see him." Keely winked and sauntered off, feeling...guilty. It was dirty pool dragging his sweet mother into their warring ways.

"Keely, sweets, can I see you for a second?"

She plastered on a smile to hide her guilty look before she faced her mother. "Sure. What do you need?"

"Follow me." Her mom led them to a small office down the hallway from the main room. After she closed the door, she sagged against the metal desk.

"Ma? What's wrong?"

"Nothing." Carolyn McKay sighed. "That's not true. With all the party preparations I haven't had time to talk to you alone." She pinned Keely with a probing look. "I'd be lax in my mothering duties if I didn't ask if you're sure about marrying Jack."

Keely's stomach clenched. "Why?"

"It doesn't exactly seem to be a love match, and when you're together..."

"Mom. You haven't seen us together except the one time we told you we were engaged."

Her gaze narrowed. "Maybe that's why I'm concerned."

Damn. Redirect. "We're both busy. He's been gone—"

"That's another thing that worries me. I'm selfish enough to want you to live here with the rest of our family, but I'm enough of a realist to understand that might not be possible with Jack's job. He'll be your husband. You'll need to be with him, wherever that is, and I doubt that'll be in Wyoming."

How was Keely supposed to allay her mother's fears when they were groundless? "My clinic is here. My life is here. My family is here. I'm not going anywhere."

"As much as it pleases me to hear that, promise me you won't marry Jack if you're not absolutely sure he's the right one."

Keely frowned. "Why do you say that?"

Her mother brushed the hair from Keely's cheek. "Because contrary to popular opinion in our family, you are *not* impulsive. This engagement blindsided everyone. I recognize the wild look in your eyes, Keely. I wore that same fearful look when I became engaged to your father. Since you were a little girl I've worried you'd never find a man who'd measure up to the pedestal you've placed your brothers and your father on."

"You don't think Jack measures up?"

"Sweetie, you oughta be asking yourself that question, not me."

A knock sounded and a second later her dad stuck his head in. "People are startin' to arrive, Caro. Who's on meet and greet detail?"

"AJ and Channing."

"Have any idea where they are?"

"No. Hang on, I'll be right there."

He nodded and closed the door.

"Snoopy damn man," her mother muttered. "Last thing, I promise. Hold out your arm." A silver bracelet dangled from her fingertips. She wrapped it around Keely's wrist and fastened it. "My mother gave this to me when I became engaged to your dad and now I'm passing it on to you."

Between each crystal bead was a steel link giving the bracelet a strength that belied the delicate look. Keely's eyes swam with tears. Her throat tightened. "Oh, Mama, thank you. It's beautiful."

"So are you. You're welcome. I hope it brings you good

luck." She kissed Keely's forehead. "I love you, girlie. Be happy with Jack. If that means you'll be living with him in Denver or the Congo, so be it. Happiness in your *own* life is all I've ever wanted for you." Her mother shuffled out.

Confused by the myriad of emotions, Keely hid in the office for another ten minutes. When she'd stalled long enough, she ventured out. She and Jack entered the main room at the same time.

Oh. My. Freakin'. God. Talk about being on a pedestal. No, the man was in a class by his handsome self. He wore a black suit that looked casual but the cut and fabric screamed expensive. No tie. He'd left the last button on his pristine white shirt undone, exposing the thick column of his throat. Keely had the uncontrollable urge to run to him, press her lips to the vulnerable spot above his collarbone and taste his skin.

But Jack didn't flash her the smile that turned her knees wobbly. He scowled at her. Scowled. At her. At her own damn engagement party.

Jerk.

Indifferent to their audience, Keely strolled across the room acting like she couldn't give a crap he'd finally shown up. Which would tick him off.

Still, his heated eyes never left hers.

She latched onto his lapels, using them to draw herself to her tiptoes. "Perfect suit for a funeral, GQ." She smashed her mouth to his for a brief, hard kiss.

Jack's hands circled her upper arms. He appeared to be hauling her closer, when in actuality, he was pushing her back. "You determined to piss me off first thing?"

"Yep. Is it working?"

"You have no idea how much."

"Oh joy, my life is complete." She spoke against his throat. "If you would've pulled a no-show, I would've tracked you down and castrated you, Jack-*off*."

"Big talk."

"How so?"

"I guarantee if you ever put your hands on my junk again, chopping it off will be the last thing on your mind, buttercup."

She snorted. "Cocky much?"

"Only when it's warranted." Jack kissed her temple and

nuzzled his face against her head. "Don't fucking push me, Keely, I'm not in the mood."

"Aw. And I so give a flying fuck what kind of bad day you've had when I've been here alone for the last three goddamn days, fielding questions about our supposed relationship."

"For Christsake, it wasn't like I was on vacation. I've been in Iowa. In cornfield hell."

"Did you say you got cornholed in Iowa?"

Jack actually growled.

She grinned. Keely one; Jack zero.

Anyone who watched them would see lovers embracing in a private moment. Not the nip Keely placed on his jaw or the answering bite he gave the top of her ear. She sucked in a harsh breath at the sharp pain. "Bastard."

"Did you miss me?"

"Like I'd miss an oozing canker sore."

Jack laughed and released her. "Now if you'll excuse me, I need to track down my mother." He pivoted on his dress shoe and sauntered to the kitchen.

Damn frustrating man. She headed the opposite direction even when she wanted to follow him to see what he was up to.

The second Jack disappeared from Keely's line of vision he closed his eyes and collapsed against the wall. Pulse racing, cock hard, mouth dry.

Dammit. That smart-mouthed cowgirl would be the death of him yet. Jesus. Did she have to look so goddamn fantastic? One look at Keely's sinfully curvy body in that skintight porn-star-meets-country-girl dress, and any objectivity sailed right out of his lust-addled brain. He couldn't think beyond stopping her insults with his mouth. His lips. His teeth. His tongue.

Get control for fuck's sake.

"Got a minute, Donohue?"

Startled, Jack's eyes opened. How had Cord McKay snuck up on him so fast?

You were stuck in a fantasy featuring your sexy fiancée, a woman who'd rather spit on you than swap spit with you.

"Sure, Cord. Glad you could make it to the party."

The man planted himself in front of Jack, arms crossed,

menace in his posture. "Here's where I'm comin' from. If you do a single damn thing to hurt her, I will gut you."

Jack waited, expecting Cord to grin and say, "Just kiddin', man, welcome to the family."

But Cord's fiery blue eyes, identical to Keely's, refused to break contact. "Understand?"

"Yes."

"Good." Cord walked past without another word. But slow enough that Jack glimpsed the knife case attached to Cord's belt.

This was going to be one goddamn long night.

For the next hour, while friends and family mingled, Jack and Keely stayed as far away from each other as possible. No one noticed, and for the first time Jack was grateful for Keely's large family.

But he watched her. Constantly. She had a dark-haired, dark-eyed baby girl cocked on her hip as she talked to her cousin Chassie. Two men—Chassie's husbands—approached, and each kissed Keely's cheek. Trevor plucked the grinning baby girl from Keely's arms while Edgard rubbed Chassie's belly and murmured to her. A blond boy streaked through their circle before rejoining the roving gang of kids—which looked to be about twenty strong.

More family members joined the group and Jack tried to place them all.

Why? It's not like it matters if you know their names. This is a charade, remember?

He listened to two older women speculating on how wild Keely's bachelorette party would be. He refilled his cup for the third time, wishing someone had spiked the punch.

The hair on the back of his neck stood up. Jack slowly turned around. Great. McKay number two. "Colby. Nice to see you."

Colby grunted. He looked around and leaned in. "Consider this your one and only warnin', Donohue. You ever hurt her, I'll gut you."

Jesus. "So noted."

"Just wanted to be up front."

"I appreciate it."

Without another word, Colby strolled back to his sweet-looking wife and rowdy kids.

Jack indulged in small talk with a couple of ranchers who'd worked with the McKays for years. But as he listened politely to talk of drought, high feed prices, low returns and government interference, his gaze continually sought Keely out. She laughed and flitted from group to group, the lovely embodiment of a free spirit. Then he noticed her hand was clenched into a tight fist at her side. Was she looking to punch someone? Who?

You probably.

For some reason, that made Jack smile.

"So as long as you're hidin' over here, I wanna take the opportunity to tell you if you harm a single hair on Keely's head, I will gut you."

His smile dried up and he looked sideways at Colt McKay.

"We clear on that?"

Jack knew his attempts to reassure the assorted male McKays that he'd never cause precious Keely distress would backfire when the "engagement" went to hell. He kept his lie simple. "Understood."

Colt nodded and meandered away.

Another two hours remained of the party. If Jack stuck to the crowds, maybe he could avoid the oh-so-fun, one-on-one threat time with Keely's remaining brothers.

As if she sensed him gawking at her, Keely cocked her head and looked straight at him. Her tight-lipped smile was better than flipping him off, he supposed, but not by much.

"Funny how my little sis ain't wearing the googly-eyed look of a woman wildly in love. She looks like she wants to punch you in the face," Cam McKay commented behind Jack.

Fan-fucking-tastic. "You know Keely. She gets mad first, listens to reason second. She'll be fine once we're alone to hash it out."

"That being said... I'm speaking off the record, not as a deputy, but as Keely's brother."

Jack waited.

"If you cause her a second's pain, I will gut you. Understand?"

"Loud and clear."

Cam grunted and shuffled off.

Imagining his bloody guts dragging in the dirt was getting

old. Maybe no one would notice if he snuck out, since most of the attendees were Keely's family and friends.

What did that say about him?

A hand landed hard in the middle of his back and Carter McKay sidled up beside him. "So you and Keely, huh? Gotta admit, I didn't see *that* one coming."

"I did," he grumbled. "I've had it bad for her since the first time I met her at your house when she was jailbait."

Carter laughed. Not pleasantly. "Good thing you never told me that before you put a ring on her finger."

"Why?"

"She's my baby sis. I gotta look out for her and make sure she isn't hooking up with some scumbag."

Jack bristled. "You suggesting I'm not good enough for her?"

"Yep. If I ever get the barest whisper you've hurt her in any way, well, fair warning, I'm gonna gut you, Donohue, old friend or not. Dig?"

"I dig."

"Good." Carter clapped him on the shoulder again. "Smart man. I see the boys are back to sneaking cookies. Gotta bust them." And Carter was gone.

Could this day get any more bizarre?

Another set of footsteps stopped behind him. Jack braced himself for a new "friendly" warning from another male member of the knife-happy, psycho McKay clan. But his mother's sweet voice rang out. "It's a lovely party, isn't it?"

"Thanks to you, I've heard." Jack hugged her tightly, feeling ridiculous at the boyish need for his mother. He was immediately comforted by her presence, her softness and the familiar scent of her always-present Jean Nate perfume. "Sorry I was gone this week when you were here."

"No worries, son. For all intents and purposes, I'm retired. I know you're a busy man. I enjoyed spending time with Keely. Such a ball of fire, that girl. And her family is wonderful."

Yeah, they're a swell bunch when they're not threatening to gut you.

His mother picked a piece of lint from his lapel. "I'm thrilled you're marrying such a perfect woman for you."

Jack's gaze zeroed in on tantalizing Keely, gesturing wildly as she talked to cluster of white-haired women. Young. Old. Male. Female. Didn't matter. She was always surrounded by people. Keely drew them to her like bees to flowers. Man, she was sweet. And hot. And pissed as hell at him.

Keely caught him looking again, and not so subtly scratched her cheek with her middle finger.

His dick stirred and he grinned at her.

Yeah, he had it bad that it turned him on when she flipped him off.

"I see you watching her all the time."

Guiltily, he returned attention to his mother. "She's my intended. Naturally I'm looking at her. Do you find that odd?"

"No. I find it sweet. You don't show that side of yourself often these days and I'm glad you're sharing it with her."

Before Jack formulated a response, his mother added, "But I am surprised you are insistent about starting a family right away." Her gaze drifted to the band of McKay offspring running amok through the crowd.

His eyes zoomed to hers. "Where'd you hear that?"

"Keely told me."

"When did Keely share that tidbit?"

"Earlier today. She said you weren't getting any younger and she didn't want people mistaking you for your kid's grandfather at school events."

What a troublemaker. That little snot-nosed cowgirl had earned serious payback.

"I recognize that *mind your own business* scowl, Jack."

Ah hell, now he'd hurt her feelings. He was batting a thousand today. "Mom—"

"I didn't mean to speak out of turn. And I understand how much you value your privacy. But to be honest, I can't wait for grandchildren to spoil. The sooner the better."

"I'm planning on getting a lot of baby-making practice in. Soon." Jack grinned when his mother gasped and whapped him on the arm.

His brother inserted himself into the conversation. "Well, ain't this just great? Us all together celebrating how my big brother stole my girl away for himself?"

"Justin David Donohue. What a horrible thing to say to your brother."

"It's true. Jack wanted, no, he *encouraged* me to break up with Keely so he could have her. Tricky, huh?"

"Get over it. That was years ago. Whatever happened between you two—" he warned Justin not to put Keely in a bad light in front of their mother, "—is over and done with. Keely and I crossed paths long before you entered the picture, so technically, she was mine first."

Justin belligerently folded his arms over his chest. "You must've worked some serious magic on her because Keely hated you, Jack. She called you—"

"Every name in the book, I know. We laugh about it now, actually. Sometimes Keely even uses it as a term of endearment." He smiled and gave his mother a one-armed hug. "Speaking of...I need to have a word with my soon-to-be blushing bride."

Jack felt Justin's glare singeing his hair as he wandered toward Keely surrounded by her friends. *Too bad, bro. You fucked up. She's mine now.* He hovered on the outskirts of the circle, waiting for his beloved to acknowledge him.

She didn't.

So Jack set his chin on her shoulder and palmed her hips, trying not to be distracted by that damned lilac scent. "Hey, baby."

Keely immediately stiffened up.

Everyone in the group noticed. He half-chided, "Relax. I won't tickle you in front of your friends." He dropped his voice. "All my favorite ticklish spots are strictly between us."

Muffled laughter.

"Anyway, can you all excuse us? I need to steal her away for a minute."

Murmured assent followed. And miracle of miracles, Keely didn't argue.

Jack clasped her hand and towed her behind him.

Halfway down the empty hallway, Keely jerked out of his hold. She put her hands on her hips. "What's so all-fired important you had to drag me away?"

"Where in the hell do you get off telling my mother, for Christsake, that we're going to start a family—a big family— right after the wedding bells stop pealing?"

Her mouth curled in an impish smile. "I was cementing our

cover, Jack. I thought you'd be happy."

He got right in her face. "Nothing about this situation is making me happy, Keely. Especially not every goddamn one of your brothers threatening to gut me—*gut me!*—like some redneck code of vengeance if I do anything to hurt poor little ol' you."

"Then you'd better make me happy, huh?" she said sweetly.

Jack crowded her against the wall, bracing his hands on either side of her head. "Try again."

"What do you expect me to say? I have no control over my brothers." Keely drilled him in the chest with her index finger. "And speaking of... Since when does *your* brother get to act all, 'You're the best thing that ever happened to me, baby', when that stupid asshole dumped *me*?"

"Fuck if I know. I have no control over my brother either."

They glared at each other.

"If you have nothing else to chew my ass about, let me go."

"Not a chance, buttercup." He searched her eyes. No teasing warmth. Just cool appraisal. "Why are you being like this?"

"Like what? Business-like? Isn't that how you wanted it between us in private? You turn the charm on and off with me whenever it suits you. Why can't I do the same to you?"

"Because even though this engagement is fake, you're not, Keely. I don't want you to become like me."

Her eyes shot daggers at him. "God, you piss me off."

"Why? What did I say?" Hell, he thought what he'd said made sense. He'd been honest with her for a change.

"Just when I want to punch you in the kidney for bein' a total jackass, you show me a part of you that ain't half-bad."

Jack's heart sped up. "Which part?"

"That part. The real, sweet, sincere side of you. You didn't toss off a sexual comment like 'I'll show you the best part of me, baby'. You act as if this is more than us cementing our cover. You act like you care about me."

"I do care about you, Keely. More than I should." Jack brushed a damp tendril of her glossy hair behind her ear, letting his finger trace her perfect, beautifully shaped jawline.

With his every inhalation, Keely's scent teased him. Warm. Flowery. Womanly. He leaned closer, drawing in a deeper breath. When their gazes clashed and Jack saw raw desire swimming in the amazing blueness of her eyes, he stopped fighting the inevitable. He framed her face in his shaking hands and said, "Fuck it," before he smothered her mouth with a blistering kiss.

Chapter Eight

She was kissing Jack Donohue. Kissing him like crazy. Kissing him like she'd fantasized about after he'd kissed her so thoroughly at Colt and India's wedding reception.

It was so much better when they were both sober.

Keely slid her hands beneath his suit coat up his muscular back. Oh man. Such a hard-toned body. Such an insistent mouth. The hint of cologne on his heated skin wafted up from his open-collar shirt. Drugged. She felt utterly drugged by his masculine scent and the sheer power of his body pressed to hers.

Jack wouldn't let their lips part for more than a second before he dove back in for another mind-blowing kiss. His tongue was hot velvet and smooth as whiskey as it glided and stroked and teased. He seduced her, reduced her to a trembling mass of need with just the power of his avid mouth.

"Sweet Jesus, Keely," he muttered against her lips. "I want you so fucking bad."

"Jack—"

He kissed her chin. "Steamy, raunchy sex is a more productive outlet for our frustrations than flinging insults."

"I agree," she moaned when his lips slowly feathered down her throat, hitting every sensitive spot with unerring accuracy.

Jack sucked the tender slope between her shoulder and her collarbone, letting his breath fan the damp spots as his tongue licked to the other side.

The gentle sweep of his thumb in front of her ear as his firm lips and sharp teeth assaulted her neck caused her whole body to quiver with unbridled lust.

"I want to hike up your skirt and fuck you right now against this wall. Raw." His mouth brushed the shell of her ear. "Hard." He blew oh so softly. "Fast."

Her sex moistened and clenched with want.

Then she and Jack were face to face. His wild eyes didn't fit his matter-of-fact tone. "Say you'll let me do every dirty thing to you I've ever fantasized about."

"You've imagined having sex with me?"

"Always," he admitted. His rough whisper launched another blissful shiver through her. "Since you were barely sixteen."

Keely blinked at him, trying desperately to believe his incredibly sweet bullshit. "Strange way of showing it, GQ."

"We both know you would've lorded it over me. I fought it. No more." He pressed his pelvis into the cradle of her hips, letting his cock rub her belly button. "Say yes."

As if she could possibly say no. Keely raked her fingers down his back, wishing her fingernails were leaving scratches from his shoulders to his tight ass. "Yes."

Jack's never-ending kisses morphed from brutal to sweet. Passion tempered with unexpected tenderness. Her head was buzzing. Her blood was humming. Her body was doing the boot scootin' boogie. The kiss waxed and waned, burned and soothed, so she almost didn't hear the giggles. When the noise finally registered, louder, Keely managed to break her lips free.

"Jack. We have an audience." She peered over Jack's broad shoulder. Her nephews and nieces were gawking at them.

When she attempted to extricate herself, his possessive embrace increased. "Who cares?"

"They'll tattle to everyone." Keely caught the eye of Kyler, the self-appointed ringleader. "Keep this to yourself, okay?"

Kyler's enormous grin revealed two empty spots where his front teeth had been. "No way." He raced down the hall in front of his entourage. In the main room, he shouted, "Hey, guess what?" The crowd quieted. "Aunt Keely and Jack are kissin' in the hallway!"

Laughter broke out.

Kyler snatched his moment in the spotlight as his due. "And they were kissin' so much they didn't even notice us. We waited, but it didn't seem like they were ever gonna stop. They were kissin' *forever.*"

Keely groaned. Her forehead fell to Jack's chest. "See? Now everyone knows we were sucking face."

Jack kissed her crown. Twice. "And we'da gotten away with it too if wasn't for them meddlin' kids."

She snickered and looked up at him. "I never would've pegged you as a *Scooby Doo* fan."

"I have *Scooby Doo* boxers."

"Aren't you full of surprises?"

"You've no idea of the surprises I have in store for you."

"Bring it on."

He made a low, sexy noise in his throat and his eyes flashed heat.

"But first, we oughta face the curious crowd, huh?"

"I suppose." Jack stepped back. He kissed her knuckles, and gestured for her to go first. "After you."

"Huh-uh, bucko. Together in a united front."

"As soon as this party is over, I'm hauling your ass back to the apartment to celebrate our engagement." His insistent voice tickled her ear. "Don't even think about chickening out on me, cowgirl."

"I am so ready for you to prove you're cock of the walk, GQ."

"Let's get this over with."

Catcalls and wolf whistles greeted them as they crossed the threshold. Someone shouted, "Speech!" Someone else shouted, "Toast!" Yet another person shouted, "Let's see another kiss!"

Jack sensed her unease and murmured, "Trust me to handle it?"

"No."

He chuckled. "Tough. There's no way to get out of it now, and I don't want you slipping up and calling me Jack-off in a fit of pique."

"Fine. Just...don't embarrass me on purpose or anything, okay? I hate that."

"Hey." He blocked her from the crowd's view. He held her chin and peered into her eyes. "Keely. I'd never do that." Jack's mouth brushed hers in a kiss so sweet and earnest her fears vanished.

More catcalls.

Jack led her to the front of the room behind the cake table. Keely kept her gaze focused on Jack's striking profile.

"Thanks to everyone for coming today. And Kyler, buddy, you've got incredibly bad timing."

Laughter.

"The truth is, I've been gone all week, and I was extremely late getting here today, which didn't please my intended at all. And she shared that displeasure with me. Several times. Loudly."

More laughter.

Her stomach roiled. Damn him. He'd sworn he wouldn't embarrass her.

Give him a chance. Trust him like he asked you to.

Keely inhaled and let it out slowly.

"Which comes as no surprise to most of you. Keely and I haven't exactly been... What's the word I'm looking for, buttercup?"

"Civil?" she supplied.

Another round of guffaws.

"Yes, we haven't exactly been civil to each other over the years. So we were more shocked than anyone when our feelings for each other changed in such a short amount of time. But the fact of the matter is, I'm absolutely crazy about her, and she feels the same about me." Jack's questioning gaze hooked hers.

She blew him a kiss. "Keep going, Jack darlin', you're startin' to get back in my good graces."

Muted laughter.

"I speak for both of us when I say we're happy to be here amidst our families and friends, celebrating what we both wanted but never thought we'd find. Thank you." He brought Keely's left hand to his mouth and kissed her engagement ring.

She laid her palm on his cheek; her fingers traced the hollow beneath his cheekbone. She would've been content with that little PDA. But Jack wasn't.

He curled his hand around her neck and yanked her forward for a prolonged kiss that damn near melted her fillings.

While she basked in the moment, pressed against Jack's body, his mouth controlling hers with possessive kisses, and clapping surrounding them, Keely almost wished this engagement was the real deal.

The photographer snapped a billion pictures. Keely's face hurt from smiling. Her feet hurt from wearing heels. And somehow through it all, Jack found a way to keep her laughing, as well as lacing every sentence with sexual innuendo.

It was enthralling. It was scary as hell because there was no going back now. They'd be lovers before the end of the night, guaranteed.

After the party ended, Keely shooed Jack away to spend time with his family while she helped clean up the party remnants.

"I have to say, Jack's little speech completely changed my mind, K."

Keely folded a pale lavender satin tablecloth. "Changed it about what, AJ?"

"About how you and Jack feel about each other. It was very romantic. Funny. Sweet without being silly." AJ snatched the tablecloth, stacked it with the others. "But I'll confess—the biggest convincer? You two making out when you weren't aware anyone was watching."

She froze. "Omigod. How many people saw that?"

AJ shrugged. "Enough."

"Great."

"We all thought it was." She sighed. "Reminds me of when me and Cord first hooked up. Man. We could not keep our hands off each other."

Keely snorted and pointed to AJ's distended belly. "You still can't keep your hands off each other."

"True. It's great to be me." She grinned.

Carolyn bustled in with a cardboard box. "Okay. The kitchen is cleaned and this is the last of my stuff to take home."

Since her mom's hands were full, Keely hugged her from behind. "Thanks for everything. You rocked it, Ma. It was a fantastic party."

"I thought so, yet I'm glad we're only doin' this once." Carolyn yawned. "Lord, I'd better get home before I fall asleep standing up. AJ, darlin', you need a ride?"

"Nah. I have my truck since Cord took the boys home."

"Good enough. See you." Carolyn hefted the box and

disappeared out the side door.

At AJ's 350 Cummins turbo diesel Chevy, Keely said, "Need a boost getting into your monster truck, el preggo?"

"No. But you can bet your butt I'll let my handsome hubby give me a hand to help me down."

Knowing Cord, that hand would go straight up his wife's skirt. Those two still acted like randy teens. Keely admitted a tinge of jealousy her best friend had found the type of love all women dream of.

She meandered to her own rig, anxious about going home, which was a total crock because chances were slim Jack would even be there yet.

Still...how would this play out? Scenarios flitted through her brain but nothing solidified. Maybe having a blank slate wasn't such a bad thing.

Trudging up the stairs, she knew she'd ditch her high heels first thing. People thought pointy-toed cowboy boots were painful? Please. Boots were bedroom slippers compared to these torturous devices.

Keely had just locked the door behind her and tossed her purse on the side table when she heard him speak.

"I was beginning to wonder if you'd chickened out."

His deep, slightly amused voice triggered tingles of anticipation. "No. My mom did all the party prep work. I couldn't leave her there to handle the cleanup."

"Thoughtful of you."

"I try."

She focused on him, slouched in a straight back kitchen chair. The glow of the backlighting gave Jack an attractively dangerous look. Barefoot, with his pristine shirt unbuttoned; his sleeves were rolled up, exposing his thick forearms lightly dusted with dark hair. Clutching a glass of amber liquid in his hand, he reminded her of James Bond—a gorgeous professional male, but ruggedly raw and masculine beneath the polished exterior. His face was shadowed, masking his emotions. But the aura surrounding him wasn't the cool and collected demeanor of a patient man. No, the air crackled with the energy of an animal ready to pounce.

Right then, Keely knew she was way out of her league with Jack Donohue. He'd push her. Control her. Force her to experience levels of need and desire she'd never fathomed.

Jack tipped the glass and sipped, studying her from his spot in the center of the room. She waited. It damn near killed her to wait, but she did it.

"So tell me, are you scared of me?"

"A little."

"Because you think I've been drinking?" He waggled the glass. "Iced tea, not whiskey."

"Good to know," she said inanely.

"Why am I scary to you, Keely?"

"Because we've been avoiding getting tangled up for a reason, and here we are, about to get seriously entangled."

"What reason?" he asked nonchalantly.

"My reason? Or what I think yours is?"

His white teeth glimmered in the darkness when he smiled. "Your reason first. And I expect nothing less than complete honesty from you, buttercup. Especially when you enlighten me with what you perceive as my reason."

Keely squeezed her hands into fists and counted to ten. Twenty. Thirty. Forty. Fifty. Sixty.

"I'm waiting," he said huskily, when she'd hit the one hundred-twenty mark.

"Here's the God honest truth. I've avoided getting tangled up with you because I'll give in to you, Jack. I'll give you everything you demand from me in bed, every part of myself I've never shared with another man. I'm a strong-willed woman. I'm used to calling the shots with men. But when I look at you, I have the overwhelming need to...surrender. I've felt the sexual heat shimmering between us since I was sixteen and I had no clue what it was."

"Are you afraid it's more than just sex?"

She shook her head. If she didn't speak, technically, she wasn't lying.

"What do you see as my motivation?" he asked, his voice barely a throaty rumble.

"You've got something to prove. To me. To yourself. Because of what happened three years ago."

Jack laughed softly. "How insightful you are, cowgirl. It's a little scary." He took another drink. "But that's not the only reason. When I saw you today? In that pretty dress that showed off every goddamn curve I've been trying like hell not to notice for the last eleven years? My dick got so hard it freakin' hurt."

Her pulse spiked.

"During the party, all I could think about was peeling the silky fabric down your body. Taking my time to enjoy every inch of your warm, beautiful skin."

"But now?"

"Now I want to rip the fucking thing off and gorge myself on you."

Keely took three steps closer to read his eyes. Oh damn. Heat and passion and hunger. For her. "So do it."

Jack was on her before she inhaled another breath. His hands tearing at the zipper on her dress. His mouth devouring hers with hot, wet, sucking kisses. They fumbled with buttons and snaps in their frenzy to get naked.

And it was still too slow.

Her dress fell to the floor, leaving her in an itsy bitsy black thong and matching demi-bra. Keely jerked his shirt down his arms and ran her hands all over his chest. Firm muscles covered with just the perfect amount of dark hair. God. He was amazing. When she hit the waistband of his suit pants, she groaned disapproval that he still wore the damn things. She tried to unhook his belt. Repeatedly.

Jack broke the kiss. "Let me."

"Tell me you have a condom."

He reached in his front pocket and handed her one. Keely ripped it open with her teeth. When his pants pooled around his ankles, followed by his briefs, she zeroed in on his cock.

Holy shit. She didn't remember it being that big. Keely dropped to her knees. She placed the condom in her mouth, circled her hand around the base of his thick cock and rolled it down the length.

"Jesus fucking Christ, Keely. Warn a guy next time."

She peered up at him. "You didn't like it?"

He put his hands on her shoulders and pushed her onto her back on the carpet. Then he joined her on the floor. He hung on all fours above her, pure male animal, his knees bracketing her hips. "I didn't say that. Lose the panties."

Somehow she shimmied the stretchy lace off.

Jack's eyes never left hers as he moved between her thighs.

He levered himself over her, matching them groin-to-groin. Lining up his cock, he shoved himself into her in one hard thrust.

"Jesus fucking Christ, Jack. Warn a girl next time."

He smiled. He was still smiling as he kissed her. And kissed her until she could barely remember how her mouth felt without his all over hers.

The heat from his body sent prickles of pleasure dancing across her skin. The ends of his hair tickled her neck as he kissed her. Her entire being was primed to blow sky high and Jack wasn't moving. At all.

Keely traced the sides of his torso, circling around to squeeze his buttocks, hoping to urge him on.

He lifted his head and stared into her eyes. "Put your hands above your head and keep your legs right where they are."

"Bossy much?"

"Do it."

She arched, forcing her lace-covered breasts against his hot chest as she slowly swept her arms up.

Jack threaded their fingers together, pressing their joined hands into the carpet and let his full weight rest on her.

Oh man, that felt good. Really, really good.

Then he began to move. A shallow stroke followed by a deep thrust. He studied her face, gauging whether he was pleasing her.

Boy-howdy he was definitely pleasing her.

His hips picked up speed. She marveled at the sheer strength of his body yet the tight control he maintained over it.

The continual friction of his pelvis rubbing over hers made her clitoris throb. Made her moan. Why wouldn't he intensify the friction and send her screaming to that elusive point of ecstasy? Whenever she attempted to arch her lower body to increase the contact, he wouldn't allow it.

"Jack. Please."

He lowered his face to hers. "No." He kissed her again, in the deceptively lazy way she was beginning to crave. His mouth seduced. His body controlled.

Keely thought she'd lose her mind. The scrape of the carpet on her backside. The damp heat of Jack on her front side. The coiling sensation inside her womb as he rocked into her. The single-minded way Jack kissed her, as if sex was just a byproduct of those deliciously addicting kisses.

After she relaxed into him, giving him the control he'd demanded, he tensed and fucked her harder. Faster. Deeper.

Her midsection tightened. Keely arched hard. This time, Jack let her grind against him. "Don't stop. I'm so close. Like that...yes!"

The pulsing, throbbing, mind-scrambling orgasmic goodness increased exponentially when Jack sucked on her neck. He zeroed in on the magical spot that brought forth her nearly rapturous moan, which would be embarrassing if it weren't so amazing he'd immediately discovered the secret spot that always set her off.

Jack slowed his strokes as he came in a drawn-out grunt. His cock pulsed inside her and her vaginal muscles automatically clamped down to prolong his orgasm.

After she'd regained her bearings, Keely blinked at him. "Whoa."

He murmured, "Welcome back, cowgirl."

"I don't know if I wanna come back. That was a damn spectacular place to be."

Jack gifted her with a cocky smile and released her hands, but didn't move off her. She touched his face, tracing the start of his hairline. The twin slashes of his dark eyebrows. His nose. His cheekbones. That strong sexy jawline.

"What are you thinking?"

"I can't believe how much I wanted to punch this fine-looking mug earlier today."

He chuckled. "I can't believe you didn't just haul off and do it."

"Hey. I do have some impulse control."

"Pity. I was hoping to see you lose all control."

Keely feathered her thumb across his well-kissed lips. "If anyone can make me lose total control, it's you, Jack Donohue."

Jack caressed and kissed her until she sighed pure contentment. "So no regrets?"

"For the rockin' sex? Hell no."

His left eyebrow quirked. "Regrets about something else?"

Yes. That this is temporary and you'll probably shatter my heart into a billion pieces when this charade is over.

"Keely?" he prompted.

"Maybe."

"That's not an answer."

"I know." *Keep it light.* "The answer will have greater...benefits if you can guess what I regret."

His eyes darkened at her challenge. "You regret bending over a haybale in Daisy Duke short shorts at age sixteen and teasing me with a glimpse of your sweet ass cheeks?"

"Nope. I did that because you were lookin' for a cheap thrill and I am an accommodating girl. Try again."

He nipped the tip of her nose. "Smartass. You regret dating my brother."

"Huh-uh. Dating him forced me to acknowledge what I didn't want in a long-term relationship. Try again."

"Regrets about the threesome?"

"Which one?"

Jack half-snarled, "You've had more than one?"

"No. I like hearing that jealous growling sound. Damn, Jack. That is sexy as hell."

"You teasing me?"

"Yep. I figure what goes around, comes around. You did your share of teasing me. Like when I stayed at your folks' house over Christmas break? You never put on more than a skimpy towel after you showered. You wanted me to salivate over this hunkalicious body."

He smirked. "Maybe. I don't regret it."

"Me either. But you did try to torpedo my relationship with Justin."

"Not for any reason beyond he would've been miserable married to you."

Ooh. That stung. Just when things were going so well. Keely turned her face away.

Jack wrapped his fingers around her jaw, forcing her to meet his gaze. "Let me clarify before you jump to conclusions. Justin would've been miserable because you're too much woman for him to handle. Don't deny you would've run roughshod over him. You'd be bored with a man you had total control over."

"Probably." She poked him in the chest. "We're getting off

the topic here. You were supposed to be trying to guess what I regret."

An unholy gleam lit Jack's face. "You regret not blowing me first thing tonight. You're in luck. I'm more than ready to let you make it up to me now."

Chapter Nine

"It's hard for me to blow you when your dick is still inside me."

Jack kissed her impudent mouth. "Be right back." He eased out and pushed to his feet, feeling her eyes roving over his backside as he strolled to the bathroom.

He tossed the condom in the trash and washed his hands. Beneath his primal satisfaction was a hint of guilt. As long as he'd fantasized about Keely McKay, nailing her on the floor wasn't his most suave moment.

Two knocks on the door. "Jack? You okay?"

"Yes." *You impatient to get my cock in your mouth?*

Crude, Donohue.

Keely pushed open the door. Her curvy frame was perfectly framed by the doorjamb. His eyes scanned her head to toe. She still wore those peep-toe fuck me pumps that belonged on a nineteen forties pinup model. Not that any model had anything on his naked cowgirl.

"Ooh, I'm intrigued by that bad boy grin you're sportin'."

"It's all for you."

Keely's gaze dropped to his erection and zoomed back up to his eyes. "Before I get to that, I need your help taking my shoes off. I lose my balance when I try."

"You want to do it in here?"

"No. My bedroom." She turned, flaunting her tight, round, perfect little ass. Talk about losing his balance. Jack almost tripped over his goddamn tongue. He grabbed four condoms from his shaving kit and followed her.

Her room was completely dark, except for a dim lamp on

the dresser. Jack flipped the light switch, flooding the room with light.

"So much for mood lighting," she muttered.

"But better for me to see all of you. Bend over, put your palms flat on the mattress and spread your legs shoulder width apart."

When it appeared Keely might argue, he merely raised his eyebrow in challenge.

She obeyed.

Jack moved in behind her, setting his hands on her hips. He traced the contours of that marvelous ass, making a couple thorough passes over the same sensitive section of skin just to see her tremble. His hands followed the line of her thighs until he fell to his knees between her feet.

Using a rough-tipped finger, Jack teased the swell of her butt cheeks past the ticklish crease of her knee, down her muscled calf to the barrier of her shoe. Then he repeated the method on the other side. As he tantalized her inner thighs with butterfly-soft touches, he caught a whiff of her sex, softening, moistening for him. His eager, demanding cock slapped his belly.

"Jack—"

"Be still." He had no intention of letting her off easy. He replicated his effort on her legs with his hot, wet tongue.

"I thought you were helping with my shoes."

"I'm a Jack of all trades."

Keely groaned.

Jack circled his hand around her left ankle. "Lift up."

She shifted. He tugged on the spike heel and the shoe popped off her foot. He kissed her anklebone and her instep before gently replacing her foot on the floor. She wiggled her toes into the carpet and sighed. "Much better."

"Good. Other side." Her right foot received the same meticulous treatment.

"My feet thank you." Keely looked at him curiously when he remained kneeling on the floor. "What?"

"Sit on the bed facing me."

"Jack—"

"Do it."

Keely bounced she hit the mattress so fast. "I knew you'd

be demanding and controlling."

"And yet, here you are." Jack placed his mouth on the inside curve of her knee. He feathered kisses up, listening to the choppy sound of her breathing. The closer his marauding mouth moved to her pussy, the more her leg muscles quivered beneath his lips. He inhaled the aroma of her lilac-scented lotion mixed with the musky perfume of her sex.

Her eyes were dark with lust as she peeked from beneath lowered lashes. Her upper teeth sank into her kiss-swollen bottom lip. An effort to keep from crying out? Pointless. He'd take great pains and great pride in making Keely come undone.

Jack curled his hands around her hips and brought her body forward to his liking, ignoring her surprised gasp. He slipped his hands under her butt and bent to lick her glistening sex. He didn't bother holding back his primal groan as he tasted her for the first time.

He could've drawn out his oral worship, built Keely to climax slowly, but Jack was crazy to feel her explode on his tongue. After pressing kisses on her closely shorn mound, he followed the cleft down to the mouth of her pussy and wiggled his tongue inside.

"Oh. Damn. That's..."

Jack withdrew and did it again. And again. He zigzagged his tongue up that gratifyingly wet slit, stopping to suckle her pussy lips, while his tongue probed her clitoris.

"Jack!"

He started working her sweet little clit. Alternating sucking with tickling flicks of his tongue and firm-lipped bites. When Keely's hands landed on his head, he latched onto that pulsing nub and sucked until she screamed.

After the throbbing slowed, her hands fell away. She flopped onto the mattress with a heavy, sated sigh. "Can I just say...holy fucking shit. That was—"

"Phenomenal? Astounding?" he supplied.

She rested on her elbows and looked at him. "Not what I expected. I thought I was giving you head. Not that I'm complaining or anything."

"Good." Jack pushed to his feet. Her avid gaze devoured his cock as he rolled the condom on. He dipped his tongue into her navel and blew across the wet spot. "Roll over."

Keely flipped to her stomach. That sexy squeaking noise escaped when he yanked her hips to the edge of the bed. Her toes barely touched the floor.

"Brace yourself for a hard, fast ride, cowgirl." Jack arranged his cock, lifted her ass so he could watch his dick disappear into her soft hot, pink flesh.

The mattress moved as Keely wiggled and widened the space between her thighs. "That's better."

"The visual is better for me too," he murmured. "Fucking hot as hell, Keely." He gripped the middle of her thighs and thrust deep.

"Yes. As hard as you want, you won't hurt me."

A snarl-like noise rumbled out and he slammed into her wet heat. Each slap of his hips brought forth her soft groan of approval. Keely fisted her hands into the comforter, keeping herself in place as his cock tunneled in and out at warp speed.

Sweat coated his face, dampened his hair, trickled down his chest and the crack of his ass. His toes curled into the carpet in anticipation, but he didn't stop. Couldn't stop.

Keely emitted a keening moan, shooting her hips back with more force. Caught within her vise-like pussy muscles, Jack had no prayer of holding back. His sac tightened, his cock swelled as it tried to break out of the latex. He came right along with her, a grunting, sweating maniac consumed with experiencing every hot pulse of bliss as his balls emptied.

"Jesus. Yes."

His strokes didn't slow even after the head rush faded. Jack kept fucking her, prolonging both their orgasms. Even in the aftermath of his release, his pelvis snapped eagerly, almost of its own accord.

Keely sagged face first into the mattress, mumbling.

What a way to end a long dry spell. Jack trailed kisses up her spine, tasting her sweat and pulled out.

She emitted a sleepy sound. By the time he'd returned from the bathroom, she'd rolled to her back.

His gaze tracked her beautiful, moist, naked flesh. Pity he'd only kissed her mouth and between her legs. He crawled up her body, stopping to tongue her rosy nipples.

"I wondered if you'd get around to that."

"That's my question." Jack propped himself on his elbow

beside her. "Do I indulge in every sexual scenario tonight because it's a one-time only offer?"

Keely mirrored his position. "Is that what you want?"

"No. Not at all. Not even close." His hand shook as he swept the damp tendrils from her neck. "Is it what you want?"

"No. Not at all. Not even close," she mimicked.

Smiling, Jack stroked her hair, twining the dark strands around his index finger. "You didn't ask what I want, Keely."

"I don't have to. I see it in your eyes, Jack."

"Busted." The woman didn't have a clue what he expected from her. "I want all of you as long as we're pretending we're engaged."

"All of me, meaning...just sexually?"

"Meaning I'll be in your bed every night."

"Oh." She frowned. "I'm a bed hog. But I'm sure that'll even out the fact you snore like a drunken pig."

Jack grinned. She had the funniest phrases. "Sounds like a fair trade."

"Snuggling up together is fine. However, I'm not doing the cooking, cleaning or pressing your snappy suits, GQ."

"But sexually speaking, anything is fair game?"

"As long as it doesn't hurt and we both are into it, yeah, I'm game to try it."

He brushed his mouth over hers. Once. Twice. Longer the third time when she didn't attempt retreat. "That's very refreshing. Most women aren't so sexually open."

"Really?"

"No lie. In fact, most women I've met are sexually repressed. They enjoy the tease and the chase. They even like the first couple times of fucking, sucking and whatever. But I've always felt..." Way to toss it out there. "Never mind."

Keely pushed his shoulder. "What? Come on. Tell me. You've always felt..."

"Like I'd been tricked. A woman will suck your dick a couple times and act like they love it. Maybe try the kinkier stuff once, but after that, no way. Women who truly enjoy all aspects of sex are a rare breed."

"Speaking as a sexually open-minded woman, I like sex. All aspects of sex. A lot. Do I have sex with whatever man trips my trigger? Sometimes. Do I feel guilty about it? No. And I do not

109

have sex with anyone besides my partner when I'm in a relationship—" she held up her hand and qualified, "—unless it's a mutual decision. I'm not promiscuous. I'm selective and prefer a guy to have the same sexual appetites and expectations I do. I am not afraid or embarrassed of my sexuality. That upfront admission freaks some men out. They want me to be embarrassed about my sexual past even when they're grateful for it."

Jack ran his hand down her arm. "Tell me about these sexual appetites and expectations. What fuels them? What feeds them?"

She rolled her eyes. "You have such an analytical brain."

"All the better to figure out exactly how I can give you what you need."

"You did. Tonight was...great, Jack."

Not the enthusiastic response he'd expected.

Maybe Keely thinks you suck in bed.

No. This wasn't about him. Normally, he'd dissect every movement. Every position. Every suck and thrust. He'd be obsessed until he figured out if he'd used a faulty technique. Not tonight. Jack understood Keely's response had nothing to do with what he did. But more what he...*didn't* do.

"But it wasn't enough, was it?" he prompted.

A shrug and then she obscured her face with her hair.

He pinched her chin between his fingers, forcing her to look at him. "Don't hide yourself from me. Ever. Your reactions, your anger, your pleasure, nothing, understand?"

She nodded.

"If this were a normal dating situation, say, we've been going out a few weeks. We have dinner or head out to the bar and come back here to have sex. Maybe I spend a few nights at your place. Maybe you spend a few nights at my place. The sex is good. We both get off on a regular basis. How long would you stay with me?"

Keely's eyes were clouded with indecision. "Honestly?"

"Complete honesty."

"A month. Maybe two."

Something—despair or hope—fluttered in his gut. "Why?"

"I'll have figured you out by then. Nothing will be spontaneous or exciting between us. I'll know how you'll react before you do." She flipped her hair over her shoulder in a confident, female move. "I'm really good at reading people, Jack. All people. Men especially. I have been since I was a little girl."

"So you're saying you'd get...bored with me?"

"Yep. You could be the nicest guy on the planet, with a steady job, a great family, a fun personality. You could treat me well, bring me flowers and chocolates, romance me, be decent in the sack and I'd still get bored with you." Keely frowned. "Not you personally—you do realize I'm speaking strictly in generic terms, right?"

"Right."

The truth sparkled like a secret gem he'd personally mined with his bare hands. Why Keely pushed him away. Why she insulted him. Why she lusted after him. Why she couldn't make up her mind whether she loved him or hated him.

Her mixed up, inconsistent responses to him were in response to his mixed up inconsistent responses to her. She couldn't get a bead on him. Jack never reacted the way Keely expected him to. She was both attracted and repelled by the idea he might actually be a...challenge for her.

That drove her absolutely crazy. And thrilled her to her toes.

Oh hell yeah. He'd push her. Prod her. Take her to sexual heights she never fathomed. He'd pull out all the stops to make sure Jack Donohue was the one man she never forgot.

"Jack?"

He smiled. "Sorry. Just thinking it's good we won't be together long. You'll be ready to move on by then."

Keely traced the ridge of his pectoral. "But I am looking forward to the time we'll be spending together. Especially now I know how compatible we are in bed."

"Mmm. And I am eager to discover what you consider kinky."

"Any time you wanna paw through my sex toy collection, let me know."

"Aren't you clever, keeping your used toys like mementos in a sexual conqueror's war chest."

Her mouth quirked. "Jealous?"

"No. I consider sex toys a one-partner indulgence." Jack followed the slope of her breast with his thumb. "After we break up, I throw them out. There's something creepy about reusing them on someone else."

"The difference is, I only allow mine to be used on me."

Jack bit back a smile. No surprise Keely set the parameters. Chances were slim any man would argue if she whipped out a vibrating butt plug and demanded he use it on her. "I'll peruse the online shopping stores and see if I find something to mix it up a bit." He yawned. "Damn. Been a long-ass day with the flying, the party and the rocking sex. I'm ready to crash."

"Me too."

He bounced off the bed and onto his feet. As he peeled the covers back, he tried to remember which side of the bed Keely slept on. The right side. So that's the side he chose.

Jack fluffed the pillows and slid between the cool cotton sheets.

She scowled at him. "You're on my side of the bed."

"Really?"

"Uh-huh. I always sleep on the right side."

"Oh." Jack paused. Keely probably expected he'd gallantly give up the right side of the bed for her.

Wrong.

"That sucks. Hit the lights, buttercup." He pulled the covers up to his chin and closed his eyes.

If Keely's disgruntled sigh was any indication, he would have no problem whatsoever keeping her off balance.

Now if he could just keep himself from falling for her.

Chapter Ten

Keely woke to an empty bed. She squinted at the clock. What the hell was Jack doing up so early? They hadn't fallen asleep until after one. Not to mention he'd woken up her up and proved for the third and fourth time he didn't need Viagra.

The aroma of coffee teased her. Yawning, she wandered into the kitchen. The silver contraption popped and hissed. Be her luck to break the damn thing if she touched it, so she opted to wait.

But no one said she had to wait alone.

The door to the bathroom was cracked open, which Keely figured was invitation enough.

Humid, piney-scented air greeted her. She debated on whether to let Jack know she was here, or to surprise him by climbing naked into the shower.

Surprises hadn't gone so well for her in the past.

"Jack? I need to sneak in and brush my teeth."

"Maybe when you're done you should crawl in here with me."

"Need me to wash your back?"

"No." The shower curtain was wrenched aside and Jack grinned at her. "I'd rather you washed my cock."

"I imagine you'd prefer a tongue bath?"

"Now there's an idea. Come on in. The water's fine."

Keely's gaze descended to his groin. His cock was already erect. Her attention wandered up his torso, over the cut muscles above his hips, the well-defined abs and the ridges of his pectorals. Yummy.

"I'm losing steam here, cowgirl."

She finally met his eyes. "Doesn't look like it to me."

Cue his raunchy grin. "I was priming myself for your morning wakeup call."

"And here I was looking forward to hot coffee. A hot man is so much better." Keely stepped over the lip of the tub and pulled the curtain closed.

Although the air was humid in the enclosed space, Keely shivered. Her nipples puckered and her skin broke out in gooseflesh.

Jack stood with his back to the water spray. His teasing smile was gone and pure male heat smoldered in his eyes. "You want to be wet for this?"

Lord. She was already wet from the way he looked at her.

His finger started at the hollow of her throat and trailed down the center of her body slowly, as he watched her reaction to his expert touch. Her nipples hardened into tighter points. Her belly quivered. Her sex swelled.

Then Jack's palms were on her shoulders and he pushed her to her knees.

That startled her. But not as much as how fast his hand gripped her hair. How quickly he guided her face to his groin. "Suck me off."

Keely opened her mouth to speak and Jack seized the opportunity to slip his thick cock between her lips. The satiny skin glided over her tongue until the cockhead hit her throat.

"Open wider. No hands. I only want to feel how you can work me with your hot mouth and sassy little tongue."

Water swirled around her knees. Spray from the showerhead left a fine mist on her skin. She sucked and swallowed, blindly reaching for the sides of the tub to find her balance.

Jack kept one hand fisted in her hair. The other hand cupped her jaw as he thrust in and out of her mouth. Fast. Then slow. But always deep. He hissed when she used her teeth.

His slippery cock was too waterlogged to discern the masculine flavor that was uniquely his. Keely relaxed her throat and angled her head, allowing him deeper entry. She simply lost herself to the moment of pleasing a demanding man. Pleasing herself by holding nothing back from him.

He murmured encouragement but didn't take it easy on her. Jack fucked her mouth how he wanted. Not asking. Taking.

It was hot as hell.

When his strokes became less practiced and more frantic, Keely increased her sucking power, preparing herself to swallow every burst of semen.

But Jack pulled out, grunting, "Don't move." Keeping one hand in her hair and fisting his cock in his other hand, Jack beat off, directing the spray of come onto her chest. His wild eyes never strayed from his intimate marking until the last spurt. He aimed that one at her face. Come splattered her lips and chin. Her tongue darted out to taste and Jack nearly roared his pleasure.

Keely almost came right then.

After Jack stopped shaking, he helped her up and let the shower spray warm her.

She tipped her head back, engrossed in the sensation of hot water pouring over her cooled skin as the evidence of Jack's passion flowed from her. Keely imagined Jack's rough hands mapping her body as painstakingly as the streaming water. She didn't open her eyes, speak or move.

I trust you. Do with me what you will.

Jack sensed her acquiescence. He held her wrists behind her back in his left hand, cupping her breast, switching sides when she moaned softly. He flattened his palm, slicking it over her belly, between her hipbones to the rise of her mound. The same time two fingers breached the wet opening to her pussy, he latched onto her left nipple and sucked hard.

At that point Keely's knees buckled.

He chuckled against the upper swell of her breast and began a full out sensual assault.

His tongue rasped her nipples. As his fingers fucked her, his thumb flicked her clit, barely there and then persistent. He'd bite down on her nipple. Suckle the sting. When she started to anticipate the pattern, he changed it.

Bastard.

It drove her mad. She loved it. She hated it.

Jack's rapid exhalations across her wet skin brought forth another full-body shiver. "You ready to come for me now, cowgirl?"

Keely couldn't seem to find her voice. She nodded.

His mouth was on her ear. "Now I know exactly how to make you speechless." Jack's hair brushed her jaw, throat and breastbone as he licked the water trickling to her nipples. He ruthlessly suckled her, impaled her on his clever fingers and stroked her clit.

She threw back her head and screamed as every nerve ending between her breasts and her pussy throbbed in orgasmic harmony.

He held on.

After she floated back from the realm of bliss, she blinked the water from her eyes and looked at Jack.

Smiling, he pushed wet hanks of her hair over her shoulder. His finger traced the vein still pounding wildly in her throat. "Good thing I put in a bigger water heater." Jack brushed his lips over hers. "I'll let you finish your shower." Then he was gone.

Keely felt too relaxed to waste brain cells fretting about how quickly the power had shifted in their relationship. Or deluding herself she'd ever had any power at all.

Jack filled her favorite mug with his precious coffee. He scrambled her brain with a prolonged good morning kiss. He even made the bed.

Guys were total putty after a blowjob.

Keely braided her hair in a single plait. She zipped a ripped pair of Levis, buttoned a faded flannel shirt over a long john top, and slipped on her oldest pair of ropers.

She exited the bedroom and saw Jack perched on the edge of the couch, papers strewn across the coffee table. His hair was mussed from repeatedly running his fingers through it—a sign of frustration.

Jack looked up and his gaze swept over her.

She braced herself for a "country bumpkin" comment and crafted a couple of snappy comebacks. But she needn't have bothered.

He merely inquired, "Where are you off to?"

"My folks' place. They're out making the rounds on Sunday

and it's the only time I can exercise my horse. Then I do whatever needs done in the barn as payment for boarding Rosa."

"Rosa?"

"Rosamonde's Red Dream is her official name, but I call her Rosa."

He sagged into the sofa cushions. "I had a horse when I was growing up. Buster. I thought he was the coolest thing ever. Drove my dad crazy that all I ever wanted to do on the farm was 'ride that damn horse'. He got rid of it the week after I left for college."

Keely gasped. "So you came home and your horse was gone?"

"Yeah. No big deal. I'd moved on by then, in many ways."

How sad for him. She wondered if his dad's attitude played a role in driving Jack from the family farm. "Well, the years I lived in Denver or I was on the road, my parents never suggested getting rid of Rosa."

"Isn't it unfair to expect them to take care of her?"

"They've bred her and made enough from the foals to cover her boarding costs. But even if she hadn't dropped a single colt or filly, they would've kept her. Eventually I'll build my own place and have room for her and the stud Jessie keeps for me." She grinned. "My current landlord is a real hardass about me keepin' pets in the building."

"Funny."

Keely snagged her Stetson off the hat rack and slung her messenger bag over her shoulder. Halfway to her truck she realized not only hadn't she said goodbye to Jack, she hadn't asked him to come along.

The day was unseasonably hot and she'd overdressed. By the time Keely finished her ride with Rosa, they were both sweating.

Keely brushed Rosa down and treated her to some oats before turning her out into the pasture. She straightened the tack, cursing her dad for leaving it such a mess week after week.

Growing up the only girl in the McKay family had been a

test of her mettle. Her father's and brothers' first instincts were to stash her in the house, under her mother's watchful eye. Sure, Keely wanted to learn to cook, can, sew and figure out how to wield charm to get her way like her mother did. But Keely also wanted to help with calving, branding, haying and butchering. She wanted to learn how to fix fence, shoot predators and rope strays.

Carson McKay and his sons worked hard so Keely didn't have to. The men in her life preferred her to be pampered. To know enough about horses and horsewomanship only to win rodeo queen pageants and hook a decent husband.

Ugh. Keely McKay had never aspired to the title of queen of the rodeo, much to her father's dismay.

From an early age, Keely smiled prettily and followed her own agenda. Her brothers and cousins blustered and threatened but always gave in to her wheedling when she begged them for help. A mix of bribery and blackmail was how Keely learned to run the haying machine and other equipment from Cord. How to rope, ride and tie from Colby. How to birth a breech calf in the dead of night from Colt. Cam taught her how to fix fence. Then he dragged her off and taught her how to fish. Carter showed her how to read the stars, start a fire from flint rocks and whittle. Kade taught her about vaccination and how to pick a good bull. Kane taught her how to dress a deer. Quinn and Ben showed her how to pregnancy-check cows. Chase let her climb on the back of a bull. Luke snuck her into the bar and taught her how to play pool. Brandt shared his extensive knowledge of horses. Tell and Dalton taught her to ride dirt bikes and how to use a beer bong.

Even her males cousins on the West side of her family furthered her life education. Her cousin Dag taught her how to chew tobacco and spit. Dax forced her to learn to water ski. Chet and Remy demonstrated how to run power tools. Nick patiently showed her how to reload ammo. Blake let her bottle feed lambs and shear sheep. Harris and Lief drilled self defense moves into her. Sebastian offered educational and financial advice.

All important things. Things her dad wouldn't have taught her.

But he taught you other things. How to two-step. How to shoot. How to break a horse. How to drive a car—a manual transmission truck and a four-wheeler. How to play cards. How to cheat at cards. How to laugh.

Mostly, her father showed day in and day out, what it meant to love. Carson McKay worshiped the ground his wife walked on. From the time Keely was a little girl, she knew she'd never settle for anything less than that type of man. That type of undying love.

So yeah, her dad purposely messed up the tack and the barn just so she'd come out on Sunday and straighten it up. That was the gruff rancher showing love. Then he'd convince her to play a game of cribbage or poker. Or to ride out to check on a pump or a horse or a sick cow. Or to sneak a piece of pie or a bowl of homemade ice cream and sit with him on the porch listening to the wind. He'd come up with all kinds of reasons to get her to stay a little while longer. And she always did.

Which is why she'd felt guilty keeping her purchase of the building in Moorcroft a secret from him. Now she was lying to him about her engagement to Jack. Although her dad would rejoice when it ended.

Keely originally figured she'd have the same *wahoo!* sense of relief, but now, she wasn't so sure. Jack Donohue had more layers, sides and facets to him than she'd imagined. He'd acted sweet and sour, kind and mean, gruff and gregarious, concerned and aloof. Maybe she'd misjudged him.

Or maybe the rocking sex is clouding your judgment.

Yeah. That had to be it.

She put thoughts of Jack and her father out of her mind as she mentally planned her week. She heard tires crunching on the gravel, but it didn't sound like her mother's Lincoln Town Car. She stripped off her gloves and hung them to dry on the hook embedded in the wooden support beams. The door squeaked as she ventured out of the barn.

Shielding her eyes from the sun didn't help cut the glare. "Dad? Mom?"

"No. It's me."

She froze. "Jack? What're you doin' here?"

"Have you ever noticed your tendency to slip into a Wyomin' drawl is more pronounced whenever you're nervous?"

Keely snorted. "You do not make me nervous. Anyway, you didn't answer my question." She moved until she saw him leaning against his Beemer.

Jack kept his arms crossed over his chest. "I had brunch with my mom and brother. Evidently my mom ended up with a piece of Carolyn's silver service. She was mortified and I volunteered to bring it back for her."

She looked at Jack skeptically. There was an edge to him, an edge that automatically made her bristle. If he was here just to return a piece of silverware, she'd eat her hat.

"Is your mother around?"

"No. She and Dad haven't come back yet. If you leave it with me, I'll be sure she gets it."

He cocked his head. "What's up with you acting so formal?"

"Jesus, Jack, make up your mind. First you accused me of reverting to a twang, now you're claiming I'm acting formal?"

"I meant you're acting awful formal for a woman who was on her knees with my dick in her mouth not five hours ago."

A blush stole across her cheeks, which pissed her off. This was how he treated her after she opened herself up to him? Screw him. "How's this for formal? Fuck. Off. You're an asshole." Keely pivoted and stomped up the porch steps.

Too bad she couldn't provide him with a dramatic exit, slamming the door after she flounced into the house and locking it behind her. But her boots were filthy and she knew better than to track mud and horseshit across her mother's floor. She sat on the edge of the boot bench.

"Would you let me—"

"Keep sayin' crude shit like that to piss me off? Hell no. Go away."

"Look. I came here to try and do something nice—"

"That comment was not nice by any stretch of the imagination." She grunted as she yanked off her right boot. "I don't know why I'm surprised we're back to you only being nice to me when we're in public."

"Or *you* only being nice to *me* when we're fucking?" he taunted back.

That did it.

Goaded beyond control, Keely whipped her dirty boot at him. At least the man had good reflexes out of bed too and he was fast enough to duck.

Jack's look of surprise was downright comical. And totally

worth it. "What the hell was that for?"

"Because I gave you a chance to leave and you didn't."

"So whipping a boot at my head is supposed to be an incentive?"

"Yep."

"You're a fucking riot, buttercup." He flashed his teeth. "And guess what? It didn't work."

"I have another boot," she warned.

"And lousy aim. You're goddamn lucky—"

"I missed on purpose, Jack-off. And *you're* goddamn lucky you're not wearing a dirt halo and a dent in your fat head." She hopped up and sought refuge in the house. Maybe her over-the-top behavior would convince the stupid, smarmy jerk to take off so she could calm down.

The porch door slammed again.

Or maybe not.

Keely took the shortcut from the back entryway to the kitchen. She scrubbed her hands in the sink and ignored Jack's gaze burning a hole in her back. When she deigned to look at him, leaning indifferently in the doorjamb, she noticed he was tapping the metal serving utensil against his palm. *Smack, smack, smack* over and over.

"Go away, Jack."

"No." *Smack, smack, smack.*

"I cannot deal with you right now."

"Tough. You brought this on yourself." *Smack, smack, smack.*

"I'll remind you you're an uninvited guest in my parents' house. I may not be able to throw you out of the apartment you own, but I can toss you out of here."

"Try it." *Smack, smack, smack.*

"Will you stop smacking that goddamn thing? It's giving me a headache."

"I'm just warming it up so the metal isn't cold when I spank your bare ass with it." *Smack, smack, smack.*

Keely couldn't help it; she laughed. "Right." She'd gone about six steps when the word, "Stop," had the effect he'd intended. She stopped.

"Do not push your luck with me any more than you already have, Keely," he warned. *Smack, smack, smack.*

Of all the freakin' nerve. Keely spun around. Her stomach fluttered. She'd never seen that look in his eye—the taskmaster with a lesson to teach. "You're serious."

"Completely." *Smack, smack, smack.*

"You really think I'm going to let you...hit me?"

"Not hit you. Spank you. Big difference. Losing your temper and throwing your boot at me proved you need to learn there are consequences for acting out against me." *Smack, smack, smack.*

"No. Way. You are fucking delusional." The continual *smack, smack, smack* was wearing on her nerves. "I haven't been spanked since I was about six years old."

In a clipped tone, Jack said, "Then it's past time you had a reminder."

"Maybe you need a reminder not to goad me," she retorted.

Silence.

A stalemate?

"I don't make idle threats. Drop your jeans and show me that ass."

"No."

"I'll have my way, Keely. You give it or I'll take it."

A small thrill surfaced. How far would he take this?

Let's find out.

She walked away. As she bypassed the living room, she realized he'd followed her. If she picked up speed, so did he. *Smack, smack, smack* echoed until she was surrounded. The noise was in her head. Pounding in her blood. Throbbing in her groin.

She took the stairs at a dead run.

Jack gave chase.

Keely shrieked. Her heart nearly beat out of her chest. Adrenaline soared and her pulse exploded. Her breathing sputtered after climbing the second set of stairs.

Then she was zipping down the hallway. Her room had a hefty lock. If she could get there first...

As she pushed the door open, a strong set of arms circled her waist. She shrieked again—which was quickly muffled when Jack lifted her off her feet and dropped her face-first on her bed.

Chapter Eleven

Jack absorbed the brunt of the fall when they hit the mattress. He quickly immobilized Keely's hands above her head and used his body weight to hold her down. Still, the woman bucked like wild bronc.

When she turned tail and ran, Jack acted like any predatory male in his position: He'd raced after her to gauge how far she'd take the battle of wills.

The question was what to do with her now that he'd caught her.

He'd ditched the cake server after she'd taken off. So he'd have to implement a different tool. His hand? It'd be hot as sin seeing his imprint on her remarkable ass, all pink and red and his.

"Don't you dare spank me, or I'll..."

That settled it. Keely was getting a spanking. Her lilac scent permeated the braid and he inhaled as much of the sweetness as his lungs would hold.

"You'll take whatever I decide to dish out. And if you weren't so goddamn hotheaded, you'd realize that I was trying to apologize for my smartass comment. But you opted to push me, so I'm pushing back."

"Jack. Please."

"Please what?" he murmured in her ear.

"Move."

"Move like this?" He slid his hips from side to side, grinding his erection into her ass. "Or like this?" He bumped his pelvis, thrusting as he rolled his hips.

"You are such a pervert."

"Just another thing we have in common, cowgirl." Jack lightly sank his teeth into the shell of her ear and soothed the sting with a soft sucking kiss.

She hissed.

His mouth returned to the curve of her jaw. "I will fuck you like this, Keely, if I choose to. Face down on the bed. Keeping my intentions unclear until the moment my cock shoves into you. Might be your cunt. Might be your ass. Might be I'll stroke my dick in your butt crack and come all over your back."

Keely shivered and not from fear.

"Hold still. Take what you've got coming to you." Maintaining his grip on her wrists in his left hand, he rolled to his left side, stretching his right leg over the back of her thighs.

She stopped struggling.

Jack rubbed his palm over her butt cheeks. Damn. Keely's ass filled out a pair of 501s to perfection. He kept stroking, building her anticipation. With his fingers around her wrists, he felt her pulse leap every time he changed direction or speed.

His first swat wasn't hard. Neither was the second. But the third and fourth—one on each butt cheek—stung his hand. Jack knew they'd stung her, even through the denim. He peppered each side with a series of fast smacks, finishing with three hard swats down low where her thigh curved into her ass.

When Keely continued to hold herself rigid, expecting more, he removed his leg and released her wrists. "I'm done. And I reward good behavior. Up on your hands and knees."

She didn't look at him, but she obeyed. Jack took a second, unbelievably humbled, unbelievably grateful, unbelievably touched by this strong woman who gave herself over into his sexual keeping without question.

He peeled her jeans to her knees, in effect hobbling her. Jack knelt on the bed, his eyes eating up the red marks he'd placed on her ass.

Fuck that was hot. He swept his palm over the marks. Literally hot. He kissed the lips tattooed on her butt cheek. Then he ran his tongue over the beautifully pinkened flesh.

"Omigod."

He laved every swollen spot. Blowing on her heated skin until she arched into him for more. Bathing his marks of possession until he smelled her arousal and saw the sweet cream dotting her inner thighs.

Jack stripped her jeans off. He placed his hand between her shoulder blades and pushed her upper body to the mattress, leaving her ass in the air. Taking a butt cheek in each hand, he lifted her up and spread her open for his mouth.

Keely gasped.

He licked her slit, from her clitoris to that sweet little asshole. He rimmed the pucker with his tongue, relishing the sexy moans of consent she didn't bother to hide.

A thrill shot through him. Keely liked his raunchy side. Her complete wantonness increased Jack's determination to please her beyond her wildest dreams.

"If this is your idea of punishment, I plan on being bad all the damn time."

He laughed and continued to torment her. He fucked her ass and her cunt with his tongue until she shook with need, whispering *please, please, please* in a husky rasp that caused his dick to jerk against his zipper.

"Turn over."

The second Keely was on her back, Jack buried his face in her pussy. He zeroed in on her clit, sucking relentlessly until Keely bucked against his mouth and came in a rush of wetness all over his face. He didn't release her juicy sex until her legs stopped twitching.

Again, Jack was humbled, seeing Keely utterly boneless, beautiful in abandon. He kissed her damp mound. The ticklish skin between her hipbones. The strange looking tattoo on her hip he suspected was a brand. The cute indent of her belly button. He looked at her, hoping she saw how much she meant to him at that moment.

No smile. No teasing eyes. She just said, "Fuck me, Jack. However you want. On the bed. On the floor. Over the chair. Hanging from the damn ceiling. I don't care. I just need to see that wild look in your eyes and know I put it there."

Her honesty floored him. Jack took her mouth in a brutal kiss. He slid his hands under her butt and lifted her, eating at those full lips. He staggered back, spun and pinned her against the wall.

He ripped his mouth away. "Help me get these jeans off."

They depantsed him. Her hot, naked skin against his drove

him out of his freakin' mind. He grabbed a handful of her warm ass, canted her pelvis and plunged his cock in deep.

"Yes. Oh God. Yes."

With her legs wrapped around his waist, she ground down on him every time he thrust up. *Slam slam slam.* No kisses. No caresses. No talking. Nothing but hard, fast fucking.

Her head fell back against the wall and she moaned, "Harder," tightening her fingers in his hair as she bore down on him with her pussy muscles.

Slam slam slam.

Keely suddenly snapped upright, a stricken look on her face. "Wait. Did you hear someone walking down the hall?"

"No."

"I did. Jack. Stop. I think my parents are home."

"So?"

"*So?* We can't do this if my mom and dad are downstairs."

Jack had just uttered the words, "You're paranoid," when Keely's mom called out, "Keely, hon? You up here?"

"Shit! Let me down."

"No. Just answer her."

"We have to stop."

He got right in her face. "No fucking way. Answer her now before she comes hauling ass in here."

Keely half-glared at him and shouted, "Yeah, Mom, I'll be right out."

Pause. "Is Jack in there with you?"

"See?" she hissed.

Jack began to thrust again. Damn. Had sex ever felt this good? He muttered, "Answer her, buttercup," against her throat and sucked on the spot that turned her inside out.

"Yes! I mean, Jack is here and we'll be done—I mean out— in a few minutes."

"Okay. We'll be in the kitchen."

"Fuckin' hell, my dad is out there too!" she whispered furiously.

"So?" His thrusts picked up rhythm.

"Dammit Jack, stop. I can't have an orgasm now."

He grinned at her. "Wanna bet?" He fucked her without pause, using his teeth on her throat until she came gasping, cursing his name, which bizarrely enough, turned him on even more. Keely pulled his hair, her orgasm was so intense. He muffled his raw shout against her shoulder as hot burst after hot burst shot out the end of his dick.

That's when he realized why the sex was so good.

"Shit. We forgot a condom."

She blinked at him sleepily, wearing the sated expression of a well-fucked woman. "Hmm? What did you say?"

"No condom."

"Oh. I'll admit I prefer ridin' bareback."

"Me too. But—"

She pecked him on the mouth. Twice. "No worries. We're safe. I'm on the pill."

"You could've told me that last night."

"We've been lovers less than twenty-four hours. It would've come up." She shrugged and tried to cover a yawn. "Let me down so I can at least fix my hair so I don't look like I've spent the last hour being fucked silly by you."

"Good luck with that." Jack withdrew and set her on her feet. "Do you want to go downstairs one at a time so they don't suspect? Or can we walk in together?"

"It's embarrassing to get caught screwing in my old bedroom as an adult when they never caught me when I was a stupid kid."

Jack zipped his pants. "You never got caught?"

"No. But I caught *them* plenty of times and that wasn't any less awkward."

"Carson and Carolyn doing the nasty? I'm shocked."

"Let's just say I had no clue what a ball gag was until one weekend I came home from college for a surprise visit, and I saw one in my mother's mouth and my father had her tied to a dining room chair."

"Really? Maybe your dad can share tips about which brand is better, since I've often wanted to gag you."

"Jack Donohue, don't you dare bring it up! I swear to God, if you—"

He smashed his mouth to hers, cutting off her protest. But his kisses didn't placate her. She pulled back and glared at him. "I'm not kiddin'."

"Relax, cowgirl. I'll behave. But I sure am hoping we're

sitting in the dining room."

Carolyn McKay slanted them both a knowing look and blithely offered them a slice of peach pie.

Carson McKay's glare could've set Jack's hair on fire. But his grin for Keely was genuine adoration. Mr. Tough Rancher was absolutely whipped for his daughter. Whipped.

Jack was beginning to understand the feeling.

"I see you cleaned up the barn again, girlie. Thanks. You and Rosa have a good ride?"

Keely wiped her mouth. "It was a great ride. We must've been gone three hours. I thought after all the party preparations and being around family yesterday you'd do something just the two of you?"

"Who's to say we didn't?" Carolyn winked. She addressed Jack. "Did your mother and Justin get off all right?"

"Yes. We had brunch before they started home. My mother was upset she'd ended up with your cake server. She made me promise I'd hand deliver it to you."

"Which is why it ended up on the floor in the living room...how?"

Keely wouldn't look at him, the coward.

Jack smiled at Carolyn. "An oversight. I got busy doing something else and must've dropped it."

Carson harrumphed but didn't demand details.

"So what's next for you two lovebirds this week?" Carolyn asked.

"Tomorrow we find out if Jack got approval on the remodel plans from historical committee. Then he'll do his thing and I'll do mine. I'm working at the clinic Tuesday through Friday."

He frowned at Keely. "Not Friday. We're flying to Milford early Friday morning. Technically we're landing in Salt Lake City and then making the two hour drive to Milford."

"That's this week?"

"I told you about it last week."

"When?" she demanded. "We had a fight before you left. You were gone right up until the party started last night and when we got home—"

"We didn't do a whole lot of talking, did we?" he murmured,

ignoring Carson's low snarl.

"Dammit, Jack, that's not funny. You said we were going to Milford at some point, but you never said when."

"Well, buttercup, it is this weekend. Friday night they're having a dinner for us. Saturday I'll do one last run through before giving them my final set of suggested updates. There's another dinner on Saturday night. However, I am hoping we can sneak out of town Sunday morning before they drag us to church."

"I can't believe this is the first I've heard of it."

Jack warned her, "You've known about this 'commitment' from the very start, Keely."

"Don't sound to me like Keely's too keen on goin'," Carson mused.

"Doesn't matter. She *is* going."

Keely sighed. "I'm not gonna have to wear a long dress and some kind of freaky head covering, am I?"

Carson laid his hand over Keely's. "Darlin' girl, if you ain't comfortable goin', then don't go. Just 'cause you're engaged to him don't mean you gotta do everything he says."

What the fuck? Jack couldn't believe Carson was encouraging his daughter to blatantly oppose him. He was her fiancé for Christsake. Keely had better realize early on that *their* relationship took precedence over every other relationship in her life.

What relationship? This engagement isn't real, remember?

Ah hell. With the intensity of the last twenty-four hours, somehow Jack had forgotten that.

Keely squeezed her father's hand. "It's okay. I want to go with Jack. This is a big potential client and he's talked about everything so much I'm looking forward to it. It's just...the timing caught me off guard." Keely smirked at Jack. "My man and I tend to fight first before we figure things out."

"Sounds like someone else I know," Carolyn muttered.

Carson's lips twitched.

"Anyway, I'll reschedule my Friday clients. No big deal. Daddy, can you ride Rosa for me this week? Since it doesn't sound like I'll be here next Sunday?"

"Sure, punkin, whatever you want."

"Thanks. You're the bestest evah."

Carson grunted, but Jack knew he was pleased.

Jack forced a smile. "Carolyn, thanks for the pie, it was delicious."

"You're welcome. You two taking off?"

He said, "Yes" the same time Keely said, "No."

They looked at each other. Measured each other.

"I have work to finish before tomorrow," he pointed out.

"So go. We have two cars. I need to redeem myself from the last cribbage game we played, where Daddy skunked me twice, right?"

"You bet, girlie. I'll get the board and the cards," Carson said and vanished from the table.

Carolyn and Keely chatted as they picked up the pie plates and headed into the kitchen.

Jack took the shortcut out the back door. He paused on the porch, propping his elbows on the railing to drink in the view. The scenery really was spectacular. No wonder Keely loved it so much.

The porch boards squeaked and Carson appeared in his peripheral vision. Jack felt like a teenage boy about to get "the talk" from his girlfriend's father. "Nice night."

"I'm just gonna say this flat out, Donohue. That girl in there means the world to me. She's been the light of my life since the day she came into this world. I'd do anything to make her happy. I always have, I always will. I trust her judgment, but son, I don't trust you. And I most definitely don't trust you with her. So if you do anything to hurt her? I swear to God I will—"

"—gut me? Yeah, I got this warning five goddamn times last night from your sons," Jack said curtly.

"I'd expect nothin' less from my boys and neither should you. But they're not the ones you oughta worry about."

"Let me guess. You are."

"Yep. Guttin' you would be too easy and not nearly painful enough. Think about it, son, because I guarantee I have been."

Jack's stomach muscles involuntarily clenched. Rather than let the threat go unanswered, he faced Keely's father head on. "I appreciate the warning, Carson."

"Have a good night, Jack." The door slammed and Carson was gone.

Engrossed in a new project bid, Jack paid little attention when Keely returned to the apartment a few hours later and headed to the shower.

But his focus was shot to hell when the scent of lilacs drifted from the bathroom. He looked up just as Keely sauntered by in her birthday suit.

She gave him a little finger wave before she shut the bedroom door.

Yeah. He was supposed to get any work done now?

Maybe Keely's naked stroll was a hint. Maybe she was waiting for him, spread out on the bed, touching herself in anticipation of him coming to her.

The door opened and out she flounced in day-glo plaid pajamas. Flannel pajamas. Pajamas that covered her from head to toe. What a freakin' waste.

With her body, Keely should wear peek-a-boo nighties crafted from sheer material that showed off her stunning curves. Lace gloves that buttoned at the wrists he could rip off with his teeth. Thongs made of silk. Sky-high heels. Or better yet, boots that came above her knees. In black patent leather. And fishnets. No, fishnet stockings that hooked to lace garters. Oh, yeah, and leather boy shorts, topped with a blue velvet bustier that matched her eyes. And a collar. Just once he'd like to see how she'd react if he slapped a slave collar on her.

"I oughta slap you, Jack, for the disgusted way you're eyeballin' my favorite jammies."

"I can't help it. I'm...stunned. More flannel? Really?"

"I'm cold. And I like to be comfy when I'm lounging around. I'm just a simple country girl with simple tastes." She pointed at his laptop. "You about done working?"

"I could call it a night if I had the right incentive."

"If incentive is a euphemism for sex, keep right on pecking away on those keys and forget about your pecker. I need some recovery time from your raw thrusting power."

That admission startled him. "Was I too rough?"

"Yes, but I loved every second of it. I'm just not used to eight instances of sexual contact in less than twenty-four hours, stud." She expelled a dreamy sigh. "And to think I didn't believe your claims about not needing Viagra."

He wanted to toss off a smart comment, but it bugged him that he might've taken it too far with her on their first day as lovers.

Like you should be surprised. Everything you do is balls to the wall, full acceleration, no breaks, no prisoners.

"Hey." Keely climbed onto his lap. "My soreness is because I haven't been in a steady sexual relationship for a while."

Jack was absurdly pleased Keely wanted to reassure him. He looped her damp hair around his palm. "Can't say I'm sorry for any of it."

"Me neither."

"So since your poor pussy needs recovery time, does that mean anal sex is out?"

Keely whapped him on the arm. "Duh. I thought I could distract you from thoughts of raunchy sex by..." She grabbed his chin. "Are you even listening to me?"

He looked in her eyes. "What? I lost any logical train of thought the second you said raunchy sex."

Keely rolled her eyes. "Sex is off the list of things we can do tonight. Want to play cribbage?"

"I don't know how to play cribbage. Do you play chess?"

"Nope. Ky and Anton and Hayden are obsessed and keep begging me to learn. But truthfully, they'd whip my ass and that would be totally demoralizing."

"Checkers?"

"I used to play Chinese checkers with Carter but that was years ago."

"We could watch TV."

She groaned. "Anything but TV."

"What do you have against television?"

"It's such a waste of time. I'd rather be hanging out with my family or my friends or doing something fun or interesting instead of sitting alone in front of the TV night after night."

Yeah, that pretty much described Jack's life of late. "Indulge me. Let me prove to you there's something on worth watching."

"Fine. But you have to indulge me tomorrow night."

Shit. He'd walked right into that one. "What's going on tomorrow night?"

"A junior rodeo. My nephews are competing. I promised I'd cheer them on." She gently smoothed her hand down the side of his face. He had the overwhelming urge to purr. "Besides, it'll reinforce our 'cover' as a newly engaged couple wildly in *luurrve,* if you go along with me."

"Will your dad be there?"

"Probably. Why?"

Because he'll probably try to throw me under a bull. "No reason. Sure I'll go. Hand me the remote."

Keely shut off the lights while he powered down his computer. She plopped right beside him. Wasn't five minutes later and she was asleep, sprawled across his lap. Not that he minded. He stretched out and she curled into his chest, not facing the TV. He didn't mind that either.

The hell of it was she was absolutely right. There wasn't a damn thing to watch. So he watched her sleep for the longest time before he carried her to bed.

Chapter Twelve

"Keely?"

She attempted to roll away from the deep, sexy, husky morning voice disturbing her sleep.

Tenacious kisses moved down her neck. Her nipples tightened into hard points when her chest was exposed to cool air.

Whoa. How the heck had he unbuttoned her top so fast? A rough, callused hand slid from her lower belly between her breasts. Clever fingers pinched and teased her nipples. Hot breath tickled the fine hairs on her nape.

As amazing as it felt, she'd been happy in dreamland. Maybe if she pretended to sleep...

An impressive erection poked into her lower back.

No rest for the wickedly horny.

Jack whispered, "I know you're awake. I want you. Just like this. Warm and sleepy and sweet."

Talk about melting her resistance. She angled her head and blinked at him. "I thought my flannel PJs turned you off."

"You could wear a burlap sack and I'd be turned on. I was just surprised by your choice of flannel." Jack rolled her flat and brushed the hair from her face. "I'm finding many things about you surprise me, cowgirl."

"I'm glad I'm keeping you on your toes."

"If I had my way, I'd be keeping you on your back all the damn time." He scattered kisses down the center of her body. "Are you still sore? We can go slow. I just...want you, like this. First thing."

Keely stared at his dark head trailing kisses south. She was as shocked by his sweetness as how easily he'd verbalized his need for her. "Jack?"

"Mmm?"

"Oddly enough, the flannel is starting to itch. While you're down there take them off." She felt him smile against her stomach.

He held a tube of K-Y. She watched him ready his cock and squirt a huge dollop on his fingers, warming the slick gel before he used it on her.

Such thoughtfulness gave her pause. But not for long because Jack was on her.

Jack's mouth covered hers as he gently smeared the lubricant inside her sex. Two fingers sliding in and out didn't hurt, but she wondered if he'd be able to go slow once his cock took control of his brain.

He levered himself over her and eased his shaft in a little at a time, watching her for any signs of pain. Once he was fully seated, he murmured, "Okay?"

"Very okay." Keely brought her knees up by his hips and ran her palms over his muscular arms. Damn, she loved his body. She hadn't had nearly enough chances to play with it.

He kissed her as he moved in unhurried strokes. The kisses were lazy and unbelievably sweet.

As they rocked together, intimately connected, the bed seemed a magical place. Dark and hot and...comforting. Keely existed in this moment of perfect intimacy. No rush to the finish. No power plays. Nothing but the feel of skin gliding on skin. Of sliding tongues and gentle kisses, soft sighs and broken breaths.

"Keely." He moaned and his orgasm released a burst of heat inside her, which triggered her own climax. He kept a steady pumping of his hips as the delicious throbbing faded. He kissed her forehead, her eyelids, the corners of her mouth.

Jack's tenderness undid her. She could deal with the snarky Jack just fine. She welcomed going toe to toe with the hotheaded Jack. But this Jack? A loving Jack? She'd been better off believing he didn't possess a loving side.

He looked into her eyes and smiled oh so softly. "Good morning." After flustering her with another lingering kiss, he sailed out of the room.

Keely realized things had been much simpler when she'd hated him. Now she wasn't sure how she felt. That could lead her to big, big trouble with this unpredictable man.

"Come on, Ky! Get 'em down. That's it. Hold on. Yes!" Keely turned and high-fived AJ. Foster, sitting on Keely's lap, knew the drill and lifted his little hand for a high five. "Man, he's fast."

"Cord has been helping him. Ky's gotta be fast to keep up with Anton. That kid has such natural talent, plus he trains like a fiend."

"Ironic that Cam, who prides himself on not being a cowboy, has a son who is a total cowboy. And a rodeo cowboy to boot." Keely squinted at her brothers behind the chutes who were helping the boys get ready. Cord patted Ky on the back. Cam doled out last minute advice before Anton's turn at goat roping.

Gib and Braxton stood on the metal fence rails beside the chutes. Colby was explaining something to his sons and they hung on his every word.

"Gib is chompin' at the bit to get into the arena."

"He's only six!" AJ said.

"Six goin' on twenty-six," Keely said dryly. Colby's oldest boy was whip-smart and redefined determined. Poor Channing had her hands full with that one.

"Where's Jack tonight?"

"Take a wild guess. Working."

"Trouble in paradise?"

Keely glanced at AJ. "What makes you say that?"

AJ shrugged. "Your answer was snippy, that's all."

Keely had a right to be snippy. After spending the day using muscles she'd forgotten she had hauling shit out of the building, she'd considered staying home. But disappointing her nephews wasn't an option.

When she'd asked Jack what time he'd be ready to go to the arena, he'd replied he had work to finish. But Keely suspected he was avoiding spending time with her and her family. He was probably watching TV.

Domini barreled down the stairs, three kids in tow. "He

hasn't gone yet, has he?"

"No, he's next after this one."

"Thank God. We got a late start. Again." She unbuttoned Dimitri's coat, then Oxsana's. Both kids plopped on the bench below them. Foster scrambled off Keely's lap to sit with his cousins. "Middle of the puddle" Liesl inserted herself right between Keely and AJ.

"Hey, Aunt Keely, guess what I got?"

Keely unwound a long blonde curl that'd gotten trapped beneath the collar of Liesl's coat. "Your daddy bought you a spaceship."

Liesl giggled. "No, silly. I got an award at school today!" She turned so Keely could see the star pinned to her shirt.

"Cool beans. What's the award for?"

"Spelling. And math. And citizenship."

"Up top, girlfriend." She and Liesl high-fived. "All three classes? I'm so proud of you."

"We are too," AJ said. "Ky shared the good news after he got off the bus today."

"Know what else?" Her pale blue eyes danced with glee. "Grandpa is taking just *me* out for ice cream tomorrow after school to celebrate."

Keely bit back a smile. Grandpa Carson was such a sucker for Liesl. "Speaking of...where are my mom and dad tonight?"

"Watching Hudson for Colt and India, and Miles and Austin for Channing. Colby said she needed a night off since he was taking the older boys to the rodeo."

"Okay, it's Anton's turn. Everyone watch," Domini said.

Anton raced out of the chute, piggin' string hanging from his mouth. He launched himself at the goat, tackled it to the ground, flipped it on its side and tied all four legs together. Then he hopped up, threw his hands in the air and took three steps back, waiting to see if the tie held. The judge nodded and held up the time. Three point five seconds, which beat Ky's time of three point eight seconds.

They whooped and hollered, watching as Ky and Anton bumped fists. In the last two years Ky and Anton had become inseparable. Add Hayden to the mix and Keely was looking at the next generation of McKay hellraisers.

Liesl leaned toward AJ. "Can I feel the baby kick?"

"Sure, honey. He's really restless tonight so you oughta be able to feel him kickin' real good."

Liesl put her hands on AJ's belly. "Can't you have a girl? There aren't enough girls in our family."

"Hey, short stuff. I was the only girl for a really long time. You're lucky you've got a little sister *and* three girl cousins."

"You'll have more girl cousins, sweetie. Macie's having a girl," Domini said.

Keely's head whipped toward her. "She is? How come I didn't know?"

"Umm. She just told us this weekend."

"I was there this weekend. Why didn't she tell me?"

AJ patted Keely's knee. "K, I know how much you hate being the last to know family stuff, but it was your engagement party. She didn't want to take focus away from that."

"Where is your handsome husband-to-be?" Domini asked.

"Screwing off."

Both Domini and AJ frowned at Keely for her word choice.

"I meant he's working, screwing off...the bad light bulbs in the building and screwing new ones in."

"Lame cover up, cowgirl," Jack whispered in her ear.

Keely jumped and spun around. The sneaky man sat right behind her. "How long have you been here?"

"Long enough." He dazzled AJ and Domini with a charming grin. "Good evening, lovely ladies. I arrived just as Anton was up. He did great. I'm sorry I missed Ky."

"Maybe next time," AJ said.

Liesl peered around Keely's shoulder at Jack. "Are you and Aunt Keely gonna kiss again?"

Jack pretended to give her question serious consideration. "Do you think we should?"

She nodded.

"Maybe later." Jack's gaze swept over Keely's face. "Sorry I'm late."

"Late? You said you weren't coming."

"No, I said I had something to finish up. Then you left in a huff."

"That's a surprise," AJ said.

"Do you mind?" Keely snapped.

"Nope. Not at all. Go ahead and fight in front of us. It's not like we haven't heard it before."

Jack stood and offered her a hand. "Come on. Let's spare young ears our squabble and have a beer."

Keely admitted a beer sounded good. As soon as they cleared the bleachers, she led the way to the beer stand. But everyone in the entire county was there and wanted to meet the man who'd "tamed Keely McKay".

"Two Bud Lights," Jack said and handed the cashier a ten, waving off the change as a tip.

Keely saw the women nudging each other and waggling their eyebrows. No denying Jack stood out, not just because he wasn't a cowboy in an arena filled with them. His forest green mock turtleneck and blue jeans accentuated his eye-catching physique and his dark good looks.

"You're scowling at me. These boots are the closest I'll ever come to wearing a pair of shitkickers."

"It's not that."

"Then what?"

"I thought you weren't coming and I'd worked up a really good mad. Now you're here and there's no reason for me to be mad, but I still am."

Jack crowded her against the wall, bracing his forearm above her head. "And just how were you hoping to use that good mad against me, buttercup? By throwing something at me so we end up fucking right where we stand?"

She blinked innocently. "Is that a possibility?"

His eyes sparked lust. "Don't tempt me. I went easy on you this morning."

"And have I mentioned how awesome it was?" She managed to sip her beer even with Jack right in her face. She didn't look away. He didn't look away.

"Aw, for Christsake, you two are adults. Get a freakin' room. Don't make me arrest you for lewd behavior."

Keely didn't acknowledge Cam. Neither did Jack.

Getting no response out of them, Cam stalked off in a huff.

They grinned at each other. Then Jack brushed his lips over hers until her mouth opened and he teased her with a flirty kiss. He tasted like beer. And Jack.

"How much longer does this go on?" he murmured.

"That kiss could've gone on a lot longer as far as I'm concerned."

He gently bit her bottom lip. "I meant this event."

"Mutton bustin' is next. It's the last event because it's the most popular. Gib and Braxton are entered." She smooched his chin. "Come on. It's probably about to start."

They held hands and made their way back into the stands.

Cord and Cam were sitting with their wives. Both Dimitri and Oxsana sat on Cam's lap while Cord held Foster on his. Liesl had inserted herself between Domini and Cam. Ky and Anton were hanging over the Plexiglas partition, trying to see into the chutes.

A number of kids stayed on and rode their sheep, but the only one who crossed the finish line was Gib.

"That kid is a natural bull rider. Channing ain't gonna keep him outta the chutes when he gets old enough to ride bulls," Cord said.

Anton piped up, "Just wait 'til you see me'n Ky ride bulls. We're gonna be world champs."

Domini shook her head. "No way am I letting you get on the back of a bull, Anton McKay."

"Aw, but Mom, if I get hurt Aunt Keely can fix me up, can't ya?"

Way to put her on the spot. "Wow. Look at the time. And you guys have school tomorrow." Keely pushed up and threw her arms open. "Who's givin' me some love?"

Liesl was the first one in line for a hug. Followed by Ky and Anton. The twins were cranky and refused to let go of Cam, but sweet Foster peppered her face with kisses. She reluctantly handed Cord his youngest son. When Keely looked over at Jack, he wore the oddest expression.

Colby and his boys were waiting at the bottom of the stairs. After more congratulations were passed around to Gib and Braxton, Colby said, "Keels, you still on for tomorrow night?"

"Yep. I'll be there with bells on."

"Come on, boys, let's get your brothers so we can go home and see how Mama is farin' in an empty house."

Everyone dispersed. Keely and Jack were stopped a dozen more times as they walked through the crowd. They finally reached Keely's truck and Jack leaned against it with a long-suffering sigh.

"You hated coming to the junior rodeo that much?"

"No. You know everyone in town, don't you?"

"Uh, yeah. I have lived here most of my life, Jack."

"I can't imagine how you kept purchasing the Brewster Building under wraps. Not only from the community, but from your entire family. From what I've seen, the McKays live in each other's pockets."

Did that bother him? "It isn't like we don't have secrets from each other within the McKay family, but we do spend a lot of time together."

"By choice?"

Keely bumped him with her shoulder. "Yes, by choice. I've always hero-worshipped my brothers, even when they weren't around. For years we followed our own paths, but it's no surprise our paths converged back here. They drive me crazy sometimes and treat me like I'm twelve, but it's fun even when it's total chaos with all the kids.

"I love bein' the cool aunt who takes them to the park. Or brings them to my place for a sleepover. Or buys them gifts that annoy their parents. I pinch hit as a babysitter whenever they need me. But I mostly like being around them all the time. Watching them grow and change. Watching how marriage and parenthood has changed my brothers. Seeing them happy..." Her voice caught and she turned away. Jack wouldn't understand the struggles her brothers faced to wind up where they were. How thrilled she was every damn day she got to watch them living their lives and being a part of it.

"Are you happy, Keely?" he asked softly.

"I'm happier now than I've been in a long time. Most days I don't think about it. Why?"

"No reason. Wondered if you'd heard that biological clock ticking."

"I'm not exactly over the hill."

"I know. I'm curious. Since your brothers have so many kids, does that mean you want a bunch of your own?"

"I don't know. Do you?"

He shrugged. "I like kids. I just never really thought about having them."

"Maybe that'll change when you find the right woman."

Jack gave her that odd look again. He pushed off the truck. "I'll see you back at the apartment."

Weird dismissal. But nothing new when it came to Jack's moods. She'd just opened the door, when Jack said, "Keely. Wait."

She half-turned toward him, hating his face was obscured by shadows. "What?"

"Don't ever change. Not for your family. Not for your career. Not for the community. Not for a man. Definitely not for me. You're perfect just the way you are."

How had Jack beat her home?

Because you sat in your truck for a good fifteen minutes trying to figure out what Jack meant.

Was that little speech Jack's way of telling her he liked her? Or worse, he respected her even when she wasn't his type?

Pointless to fret about now. She trudged up the stairs, not knowing which Jack she'd find. Angry? Demanding? Sweet? Aloof?

The apartment was dark. No TV. No blue glow from his laptop. She wandered to the small bedroom, wondering if he needed alone time. She honestly couldn't blame him; her family was overwhelming, especially to a loner like Jack.

Nope. Not there either.

Her bedroom was pitch black. He'd even closed the curtains, cutting off the lone sliver of light from the streetlights at the front of the building.

"Jack?"

No answer. Rather than risk waking him by turning on a light, she rummaged in her pajama drawer in the darkness and grabbed the first thing she'd found. She stripped and yanked on the oversized T-shirt. As soon as she'd crawled between the sheets and situated herself, Jack spoke.

"You're as wiggly as a worm."

Keely spooned behind him. "You're as hot as a furnace. You feeling okay?"

"Just feeling a little...melancholy. No big deal."

Wow. Stoic Jack confessed a crack in his emotional armor. "Was it something I did?"

"No." He sighed. "I don't even know how the hell to explain it."

Keely kissed the middle of his back. "Try."

He didn't say anything for the longest time. Finally, he said, "Being around your family makes me miss my dad. Mostly it reinforces my regret of all we missed out on. Granted, we never had an easy relationship, but I thought we'd have time to change that. Your family makes it look so effortless."

"It's not. In fact it's hard living so close. Seems I'm always overstepping boundaries. Or they're overstepping mine. I hated when my brothers were gone and I can't imagine only seeing them once a year. But sometimes I wonder if distance isn't better. Makes the heart grow fonder and all that jazz."

"Can you really see yourself living someplace else?"

Keely's non-response spurred Jack on.

"See, that's where we're different, Keely. I never saw myself living on the farm permanently. Not even as a kid. I couldn't wait to get out and establish my own identity."

"Was it that awful growing up there?" she asked.

"I hated the constant backbreaking work. I watched my dad toil, year in year out. For what? He and my mother lived hand to mouth. It wasn't like he spent quality time with us. He liked his whiskey and he liked his quiet. He didn't have a great relationship with us kids because he couldn't be bothered to make the effort. So as I watched your brothers, with their kids, how they're all such great fathers, I wondered if I'd inherited my father's worst qualities. If I was ever lucky enough to reproduce, if I'd be a shitty father because that's all I know."

She had to tread lightly, since this was the first time Jack had opened up to her. It was as enlightening as it was heartbreaking.

"I never wanted to be like my dad. It's sobering when I consider I am just like him. I'm not a farmer, but what I do for a living is my personal measure of who I am as a man."

"Jack—"

"But even now, I don't make the effort with my mother. Or Justin. Or anyone else. I'm stuck in this fucked-up cycle and can't seem to change it."

"Do you want to change it?"

His body stiffened. "Look. Just forget I said anything and go to sleep."

Ooh. Dismissed again. Luckily she'd gotten used to mood swings when she lived with Cam. Keely pushed away from his warmth and sat on the edge of the bed.

Jack rolled over. "Sorry I snapped. You don't have to go. Stay."

Keely ignored his assumption she'd leave when he finally reached out to her. No way. She was sticking. She was annoying that way. She rooted round in her nightstand drawer until she found the pouch at the back. Palming it, she slid back between the sheets. "I'm not goin' anywhere." She traced the frown lines on his forehead. The rise of his sharp cheekbones. The tensed line of his jaw. The grooves bracketing his sinful mouth. When he closed his eyes and sighed, she knew tonight he needed her to soothe him.

She straddled his pelvis and knocked the pillows aside, pinning his arms above his head.

His eyes flew open.

"Stay still." Keely urged his lips to part, allowing her to direct the openmouthed kisses she craved. She tested his reactions as she explored his mouth. Sucked on his tongue. Licked and nibbled and bit as long and as methodically as she pleased. Jack was an active participant, but he didn't try to wrest control.

She slid her lips up and down his neck. Tasting. He arched when Keely hit a sensitive spot with her tongue. He groaned when she sucked on the tendons straining for attention. She scattered kisses across his pectorals, relishing how the downy chest hair teased her cheek. Mmm. He smelled terrific too.

"Keely—"

"Let me, Jack." The tip of her wet tongue flicked his nipple. "Or do you want me to stop?"

"No! I just—"

"Then be good, bad boy, or I will stop."

Jack slumped into the mattress with a terse, "Fine."

She bent to her task of mapping his pecs with her mouth. She traced the cut muscles with her tongue between lapping at his nipples. "I've never seen you working out, so how is it that you maintain such a studly body?"

"I work out at home while I'm watching TV. I've used the

weight room in the community center several times since I've been here."

"I'm glad. So—" she licked his right nipple, "—very—" she licked it again, "—very—" and she blew across the wet skin, watching that already taut nipple tighten further, "—glad."

His hips shot up. "You're killing me with that mouth of yours."

Keely painted wet swirls on his abdomen, paying meticulous attention to that luscious six-pack. She dipped her tongue into his belly button; his cock jerked against her neck. She swept the pearly bead from the head and placed a smacking kiss on the middle of his shaft. "Scoot up and spread your legs."

He moved so fast she suspected he'd gotten fabric burns on his ass.

For a minute, Keely admired the bounty before her. She'd seen her share of cocks, but she admitted Jack's cock was beautiful. Big. Long and thick. The shaft itself was wide enough she couldn't circle her index finger and thumb around the girth. His black pubic hair wasn't too long or too short. She appreciated his manscaping.

She nuzzled his groin, inhaling the ultimate masculine scent that was as familiar as it was unique. She brought the pilfered pouch within reach and angled her head to suck his sac.

"Sweet Jesus."

Man, she loved the way he groaned as she rolled his balls over her tongue. Sucking both together, then one at a time. She released them and flicked her tongue up the ridged vein of his cock until the tip reached the sweet spot below the head.

Keely half-expected he'd be watching her intently with those sexy hooded eyes, but his head was on the mattress. His eyes were closed. He wasn't relaxed, but he'd probably forgotten their entire conversation.

As much as she'd enjoyed taking her time, Keely ended the sexual teasing. She wanted Jack's orgasm. She'd earned it. She swallowed that velvety heat into her mouth, just holding it there.

Jack didn't grab her head. He didn't force his hips up. He stayed still and emitted another rough-edged moan.

She slipped the Fukuoko 2000 onto the tip of her finger. She brought more of his cock into her mouth, letting the wetness guide him deeper. She sucked hard as she released the length back, letting her teeth nip the upper rim of the head as her tongue fluttered below it. Keely did this over and over.

It wasn't long before he rasped, "Goddamn. Keely. Please."

Her head bobbed faster, keeping the strokes shallow. She flipped the tiny switch on the mini "massager" and placed the vibrating tip on the strip of skin behind his balls in front of his anus.

"Holy fuck!"

And Jack was toast. The instant his balls constricted, his cock hit the back of her throat and she swallowed each hot spurt. He came so violently, the bed shook. When she figured she'd sucked every last drop and most of his brainpower, he slipped free from her mouth.

Several minutes passed. He didn't say anything. He didn't reach for her. And Keely suddenly felt very unsure of herself and almost...shy. She pushed onto her knees, ready to flee.

But Jack hauled her against him so she sprawled across his chest. He took her mouth in a savage kiss. After he finally relinquished her lips, he buried his face in her neck.

"So I guess you liked that after all?"

He swatted her ass. Hard. "You even have to ask?" He dusted delicate kisses on her cheek. "That was fucking amazing. Thank you."

"I loved doing it."

"I could tell." He breathed in her ear. "Did having my cock in your mouth turn you on? If I slip my hand between your legs will I find you wet?"

"Drenched."

"Maybe I should take care of that for you."

"Or I could take care of it myself and you can watch."

Jack's entire body went rigid. Then he growled, "Show me. Now."

Keely straddled him again, staying up on her knees. "This won't take long." She smiled naughtily and brought the Fukuoko to her mouth. She watched Jack's face as she licked it.

A dark hunger shot through his eyes and he growled again.

She set the plastic tip directly on her clit, flicked the switch and closed her eyes. Because she was primed from blowing Jack, that tightening, tingling sensation didn't build; it sideswiped her. Immediately. Keely climaxed with a sharp gasp.

His slow, sensual smile brightened his face. "You weren't kidding about fast."

"Nope."

"Sexy as hell. Next time I'll be in charge of the vibrator selection, as I know you've squirreled away a whole box of them."

"Deal." Keely shoved the Fukuoko in the pouch, threw it on the nightstand and crawled into Jack's arms.

Before she drifted off, he whispered, "Thanks, cowgirl."

Chapter Thirteen

Due to a light schedule, Keely left work early. She drove to Moorcroft to check on the building process before she headed out to Colby and Channing's.

Jack was in a foul mood. He wasn't yelling, but speaking in clipped tones, wearing that don't-fuck-with-me look. Eyes hard, mouth flat, eyebrows drawn together. Plus, his hair nearly stood on end from jamming his hands through it.

Might make her a chickenshit, but she steered clear of him.

Chet and Remy were covered in dust and grime, leaning against the wall by the back door. Keely approached them cautiously. "Hey guys."

"Don't ask how it's goin', 'cause I'll tell ya right now, it ain't goin' well, cuz. Not at all," Chet said.

A knot formed in her belly. "What happened?"

Remy took a long pull off his water before answering. "Nothin', that's the problem. Before we can get to the actual remodeling part you've contracted us for, we have to tear down all the ruined materials and haul them out. That's what's taking the bulk of time you've allotted. Jack ain't happy about that."

"Why not? That's part of the process, isn't it?"

"Yes. And no. We worked all damn day clearing out the lathe and plaster in the first room upstairs. One room. Out of all these rooms."

"And we weren't slacking either," Chet added.

Her confused gaze moved between them. "I don't understand."

"I know you don't, sweetheart. But the truth is, you need to hire a demolition team to come in here and get it ready for us to start. We've done our best to work around it, but the truth is..."

Chet and Remy exchanged a look.

"The truth is what?"

"The truth is: that's not their job, Keely."

She whirled around and faced Jack. "What?"

"They've been busting ass hoping it'd get easier, but it hasn't. Neither the work nor the fact they should've told you from the start that teardown wasn't configured in the contract."

Keely stared at her cousins with total mortification. "Is that true?"

Remy blushed. "Yeah. It's true. We didn't want you to feel bad. You're family and we wanna help you. Like Jack said, we thought we might be able to do the teardown easy, but we can't. And now we've fallen behind, not only on Jack's timetable for this project, but on our other construction projects."

Not only was she fucking up her own project with her ignorance, but Jack's, as well as those West Construction had committed to. Keely had the overwhelming urge to hide her face in shame.

Buck up. This is what big girls do. Own up to their mistakes and make amends.

"I appreciate you guys finally telling me. I hate to think how much longer this might've gone on if Jack hadn't forced the issue." She attempted a smile. "Since we're being upfront with each other, I'll need timesheets for you both for the last week so I can pay you for the teardown you've already done."

Chet protested. "Keely. That's not necessary."

"It is. You work hard. I won't screw you out of money because you're too nice of guys. It ain't your fault I'm just your clueless little cousin, okay? I *can* pay you."

Another silent communication passed between the brothers. Remy said, "All right. We'll have the paperwork filled out and here tomorrow."

"Thank you. You guys know any companies I could hire to come in and finish the teardown? So you can get started on your end?"

"I know of one outfit from Meeteetsee, but last I heard they were starting a project in Livingston, Montana."

"And they ain't cheap," Remy pointed out.

"How much money we talkin'?"

Chet shrugged. "I'm guessing...about fifty, sixty."

"Fifty or sixty what?" Keely asked.

"Fifty or sixty thousand dollars. I believe that's a low number, even for around these parts," Jack inserted.

Keely's eyes nearly bugged out of her head. Holy shit. That amount would eat a huge chunk of her budget for the first year. But if she didn't get it done...the clinic couldn't open. As it looked right now this dream of hers was nothing more than a pipedream. Her eyes burned hot with unshed tears.

Bawling wouldn't solve a damn thing. She needed to think this through. Like she should've done from the beginning. It embarrassed her she'd gone off half-cocked, believing she had the construction portion of the project under control.

"We'll help in whatever way we can, Keely, you know that," Remy said quietly.

"I do know that." She looked at her watch. "I also know I'm late for my babysitting gig with Colby and Channing's hellions. I'll see you guys tomorrow."

Jack didn't chase Keely down because she needed time to process her mistake. Later tonight they could discuss solutions like rational adults. He pointed to Chet's cooler. "Got anything stronger than water?"

"Sure." He pulled out a bottle of Coors Light. "Here."

"Thanks." Jack cracked the top, tempted to drain it in one swallow.

"So can me and Remy ask you something, Jack, without you getting all pissed off at us?"

"Give it a shot, but no guarantees."

"How come you didn't tell Keely she needed to budget separately for teardown? Especially since you were helping her figure out what it'd take to get this place up to snuff?"

"An oversight. We've all made them," he lied. "I'm kicking myself same as you guys are."

"She's a fiery, independent woman. This oversight will drive her crazy. She'll blame herself, lose confidence, close down..."

"And then she'll pull up her bootstraps and do what needs done," Remy added. "She ain't the type to stand around, wringing her hands and waiting for someone to rescue her.

Which is damn amazing when you think about it. She could've turned out so much differently."

"Amen, bro."

That startled him. "What do you mean?"

"We've—her brothers and cousins on both the McKay and West side—looked out for her. She wouldn't have had to do nothin' but stand around and look pretty and helpless. But that's not what Keely is made of. That's not who she is now, or who she was even when she was a girl. She don't want nothin' handed to her. She learned to do things for herself. If she didn't know how to do something, she found folks to teach her. We admire the hell outta her for standing her ground when it'd be easier to give in."

"To her family?

"Yeah. God love our McKay cousins, but they would've put the kibosh on her buying the building straight away. They would've accidentally made Keely feel stupid for trying to do something without their help."

Jack scowled.

"Don't get us wrong," Chet said. "They ain't cruel to her. And hell, I don't even think they realize they're doin' it. But because they're all older males, they don't see Keely in an adult role. They treat her like a little girl. And they'd see purchasing this building as another one of Keely's whims. We knew how much it meant to her, fulfilling this lifelong dream. We also know that if this clinic project falls through, her family will act like it's no big deal, when it will crush her."

"Which is also why if she don't have the money to hire someone to do the teardown, she absolutely will not ask anyone in her family for financial help," Remy pointed out. "Hell, she'll be here with a crowbar and do the whole thing herself."

They were lost in their separate thoughts until Jack felt Chet and Remy's curious gazes on him. "What?"

"Since you and Keely are gonna get married, if she finds a company that'll do the teardown, would you be willing to pay for it?" Chet asked carefully.

Another tricky question. "I'll do whatever it takes to help her. But we all know she won't take money from me. It's not because I can't afford it, but it'll be a matter of pride to her."

"Yeah, she wasn't none too happy to find out you owned

the Sandstone Building, was she?" Remy mused.

"No. I'm living with her and she's still paying me rent. So as much as you guys didn't want to see her brothers crushing her dreams, I won't play a part in making her feel beholden to me. She hired me. She's paying me. In her mind when it comes to the building stuff I just work for her. Period."

Remy and Chet exchanged a skeptical look.

"You saw how Keely acted. Did she fly in here and lay a sloppy kiss on me? No. Did she cry on my shoulder when she discovered she'd made a big mistake that would cost her a pile? No. She bucked up, offered to rectify things with you two and she treated me like she would've any other employee." Truthfully, her behavior stung like hell. But this situation wasn't about him.

"I get what you're sayin', Jack, I really do. I just wish there was some way to help her without any of us trying to sneak her money."

A solution started to form. "How many guys are on that crew out of Meeteetsee?"

Remy scratched his chin. "Probably a dozen. Why?"

"If they had a dozen guys on the clock, how long would it take to teardown this place?"

"Three days. But that'd probably be milking it. Customers would freak if they thought the company could make fifty thou in a single day."

"But if we could get a dozen guys here, say tomorrow. For all day, would you two be willing to help me supervise what gets torn out and what stays?"

Chet and Remy nodded at each other. "Absolutely. What did you have in mind?"

Jack grinned. "I'll tell you, but you've got to promise me that Keely won't ever find out."

Jack called Carson McKay. He was actually relieved the ornery SOB answered with a gruff *hello*.

"Carson. Jack Donohue. Got a minute to talk?"

"Only about that long. I gotta get Caro pretty quick. What did you need?"

"First off, Keely can't know I called you about this."

Carson harrumphed, which Jack took as assent.

Jack spun a tale about the company Keely hired for the teardown backing out. How it could jeopardize the entire clinic project because of time constraints. Keely was mightily upset, but she didn't want to inconvenience anyone in her family by asking for help.

"That girl. Don't she know we'd do anything for her?" Carson said with exasperation.

"Which is why I called you. If you show up at the building tomorrow with a bunch of guys ready to work, under the direction of me and Chet and Remy, Keely won't lose a single dollar, or a day on the timeframe of getting the building up to speed."

Carson was quiet for a minute or so but Jack suffered through it. Finally he said, "I'll take care of it. But I wanna know why you ain't takin' credit for it?"

"I don't have to tell you Keely McKay is stubborn and filled with pride. If I arranged to fix it she'd see it as me meddling in her business. And trust me, when it comes to that building, my relationship with her is *all* business."

He snorted.

"If you show up with her brothers and assorted cousins wanting to help her out of a jam...she'll see it differently. Plus, all of you will have been involved in some part of the process, of this project that means everything to her." Jack paused. "She helps out her brothers all the time. In fact, she's watching Colby's kids right now. It'd be good for your family to pay back that kindness when Keely needs it the most and expects it the least. And trust me, she needs it."

Another bout of silence.

"You got all the bases covered, son, and I can't fault you for lookin' out for her, in fact, I appreciate it. But how's that snoopy girl gonna believe I just *happened* to hear about her building troubles?"

"Easy. Chet and Remy. Just tell her you stopped by last night to see the progress after talking to her on Sunday. Chet and Remy mentioned issues with the teardown process. You went home, made a few calls and set up an old-fashioned barn raising in reverse."

"You sure you ain't a politician, Jack?"

"Hell, no, Carson, you sure know how to throw an insult like a damn dagger."

Carson chuckled. "See you tomorrow. But if this scheme backfires? I'm rolling on you first, guaranteed."

Jack said, "I'd expect nothing less," to the dial tone.

Although Jack was restless, he dragged his laptop into the bedroom and caught up on paperwork. He figured trying to sleep was pointless, so it shocked him to wake up at one in the morning completely disoriented. He stacked his papers, powered down his laptop and wandered into the living room.

There she was, fully dressed, asleep on the couch.

A protective feeling expanded in his chest. He wanted to take care of her. And not just tonight. Jack lifted her into his arms.

She blinked her eyes sleepily. "Jack? What are you doin'?"

"Tucking you in bed. You fell asleep on the couch, buttercup."

"I got home and thought about watching TV but I couldn't figure out how to turn it on. I'm hopeless with everything today."

"Don't say that. I'll show you tomorrow." Jack kicked the bedroom door shut.

"I swear I just closed my eyes for a minute. Those kids of Colby's wear me out."

He set Keely on her feet by the bed. He undressed her down to panties and a tank top. She crept under the covers.

Once Jack was in bed, she wrapped herself around him. "You know, GQ, I'm kinda starting to like you a little bit."

He kissed the top of her head. "Same goes, cowgirl."

The next morning Keely started her day with less enthusiasm than usual. Jack had made coffee but he was already gone. He'd left a note by her favorite mug, reminding her she'd promised to pay Chet and Remy for the teardown work today.

The last thing she wanted was to drive to Moorcroft and face her failure. She'd thought about the problem and hadn't found a viable solution besides hiring a demolition company and trying to keep on schedule. Jack had allotted six weeks. They'd nearly burned through two already.

Jack. He'd been so sweet again last night. Carting her off to bed. Tucking her in hadn't made her feel like a child; it'd made her feel cherished. Yesterday when she learned she'd fucked up big time, Jack hadn't belittled her for her ignorance. He hadn't swooped in and offered to fix it for her.

Would you have taken his help if he'd offered?

No. No matter how good his intentions were, Keely couldn't take money from him. It was her mistake; she'd find a way to fix it.

When she pulled up to the building an hour later, trucks were parked everywhere. Ten industrial-sized Dumpsters lined the parking lot. What the hell was going on?

She cautiously entered the building amidst the banging and hammering. Male voices echoed. Inside the main room, she gasped. The entire upper floor was an empty shell.

Keely called out, "Chet? Remy?"

And whose head popped out first? Her father's.

"Daddy? What on earth are you doin' here?"

He wiped his hands on a bandana and ambled toward her. "Now hear me out, Keely, before you go getting that look on your face."

She opened her mouth to demand, "What look?" but settled for, "I'm listening."

"Last night I stopped by to see you."

"You did?"

"Talked a bit with Chet and Remy. They indicated you were havin' issues with getting this place tore apart. So I went home and got to thinkin'."

"Always dangerous," she murmured.

He flapped the bandana at her. "Smarty pants. Anyway, destroyin' stuff is what many of the McKays do best." He grinned. "I made a few calls. And here we are, doin' our best to tear this place down so the West boys can build it back up."

Keely didn't say a word. She was absolutely stunned. And touched. And about to break down and sob.

"Girlie, it scares me when you get all quiet."

She couldn't speak around the lump in her throat.

"Aw, hell, you ain't pissed off are ya?" He sighed softly, nervously wiping his hands with the bandana. "I just wanted to help out. Seems like you don't need me now that you're all grown up."

No way could she stop the tears, or from launching herself at him. "Daddy. I-I can't—"

"I know, baby girl," he soothed. "It's okay."

Keely breathed him in, sun-warmed cotton and honest sweat, coffee and Red Man tobacco, English Leather cologne and the hint of her mother's perfume. Scents that offered her comfort, security and assurance like nothing else in her life. She whispered, "I'll always need you. Always."

"Good to know." He squeezed her so strongly she could scarcely breathe. She cried harder when he gruffly said, "I love you, baby girl."

After her dad released her, Keely wiped her tears with her fingers. He handed her a hankie with a crusty, "Here. Don't understand why the sex that's always cryin' about something never remembers a damn hankie."

She laughed. "Thanks, Daddy."

"Anytime, punkin. You ain't gonna believe all they got done already. Chet and Remy are supervising. So's Jack. He's a damn taskmaster."

"How well I know that."

Inside the building, she could barely hear above the sounds of progress. Cord and Colby worked upstairs with Carter. In the backroom, Chet and Remy pulled out wiring while Trevor and Edgard gently pried off mopboards.

Colt, Quinn, Ben and Kade were ripping out lathe and plaster in the front room. Kane, Cam, Brandt, Dalton, Tell and her uncles Calvin and Charles were removing sections of ceiling. Whoa. Carson McKay had called everybody. Her assorted male relatives smiled at her and returned to the grind.

Her dad started toward the front door and Keely snagged his arm. "I can't believe—"

He winced.

"What's wrong with your arm?"

"Nothin'."

"Let me see it."

He showed her the inside of his left forearm. Beneath the

rip in his shirt was a bloody scratch.

"What happened?"

"Me'n Jack were bustin' a cabinet outta the bathroom. Damn thing sliced me."

"Come on. I'll fix you up." Outside, Keely unearthed the first aid kit from underneath the front seat of her truck. She swabbed the area with a disinfectant pad, smeared on antibiotic cream and covered it with a square bandage. She even placed a healing kiss on it. "There. Good as new."

"Thanks. Your mama's gonna give me hell for rippin' my shirt."

Keely rolled her eyes. "Mama never gives you hell about nothin'."

He bussed her forehead. "How little you know, girlie." He ambled around the corner.

That's when Keely saw Jack waiting on the steps. Buoyant, she made a beeline for him and he caught her in a tight hug. She swallowed his surprised laughter with a deep kiss that turned unexpectedly gentle. She whispered, "Thank you."

"For what?"

"For tucking me in last night. For making coffee this morning. For supervising this teardown even though it isn't part of your job description."

"My pleasure, buttercup."

"I'm sorry I can't stick around and help since I rescheduled my Friday clients for today."

"Don't sweat it. With this many guys, it'll be done fast." Jack rubbed his lips over hers. "And for being McKays, they take direction surprisingly well."

Keely rested her forehead to his, feeling all choked up again.

"Baby. What's wrong?"

"How am I ever supposed to repay them, Jack? Thank you isn't enough. It's above and beyond even for family."

"Not for them, it's not. They're doing it for you, *because* of you."

"Sometimes you are so nice I can't believe I ever hated you."

He kissed her again. Longer. Deeper. Sweeter.

"Get a room," Cam yelled out.

"Get back to work," Remy added.

Male laughter echoed.

"They're gonna give you crap for the rest of the day for that lip lock, GQ."

"I'm up for the challenge."

"Good. I'll see you later."

Lucky for Keely the day didn't drag as much as she'd feared. She finished at the clinic and drove back to Moorcroft, anxious to see the changes.

Dusk had fallen. The vehicles were gone. She unlocked the back door and ventured inside. She didn't need a spotlight to see the differences; the place was empty. Completely empty. Walls gone. Ceiling gone. Plumbing gone. Electrical gone. The space was a blank slate. A clean canvas.

For the first time it felt like hers.

Keely tried to envision where the spaces would be divided into patient rooms. What the refurbished woodwork would look like. If the tin ceiling would gleam after one hundred years of grime was removed.

Giddy, she spun around on the wooden floor, arms flung open wide, laughing. Trying to capture the moment—her dream was finally within reach.

Chapter Fourteen

Jack was ready to walk out the door when Keely whirled in like a tornado. Her mouth ran a million miles an hour.

"So I drove back to Moorcroft after I got off work and I'm stunned. I cannot believe they finished all of it today. I'm peeing my pants I'm so pumped."

"There's a visual I needed, Keely."

She took in his appearance. "Where are you goin' all duded up?"

"Out with Carter. Wearing clean pants and a sweater hardly qualifies me as duded up," he said dryly.

"Whatever you say, GQ." She bussed his cheek. "You look nice and smell even better. What're you guys doin'?"

"Eating first, then hashing through details for a couple projects I've lined up for him."

Keely looked at him quizzically. "You Carter's pimp?"

"In a manner of speaking. He's greatly underappreciated in the western art world." He adjusted his sleeves. "No big deal. I do what I can to get his name out there. Pass along commercial contacts."

"I never knew you were so invested in Carter's career."

"And you can't tell anyone, either," he warned. "He'd be pissed as hell if he thought I'd blabbed to you."

"But we're in *luurrve*. You're supposed to tell me everything." Keely left a smacking kiss on his mouth. "Don't worry, my lips are sealed. I'll see you later."

"Where are you going?"

"My dart league starts at eight."

Jack narrowed his eyes. "You play in a dart league? Why

didn't I know that?"

"I figured you'd think it hopelessly lowbrow so I didn't mention it." She hopped from foot to foot as she took off her boots. Then she sailed into the bedroom.

He followed her and leaned against the jam as he watched her undress. "How long have you been playing darts?"

Keely whipped off her shirt. "In a league? Six months. But Colt taught me to play when I was a kid. I was a lousy shot with a bow and arrow. He thought darts might teach me hand-eye coordination, but I just ended up liking darts more than shooting bow." She flipped through the hangers in the closet.

"What other hobbies do you have that I don't know about?"

"Darts ain't exactly a hobby. It's an excuse to hang out with my friends and drink beer. They've been trying to get me to join a volleyball league but it doesn't interest me. I'm in a book club, but half the time I don't read the damn 'literary' books they pick because they're total downers."

"What would you rather read?"

"Erotic romances." Keely winked. "As far as other activities? I'm on the volunteer list for the community center and fill in when someone's sick or on vacation. Oh, and I like to dance."

Jack wondered if her excessive social calendar was because she didn't like being alone. "You don't ever stay home and relax? Kick off your boots and stay a while?"

"Sure. But my idea of relaxing and yours are way different."

Why did he bristle? "Meaning what?"

"I relax when I'm asleep. Reclining in front of the TV as a way to relax? No thanks. I'd rather do things with real live people instead of pretending what happens on a sitcom or dramedy or reality show matters. Connections matter to me. And there's nothing more relaxing than laughing with family and friends." Keely buttoned the last button of the India's Ink dart league shirt.

For Christsake. This woman played in a dart league sponsored by a tattoo shop. She had tattoos. She drove a dirty pickup. She had fifty different colored pairs of shitkickers. She had a social life to rival Paris Hilton's. Did he have a single thing in common with her besides phenomenal sex?

Yes. You need each other to get your careers on track.

Sometimes Jack forgot the big picture. Sometimes he forgot

their relationship wasn't real. What really pissed him off was sometimes he even forgot Keely wasn't his type.

"Speaking of families. Last night Channing dropped the bomb she's having a girl! No one tells me anything important these days."

"Well, it's important you don't make plans for tomorrow night because we need to talk about the Milford trip."

"But Thursday night is my night to—"

Jack held up his hand stopping her protest. "I don't care if it's your night to shoe horses or to craft quilts or to can pickled beets. I need you here."

"Fine." Keely brushed past him. In the doorway to the bathroom she turned. "Have fun with Carter. But don't wait up for me."

Don't wait up for me.

Jack ground his teeth together. Three hours had passed and her parting shot still rankled.

"Jack? Buddy? You're gonna have an embolism if you keep scowling like that. So tell me what's up."

"Your sister drives me fucking crazy."

"And that's news?" Carter laughed. "The fact you two haven't killed each other by now is newsworthy. Never in a million years would I have predicted you two as a couple."

"Join the club."

"So tell me...what did my little sis do to piss you off? Earlier at the jobsite you guys were goin' at it hot and heavy. I thought my dad was gonna get the hose out and spray you down."

Jack scraped his hands over the razor stubble on his jaw. "I don't understand why she has to be doing something all the time. Why can't she just stay home? It's like she can't stand to be by herself."

Carter didn't say anything.

At first, Jack wondered if he'd overstepped his bounds. Then he worried Keely had kept something important from him. "What?"

"Keely didn't tell you how she's spent the last five years?"

Jack squirmed. He should've kept his mouth shut. He should know all about his fiancée's past. If he showed his

161

ignorance, Carter would get suspicious.

"Jack?"

He shook his head.

"It figures she didn't fill you in." Carter signaled the waitress for another round.

When Carter didn't start talking, Jack got both worried and pissed off. "You can't drop something like that into conversation and leave it there to fester, McKay."

"It's not festering, Donohue. I'm debating."

"On what?"

That blue gaze identical to Keely's pinned Jack in place. "On if I should keep my big mouth reputation in the family and just flat out tell you, or if I oughta let it fester so you're forced to ask Keely about it. Part of me thinks if she would've wanted you to know, she would've told you herself. But part of me thinks it's your right to know."

When the waitress swung buy with more beer, Jack ordered two shots of Wild Turkey.

Carter leaned back in the booth. His posture wasn't lazy, but challenging. "If you think getting me drunk will make me spill my guts, you're barking up the wrong tree, pal."

What was up with this family and the colorful colloquialisms? "The shots are for me, not you."

The silence stretched between them until the waitress brought the whiskey shots. Jack drained one and set the other aside.

"You're a lot like her, you know."

Jack's gaze shot to Carter's. "Keely?" He snorted. "Right. Talk about oil and water. Fire and ice. Concrete and glass."

His comment must've alleviated Carter's misgivings. He set his elbows on the table. "If I tell you this, Jack, I need your word that you will not tip off Keely that you know."

"I won't."

"After Cam and Domini got married we were all together for some family holiday. The kids were watching a movie in the family room, the babies were asleep and it was just adults around the dining room table, which rarely happens. We're bullshitting, teasing one another, like we always do, when someone, I don't even remember who, tossed off a comment about Cam not pulling his weight with the ranch—a total joke, right? I mean, we'd just gotten Cam interested in being part of the family again and none of us wanted to fuck that up. So they start picking on me and I volleyed it back, and the next thing we were all ragging on Keely.

"Even before she'd moved into Domini's apartment she'd disappear for days—sometimes weeks on end. As far as we knew, she worked part time at the VA in Cheyenne a couple days a month and that was her only job. We wondered if she had a guy on a string keeping her away from home. So we teased her about being too busy chasing tail to get a real job, or to help out at the ranch. I'll admit we were total dicks to her, bringing up stupid shit she'd done in the past. Treating her like she was a bratty preteen. Questioning her work ethic after living in the big city. Normally Keely would fire insults right back, but she got quieter and quieter. We were so busy ribbing her we didn't notice."

Jack's gut knotted—not from the shot of whiskey.

"Eventually we pushed her too far. Keely stood up and said the reason no one in our family knew what she'd been up to during her trips to Cheyenne was because we were all a bunch of self-absorbed pricks and hadn't bothered to ask about her life. We all sort of looked at each other in shock and realized she was right.

"When she wasn't working at the VA or private hospitals in Cheyenne and Ft. Collins, she was moonlighting on the rodeo circuit as a sports med tech for extra cash. The reason she didn't have energy to expend on her measly portion of the testosterone ranch was because she was exhausted."

"Measly portion of the ranch?" Jack repeated.

Carter stopped to sip his beer. "Long, involved legal gibberish I won't go into."

But Carter did detail the personal sacrifices Keely made for Cam to get him back on track after his discharge from the army. Putting her schooling on hold, keeping her assorted relatives at bay at Cam's request, even angering them and shouldering the blame. Jack was beyond stunned, listening to the depth of Keely's commitment to her family, hearing about her generosity and her determination—to the exclusion of fulfilling her own dreams.

"The hell of it was after we all compared stories, we realized as well as Keely knew all of us, we didn't know her as an adult at all. That's what hurt her the worst."

"I imagine it did." Jack knocked back the other shot, struggling to control his emotions, mostly his admiration for the woman who acted out of love with no expectation but to be loved in return. It was damn humbling to realize he'd never had that deep connection with any one person, let alone the sheer number of people Keely connected with on a daily basis. The sheer number of people who benefited just from having Keely McKay in their lives.

What would it be like to be on the receiving end of such devotion? Or to have the balls to give it back in return without fear?

"Jack?" Carter prompted. "What's wrong?"

Everything. "Nothing. Just trying to wrap my head around all this about Keely. AJ didn't know what she was up to? What about Chassie? Or Ramona?"

"My guess is Ramona knew what Keely was doing. AJ and Chassie are wrapped up in husbands and kids, whereas Ramona is single and probably understands Keely's drive."

"So what happened afterward?"

"We groveled. Big time."

Jack laughed softly. Even when his heart broke a little for the woman who gave so much.

"She cried a lot and called us names, but she forgave us because she's just that way. Girl's got a heart as big as Wyoming." Carter rubbed his chin. "My point is, you are more like her than you realize, Jack. You both work hard to keep your personal and professional lives separate. I figure she's entitled to be out every night of the week if it makes up for all the years she didn't get to have fun."

"Fun? Weren't you the one who told me she was such a wild child?"

"In high school," Carter scoffed. "That was a decade ago. She might've mixed it up a little when she first went off to college in Denver, or cut loose when she came home, but her life changed after Cam was injured."

That made sense. But why hadn't Keely shared any of this? Didn't she trust him? Especially after he'd opened up to her about his family issues? He took a deep breath, trying to relieve the tension distorting his muscles. "I appreciate you telling me."

But Carter wasn't paying attention to him. His focus was beyond Jack's shoulder. He muttered, "Fuck."

"What?"

"Nothin'. I'm getting tired. Now that we're done with business we oughta hit the road."

Jack squinted at the clock. "It's ten. You don't have the wife and kids here. I'm not all in for getting shitfaced, but why are you so eager to leave?"

"No reason. Just tired."

Then Jack knew. Keely was here. The question was: who was she here with? "Where is she?"

"On the dance floor."

He wished he had another goddamn shot to suck down. "Alone?"

Carter shook his head.

Jack snarled.

Before he bolted, Carter grabbed his forearm. "It's just her friend Michael. Don't go after him."

"It's not Michael I'm going after."

"Jack—"

"Don't wait around." He tore his arm from Carter's grip and exited the booth.

Jack didn't barrel up and pull Keely off the dance floor. He watched from the shadows, planning to ambush her. If she fought, he'd drag her out of the damn bar by her hair.

When had he started giving into his caveman mentality?

The fast song ended. Some crap with too much slide steel guitar and a mournful fiddle started. His ears threatened to bleed. He hated country music. But he wouldn't stand by and let another man hold his woman.

Jack stalked to the dance floor. The guy with his hands on Keely leapt back.

"Keely and I are just friends. We were just dancin'."

Keely whirled around. "Jack? What are you doin' here?"

"Surprised to see me, buttercup?" He gave Michael a feral smile. "Get lost."

The guy left skid marks he dashed off so fast.

"Oh. My. God. You did not just—"

Jack grabbed her, plastering their bodies together. He put

165

his mouth on her ear. "I warned you. The only man allowed to touch you is me. That includes dancing. So make nice or I will make the rest of your night a living hell."

"You don't scare me."

He chuckled. "Oh, cowgirl, that was the wrong thing to say." He spun them and in the process slipped his thigh between her legs. Every time he moved, he ground the hard muscle into her pussy.

She hissed, "Stop it."

"Why? You aren't scared of me, remember? You aren't scared if I keep this up I'll make you come right out here on the dance floor?"

"Don't."

"You want it. Your body is quivering." Jack nuzzled her cheek. "I feel your nipples poking into my chest. You're excited. If I wiggled my hand into your jeans right now, would I find you wet?"

"Why are you doin' this?" she demanded.

"Because I can. And you'll be goddamn lucky if making you come out here is all I do to you tonight."

In a fit of pique, Keely attempted to turn her head away.

Jack was having none of it. He forced her chin up and sealed his mouth to hers. She reacted as he expected: she fought him for five seconds and kissed him back with equal abandon.

Throughout the kiss and the slow dance he kept grinding his thigh into her clit. Rubbing back and forth the way that set her off. Her sex was fire hot riding his leg. His heart pounded as hard as hers.

Keely clenched her shaking thighs around his, a signal she was close to exploding.

He slid his leg away, allowing his lips to cling to hers for several heartbeats before he broke his mouth free.

"Jack. Please."

"I will let you come on one condition."

"What?"

"You will follow me as soon as this song is finished. No questions asked. No saying goodbye to your friends. Just you and me, Keely, settling this *my* way, however *I* see fit."

"Yes."

"Right answer." Jack shoved his thigh back to where she most needed it. "Close your eyes. Feel the friction of the fabric on your clit. Is your pussy hot and throbbing? Wishing my cock was riding you instead of you riding my leg? Do you know how hard my dick is right now? You do that to me. Make me so fucking hard I can't see straight." Jack's mouth returned to her ear. "Come on me. I want you so wet and hot that you soak through your jeans and leave a wet spot on mine."

She started to come and he swallowed her cry in another hungry kiss.

As Jack felt the pulsing and tightening of her cunt around his thigh, he clenched his quad harder, increasing the pressure. He stroked her hair. To anyone watching, they appeared to be a couple lost in a sweet moment.

Keely finally unlocked his leg, dropping her forehead to his chest as she tried to level her breathing.

The song ended. Jack led her off the dance floor, past the bar and down a deserted hallway. He checked both ways and dragged her into the men's room. Better bet than the always-busy ladies room. Inside, he flipped the lock.

Panic flitted through Keely's eyes. "Jack—"

"Not a word." He faced her body toward the door. In no time he unhooked her rhinestone belt and unzipped her jeans. Flattening his palm on her abdomen, he followed her damp mound until his fingers met creamy wetness. Fuck she was hot. He jerked her jeans out of his way. "Hands above your head."

Jack loosened his pants and yanked his boxers to his knees. Pressing his left hand over her pussy, he angled her pelvis and aligned his cock. Her warm, wet heat beckoned him. He flexed his hips and impaled her.

"Oh God."

"Fast and dirty, cowgirl." Jack plunged in and out, gritting his teeth against coming immediately. The incessant pleasure of fucking her was almost too much. "I wanted to ream your sassy little ass. But I'll save that for when I have you bound, at my mercy."

She whimpered.

Jack hammered into her without pause. Sweat dripping into his eyes. Snaking down his spine. His primal side urged him to use his teeth to mark her. On her shoulder. Her neck. So when she saw the symbol of his passion she'd remember who had the right to touch her. To pleasure her. He rotated his hand and stroked her clit with his middle finger.

"Yes. Don't stop. Faster."

She was so wet keeping hold of that slippery nubbin proved difficult. He curled his fingers and pinched her clit with his knuckles. Squeezing as his cock rammed into her.

Blessed release teased him. His muscles tightened from the base of his neck clear down between his legs, yanking his testicles up. He shot like a rocket. "Jesus, fucking Christ."

Keely's pussy convulsed around his cock, every rhythmic pull brought him deeper into her slick feminine heat. He couldn't stop pumping his pelvis because her climax triggered a second one for him.

Holy fuck. That'd never happened before. He let his head fall back as he rode out another set of hot pulses.

His mind blanked. Finally the *drip drip drip* of the faucet and the *tick tick tick* of the heater roused him, the sounds mingled with their broken breaths.

Jack eased out and Keely's legs buckled. He wrapped his arms around her waist, holding her upright. "I've got you." He stroked her hair, soothing her. Petting her until she found her equilibrium. "You okay to get dressed now?"

"Um. Yeah."

As Jack righted his own clothes, he considered apologizing to her for his obsession with needing to nail her, right fucking now, in a bathroom of a honky-tonk. But Keely didn't appear to have any regrets. God knew he didn't. He kissed the back of her head and whispered, "You need help?"

"I don't know. I just..." Her body shook. "Jack. We're gonna kill each other if we keep this up."

That was putting it mildly. "I know."

"It freaks me the hell out."

"Me too. Come on, let's go home."

Chapter Fifteen

Keely gazed at the vast nothingness. Dirt in shades of orange, tan and dusty gray. Scraggly trees. An endless horizon with mountains too far away to trust the vista would improve.

And people thought Wyoming was ugly? Had they ever been outside Milford, Utah?

"I heard that sigh." Jack rubbed his rough thumb across her knuckle. "You okay?"

No. As strange as it was to be heading into Jack's territory, so to speak, convincing his clients they were madly in love, it was stranger yet to be holding Jack's hand. Just because they both wanted to. Or maybe they needed to.

After the "bathroom incident" Jack had started acting proprietary all the times, not just in public. Part of her believed his response was in preparation for this event. Another part understood Jack had staked an invisible claim on her. A claim he wasn't ready to verbally own up to even when he'd physically left his mark on her.

Keely had no clue how to feel about that.

After she'd returned home from the bar that night, Jack whisked her off to bed. His solicitous caresses lulled her to sleep.

Then last night, he'd picked up dinner and they'd detailed the Milford trip. Afterward, he coaxed her into wearing a hat as she rode him cowgirl style on the couch. The sexy, fun romp had shown a playful side of Jack. When they'd tucked themselves in for the night, Jack insisted on twining his body around hers.

It was enough to make a girl think he loved her.

It was enough to make a girl fall completely in love with him.

Only a foolish girl would believe this situation is more than a business arrangement. Once you both have what you want, the Jack and Keely show will be over forever.

Keely didn't consider herself a foolish girl, but she'd never been so confused about love before, mainly because she'd never been in love like this. It scared her to death.

"We're about twenty miles out," Jack said.

"Please tell me the topography improves."

"Not even slightly. They set a town in the middle of this because there's water nearby and the railroad goes through."

"I know why my great-great grandfather landed in Wyoming territory. Being tied to the land for generations is an incentive to stay. But what would make someone move to Milford now?"

"Why do people move to Sundance?" he countered.

"Not many do. They've got more money than God and can afford the outrageous land prices, and don't have to rely on earning a living locally."

"That's a harsh assessment for your beloved hometown."

She shrugged. "It's true. We are reverse snobs. Any of those 'new-age' types who try and gain a foothold in the community have a hard time. Most don't stick around long. We don't like change. We like our guns, we like our beef, we like the money from coal and oil. We like to challenge anyone who tries to take it away from us. If you don't embrace all that is our western way of life...well, we ain't got time for ya."

Jack tapped his fingers on the steering wheel. "So when Henry asks where we're going to live after we're married, you'll say...?"

"We'll split our time between Colorado and Wyoming for now, but after we start having babies, we'll settle in Sundance because it's a good place to raise kids and I have lots of family around the area."

He shot her a sideways glance. "That sounded a little rote."

"That's because it's what you want me to say."

"It's not what you'd say?"

"Nope."

"What would you say?"

"I'd say it didn't matter where we lived because anywhere

you are is my home."

Jack sent her another look, a softer one. "Keely—"

"Don't worry, I won't be morbidly sappy and embarrass you." She pulled her hand from his, needing to distance herself. "Thanks for not making me listen to that jazz crap for the last two hours."

"Same might be said for you saving my ears from the noise pollution that passes for country music."

You didn't seem to mind it the other night when you gave me an orgasm on the dance floor during "You Look So Good In Love".

Yeah, she wasn't bringing up that reminder.

Jack pointed. "Here we are."

They crested a rise. The town spread looked like any ordinary small town. But as soon as they hit the city limits, Keely could see the difference. It was...clean. The houses were well maintained. No rusted swing sets or broken down bicycles. Once they passed into the commercial area, there was more diversity. No regular billboards, say nothing of flashing billboards.

"Whoa. It's like...the flashback to the town's past in the movie *Back to the Future*."

"Exactly!" Jack grinned at her. "You'll freak when you see the clock in the town square. It's right outside our hotel."

Keely gawked at everything. Jack pointed out the architectural details he liked and loathed. He waxed poetic about the potential, meshing visions with reality, style with modern amenities. Happy as she was to hear his excitement about his work, he lost her a couple times. She half-feared Jack would blame her if he wasn't awarded this job. But he wouldn't have a shot at the project at all if it wasn't for their fake engagement. Yet, she had an uneasy feeling.

"Keely?"

Her attention returned to him. "What? Sorry."

"Was I boring you?"

A dutiful fiancée would lie and make him feel good. "Maybe some." Shit. She waited for him to toss an insult back at her.

But Jack released a resigned sigh. "I'm told I ramble on sometimes. If it appears my client's eyes are glazing over when I'm talking, could you give me a sign?"

"Sure. Got a sign in mind?"

"Tap on your chin with your index finger?"

She thrust out her chest in a sex kitten move. "Or I could just flash them my tits, baby."

Smiling, Jack said, "I'm the only one who gets to read that sign, buttercup." He kissed her. The quick peck morphed into something...more.

A rap sounded on the window.

They broke apart guiltily.

A middle-aged bellman in a spiffy red tasseled hat smiled through Keely's window. "May I help you out, miss?"

"Uh. Sure. Thank you."

Jack popped the locks and the trunk. The bellman lifted the bags out and wheeled them to the front desk. Another red-hat-wearing bellman held the door and Jack slipped him the car keys.

Keely noticed the matronly woman at the check-in desk also wore a red uniform, complete with tasseled hat. Had she somehow stumbled into a Shriners secret hideout?

"Mr. Donohue, so happy to have you back at the Milford Inn." The woman behind the desk beamed. "And this lovely young woman must be your fiancée? Kelly McKay?"

"Keely," she corrected gently. "Two e's, one l. Common mistake."

"Oh. I'm so sorry. Such a pretty name. I'll just get that changed." Her fingers flew across the keys. "There. Done. I have you on the second floor." She slid the key card envelope across the desk. "Horace will help you with your bag."

Keely felt like an idiot looking to Jack for direction. Normally she'd take the bag herself. In this situation was she supposed to let her fiancé haul the luggage? Or let the man decide to hand the responsibility to the bellhop?

Jack smiled at Horace. "You can take my bag up to my room too." He handed the man a folded bill.

"Mr. Donohue is on the third floor." She passed a piece of paper with the room numbers to Horace and he rolled the suitcases to the elevator.

"Here's your key, Mr. Donohue. Please let us know if we can assist you in any way during your stay. Don't forget if you need room service, it's available twenty-four hours a day."

"Much appreciated, Mrs. Trudeau." Jack slipped his hand

into hers and they strolled out the front door.

After half a block, Keely dug her heels in and faced Jack. "Separate rooms? On separate floors? Really?"

"Very old fashioned, I know, but you can't say I didn't warn you." He squeezed her hand. "It's one line we can't cross, Keely, sneaking into each other's rooms."

"Then I'm glad I brought my vibrator."

Jack choked out, "You did?"

"No, you're so easy. But we can have phone sex, right?"

"It's only two nights." He rubbed his thumb over her wrist in a lazy, sexy manner and she knew his eyes smoldered behind his sunglasses. "Have you gotten so used to having me in your bed you'll miss me if I'm not there?"

"If I say yes?" she asked coyly.

"Then I'll have raunchy phone sex with you."

"If I say no?"

"Then I'll still have raunchy phone sex with you."

"Like I said, GQ, you're easy." A total lie. Jack Donohue was the least easy man she'd ever known.

In the hour they wandered, several shopkeepers came out to greet them. She counted three hair salons and two barbershops. One large drugstore. Two furniture stores. Three diner-type restaurants. Assorted boutiques, featuring purses, costume jewelry and shoes. Those fancy, exclusive shops made her break out in hives.

Keely wasn't a "shopper" any more than she was a girly-girl. She bought her clothes at western stores or outlet malls. She didn't spend time agonizing over what to wear, although she had a weakness for funky cowgirl boots. She managed to slather on makeup most days, but not in excess.

Her one indulgence was lilac-scented lotion and oil from Sky Blue, a company her cousin Kade's wife, Skylar, owned that specialized in naturally made beauty products. But she probably wouldn't have bothered if the store wasn't right below her apartment.

With Jack gone in meetings all day tomorrow, hopefully she'd have time to explore on her own.

A horrible thought struck her. What if the wives of the committee members had planned her day for her? What would she do?

Buck up. This is important to Jack.

"Keely? What's wrong?"

She smiled at him. "Nothing. We should go back to the hotel so I can freshen up before dinner."

They parted ways in the hotel lobby. Probably so the front desk could report she and Jack weren't sneaking in a quick fuck before happy hour. Right. No cocktail hour in Milford.

Keely hung up her clothes and checked out the room. Tall windows covered in chintz and velvet draperies. Fussy furniture with spindly legs and loud fabrics. The headboard was wood gilded with gold. Fancy place. Too fancy for her taste. She preferred a relaxed, casual atmosphere where she wasn't afraid to put her boots on the coffee table.

Maybe she should take a nap. They'd stumbled out of bed at the butt crack of dawn to drive to Rapid City. After hopping a plane to Salt Lake City, they made the two-hour trek to Milford via rental car. She yawned and closed her eyes.

Her cell phone buzzing on the mattress woke her. "Yeah?"

"I'm out of the country for three freakin' weeks and I come back to find out you're engaged? To Jack Donohue of all people? Jesus. What the fuck, Keels?"

"I missed you too, Ramona."

"Sorry. It just caught me by surprise. I got the text message with the engagement picture and the engagement party invite from Aunt Carolyn. But no squealing phone call from you. No gossipy tidbits from our other relatives about you being knocked up... They all expressed the same WTF reaction I had. So tell me K, is it true?"

"Yes. It was fast." She offered the condensed version of her courtship with Jack.

"Do you love him?"

"Yeah, I do." At least that much wasn't a lie, but it wasn't any easier to admit. She'd done the one thing he'd warned her about and she'd feared: she'd fallen in love with him.

Ramona didn't say much. "Are you at home right now with the new stud of your life?"

"No. Jack has a client thing in Utah and I'm with him. Where were you gone to for three weeks?"

"Hell," Ramona said with no sarcasm. "I fired my travel coordinator the second I had cell service in the States. Trust me, you do not want to hear me whine about the Orient." She paused. "You okay? For being wildly in *luurrve* and all, you don't sound like your chipper self."

"I'm nervous about meeting Jack's clients. I do not want to say or do anything to fuck it up."

"You'll be fine. You're charming, funny and you can drink any man under the table. At least you used to, but damn, you've been dull as dirt the last few years, cuz."

"Ramona!"

"Kidding. Sheesh. Should I build up your confidence with serious stuff since your sense of humor has vanished?"

"Yes, please."

"Let's start with the obvious. What are you wearing tonight?"

Keely rolled her eyes. Ramona lived the code "clothes make the woman" and truly believed all that fashionista crap. "I'm wearing my emerald moleskin skirt, brown boots with the orange and green butterflies, a slim-fitting, button-up shirt in dark tan and a brown bolero jacket."

"Good. How many events do you have to dress for?"

"One more tomorrow night and that's formal."

"What else did you pack?"

Keely described her engagement dress.

"It sounds perfect, but showcase your personality by adding a splash of color. Look for a funky scarf in those shops you're hitting tomorrow."

Funky. Right. Milford, Utah didn't like funky.

"Oh, and I'm sending you a box of samples I picked up. One pair of jeans will make you look totally hot. You'll be a trendsetter in Sundance."

"Another dream realized," she said dryly. She tacked on, "Thanks, Ramona," lest her cousin stop sending her free, cast-off western clothes.

"I've gotta run, hon, I just wanted to send my love and give you congrats on hooking a hottie. Does he have a big dick too?"

"Yep. And he knows how to use it."

"Bitch. Call me next week when you get the clothes."

"I will. Thanks."

"Knock 'em dead, Keely. I have total faith in you."

After she hung up she stared at the ceiling. "At least someone does."

Keely swore she'd make the best of the next two days, her last two days with Jack as his fake fiancée. She'd smile and act happy, even when it hurt that this make-believe situation was nearly over.

Too bad her feelings for him were real.

Jack nearly swallowed his tongue when Keely stepped from the elevator. And he was damn glad he had a suit jacket on to cover his immediate erection.

Holy fuck. She was a goddess.

He was used to seeing her dressed casually, wearing jeans, minimal makeup and her ever-present cowgirl boots. The outfit she'd chosen wasn't overly dressy. Her choice of earth tones fit her personality. Yet the cut and color of the clothing let her natural beauty shine through, so you didn't notice the clothes, but the woman.

His woman.

Keely approached him with a cautious smile. "Hey."

He reached for her hand and kissed her palm before threading their fingers together. "You are absolutely exquisite."

She blushed. Shifted from boot to boot, apparently stunned into speechlessness.

"Come on. It's a short walk and I cannot wait to show you off."

Her blue eyes sparked fire. "I am *not* a show heifer, Donohue."

Jack was relieved her fit of nerves had passed. "There's my feisty fiancée."

They were quiet as they strolled to the restaurant. The hostess showed them to a small banquet room filled with people. Keely's hand tightened around his.

"Relax, buttercup." Jack put his mouth to her ear. "If you're nervous, just imagine them in their underwear."

"You're the only person I want to imagine that way. You really want me staring at your crotch all night?"

"Whatever works."

"Jack! My boy, how are you?"

Jack grinned at Henry Smith, a balding, barrel-shaped man with two chins and a politician's smile. He thrust out his hand to shake Henry's hand vigorously. "Henry. Great to see you again."

"We are pleased to have you back."

"I appreciate the second chance." He curled his arm around Keely's shoulder and brought her forward. "This is my fiancée, Keely McKay. Keely, this is Henry Smith, the brains and power behind the Milford Historical Preservation Committee."

"Brains and power, bah." Henry delicately shook Keely's hand. "A real pleasure to meet you, Keely. Although, I'll admit to being surprised when Jack told me about your engagement. He'd never indicated in his dealings with the committee that he was involved in a serious relationship."

"Oh, Jack keeps his personal and professional life separate, so I'm not surprised," Keely said with a smile. "To be fair, I'd not heard of you either."

He chuckled. "Well, I can certainly see why he'd want to keep such a beautiful woman all to himself. Have you set a wedding date yet?"

"No. But my parents did throw us an engagement party last weekend."

"How marvelous. My wife, April, whom you'll meet shortly, will be so disappointed she didn't get to send a gift."

"Not to worry. I do have pictures of the party I'd love to show her."

Jack patted her shoulder. "Keely. Sweetheart. I'm sure Henry and April aren't interested in—"

"Nonsense. We'd be delighted to see them," Henry said. "And we would love an invite to the wedding."

"We're still working out schedules and details. I have a large family, and naturally I want all of them to be in attendance. It's tricky trying to figure it all out."

"I imagine." Henry smiled at Jack. "Shall we catch up with the other committee members while we're waiting for dinner to be served?"

"Absolutely." Jack kept Keely close by because he could tell she was still nervous. These people made him uneasy too. As if they were waiting for him to fuck up and say or do something to take him out of the running for the job.

Why does this job matter to you so much? You'd rather pretend to be someone you're not? Just so you can flip Baxter the bird?

No. That wasn't it... Was it?

"Jack?"

He refocused on Keely, not his burst of self-doubt. "Yes, sweetheart?"

"It's time to eat."

"Good. I'm starving."

The committee separated them. The men sat at one end of the table and the women at the other. Jack forced himself to concentrate on business and not how Keely was faring.

He snuck looks at her every so often. She was smiling, engaged in conversation, but she'd barely eaten two bites of her meal. Dessert was a gingerbread cake, dry as dust. Keely picked off the maple frosting and drank lots of water.

On a professional level, the meal was a success. Jack pointed out permit issues other companies under consideration might've missed. During their partnership, Baxter had left those details to Jack. And Jack had heard through the grapevine Baxter had been fined on other projects because of oversights. When he learned that BDM hadn't made a formal pitch to the Milford Committee yet, Jack kicked himself for opening his big mouth, because he'd just given Baxter another advantage.

Once the table was cleared, several people left and others changed seats. Jack motioned to Keely to take the empty chair beside him.

They'd barely situated themselves when Henry addressed them. "So, Jack, since you kept us in the dark about your lovely Keely, we're anxious to hear how you two ended up engaged."

Murmurs of assent sounded from around the table.

Jack said, "It's sort of complicated—"

Keely patted Jack's hand on the table. "Jack, darlin', no offense, but you're a man and you don't do this story justice. Why don't you let me tell it?"

Soft laughter.

He bared his teeth at her in warning. "Go ahead, sweetheart. But I'll jump in if you get something wrong."

"I'm never wrong."

"See what I'm up against?" he said innocently to the men.

They all nodded.

"If you would've told me a year ago I'd be engaged to Jack Donohue, I would've said you were plumb crazy," Keely said. "See, Jack and I hated each other."

A few gasps sounded.

Jack withheld a groan. Dammit. She'd better not fuck this up.

"Maybe hate is too strong a word. We disliked each other intensely. I've known Jack since I was sixteen. He and my brother Carter became best friends in college and Carter dragged Jack home to the ranch one weekend. We detested each other on sight. He was rude and mean."

"And she was a total spoiled brat," Jack inserted.

Laughter.

"Needless to say, our paths have crossed many times over the years. We never moved past the 'I can't stand to look at you' stage. In fact, it was worse the more time we spent around each other."

"It was much worse when you started dating my little brother."

"And his brother Justin...dumped me."

Muted female murmurs of understanding.

"Did you swoop in and mend the pieces of her broken heart?" April Smith asked dreamily.

Keely leaned forward. "No, he did not. We ended up swapping insults at my brother Colt's wedding reception."

She took a drink of water; the tiny pause let the drama build.

"Fast forward to six months ago. I bought an old building in Moorcroft that needed serious renovation. It was also listed in the Wyoming Historic Register, and I don't have to explain to you all what a nightmare that is."

Laughter.

"The bottom line is, I didn't like Jack personally, but professionally, I knew no one was better qualified to help me with historic renovation project than Jack Donohue. I swallowed my pride and called him. He swallowed his disbelief and met with me. And miracle of miracles, we didn't exchange one insult at that first meeting. Once we hashed through the business end...well, two years of no contact gave us an entirely new appreciation for one another. We saw each other in a whole different light. Because our past history was so...volatile, we didn't tell anyone we'd fallen in love. No one in our families would've believed it."

More laughter.

"Keeping our feelings private allowed us time to understand and accept how deep those feelings really are."

Hell, that sweet story choked Jack up and he knew it was a damn lie. He didn't care if the committee disapproved of a PDA; he had to kiss her. He pressed his lips to hers, letting her warmth and sweetness flow through him.

"Oh my, that is about the most romantic thing I've ever heard," April gushed.

When Keely stared into his eyes, for a second, Jack believed every word she'd uttered was the gospel truth. He murmured, "Keely—"

"Was his proposal as romantic?" April interrupted, breaking the moment.

"Not even close."

Laughter.

"Hey, it wasn't *that* bad," Jack argued.

Keely lifted a brow. "Shall we let them decide?"

April clapped her hands. "Oh goodie, yes, tell us, tell us!"

Jack suspected April didn't get out much. Or didn't have romance in her life. He shot a sideways glance at Henry, discreetly picking his nose.

"It was late afternoon in my decrepit old building," Keely began. "We were dusty and dirty from working all day. I was sweeping up the millionth dustpan full of mouse droppings, when Jack yelled across the room, "Hey, buttercup, marry me."

Female groans.

Jack grinned. "Keely, my love, that wasn't how it went down at all. We *had* been working hard all day. But when I looked at you, the golden glow of the late afternoon sun shining on your hair and face, I didn't care you were dusty and dirty. I didn't care you were sweeping up mouse droppings. All I saw was the most beautiful woman in the world. I knew right then I wanted to spend the rest of my life with you." He brought her hand to his mouth and kissed her knuckles.

Keely blinked at him. Repeatedly.

Shit. Was she blinking back tears?

"Jack definitely wins as the most romantic version."

He broke eye contact with Keely to smile at Henry's wife. "See? It's all about perception."

Keely set her left hand flat on the table. "It also helps he bought me a huge engagement ring."

Jack was frustrated Henry insisted on talking politics and sports, not about the restoration project. Keely had held her own tonight, but she looked wary when April volunteered to walk her back to the hotel. After they left he managed to sneak away to make a phone call.

Half an hour later, his cell phone rang as he entered his hotel room. "What's up, buttercup?"

"Imagine my surprise when I heard a knock on my door. I was hoping you'd snuck past the guards to have your wicked way with me. I wasn't expecting room service." He heard the smile in her voice. "I certainly wasn't expecting steak, a side of bacon and a gooey chocolate brownie. If you were here, Jack Donohue, I'd kiss you."

Making her happy made Jack grin like an idiot. "What else would you do?"

"Snarl if you tried to snatch even one small bite. Sometimes you are so sweet I can't believe..." She cleared her throat. "Anyway, thank you."

"You're welcome." He stretched out on his bed. "Now about that phone sex..."

"Not tonight dear, I have a headache."

He laughed.

"Seriously. Two days of us not making—" she paused, "—loud noises as we're fucking like animals would be good for us."

Had Keely almost slipped up and said...making love? It wasn't love between them, just great, raw, anything-goes sex. Just a byproduct of their deal. She knew that, right? She hadn't actually believed any of the romantic crap they'd spewed tonight, had she?

Didn't you believe it?

"No changing my mind on this. And can I just say you

looked absolutely yummy tonight? You sure do fill out a suit, GQ."

"Keely—"

"I'll see you sometime tomorrow, Jack. Sweet dreams."

Chapter Sixteen

The second day in Milford had gone better than the first. The committee was enthusiastic about the additional changes Jack suggested. He'd nailed the presentation.

Once again he and Keely were separated during the formal dinner. Afterward, she was surrounded by various women, leaving him no chance to speak to her alone. When he'd finally returned to the hotel two hours after she'd left, Keely hadn't answered her cell phone. He asked her about it this morning, she claimed she'd forgotten her charger and the battery was dead.

Jack looked at her, sleeping in the passenger seat of his car. She'd slept the entire way from Milford to Salt Lake City. Ditto for the short flight to Denver. Keely had wandered off by herself in the Denver airport to browse the gift shops. On the flight from Denver to Rapid City she'd stared out the window. And she'd fallen back asleep shortly after he'd pulled onto I-90. Jack was frustrated because this...retreat wasn't like her.

Outside of Spearfish, he said, "Do you want to stop someplace and eat?"

"No. I'm not hungry."

"You sure? You haven't eaten much today."

"I think I know when I'm hungry."

"Maybe *I'm* hungry."

"Then stop the goddamn car and get something to eat. You're drivin'."

Surly cowgirl speak. Yeah. She was pissed all right.

Jack ignored her until they reached Beulah. He exited off the interstate. The only thing open was an Exxon station.

Scratch that idea.

As he stopped at the lone stop sign, he noticed a gravel road. Posted on each side with a DEAD END sign and a Beulah Municipal Cemetery sign.

He hung a sharp right.

"If you hafta take a piss, there was a gas station right back there. You don't seem like the type to whiz in the weeds anyhow."

Jack didn't answer. He drove past the cemetery to where the road ended. He shut off the car, pocketed the keys and climbed out.

A few minutes later Keely bailed from the car and lashed out at him. "What the fuck is goin' on, Jack?"

"You tell me."

"You're the one who drove us out here."

"You're the one who hasn't said more than two dozen words to me since we left Milford."

"You complain when I don't talk as well as when I talk too much? I guess there really is no pleasin' you." Keely started down the road at a good clip.

"Where are you going?"

"Home."

"It's a long walk," he yelled.

No answer.

Jesus. The woman spiked his temper from zero to furious in less than sixty seconds. He took off after her.

Her body language gave no indication she noticed.

When Jack caught her, he immobilized her and widened his stance so she couldn't knock him off balance when she started to thrash.

And she fought him like a wet cat. She cursed, screamed and flailed against him. To no avail. Jack held his ground. They'd have it out right here, right now.

When Keely stopped struggling, he breathed a sigh of relief, even when he suspected her submission would be short lived at best. "You done fighting me?"

"Let me go, Jack. Right now."

"Why won't you talk to me, buttercup?"

"Don't call me that anymore!"

"Fine. Why won't you talk to me, Keely?"

"Because there's no point. It's over."

Jack frowned. "What do you mean *it's over*?"

"All of this." She tried in vain to gesture with her trapped hands. "This stupid fake engagement is over. Us bein' nice to each other is over. Done."

He spun her around to face him but kept hold of her biceps. "What in the hell ever gave you that idea?"

Keely dropped her chin to her chest.

He shook her a little. "Look at me goddammit."

When she finally opened her eyes, Jack saw a sheen of tears. "Keely."

"You got what you wanted, Jack. We both know the trip to Milford was a total success. They'll award you the contract, guaranteed. And after next week you can sign off on my project, with the exception of the final inspection. There's no reason for you to stick around Sundance."

He gaped at her. Keely really believed she wasn't reason enough for him to stay?

She's right. You don't need to stick around.

But he wanted to stay. The thought of leaving her left an ache he couldn't explain. Or justify. But he sure as hell needed more time to figure it out what the hell it meant.

"See? You can't argue with my logic."

"Don't tempt me to argue with you, cowgirl, because you know how much I get off on it."

Keely didn't even crack a smile.

"We're not done. Far from it. Have you forgotten I demanded a minimum of a month from you for this engagement? We're at what...three weeks? And don't you think it would be suspect if we broke off all contact the same week I signed off on your project? Right after we returned from Milford? You ready to deal with the explanations on that?"

"No. But—"

"Listen. Can we just let this...relationship fade away on its own? Spend as much time together as we can this week in Sundance?"

Her entire posture stayed tight. Closed off. Skeptical. "Why?"

"A week from today there's a job I have to be on site for

until it's finished. I'll be gone for three full weeks. But this week and especially next weekend, I need you to keep up this pretense." Inwardly, Jack winced at his word choice. What had developed between them hardly felt like make-believe.

"What's going on next weekend?"

"Convention in Denver."

Keely scowled. "First I've heard of it. A lot has happened. You can't expect me to remember all of it."

I'll remember all of it. The way you taste first thing in the morning. The sweet scent of lilacs surrounding me last thing before I drift off at night. Your eyes glaring at me with anger. Your eyes devouring me with hunger. Your laugh. Your determination. The unquestioning love you have for your family. The way you make love with your heart and soul as well as your body. I'll never forget any of that.

"Jack?"

"I swore I told you. This is our annual Professional Preservationist's Society meeting; it just happens to be in Denver this year. I've already booked us a suite at the Adam's Mark downtown."

"When would I have to be there?"

"By six o'clock Friday night for a cocktail party and a dinner."

"Will we have separate hotel rooms?"

Jack got right in her face. "No. Way. You will be in my king-sized bed all weekend."

Something shifted. Keely reached out and fiddled with his collar. "Did you miss the sex the last two days?"

"No, I missed sleeping with you." Jack slid his hand up to cradle her beautiful, but strangely sad face. "Did you miss it?"

"Yeah."

It wasn't like Keely not to elaborate. So he took it upon himself to fill the void. "I was so horny I had to whack off. Twice."

She blinked with surprise. "You did?"

"First thing in the morning I relived our first shower. How amazing it felt shoving my cock in your mouth. How hot it was seeing my come on your face."

"What about the second time?"

"The second time I thought about all the positions we

186

haven't tried yet. Sixty-nine. Reverse cowgirl. Or in your truck, which is a personal fantasy of mine, believe it or not."

"A truck fantasy, GQ? How rural."

"And it's a crude and lewd fantasy too." He crowded her. "My dick buried in your hot little ass was the visual that sent me over the edge. Imagining you on your hands and knees with those sexy butt cheeks spread wide. Watching my dick disappear into that tightly puckered pink hole. You're not a virgin to anal sex, but I'll bet my cock is bigger than anything you've had. The thought of how hot and tight you'd be as I rammed into your back door. Jesus, Keely, I shot all over my hand. And I used the come to get myself off again, imagining you still bent over as I whacked off all over your ass. Seeing my come sliding down the crack of your butt and running into your asshole."

Lust glittered in her eyes. "Graphic much?"

"You love it."

"I do, but that's three times you jacked off, not two."

"I wanted to see if I could get you so hot and bothered just from the verbal description of what I want to do to you that you forgot to count." He feathered his lips over hers, testing her response.

And there it was. Keely's hungry, unabashed need. Giving him everything, holding nothing back, she was his equal in every way. He wanted her in every way.

"I want you, Keely. Right now. Up against the car." Jack dragged his mouth down her neck, leaving sucking kisses.

Keely stepped back. Way back. "Huh-uh. I will let you fuck me in the men's bathroom at the Golden Boot, but I draw the line at screwing outside the cemetery in Beulah."

"Fine. But hold that thought until we get home."

"If you're lucky."

Jack kissed her again. "I'm feeling very lucky."

Could Keely spend another week with him? Without Jack figuring out she'd fallen in love with him?

Yeah. Don't act like a complete freak like you've been doing all day. The no talking, no looking, no touching reaction is a dead giveaway. Fuck him, insult him and he'll never guess anything has changed.

Even when everything had changed.

She filled the rest of the drive with stories of how she'd spent Saturday, a captive audience with April, Phyllis and Georgette. Shopping, lunch and a three-hour tour of the town. Fielding pointed questions about her religious affiliation. Fielding pointed questions about being a "working woman". Fielding pointed questions about what it was like to be with a devastatingly handsome, completely charming, totally put together man such as Jack Donohue.

Jack preened when Keely relayed the women's flattery.

"Of course, I couldn't tell them you're the ultimate package because in addition to your stunning good looks and mouth-watering physique, you have a big cock."

"There's my sarcastic cowgirl."

"Miss me?" she cooed.

"Like an oozing canker sore."

She laughed. "We've come a long way in three weeks, haven't we?"

"Yes, and amazingly, with no knife wounds."

They pulled into Sundance as the sun turned the hills bronze, reflecting gold across the valley, showcasing the beautiful landscape she'd never tire of looking at. Keely breathed deeply.

"Why the contented sigh?"

"Because I'm home. Every time I come back from a trip I realize how much I love this place and how I never want to leave it."

"Never?"

"Never. Everything I've ever wanted is right here. Why would I leave what makes me happy?"

He didn't comment, but she hadn't expected him to.

At the apartment, Jack dragged the suitcases upstairs. Then he dragged her straight into the bedroom.

"Keely." He framed her face in his hands and blew her mind with an infinitely gentle kiss.

She didn't let him speed race them to the next level of seduction. She kept kissing him. Wetly. Deeply. Softly. Firmly. No rush; she wanted to savor him.

"Naked," she murmured between flirty kisses. "Completely

buck-assed nekkid. We're usually in such a hurry we still have half our damn clothes on."

Jack leisurely undressed her. She unclothed him with equal deliberation. He stripped away the quilt and eased her onto the mattress. Kissing a path down her body, he inadvertently tickled her bared flesh with his hair. Keely adored his too-long mop of glossy black. It fit him.

His mouth proceeded straight to her pussy. He groaned and lapped at the wetness. "I could taste you for hours."

"I'll take you up on that another time. Right now, I need you."

He situated his hands by her shoulders and kneed apart her thighs. "You ready?"

"You asking? Instead of taking? You hit your head or something?"

"Smartass." Jack's thickness filled her in a slow, sweet glide that satisfied more than the sexual ache in her body. "Put your legs around my hips," he urged.

Keely rocked up to meet his relaxed thrusts.

But Jack reset the pace to slow-mo, while intently peering at her face. "You're beautiful. I don't say that enough."

Don't say it again or I might believe it means something.

"Let me take care of you."

Forever? Or just for tonight?

"Look in my eyes when you come, Keely."

He flexed his hips at the end of every stroke, propelling his cock deeper, but keeping the withdrawal of his shaft agonizingly unhurried.

"Jack—"

"My. Eyes. Don't look away. Show me what I do to you."

She concentrated on the telltale tug in her womb. It took all her self-control not to grab Jack's ass and greedily chase down the orgasm, grinding her way to bliss via his body. Letting him bring the pleasure to her.

When Keely's pussy muscles contracted and her clit started to throb, she locked her gaze on Jack's slumberous eyes and came in silence. No keening wails or soft gasps. No arching or straining. The orgasm was no less intense for the quietness.

Heat expanded inside her as Jack came in the same intense stillness. Watching her with focus equal to what she'd given him.

It was as strange as it was wonderful.

Jack buried his face in her neck. "Fall asleep with me like this, Keely. Just for a little while."

Another unusual request. But she wouldn't deny him. Keely was beginning to believe she wouldn't deny him anything.

The next night Keely stripped off her clothes the second she'd closed the apartment door.

"Now that's what I love to see. Eagerness to get naked with me, buttercup."

She scowled at Jack in his usual place on the couch. "No time for slap and tickle. I'm late."

Thud. Boot one hit the ground. Thud. Boot number two hit. She raced into the laundry room and dumped the stinky bundle, then zipped to the bathroom.

"Late for what?" Jack yelled.

"Colt's basketball game starts in fifteen minutes." Keely flipped the handles and the shower kicked on. She twisted her hair in a clip on top of her head and climbed in.

"Why didn't you go straight to the game from work?"

She shrieked. Jack stood at the end of the tub. Gawking at her. Not at her face, either. "Do you mind?"

"Not at all." His eyes ate her up. The man actually licked his chops.

"I repeat. No time for water games." She faced the water and rinsed.

After she finished, Jack handed her a towel.

"Thanks. My last patient showed up for her therapy session with a case of the flu and she barfed all over me." Keely shuddered and toweled off. "I'm surprised you didn't smell it when I walked in."

"All I smell is my sweet Keely."

"Horny bastard." She resisted snapping him with the towel after her mind glommed on to his use of the word "my".

"Does that barfing thing happen often?"

"Often enough that I keep a change of clothes in my locker. But I'd forgotten to replace them because I haven't done laundry in a coon's age."

"How long exactly is a coon's age?"

"Halfway between the twelfth of never and when hell freezes over."

"You're in a mood."

So was he. She hustled to her bedroom and bent over to open the bottom dresser drawer. Down to her last pair of clean jeans. She'd have to do at least one load of clothes tonight. She turned and Jack was right there. With that look. The look that thrilled her. The look that warned her she'd be late for the damn basketball game. "Jack—"

He dropped to his knees.

"I really don't have time—Omigod! You so don't play fair." Her feet slid on the carpet as she automatically widened her stance.

Jack chuckled against her sensitive flesh and licked her slit from top to bottom. Then from bottom to top. "Tasty. Bet I can get you off as fast as your vibrator."

"Ah. Sure. Yeah. Okay. Go ahead and try."

"Thought you might say that." His thumbs pulled back the delicate skin at the top of her mound, leaving her fully open to his skillful mouth. He lashed her exposed clit with quick whips of his wet tongue.

Keely groaned.

He'd didn't relent. He kept up a hot, wet vibration on that bundle of nerves until her legs trembled. The instant her breathing changed, Jack sealed his lips around the swollen nub and sucked.

"Oh God. Jack."

He sucked harder.

"Yes. Like that." Keely splintered in a dozen directions. Black and white spots ruptured behind her eyelids. Blood rushed like a raging river through her body. Her consciousness floated to another dimension—the whole nine yards of orgasmic satisfaction.

Oh man. She'd needed that. Bad. How had Jack known?

She cracked open her eyes and glanced down at him.

He suckled her pussy lips, together with her clitoris, one last time before releasing her.

"That was...mmm. A great surprise."

"I couldn't resist. I love going down on you." He stretched up. "And we still have time to make it to the basketball game."

"We?" She froze. Jack wanted to tag along to a social event with her family? She thought after the weekend in Milford he'd become a hermit.

"Makes me insane to sit here alone, knowing you're watching a bunch of half-naked sweaty guys racing up and down the court."

"My brother and my cousin Buck are two of the guys, so eww." She slipped on a plain pink thong. Out of underwear. Down to one bra. The red and green Christmas bra patterned with presents and sported a big red bow in the center of her cleavage.

Jack stared at her chest with that look. "I'm opening my present right when we get home."

Wednesday night...

"You don't have to come."

"I want to come."

Keely whirled around. "Why? So you can fuck me in the men's bathroom at the Golden Boot again?"

Jack beamed his cocky grin. "No. But if you ask me real nice I'll consider it."

"Pervert."

"Sticks and stones, cowgirl."

Argh. "You hate darts."

"No, I don't."

"You hate country bars."

"No, I don't."

"You can't deny you hate country music, which is all they play at this country bar."

"True. But watching your fine ass in skintight denim as you're bending forward to throw a dart?" Jack's gaze redefined lewd. "Buttercup, I doubt I'll hear anything over the pounding in my heart."

"You mean the blood pounding in your groin," she shot back.

"That too. You bring out the beast in me."

How well she'd learned that. Twice.

Keely retreated to the bedroom, flashing back to last night.

The frantic call from India, begging her to drive out to the Sky Blue manufacturing plant and pick up three boxes of lotion she'd forgotten to stock. Poor pregnant India had babbled about an A.A. meeting, Colt helping Trevor and Edgard, and her sweet baby Hudson being a brat. Keely assured her frazzled and highly hormonal sister-in-law she'd take care of it.

Oddly enough, Jack had volunteered to ride along. Odder yet, after loading up the boxes he hadn't seemed eager to leave. He and Kade shot the breeze, while Keely heard all about Eliza's preschool. Peyton and Shannie, not to be outdone, talked a mile a minute about the new kitties in the barn.

Once they'd started home, Jack demanded the price for his help: fulfillment of his fantasy of fucking in her truck.

After they'd parked in a secluded turnout, Jack was on her—all possessive, challenging male. He sprawled in the passenger's side and bid her to masturbate for him. Slowly. As soon as she got off, he hauled her onto his lap. She bounced and ground on his cock; he focused his full oral expertise on her nipples. Pinching, sucking, licking. Even the biting wound her arousal tighter.

Jack gripped her ass cheeks in both hands, pounding into her cunt forcefully. His orgasm was hot and wet and messy and it sent Keely spiraling into subspace.

As she drifted back, she was vaguely aware of Jack toying with her asshole. Teasing those blood rich nerve endings with the rough pad of his thumb. Then something slick slid into her anal passage.

"Relax," he murmured against her throat.

"What the fuck did you just shove up my ass, Donohue?"

"Anal beads. The small set."

"You have more than one set?"

"I told you I planned on shopping for new sex toys. Does it feel good?"

"No."

"Liar." He nibbled her ear. "You're wearing them until I take them out."

Excitement unfurled in her belly. But she couldn't give into him so easily. "And if I say no?"

"You won't."

She squirmed in her seat on the drive back to Sundance. Jack ignored it. In fact, he barely looked at her until they were in the apartment.

But when Jack looked at her? Man oh man. Gone was the sophisticated, charming architect. The man who'd loomed over her was primitive male. Wild. Intent on conquering, claiming and marking his territory.

First, he took her mouth in a savage kiss. Next, he had Keely naked, facedown on the bed. Her heart pounded crazily. Not out of fear, but out of feminine pride. She'd never affected a man this powerfully. Never. And to affect such a strong man as Jack Donohue to the point he lost all control and became a raging beast in his quest to have her? That was a heady, once in a lifetime feeling. And she was damn well going to savor it for as long as she could.

Jack's body heat scorched her back as he angled her ass in the air. "Do you want your vibrator?"

That was his way of saying she'd have to get herself off because her pleasure wasn't his concern. This was all about him.

It was fucking hot as hell.

"No."

Jack growled. Hot, wet, openmouthed kisses trailed down her spine until his mouth met the handle of the beads. Very delicately, he licked around her stretched opening.

Lust slammed into her hard and Keely locked her knees.

He eased the beads out. Then cool gel and one slippery finger pushed in and out of her hole. More gel. Another finger.

Oh, shit it burned. She held her breath until Jack commanded, "Breathe. Loosen up. Let me in. That's it." Then he screwed three fingers in deep and completely out. Satisfied by his preparation, Jack pulled her ass cheeks apart. The crown of his cock nudged her anus.

Keely breathed out as the thick head popped inside the ring of tight muscle. Before she registered the sharp pain, Jack slid the shaft into her anal passage. No stops. He fed his dick in until his balls slapped her pussy and he couldn't go any deeper.

She concentrated on the musky scent of sex and sweat. Would Jack ask if she was okay? Or give her an erotic play by play of how tight and perfect her ass felt clamped around his big dick?

Jack did neither.

He fucked her without restraint. Withdrawing the plump cockhead completely every time he pulled out. He'd rest the tip on her spasming hole and slam back in. Over and over until she began to anticipate the burning scrape of retraction. Began to crave it. She braced herself for the sweet agony of pleasure mixed with bite of pain as Jack plunged back inside her clenching channel in one solid thrust.

A strange buzzing built inside her head as he reamed her. Proved he owned her.

Jack finally spoke. "Bear down on me. Harder. Sweet mother of God." He shoved hard, stilled behind her and roared.

She felt every hot spurt as he filled her ass with his seed. She milked every drop, until the continual clenching and unclenching of her interior muscles set off a vaginal orgasm that stole her breath.

His body shuddered as he experienced her contractions. He didn't attempt to pull out of her bowels. For the longest time Jack let that big dick stuff her to the point she almost got used to it.

Almost. Then he growled, "Again."

Yeah, she'd been a little sore this morning. But Keely didn't regret a single minute.

"Keely?"

Startled out of her vivid flashback, she faced Jack, lounging in the doorway to her bedroom. "What?"

"If you really don't want me to come to the bar and watch you play darts tonight, I'll understand. I was just giving you shit."

The vulnerability Jack showed her on occasion, like now, like last night, still had the power to move her. And because he was willing to share that side of himself with her, she grinned.

"Okay. You can come. But if I hear one caterwaulin' or goat-yodelin' comment about the music, you're sittin' in the truck."

Chapter Seventeen

Two days later...

Jack paced in his condo, waiting for Keely to arrive. Why had she insisted on seeing where he lived?

Because you're supposed to be engaged, dumbass.

He inhaled a deep breath. For Christsake, he shouldn't be embarrassed. He'd paid a shitload of money for this high-rise condo with a view of the Rocky Mountains.

Jack gazed at the jagged peaks that were covered in snow year round. As a South Dakota farm kid, raised on the flat prairie, he was amazed every time he looked at the majestic mountains.

Yet the view outside presented his living room in an even more pitiable light. He hadn't spent time or money decorating besides adding two black leather reclining Lazy Boy chairs. True, Jack had forked over serious bucks for the top of the line entertainment system with a gigantic digital flat-screen TV, and theater quality surround sound. His massive collection of DVDs was arranged alphabetically on the shelves of the entertainment center that encompassed the entire wall.

The phrase "entertainment center" caused a snort. He'd never entertained here. Never cooked. Aside from his cleaning lady, he'd never invited a woman over. He feared looks of pity or worse, calculated looks of home improvement ideas.

Working out of his home meant no water-cooler type conversations with his coworkers—but after the ugly situation with Baxter and Martine, he considered that a benefit.

Since Jack had moved to Colorado from Chicago, making money took priority over making friends. And yeah, maybe he had crawled into a hole after Martine ditched him for Baxter. No one could blame him for holing up and licking his wounds.

It's been three years. Get over it. You've got a chance to have a better, fuller life.

With Keely McKay? Despite her sexual appeal, the sweetness she masked beneath insults, her thoughtfulness, her ambition, her sly sense of humor and her tendency to give all of herself to those she cared about, Keely was not the type of woman he expected he'd spend his life with. She'd never leave Wyoming, never venture far from her family, which led him to believe she had a narrow view of the world.

Any narrower than yours?

Jack admitted spending the last few weeks with Keely and her family and friends proved his life was empty outside of working hours. No real relationships. No group of male buddies to invite over to catch a Broncos or Rockies game.

The one solid friend he'd kept throughout the years was Carter McKay. Jack figured after Carter married Macie the friendship might cool. But if anything, they'd gotten closer. Carter and Macie welcomed him into their life. In the last six years he'd enjoyed every moment spent at their house in Canyon River with their three wild boys.

Maybe you aren't as allergic to the notion of home and hearth as you've deluded yourself into thinking you are.

Then again, maybe Carter continued their relationship because of Jack's ability to track down art commissions. If that perk ended, would Carter still call him? Or worse, what happened after the engagement with Keely went south? Would Carter blame him and cut all ties?

That thought absolutely paralyzed him.

The intercom buzzed and his heart rate rocketed. He depressed the button. "Yes?"

"A Keely McKay here to see you sir."

"Thanks. Send her up."

He paced, feeling edgy and nervous in his own skin.

Two brisk knocks. Jack opened the door, took one look at her beautiful face and everything inside him calmed. "Hey. Come in. How was the drive?"

"Uneventful."

She skirted the plain white wall dividing the entry foyer

from the living space. In the living room she wandered to the floor to ceiling windows. "The years I lived in Denver I always wondered what the view looked like from up here."

"And?"

"Still makes you feel far away, doesn't it?"

He didn't quite know how to respond to that.

Keely meandered to the dining room, which didn't have a table, but a drafting table, a Bowflex and weight sets. She moved through the kitchen. Her gaze swept over the breakfast bar. The double sink. The double ovens. The built in dishwasher. The island with a Jenn-aire range inset into a marble countertop. The sub-zero refrigerator. She didn't say a word—good or bad—as she rounded the corner and headed down the hallway leading to the bedrooms.

Jack's whole body went on full alert.

She poked her head into the main bathroom. He could almost hear her assessment: nothing fancy. Boring white walls, white sink, white toilet, white tub/shower combo and white tiled floor.

She entered the second bedroom, which served as Jack's office. Two oversized drafting tables lined the longest wall. A mahogany desk anchored one end of the room. He'd converted the walk-in closet with shelves for storing building plans and to house his collection of books on restoration as well as photographic books. The only wall not covered in shelf space was plastered with an enormous map of the U.S. dotted with colorful pins.

"These pins are where you've done restoration projects?"

"Yes."

"What a cool way to see all you've accomplished."

Jack smiled. Keely would see it as a positive. Whenever he was frustrated with project plans, he saw the pins denoting finished projects and it motivated him to continue.

"This is a great space and all cozy with books, but where do your clients sit?"

"I don't bring clients to my home, Keely."

She faced him. "But you don't have another office someplace?"

"No. Most of the initial business is conducted over the phone. I travel to where I'm needed, hence no need for a formal office space. A PO box, an Internet connection, a phone and I'm good to go anywhere."

"Oh. Well, I thought..." Her eyes darted away. "Never mind."

"What?"

"I thought since you're a historic preservation specialist you'd have a funky, cool office in a nifty building you restored. With pictures of the work you've done. Nothing fancy, just..."

"Something besides an overfilled second bedroom in a modern condo in Denver?"

She blushed. "I guess."

"I had an impressive office when I worked in Chicago. Evidently the conference table in the meeting room was a favorite place for Martine and Baxter to fuck, so I'm soured on formal office suites."

"You don't have to snap at me, Jack, for asking a simple question." She wheeled around.

Jack caught her wrist as she stormed into his bedroom. "Sorry. My place isn't anything remotely cool... Basically it sucks and I'm embarrassed. There's no personality and I've lived here for three years. It's like I just moved in."

"Or are expecting to move out," she murmured.

He hadn't thought of it that way.

"Is this your bedroom?"

How he wished he could lie, because this was one ugly-ass, bare-ass room too. A plain boring brown comforter on the king-sized bed. One nightstand. One dresser. Both brown wood. No chairs. "At least the shitty décor in here fits with the rest of the place."

"You do live here like you're waiting for your life to start someplace else."

Another perceptive, yet jarring comment.

Keely moseyed into the closet. "Omigod, GQ. Do you really wear all those suits?"

He squinted at the orderly line of jackets, suit pants and shirts. The dozens of ties folded over tie racks, separated by color. The pairs of dress shoes in black, light black, brown and light brown. His casual clothes were stacked on the opposite side, a considerably smaller selection.

"Yes. I wear them all."

"Since you don't have clients come here, when you get up

in the morning to go to work in your office, in the next bedroom over, do you actually put on...an entire suit?"

That would seem ridiculous to her. Hell, it seemed ridiculous to him. "Sometimes," he admitted. "If I have to go out later I usually wear a suit. I'm more comfortable in suits than I am in jeans, Keely. It's just the way I am."

"Which is a damn cryin' shame, because you fill out a pair of jeans very nicely. However, I can hardly see your very fine ass or your impressive junk when a suit coat covers the front and the rear."

"It conceals a big problem whenever I'm around you, buttercup."

Keely fingered a pile of sweaters, arranged by color. "I live in jeans. I hate getting dressed up. But I will, when the occasion warrants it." She jammed her hands in her pockets. "Did you have help organizing your closet? It's so tidy."

"I have help choosing my wardrobe, but I manage to hang things up all by myself," he said wryly.

Keely gaped at him. "Someone helps you shop?"

"I've dealt with two men's clothing stores in Chicago for a few years. My personal shopper knows what I like."

"I've never met anyone with a personal shopper and wardrobe consultant. My God, you *must* be filthy rich."

He skirted the *rich* issue. "Do you think I'm a pansy-ass because I care how I look?"

"No. Those shoppers are worth every penny because you always look smashing."

"Smashing?" Jack groaned. "Fuck. That word makes me sound like a metrosexual."

"You're all hunky, hot, real man, in my experience, so not to worry." Keely ducked out of the closet to sit on the bed. She wore a strangely pensive look.

Shit. Maybe she did think he was a fucking pussy because he didn't have a closet full of Wranglers, shitkickers and flannel. "What?"

"I'm going out on a limb here. You don't have a revolving door to your bedroom, do you?"

He shook his head, less self-conscious about his pathetic sex life than his dismal apartment. "As a matter of fact, you're the first woman I've ever asked into my bedroom, Keely."

The look of surprise melted into a look of pure seduction. Keely reached up, wrapped her fingers around the knot in his tie and tugged hard. "Whaddya say we christen the bed?"

"I'm not sure—"

"I am." Using the tie, she pulled his face closer to hers. "If you're afraid I'm gonna muss your snappy suit, GQ, you'd be right. But I happen to know you've got a whole closet full of replacements, so buck up and fuck me."

Jack's dick was as hard as a steel beam upon seeing the wicked gleam in her eyes. He crawled over her and backed her into the middle of the bed. "Strip."

But Keely flipped Jack on his back. Straddling him, she said, "Nifty trick, huh?"

"With five older brothers, I'm not surprised."

She kissed him, letting the glide of lips and tongues heat them both up. Between kisses, she whispered, "Let me take care of you, Jack."

"Anything you want. I'm yours."

"Then I'll take you." Keely rolled off the bed, whipped off her clothes and climbed back on top of him. The woman was something—all naked, soft, bouncy female parts.

Her fingers unknotted his tie. She left it undone beneath his collar and worked the buttons free, spread the shirt open, leaving his chest exposed. Next she unbuttoned, unzipped and removed his pants and boxers.

She nibbled the column of his throat. Her hands mapped every ridge and muscle on his chest. "Doesn't this feel naughty with me buck-ass nekkid on top of you, and you still wearing your shirt and tie? Like I'm your wicked secretary and we snuck off so I could take...dictation?"

Jack laughed softly. "Oral?"

Keely bit down on his left nipple and he arched up from the sheer pleasure of it. "You like the rough stuff, boss?" She bent her mouth to his right nipple and did the same thing.

"Keely—"

"Here's a memo. If you don't zip it I'll stop touching you."

"Shutting up now."

She tasted and tormented his upper body until Jack thought he'd shoot like a randy teenage boy if she ever put her hand on his dick.

But she avoided his cock. Even when it was jerking, leaking and begging for her attention.

Keely kissed him all too briefly and pushed up on her knees over his pelvis. She touched his lips with her index and middle fingers. "Open."

He parted his lips and drew her fingers deeply into his mouth, getting them good and wet.

She murmured, "You do that so well, Jack." Then she trailed her wet fingers down her slit and plunged them into her pussy.

His cock slapped against his belly.

Keely's free hand pinched her nipple hard. She moaned loudly as she continued to fuck herself on her own fingers.

Jack watched Keely raptly, beautiful in abandon.

She locked her gaze to his and pulled her fingers out of her sex with a wet sucking sound. Then she pressed them to his lips again.

He sucked, growling at the dark, sweet taste of her juices flowing over his tongue.

"Am I wet enough to take full dictation?"

"Yes. Goddamn, Keely you're making me crazy."

"Good." She slanted her mouth over his and sank down on his cock to the root.

She rode him hard. Her tits bounced sexily as she dangled above him, her head thrown back. Repeating the motion and the rhythm, bringing them both to the edge.

Jack grabbed a handful of her ass and directed her to pump her hips faster. He couldn't hold back and as his balls tightened. The combination of arching his pelvis the same time as her cunt muscles clamped down on his shaft made him shout until his throat hurt.

A blank sense of peace floated over him.

Sweet kisses roused him. He flipped his eyes open. Shit. Had Keely come?

She pressed her forehead to his. "To answer the question I see in your eyes, yes, I got off. You didn't leave me wanting. You never leave me wanting, Jack."

"That's a relief. I sort of blacked out there at the end."

"Exactly what I was aiming for." Three more flirty kisses and Keely smiled against his cheek. "Bed christening complete."

Saying *thank you* seemed lame and pathetic, but he muttered it anyway.

"My pleasure. Next go around let's break in the reclining chair in your living room. Oh, and for that one? I'll want you to wear a brown suit coat. And the Scooby Doo boxers."

Keely insisted on driving her truck to the hotel, mumbling about getting stuck in the city without a means to escape.

After they'd checked in, Jack donned a different suit. It amused him to see Keely fussing as she readied herself for the cocktail party. She rarely primped—she didn't need it, she always looked utterly breathtaking—but she took extra time with her makeup.

She sighed. "Should I put my hair up?"

He moved behind her in the big bathroom mirror and kissed her shoulder. "No. Your hair is beautiful the way it is."

"Beautiful? It's stick straight and boring and—"

"Perfect. Leave it. I love it."

"You do?"

"Mmm-hmm."

"Fine. What about my makeup? Should I add more eyeliner?"

"Keely. Stop. Breathe. Buttercup, you look terrific."

She inhaled and let the breath out slowly. "I'm nervous."

"Why? This is no different than Milford. You did fine there. Better than fine. Just be yourself."

As Jack walked out of the bathroom, he thought he heard her mutter, "That's what I'm afraid of."

The banquet room was packed and the cocktail party was in full swing when Jack and Keely entered. She refused a drink, as the choices were only red or white wine.

Once his colleagues noticed them, they were swarmed. The men wanted a closer look at Keely. The women were sizing her up as well, which increased Keely's nervousness. She kept tugging at her dress and fiddling with her hair.

Ten minutes into the social bullshit, the moment Jack had been waiting for arrived: Baxter and Martine approached them.

Baxter stuck out his hand. "Jack! Good to see you, buddy. We must've missed each other during the seminars."

Jack returned Baxter's vigorous handshake. "Good to see you too, Baxter. I made a couple of the morning sessions, but Keely was due in this afternoon so I'm afraid I skipped out." He placed his arm around Keely's shoulder, urging her forward. "Baxter, this is my fiancée, Keely McKay. Keely, Baxter Ducheyne, my former business partner."

Keely smiled offered her hand. "Pleasure to meet you."

"The pleasure is all mine. Allow me to introduce my wife, Martine."

Martine offered her manicured fingertips. "Kelly. I'm sure we'll have plenty of time to chat later." Then Martine's lipsticked mouth bestowed a tight-lipped kiss on each of Jack's cheeks. "Jack. Darling. How marvelous to see you. You're looking devilishly handsome as ever."

Jack ground his teeth at Martine's mispronunciation of Keely's name. He managed a civil smile. "You're looking...rested."

Baxter chuckled.

Martine allowed a brittle laugh and addressed Keely. "Isn't this awkward. I'm sure Jack told you about our past relationship. Whenever our paths cross and he's so cool, I realize I miss the divine compliments he used to lavish on me."

He withheld a snort. Lavish. Right.

Keely blinked innocently at Martine. "You and Jack had a fling? Really?" She half-elbowed Jack in the gut. "Seems *someone* forgot to mention that tidbit to me."

Martine's eyes narrowed first at Keely, then at Jack, as if she couldn't believe she hadn't rated mention.

Jack leaned over to brush a soft kiss on Keely's temple. "Sorry, sweetheart. We've been preoccupied, haven't we?"

"Yes, we were all quite shocked to hear the playboy had been caught." Martine's gaze lingered on Keely's midsection. "I assume since the engagement was so quick, a hurry-up wedding is to soon follow?"

That bitch thought Keely was pregnant. Jesus Christ. How had he ever been attracted to her? The woman was an absolute nightmare. "No, we haven't actually set a date. Next year, maybe. She's wearing my ring. That's what matters to me."

"Oh, yes, let me see the ring," Martine cooed.

Keely held out her left hand.

All Jacked Up

Martine scrutinized the diamond. "Lovely. What is it? About seven carats?"

"Nearly eleven," Jack said. "A daily reminder that Keely ranks above a perfect ten in my eyes."

Keely swallowed hard. To anyone else it'd appear she was overcome with emotion, but Jack knew she was choking back a snort of disbelief.

"A Tiffany creation?" Martine asked.

"No, Harry Winston." Might be petty, but he knew that'd grate on Martine. She'd always dropped hints about wanting jewelry bearing that exclusive name and he'd never indulged her.

"I hope you'll accept my sincerest congratulations," Baxter said. "It's good to see you smiling again, Jack."

"Yes, thank you. I have quite a bit to smile about these days. We'll see you later." He steered Keely away.

When they were alone, Keely said, "You actually fucked her? Dude. Did her forked tongue feel exceptionally good on your dick or something?"

Jack grinned. "She didn't 'do' that more than once, if I recall. My taste has improved markedly, hasn't it?"

"Yes. So has your bullshitting ability." Keely peered into his eyes. "A daily reminder that I'm above a perfect ten? Please. Jack. I almost gagged."

"Mmm." He kissed her. Twice. "Why do you think I got us out of there so fast?"

"Smart move. After that...I need alcohol so badly I'll even drink a shitty glass of wine."

"Hang tight. I'll be right back."

After dropping off her wine, Jack left Keely in the midst of a group of his colleague's wives. She'd done this meet and greet before with great success and she didn't need him holding her hand, especially when he had business to discuss. Keely was tough. Smart. She could hold her own with anyone. She'd do just fine.

This party was Keely's worst fucking nightmare.

First, she was underdressed. *Way* underdressed. The women in attendance wore smart, classy cocktail dresses that probably cost more than her truck. The frumpy little engagement dress which'd worked in so well in Wyoming and Utah made her look like an escapee from *Hee Haw* in this ritzy setting.

Second, her feet hurt. She'd worn heels, but checking out the other women's expensive shoes, flip-flops would've been a better footwear choice. And would've garnered fewer, "Are those shoes from Payless?" type of raised eyebrows the females aimed at her poor aching feet.

Third, no beer. What kind of party didn't have a cash bar that served beer? Which served as another reminder of how hopelessly low class she was. How out of her league Jack was.

Fourth, Mr. High Class himself had abandoned her. Completely. No looking back, no encouraging smiles from across the room. He'd ditched her in a nest of snakes.

Even the women's clattering bracelets and earrings sounded like rattles—but she doubted she'd get any warning before they struck.

"You're from Wyoming?" a brunette with far too many Botox injections asked.

Keep it simple. "Yes."

"I've never actually met anyone from Wyoming," another brunette with beady black eyes commented. "What on earth do you do there? *Is* there anything to do there? Or is that why the state is so meagerly populated? Because no one can stand to stick around?"

Female laughter.

Keely blushed.

"Oh, I'm sure *Kelly* can regale us with plenty of quaint little tales from her life in the Wild West, Laura." Martine sipped her white wine. "I imagine you have a horse?"

"Actually, I have two horses. One—"

"So you don't have a car?" Martine snarked back.

"Of course I have a vehicle. A truck."

Snickers.

"With mud on the tires, a gun rack and a bale of hay in the back?" a snide blonde sidekick of Martine's tossed out.

"Oh, Reagan, don't forget country music blaring as she's driving down the gravel road to take care of her horse," the another brunette threw in.

"*Horses*," Martine corrected sweetly. "She owns more than one, remember? I'll bet one's a real stud."

Laughter.

"How does Jack feel about letting you ride another stallion?"

Don't say a word.

"No, seriously, Kelly. We're pleased for you and Jack. Even if we're a bit surprised by his...choice." Martine flashed her fangs. "You have been married before?"

Keely frowned. "No. Why would you—"

"I just assumed girls in your neck of the woods married early. Anyway, I'm sure your family is pleased you caught a man like Jack."

Caught. Like I laid out a trap line? Give me a fuckin' break.

"Does Jack get cattle or land or pigs or something after you get married?" the nasty blonde asked with mock-sincerity.

"Or forty acres and a mule?" another added.

Martine admonished her. "Theresa! That was not nice. I'm sure that 'bride price and dowry' nonsense is a thing of the past." She peered at Keely through slitted eyes. "Isn't it?"

Tittering and whispers.

Keely wanted to crawl into a hole and die. This situation was beyond any horror she'd ever encountered. Nothing would make these women be civil to her. They saw her as fresh off the farm meat and decided to cut her down to size, one petty, shallow little slice at a time.

Fight back.

No. She wouldn't embarrass Jack in front of his colleagues, which meant no firing off rude suggestions. She'd suffer the humiliation with whatever dignity she could muster. But if Jack wanted to hang around with his vicious friends after dinner, she'd plead a headache and return to the room.

Don't you mean slink off to your room like a whipped pup?

Backing down and biting her tongue was a new experience. These blowhards needed a serious smackdown, but Keely McKay couldn't wield the verbal paddle tonight. Or any other night.

People started drifting into the banquet room. Keely didn't budge, praying the pit vipers would slither off. Maybe she could regroup with others who weren't so incredibly vile. But mostly she hoped Jack would come save her.

So much for her feminist mantra of not needing a man to rescue her.

Martine whispered loud enough for all her friends to hear. "I realize you're used to hearing a dinner bell clank as a signal for chow time, but if you follow the herd you'll realize they're starting to serve dinner."

"Thank you." *You miserable, tight-assed sow.*

"Or you can just come along with me since we're sitting together."

Sheer panic arose. She wasn't sitting with Jack?

Martine's lips curled into a sneer. "Oh, you poor thing. Didn't Jack tell you? Typical of him, he's so aloof and unconcerned for anyone except himself. At these events they separate the men and women. So the men can talk business and the women...well, you can imagine how fun it'll be, us getting to know you over five dinner courses."

Her stomach lurched. She doubted she'd be able to choke down a single bite.

And if Keely thought it couldn't get worse, she was sadly mistaken.

Theresa asked if she chewed tobacco.

Reagan asked if she used hay as toothpicks.

Laura asked if she hunted and killed her own food.

Martine asked if she made all her own clothes.

After they tired of making fun of her, they took great joy in ferreting out how rural Keely was. They gasped upon hearing she'd never been to New York City. Or the Caribbean. Or the Orient. Or Europe. She'd never heard of any of the clothing, shoe and handbag designers they yammered on about ad nauseum. She'd never attended an opera or a Broadway play or the ballet. When Keely admitted she'd been to an art opening—namely her brother Carter's—they'd rolled their eyes. "Western" art wasn't real art.

Keely hadn't anticipated Martine's snideness. But it'd gone beyond Jack being her former lover type of jealousy. And Keely didn't understand why Martine bothered to engage in the "Kelly is a low class bumpkin" attack if she believed Keely so far beneath her social stratosphere.

The meal, the insults, the sheer horror of the night dragged on. And on.

During a pause in the speaker's program, Keely retreated to the ladies room, debating on whether she should cut bait and run. When she exited the stall, Martine was freshening her lipstick at the sink.

Keely couldn't muster a smile. Or even meet Martine's cruel eyes in the mirror. She washed her hands slowly, hoping Martine would leave.

No such luck.

Martine waited while Keely dried her hands. Naturally, they appeared to be the only ones in the bathroom.

"You won't hold onto him, you know."

Keely didn't respond.

"I know Jack told you about me. About us. I'm sure he also told you I left him for his partner. But I'll bet your frumpy dress he didn't cough up the truth about why I left the gorgeous, sexy, charming Jack Donohue for an older man?"

For money hovered on the tip of Keely's tongue.

Martine slithered closer and Keely forced herself to hold her ground. But she refused to look at her.

"Jack is a workaholic. I suspect he has something to prove because of his humble background. I didn't mind his obsession with business when we were first together. He was so dynamic I forgave him. Eventually I couldn't continue to overlook the missed dinners. The broken plans. The ruined vacations. The last minute cancellations because he prioritized business over everything. He had few friends. He had nothing to do with his family. Jack is all about work. He will do absolutely anything to get ahead in this business."

A strange tingle worked its way down Keely's spine. Much as she hated to admit it, there was a lot of truth in that statement.

"When he deigned to spend time with me, he expected that time to be spent on my back in his bed. Yes, Jack was an amazing lover, but I found his sexual appetite to be rather primitive and excessive. More kinky than I was willing to give him. I'll bet he's found that 'anything goes' dirty girl type of kink with you?"

Do not blush.

Martine sighed. "I can see by your stubborn silence you

don't believe me. I pity you. I've been where you are. I'm lucky
Baxter could see I was unhappy whenever I went to Jack's office
and Jack wasn't there. Baxter treated me as I deserved,
lavishing time and attention on me. He's given me everything
I've ever wanted. Baxter and I are well suited, which between
us, bothered Jack far more than anything else about the
situation. Jack knew no matter how much money he made or
how successful he'd ever become, he'd always be trying to prove
to everyone and to himself that he was good enough for me."

Keely's mouth fell open at Martine's completely asinine
assessment of Jack. But she finally met the snake eyes in the
mirror. "You honestly believe if you and Jack would've stayed
together, it would've been because he accepted he'd...married
up?"

Her eyes were chips of ice. "Better than marrying down."
Those revulsion-filled eyes raked her head to toe. "Good God.
Could you be any more of a country mouse? You don't even
know how to properly dress yourself for a business function.
How embarrassing for Jack. He's really scraping the bottom of
the barrel with you, isn't he?"

Bull's-eye. Martine's maliciousness torpedoed any remnant
of Keely's confidence.

"Don't kid yourself he'll actually go through with marrying
you. Every year, it's the same sad story. Jack shows up at the
conference with his latest piece of ass. Young. Hot. Oblivious.
Everyone knows he's trying to make me jealous. Trying to prove
to his male colleagues what a stud he is. We all laugh. It's so
pathetic. I'm sure you noticed all the staring and whispering
you attracted. This is a small community, and you'll find no one
will take the time to befriend you. What's the point? This time
next year you'll be gone."

*Don't cry. God, do not give this woman the satisfaction of
seeing your tears.*

Martine rearranged wisps of her hair in the mirror. "I feel
sorry for you. You're as gullible as you look and you've fallen
hard for Jack's charm. My best advice is to keep that ring he's
given you. It'll buy you a new horse or repairs on your truck or
whatever pitiful thing you need after he dumps your mousy ass
back in Wyoming." She twirled on her heel and flounced out.

Blood scorched Keely's cheeks. A sick feeling of betrayal
and finality settled deep in her bones. She wasn't sure she had

the strength to move. But she didn't have the strength to stay either. Not in the bathroom, not in the hotel, not in Colorado. Not with Jack.

Go home. It's where you belong. She felt like Dorothy in *The Wizard of Oz,* when the phrase "There's no place like home" repeated in her head as she trudged back to the room.

In something of a daze, Keely changed her clothes and packed her suitcase. Rather than chancing running into anyone, she bypassed the elevators and hoofed it down the stairs to the garage level where she'd parked her truck. Oddly, it fit her frame of mind to discover she'd parked on the lowest level.

After she'd cleared the Denver city limits, she realized she was in no shape to drive to Sundance. Holing up in hotel didn't appeal to her. She didn't want to see anyone she knew or talk to anyone she knew. Confessing Martine's degrading remarks would be bad enough. But hearing platitudes about how she shouldn't let Martine's insecurities affect her would be much worse.

Martine's words had cut to the bone. Maybe they were just nasty barbs, but barbs stung whether the connection with them was intentional or accidental.

All Keely wanted was to reconnect with herself. To remember who she was.

On autopilot, she drove to the refuge she'd fled to the years she'd lived in Denver. She'd always found herself here. But before she climbed out of her truck, she curled up in the bench seat and cried.

Chapter Eighteen

Jack had tuned out the speaker's drone an hour ago. About the last time he'd seen Keely.

And whose fault is that?

His. He'd been busy networking and hadn't realized Keely had gotten stuck with the coven at Martine's table until the dinner was over.

His gaze zeroed in on her empty chair again. Where the hell could she have gone?

Clapping echoed as the speech finally ended and he distractedly joined in. Immediately Jack was on his feet. When his colleagues stopped him to talk, he couldn't very well walk away, since he'd attended the conference to work. By the time he'd made it out of the banquet room, another twenty minutes had passed. And still no sign of Keely.

Jack was starting to get worried.

"Jack?"

He turned as Gina Arguello approached him. When Jack lived in Chicago, he'd collaborated with Gina's husband Donnie on a couple of projects and he'd been to their house for the occasional barbecue. "Gina. Nice to see you. How are the kids?"

"Getting big and ornery." She hesitated and twisted her wedding ring around her finger. "I'm happy to see you here. I know the last couple years were rough on you."

"Brutal. But things are looking up. Was there something you needed?"

"Ah. Well, I don't know if it's my place to say this or not, but I accidentally overheard a conversation between your fiancée and...Martine."

"When?"

"An hour ago."

An odd feeling of foreboding replaced any sense of relief. "Where was Keely when you heard it? Because I've been looking for her."

Gina blushed. "In the lady's room. I'm pregnant and I wasn't feeling well after dinner so I went to the restroom. I was about to come out of the last stall when I heard Martine start in on her."

Shit. "What did she say?"

"Martine went off on this tirade about you. Then she started belittling Keely. It was vicious. If I thought I'd felt nauseous before, it was worse by the time Martine finished with her."

Jack forced himself to stay calm. "Tell me all of it." When Gina finished, Jack stared at her in absolute horror.

"I know I should've jumped in and put a stop to it, but I don't want to tangle with Martine. Ever. Donnie needs the consulting work with Baxter, especially with another kid on the way. I'm sorry—"

"It's okay, you don't have to apologize. There's no way to stop the shit that Martine spews. Do you know where Keely went after Martine left?"

Gina shook her head. "I planned on talking to her and telling her Martine was full of lies, but when I left the stall, Keely wasn't around."

He squeezed Gina's arm. "Thank you, Gina."

His gut was tied in a mass of knots.

Stay calm.

As he walked to the elevator, Jack dug out his cell phone and called Keely. Automatically the message kicked over to her voice mail.

Stay calm.

He drummed his fingers on the handrail as the elevator whirred up to his floor.

Stay calm.

Jack even managed not to take the length of the hallway at a dead run.

Stay calm.

He inserted his key card and called out, "Keely?"

No answer.

When he saw her key card on the dresser but no suitcase, all calmness evaporated.

She was gone.

"Goddammit straight to fucking hell, Keely McKay. Where the hell did you go?"

Jack called her cell phone again. He left another message.

Over the next hour, Jack called her cell phone twenty-seven times. He called her home phone twenty-nine times.

After nearly wearing holes in his shoes from pacing, he called information in Sundance. His heart raced as the phone rang. An irritated female voice snapped, "You'd better have a good reason for calling me this late, whoever you are."

"AJ. It's Jack."

She went on alert so fast he felt her panic through the phone lines. "What happened?"

"Keely's gone. She's not answering her cell phone and I'm going crazy."

"What did you do to her?"

"Nothing! I swear. We were at a business banquet, we got separated at dinner and evidently an old...girlfriend of mine said some upsetting things. Keely left without a word to me. I only know that much because a woman overheard their conversation."

"So you guys weren't fighting again?"

"Not this time."

"When did this happen?"

"At some point in the last two hours she got in her truck and took off and... Shit, I'm worried because I know she's upset. Jesus. *I'm* upset. And I will wring her neck if I find out she's driving all the way back to Sundance this time of night by herself."

AJ was quiet. "Let me try calling her. Maybe she's just not answering your calls."

Jack closed his eyes. "Thank you. Call me right back. Please. And if you do talk to her, tell her I'm sorry. So goddamn sorry and I had no idea that she'd gotten stuck—"

"Jack. Calm down. Let me try her first before you start relaying all the things you want me to tell her, okay?"

"Okay."

He flexed and smacked his fist into the mattress while he waited for AJ to call. His phone rang five minutes later. "What did you find out?"

"She's not just ditching your calls. She didn't answer when I called from my cell, or from the house phone, or even from Cord's phone."

Fuck.

"Either she's really really pissed or she's driving through Wyoming where there's no cell service."

"That doesn't help much."

"I don't know what else to tell you."

He didn't buy it. "Where is she?"

"I don't know."

"She's your best friend. What's your gut feeling? Is she driving home?"

AJ sighed. "My gut feeling is no. She needed time alone to sort things out and she's smart enough after the accidents in her family not to act rashly when she's upset."

"Where would she go?"

Silence.

Jack knew AJ knew exactly where Keely had gone. "AJ. I know your first loyalty is to Keely. I get that. I wouldn't ask if I wasn't losing my fucking mind. Jesus. I need to make this right. She walked into something tonight that had nothing to do with her and I didn't warn her. That part *is* my fault, okay? But that also means I need to fix it. Christ. I'll do anything to fix it. Please. Just help me find her."

AJ sighed again. "When we went to school in Denver and we were missing home, we'd head to the Quarter Past Midnight Stables. Keely got chummy with Darla, the owner, and exercised horses and cleaned stalls for fun. After I married Cord and moved home I know she spent lots of time there."

Sounded like Keely. Making friends all over the damn place and finding fun and solace in a damn barn. "What if she's not there?"

"There is another place she's goes, but it's much closer to home. We'll cross that bridge if it comes down to that."

"Thank you, AJ."

"You're welcome. After you find her, make her call me, Jack Donohue, so I know she's okay. Or I swear to God I will sic her brothers on you. One at a time. Before I call Carson."

The wrath of an angry pregnant woman scared him almost as much as Keely's dad. "I promise."

Jack went to find his cowgirl.

Two vehicles were in the parking lot at Quarter Past Midnight Stables. A Dodge Ram with Colorado plates and Keely's dirty, beat up black Ford. Jack almost kissed the bug-covered grille.

The office door was unlocked. A buzzer sounded and within a couple minutes a bleary-eyed woman appeared in the enclosed office space. She slid open the glass partition. "Help ya with something?"

"Ah. Yeah. I'm looking for Keely McKay."

The bleariness vanished and her focus turned razor sharp. She flipped her long, gray braid over her shoulder and folded her arms across her abundant cleavage. "And who would you be?"

"Jack Donohue."

"Never heard of ya." She slammed the partition and turned her back on him.

Jack rapped on the glass. "Darla? AJ McKay said I could find Keely here. I saw her truck in the parking lot. I know she's here somewhere. Please. I need to see her."

Darla whirled back around but didn't open the glass window.

She studied him. "You say you talked to AJ?"

"Yeah, she gave me hell too."

"I always liked that girl." Darla shook her finger at him. "Keely's in the south white barn. If she don't want you here, I'll escort you off the premises with my shotgun, we clear?"

"Yes, ma'am."

Darla hit the switch that unlocked the gate.

Jack forced himself not to run when he saw the white metal siding of the barn on the south end of the property. The door was already open. The pungent odor of horseflesh and horseshit blasted him as he walked in.

The dim lighting revealed little beyond twelve stalls lined up, six on each side. Very quietly he started down the center section and tiptoed past curious horses until he found her.

Keely had her back to him. Her glossy black braid hung past her shoulder blades. She wore a flannel shirt with the sleeves rolled up. Faded jeans tucked into old shit-covered boots. One hundred percent country cowgirl. One hundred percent his.

Keely McKay *was* his. She belonged to him.

The self-admission was not the shock to his system he'd imagined. He suspected he loved her all along and he'd fought it, creating elaborate excuses and lying to himself that sex and circumstance made him feel this way. But as Jack looked at her, he really saw her. Her. The woman who owned him.

He'd found the once in a lifetime, bone deep, straight to the soul kind of love he'd never believed in.

For the longest time, Jack watched the woman he loved combing the Quarter Horse. Murmuring to it, running her hand across the withers. Keely pressed her face into the horse's neck and tried to keep her shoulders from shaking as she cried.

Her every tear felt like a drop of acid on his heart. Jack didn't deserve her, but he took a step toward her, toward their future together anyway. Would she let him soothe her? Kiss away her tears? He'd promise her the damn moon if she'd stay with him. If she'd give him another chance.

But would she ever love him the way he loved her?

Keely swiveled around at his approach, eyes swollen and nose red from crying. She still looked beautiful. His gut clenched knowing her misery was his fault.

When she didn't yell at him, insult him, or ask him what the fuck he was doing here, Jack knew he had an uphill climb. A spitting mad Keely he could handle. But Keely seemed...defeated. And he didn't know how to handle that. Waltzing in here and declaring his love for her would only muddy the waters. She probably wouldn't believe him anyway. It'd keep.

"How'd you find me?"

"I called AJ."

She stopped brushing the horse for a second. Then she resumed the long strokes. "I'm gonna kick her ass. She shouldn't have told you."

"I begged her."

"Why? I'm surprised you even noticed I left."

"I did. Look. I'm sorry you got stuck with Martine tonight."

"Are you really?"

"Yes. Did Martine really corner you in the bathroom?"

Keely didn't miss a beat in her horse grooming. "How did you find out?"

"A woman named Gina overheard the conversation."

"Fuckin' awesome. Did this Gina laugh about it when she told you?"

"No. She's not like that, Keely."

"Well, she'd be about the only one in that lousy group of women." *Brush brush brush.* "Anyway, it doesn't matter."

"It matters to me."

A snort. Hers or the horse's?

"Why'd you leave without telling me?"

"Because I don't answer to you, Jack, and I didn't need your permission to leave. I needed to get away."

"From me?"

She shrugged.

Jack dry-washed his face and forced himself to stay calm. "Fine. But I'm here. Will you talk to me now?"

"Nothin' left to say."

"You're wrong."

"I was wrong about a lot of things."

Silence.

Fuck being polite. "Me too, Keely. Wrong to insist you go to that stupid cocktail party in the first place. Wrong to leave you at Martine's table, subjected to her ugly whims. Wrong not to notice you were gone until it was too fucking late. If anyone is in the wrong here, it's me. Not you."

Keely spoke lowly to the horse. Gave him one last pat on the rump before she picked up a bucket and exited the stall.

Jack stood aside from the gate to let her out. She never looked at him. He was undeterred by her coolness and he followed her to the tack room.

She put away the supplies and hung the bucket on a wooden peg. Ignoring him. Killing him with aloofness.

"Talk to me, goddammit."

"What do you want me to say? I went so far beyond my

comfort zone tonight that I lost myself? But in some respects it only made me realize how different we are?"

"We're not that different."

"Really? I don't live my personal or professional life in the shadow of expectations from others," she shot back.

"And I do? That's the type of man you think I am?"

Finally Keely looked at him. "That *is* the type of man you are, Jack. Instead of being who you are on the inside all the time, you change who you are to fit the circumstances."

That stung. But it wasn't the point. Why was Keely making this about him? *She* was the one who'd been ambushed by Martine. *She* was the one who'd bolted from the party. And not because she'd suddenly realized some startling truth about his business acumen—or lack thereof. She was focusing on him, his flaws, rather than the issue at hand. How badly she'd been hurt.

Clever. Sneaky. But he wouldn't let it slide.

Jack stalked her. Her spine hit the tool bench; he curled his hands around her biceps. "I'm sorry. I'm a total and complete fuck up. A total and complete jackass. I will let you yell obscenities and scream insults at me to your heart's content, but first I need you. I need this." He lowered his mouth to hers and kissed her. He kept kissing her until she responded with the sweetness, goodness and heat that filled the empty part of his soul. He hadn't understood the depth of the missing piece until she came into his life.

He whispered kisses along the elegant line of her neck. "Please. Come back with me, cowgirl."

"I can't."

"Or won't?"

"I won't be paraded through the hotel like a naughty child who's run away and is back to face the music. And it goes beyond me not wanting to run into Martine."

"Does it go beyond you not wanting to be with me?"

"I don't know."

Another direct hit. "Well, buttercup, you can't sleep in this barn, though I'm sure you'll point out as a Wyoming tough girl you've done it more than once."

"That would be true. And horses are better company than people. They don't judge. They don't talk back."

"Yeah, but they smell like shit and try to throw you on your ass at every opportunity." He saw her lips twitch. "Besides, I won't let you drive back to Wyoming this time of night by yourself. Whatever you do, stay here, or go back to the hotel, I'll be with you."

Keely absentmindedly brushed tufts of hair from her cheek. "I'll stay at your condo until I can leave tomorrow."

"Keely—"

"Either I stay at your place or I hit the road. Choose."

"My place it is."

They'd crawled under the covers; a chasm yawned between them as wide as the bed. Close but not touching. Not sleeping. Keely faced away from him. He stared at the ceiling, a million thoughts raced in his head. None coherent.

Jack finally asked her the question that'd bugged him all night. Been bugging him for years, actually. "Keely, do you think I'm shallow?"

She rolled over. "Sometimes. With some things. But I don't think you're as shallow as you pretend to be."

Jack frowned. "Meaning what?"

"If you wear expensive suits, live in a swanky condo and drive a pricey car, people will think you're successful."

"That makes me shallow?"

"No. That makes *them* shallow because that's all they see. Are you successful because you care about other people's perceptions? Or are you successful because you want to be?"

"What do you think?"

"I think you're successful because you love what you do, Jack. The money is just a bonus."

He smiled in the darkness.

"But it's easy to get trapped in that name brand mindset. To start to believe that what's on the outside—what you wear, where you live, what you drive, where you've been—is more important than who you are inside those trappings."

"So you saying appearances don't matter at all?"

"Yes, appearances do matter, but it shouldn't define you."

"Does it define you?" he countered.

"No. What if I'd tracked you down in the banquet wearing my stable-cleaning clothes? If you'd pretended not to know me, that's shallow. If you'd kissed my cheek and said, 'Darlin', next time leave the shitkickers at home,' that's caring less about appearances because you were happy to be with me."

Jack seized the chance to turn the tables. "Would you be happy to be with me, Keely? If the reverse was true?"

"Meaning what?"

"Say I accept your dirty boots and western quirks. Say you accept I'm a suit-and-tie-wearing guy. Say I'm madly in love with you. You're madly in love with me. Would you give up your way of life to be with me?"

"Way of life?" she repeated.

"Would you move away from your home in Wyoming to live with me in this condo in Colorado? Or are you so set in *your* ways that you wouldn't consider it?"

"What does that have to do with being shallow?" she demanded.

"Don't you think it's shallow that you won't consider living anywhere besides Wyoming?"

"Not the same. Not at all."

"Really? You don't look at me with pity because I live in a high rise and wear a monkey suit? The same way those women pitied you for what you wore and where you lived?"

Sticky silence.

Jack wanted to tell her he wasn't just hypothesizing. Would any kind of long term, real relationship have to be solely on her terms?

"Maybe I am shallow," she said in a small voice. "I never thought of it that way. You definitely gave me something to think about."

"Keely. You misunderstood."

"The hell I did. I'm happy in my own skin. I could be happy anywhere if I was with the person I loved. But it's a moot point anyway."

"Why?"

"Because you *don't* love me. And I don't pity you for the way you live as much as you pity yourself."

"Hey, that's not fair."

"Nothin' ever is. Good night, Jack."

She jerked the covers so tightly around herself he only saw a lump on the other side of the bed.

Cocooned as she was, she wouldn't have heard his *But I do love you* rebuttal, but he said it anyway.

"I wish you'd change your mind."

"I'll text you and let you know, okay?"

"Okay." Jack scrambled her brain with a kiss with equal parts fire and sweet regret.

Keely watched the elevator doors close and returned to his condo. She spent a considerable amount of time staring out the window contemplating her options.

Wow. Big choices: Stay or go.

Her cell phone blared "One Hot Mama". Smiling, she said, "Hey, AJ. What's up?"

"My feet. Foster is down for his nap. Ky and Anton are helping Cord. So I have time to grill you about what the hell happened last night."

Where to start? "Jack was too freakin' busy being a businessman to notice I was miserable with his asshole associates' wives. I got tired of being the lowbrow entertainment and left. Oh, and piss off for telling him where I went, AJ."

"What was I supposed to do, K? I've never heard calm, cool and collected Jack Donohue that upset. I figured something major had gone down if you'd bolted. So sue me. I wanted to make sure you were all right just as much as he did. You know how we all hate it when you just take off and no one has a clue where you are."

Keely closed her eyes and let her head fall into the headrest. Sometimes getting away by herself was the only way she could clear her head. Her family didn't understand, so she'd stopped trying to explain and just took off whenever she needed.

"Here's where you tell me what happened," AJ prompted.

"It was a fucking nightmare."

"Still doesn't explain anything, K."

She struggled to put it in a context that didn't sound hopelessly high-schoolish. "Remember when you first moved to Denver? We went to that party over at Tim's house and you had an awful time? Back at the apartment you cried because you'd felt totally out of place, like my hick cousin who'd never been to the big city? That describes last night.

"But replace the obnoxious jocks with Jack's colleagues. Replace the snotty sorority sisters with snooty colleagues' wives. I wore the wrong clothes. I wore the wrong shoes. Hell, I think they sniffed to see if I had cowshit on me. Plus, the ringleader was Jack's old flame and she made me feel small enough to fit into a thimble—before she cornered me in the can to reinforce what a total fuckin' loser I am. It was horrendous, AJ. All I wanted was to go home."

AJ paused thoughtfully. "So you ran?"

"Yep. And I hid." *And I realized I'm a total idiot for falling in love with a man I can't have because he sees me the same way they do: A hick country girl who'd never fit in his world.*

"You never run. You always stay and fight."

Keely sighed. "I know. But I was in way over my head."

"So next time you're in that situation? What happens?"

It won't happen again. "I don't know."

"Keely. Listen to me. Sounds like these social events are a big part of Jack's professional life. You can't run every time. You have to find a way to deal with it in a way that works for both of you."

"My way to deal? I'd tell Martine and her cronies to fuck off. But I can't because it'd reflect badly on Jack."

"True. But you've got no reason to hide and hang your head in shame for not being good enough. So what if you wore the wrong clothes? You've got a college degree for cripesake. You've worked for the PBR, the PRCA and the VA. You're part of one of the oldest ranching families in Wyoming. You're on your way to being a businesswoman in your own right. Plus you're generous and funny, everyone who meets you loves you, not to mention you are beautiful inside and outside. If they can't see that—"

"They don't. And I don't feel like I should have to defend my life or explain who I am to anyone."

"Does Jack know that?"

"He does now. I don't want to change, AJ. I'm happy with who I am."

"Then screw 'em. What the hell do you care what some hoity-toity wives think? They don't have any power in Jack's career. Isn't that why they're called trophy wives? They're worthless ornamentation. I say show up tonight in your hottest, most flattering western outfit and flirt shamelessly with all their husbands."

"Great plan, AJ."

"Seriously. If they already dislike you, what're you out? They smacked your pride; hit 'em back where it hurts. We both know, sista, when you're on, you're on. No one can top you in the charm department. No one can top you in the looks department. Let that wild child out, Keely West McKay. She's been caged too long."

Keely laughed. God, she loved AJ. She was the best friend in the history of the world. "That'd definitely stir things up."

"Will this 'in your faces beyotches' response cause problems in your relationship with Jack?"

When she and Jack broke up, AJ could convince everyone she'd seen it coming due to their divergent philosophies. "Maybe."

"Then what are you out?"

Nothing. Or everything.

"Just think about it. When will you be home?"

"Tomorrow."

"Good. Come over, I'll crack Cord's expensive tequila for you and we'll talk more. I love you, K. You're the best person ever. Don't believe differently."

"Love you too, and thanks."

She hung up and stared out the window again.

Hell. Maybe AJ was right. If Keely McKay was going out, maybe she should go out with a bang instead of a whimper.

Chapter Nineteen

Keely was twenty minutes late for the pre-dinner cocktail party. Not intentionally—it'd been difficult finding a parking place big enough for her truck. She'd wound up on the bottom level of the parking garage. Again. Not a good sign.

Wrong. You've got no place to go but up.

True. With each step into the hotel her inner cheerleader kept up a brisk, *You can do this! You can do this!* She was doing it; she just wasn't sure how smart it was.

After she'd sauntered in, the banquet room hushed in a collective pause she'd seen in movies.

Fuck 'em. Let 'em stare. This is the real me. Proud to be one hundred percent pure Wyoming cowgirl. If they didn't like it they could take a flying fuckin' leap. So could Jack.

Keely wore a pair of dark blue, skintight bootcut jeans with deerskin leather fringe running down the outer seam of each leg. The fringe made a cool *flap flap* noise as she walked. She'd threaded her rainbow crystal b.b. simon belt through the belt loops and tucked in her favorite baby blue camisole to showcase the horseshoe-shaped rhinestone buckle. Lastly she'd donned a vivid blue long-sleeved shirt, embroidered with cornflowers, finished off with pearl snap buttons. Her feet sported scuffed up ostrich skin Ariat boots.

Baxter Ducheyne approached her first and his piggy eyes slowly scrolled over her. She forced herself not to shudder at his leering smile. He thrust out his sausage-fingered hand. "Keely. Lovely to see you again."

"The pleasure is all mine, Baxter," she lied. "Have you seen Jack? I didn't meet many people last night after I left the dinner." *Thanks to your vomit-inducing wife.*

"I'm sure Jack's here someplace. Don't you worry. I'd be happy to introduce you around," Baxter assured her.

Keely oozed folksy charm. At one point, she realized a half dozen men surrounded her. A lanky man with a pronounced goiter and Fabio's flowing hairstyle had spoken to her. "I'm sorry, sugar, what did you say?"

"I-I wondered if you'd like a glass of wine?"

"Actually, I'm more of a beer girl."

Male chuckles.

"Did the hotel provide a full service cash bar tonight?"

"Umm...no. Sorry. Just wine."

"Snooty bastards. Nothin' wrong with beer and we are in Coors country after all."

More chuckles.

Keely placed her hand on Fabio-aka-Ichabod's arm. "Thanks for asking. I'd love a glass of ice water."

He beamed. "Be right back."

"I disappear for a few minutes and you've got someone else playing fetch and carry for you?"

Jack's sexy husky voice caused a ripple of desire. She turned; Jack's handsome, perfect face was right there. Green eyes rapt, full mouth curved into a smile. Without preamble, he pressed his soft, warm lips to hers, kissing her soundly.

Keely melted into him.

"You're stunning as always, cowgirl. Except I'm disappointed you're not wearing your lasso."

"I left it upstairs on the bed." She winked and hip-checked him. "For later."

More laughter. Man. She was on a roll.

"I see you've met some of my colleagues."

"Baxter was thoughtful enough to provide introductions to the gentlemen I missed last night."

"Now, Baxter, don't you be trying to steal another woman from me," Jack chided.

The guys in the group didn't know whether to laugh.

Baxter finally grinned. "If I would've known Keely was in your future, Jack, I might've waited to steal her instead."

"Nice to know I'm that expendable," Martine said drolly behind them.

"Martine. Sweetheart. You know we were joking," Baxter said, drawing her into the circle.

The others in the group scattered, leaving the four of them alone together.

Martine ignored Baxter, granting Keely a head to toe inspection. "How sad you thought this was a costume party, Kelly."

"It's *Keely*, not Kelly, but I'm sure at your age it's hard to keep names straight." Keely flashed her teeth. "And thank you for noticing my outfit, although these are my everyday clothes. No point in wearing my best duds when there's *no one* here I need to impress."

"I'm most impressed with you when you're wearing nothing at all," Jack mock-whispered.

She half-shoved him. "You are insatiable, Jack Donohue. Behave in public."

"Always, but never in private. If you'll excuse us, I need a minute alone with my beautiful bride-to-be." Jack steered her to an alcove that wasn't private in the least.

Keely smiled. "Surprised to see me?"

"Very." He curled his hand around her neck, stroking his thumb along her jawline before smooching her lips with softness and sweetness. "I'm very happy to see you."

"Yeah? What is on the agenda tonight?"

"Dinner, followed by a long, boring annual meeting. Then I take you up to the room and fuck you until you scream my name."

"Feeling confident?"

Jack frowned. "Never when it comes to you, buttercup."

Whoa. Not a response she'd anticipated.

"Let's mingle so we can get the hell out of here as soon as possible when it's over," Jack said.

During dinner they sat with a couple from Chicago, as well as Jack's other colleagues who'd ragged on him for his hermetic state in the last few years. Keely enjoyed herself more than she'd expected. Jack was attentive, not overtly obvious, but acting as if he genuinely cared for her.

She and Gina slipped out when the business meeting

started, intending to hit a downtown toy store. Since Gina had forgotten her purse in her room, Keely waited in a quiet reception area around the corner from the main bank of elevators.

The quiet didn't last long.

"Well, if it isn't the wannabe queen of the rodeo."

Keely counted to ten before she deigned to glance up from her cell phone. "Well, if it isn't Mrs. Ducheyne." *More like Mrs. Douchebag.*

"You think you're brave and cool showing up dressed like that?" A dismissive gaze flickered over her.

"Wow. You really have nothin' better to do than to try and harass me? Why do you care what I wear if I'm so inconsequential to you?"

"I couldn't care less. You're embarrassing yourself again."

"Sort of like your little pep talk in the bathroom was supposed to embarrass me? Did you believe your lies had the power to send me packing? Wrong. Wyoming women are made of sterner stuff."

"Tackier stuff for certain," she sniffed.

"Ooh, and it was so classy to have your jealous rant about Jack...in the crapper?"

"Jealous? I don't—"

"I don't know which we laughed about more, your ridiculous yarn about Jack bringing bimbos to this conference, or your bizarre belief Jack's still carrying a torch for you. Talk about being embarrassed for you, lady. Jack was over you three years ago."

"And how do you know that?" Martine snapped.

"Because Jack and I ended up together at my brother's wedding reception in Wyoming a month *before* you 'left' him for Baxter."

"You're lying."

Yep. But it served Martine right. "I've known Jack since I was sixteen, Mrs. Ducheyne. I found it...enlightening at our engagement party last month that his mother and brother knew zilch about you. If Jack couldn't be bothered to tell his family about your relationship, really, how important could you have been to him?"

Martine glared but she didn't storm off. Probably trying to

formulate a snarky comment about Keely's hair or clothes, since that was the extent of her insult repertoire.

"The truth is: it bugs the living shit out of you that you made a mistake dumping him. You can't help but compare sexy as hell Jack Donohue, to the stodgy, pudgy old timer you settled for. Especially when you see Jack is happy and successful without Baxter."

"Successful?" she sneered. "That's a stretch."

"Wrong. I'd bet your matronly purse Jack gets the Milford restoration project because I was there when he pitched it. They love him and they loved his ideas."

Her eyes turned shrewd. "You were there?"

"Yes. And besides that project, Jack is contracted for my historic building, a courthouse in Montana and two projects in Iowa. That's just through the end of this year."

"What do you mean 'my historic building'?" Martine demanded.

"Jack is supervising the restoration of a historical building which will house the rehabilitation clinic I'm opening in Moorcroft."

"A freebie for you? How charitable. I doubt he's spending much time on it since he's so...busy." She made quotes in the air with the word *busy*.

"Since he's been working out of our apartment in Sundance, it's not a long commute for him to Moorcroft."

"You're living with Jack in Wyoming?"

"Didn't know that, did you?"

Martine's face darkened.

"Jack and I have a history. We have a future. So I'll say this as simply as I can. Stay away from me. Stay away from Jack. If you ever corner me in a bathroom again? Be prepared for me to come out swinging."

The elevator pinged and Gina rounded the corner. Once she saw Martine she tried to backpedal. "Oh, sorry, I'll just wait over—"

"No, I'm ready for some fresh air." She walked away, head held high.

Inside the elevator car, Keely laughed. "What a pretentious bitch. I can't believe I almost let her get to me."

Gina said, "She scares me. She scares everybody in this

organization."

"Not me. Not anymore."

As Keely said it, she really believed it.

After she'd purchased gifts for her nephews and nieces, and a surprise for Jack, Keely returned to the hotel room. She had no idea how long Jack would be stuck in the meeting.

To kill time, she filled the garden tub and added scented oil. She slipped beneath the bubbles, sighing at the rare indulgence. Nestling her neck into a towel, she sipped the beer she'd liberated from the room fridge.

Keely blanked her mind to everything except the hot water caressing her skin. The soft popping of soap bubbles. The tart taste of the cold beer.

But her conversation with Martine bobbed to the surfaced like a rotten apple. She'd met plenty of people in her twenty-seven years who didn't like her. But always for a reason, not simply because she existed.

No, Martine doesn't like you because you have Jack.

What a laugh.

How much did it suck she was in love with a man she couldn't have? Sure, she could have him tonight, his body, his undivided attention, his sexual expertise. But come tomorrow morning, they'd say goodbye. He'd be gone for the next three weeks. During which the majority of her building remodel would be completed. During which he'd most likely be awarded the Milford project. During which she'd have a breakdown, knowing she'd never find a man who'd hold a candle to Jack Donohue.

In retrospect, that's what she'd always been afraid of—falling in love with him. It'd been easier to hate him.

"Now there's a pretty sight," Jack drawled.

Keely jumped. In the depth of her forlorn thoughts, she hadn't heard him come in. But she didn't open her eyes, not wanting him to recognize her melancholy.

"But what's put the frown on your face, buttercup?"

The thought of losing you. When I never really had you.

She absentmindedly waved the half-empty bottle at him. "I figure you'd be pissed when you saw me drinking a ten dollar beer out of the mini-bar."

"I can come up with an inventive way for you to pay me back."

"I'll bet." Keely swigged and let the bottle dangle by the outside of the tub. "How was the rest of your meeting?"

"Long and boring. Pointless. Did I mention long and boring?"

"Yes."

"How was your shopping excursion with Gina?"

"Expensive. Lord. Why do I have so many nephews and nieces? I limited myself to spending ten bucks on each kid and I still walked out two hundred dollars poorer."

"You love them and you're not really complaining."

Keely smiled. "How true."

"Would you rather I face you or sit behind you?"

That question made her eyes fly open. Oh wow. Jack was totally, gloriously, buck-assed nekkid. Totally, gloriously, buck-assed nekkid and fully aroused. And holding two beers. He really was the perfect man. She scooted forward, splashing water everywhere. "You can sit behind me."

"Somehow I thought you might say that."

Jack handed Keely the beer. When he stretched out in the tub, she was enveloped in his substantial presence—all muscles and heat and hot, hard man.

Definitely not getting over him any time soon.

She situated herself between his thighs. Her spine pressed into his chest. Her head seemed to fit in the curve of his neck perfectly.

He'd dimmed the overhead lights and the lamps from the bedroom offered a golden illumination. Had Jack meant the setting to drip of romance? Probably not.

Jack's free hand gently stroked her arm as it rested on the edge of the tub.

He sipped. She sipped. The water had cooled. She lifted her foot and cranked the hot water tap with her toes. After it'd warmed, she slumped back against him.

"What talented toes you have, Miz McKay."

"Only trick I can do with them, unfortunately."

"Pity. I was hoping you could juggle."

"Sadly, I never learned to juggle. How about you?"

"I used to juggle. Haven't tried it in years."

"I imagine it's a lot like riding a bicycle."

"Maybe."

"Would you try to juggle for me?"

"Would it turn you on?"

"Most likely. Everything you do turns me on, Jack." Dammit. Why had she said that?

"Then absolutely I'll juggle for you." Jack kissed the slope of her shoulder and her skin broke out in goose flesh. "Have I mentioned how much I love this section of your skin?"

He repeatedly dragged openmouthed kisses over the bared flesh. Prickles of goose bumps followed in the wake of his marauding mouth. "You're so responsive to me," he murmured.

"Jack. God. Stop."

"Stop?"

"For now. I really was liking bein' nekkid with you in the tub, relaxing, drinking our very tasty, very expensive beer."

"Mmm. Me too." Jack flicked his tongue up the cord in her neck. "But once the beer is gone, you're mine."

Promise?

Dammit, Keely. Don't go there.

For a long while they didn't speak, just continued floating together in relaxation.

"Tell me what you're thinking," Jack said softly.

"I'm thinking about you."

"What about me?"

"That there's a lot I don't know about you."

"Ask me anything." He pressed a kiss by her temple. "My life is an open book for you."

Keely bit back the obvious *How do you feel about me?* question and blurted, "Have you traveled to Europe since your career is all about studying architectural details?"

He skimmed his fingers across the surface of the water. "No, I haven't. Never really wanted to, to be real honest."

"Why not?"

"I travel a lot as it is. So for me, the perfect vacation wouldn't involve any travel. No sightseeing. None of that typical tourist stuff."

"You'd prefer one of those 'stay-cations' people on the

coasts talk about?"

"Spending a week in my condo would never be considered a vacation," he said dryly.

"Your bed is comfy."

"I'd be all over a stay-cation if you were in my bed for a solid week, cowgirl."

Keely nipped her teeth into his jaw. "Smartass. I'm serious. So...since we're pretending to be engaged, where would you take me on our pretend honeymoon?"

"A private island. Where the sun is hot, the sand is soft, the water is warm and clothing is optional. There's no one around but us. Two solid weeks of alone time, doing whatever struck our fancy."

"I'd be well versed in getting sand out of my ba-jingo."

"*Ba-jingo?*" Jack murmured in her ear. "I knew you watched TV. Eliot on *Scrubs* is the only one I've ever heard use the word ba-jingo."

She smiled. "Busted. After AJ married Cord, I spent hours wallowing in reruns on TBS and figuring out what to do with my life."

His throat muscles worked as he swallowed a drink of beer. "Is that when you came up with the idea for a clinic?"

"Sort of. I started traveling with the sports medicine team on the rodeo circuits. The rehabilitation aspect appealed to me, but long term, not short term. It was great practical experience. Not only did I earn college credits, it was sheer heaven putting my hands all over hot cowboys and going to the rodeo for free every night." Jack snarled softly and she loved that he was jealous. "But I didn't really put it all together until after Cam's war injury."

Jack's wet fingers trailed up her arm. "I know Cam's experience was hard for the whole family, but Carter indicated it was rougher on you. Is that true?"

"Yeah." Keely swigged the last liquid from the bottle and set it aside. "Not only because I lived with him and helped him get back on his foot—ha ha—after he returned from Iraq. See, Cam and I have always had an unusual bond in that we both knew we'd never be part of the McKay ranching operation as adults. Cam out of choice; me out of gender."

He stilled. "Your dad cut you out of your ranch heritage

because you're a woman? Jesus, Keely, that's archaic. And how the fuck is that fair to you?"

She curled her free hand over his, surprised by his vehemence on her behalf. "It's not like that."

"Then explain how it is. Because before my dad died, even when he knew I'd never take over the farm, he gave me the choice. Sounds like Carson isn't giving you that same option."

"I do have a stake in the McKay Ranch, smaller than my brothers'. Which it should be because I don't help with day-to-day operations. I draw a salary from the profits, if there are any. I take the minimum amount and leave the rest of the cash for operations. Cam is the same. So is Carter, although, because Carter lives in Sundance half the time, he's more involved."

Jack squeezed her hand. "But where does that leave you?"

His sweet concern allowed her to be honest about the situation, maybe for the first time. "It leaves me looking for my place in the family and in the community. Buying the building was the first step to being on my own as an adult. As Keely McKay, proprietor of a medical establishment, not Keely McKay, unfocused wild child."

"Does that moniker bother you?"

"Not anymore. It's not who I am. I did what I did. Reap what you sow, blah blah blah. Some of it was stupid, but nothin' worse than anything anyone else my age was doing." She laughed. "There were bets I'd be pregnant by a cowboy and married by seventeen, divorced by nineteen, remarried to another cowboy by twenty-one. I'd squeeze out a couple more kids, end up divorced again, and about the time I turned twenty-five, I'd settle down with a local rancher my parents approved of. Of course, no one knows the ins and outs of our family line of ranch succession. Even if I do marry a rancher, he'd better have his own spread because he won't get an inch of McKay land."

"Not even if he's married to a McKay?"

"Nope. All male succession, remember? So the direct descendants, my dad and uncles, had to legally change everything so the ranch stays a patriarchal line after I was born."

"So you get nothing?" Jack demanded.

"I got everything," she said quietly. "I got to grow up on the most beautiful place on earth surrounded by all the people I love. I still can traverse any part of McKay land any time I want. But as far as me ever getting controlling interest in the McKay Ranch? Won't happen." Keely shivered because the water was getting cold. "So I always wondered if the cowboys were sniffing around me because the biggest part of my feminine appeal was my connection to the McKay land."

Jack set his beer bottle aside and curled his hand around her jaw, forcing her to look at him. "Rest assured. Your appeal is not due to your family name or some piece of Wyoming dirt."

"Really?"

"Really. It's you, cowgirl. Plain and simple. And I'm not after your land."

"What are you after, Jack?" *Please say my heart.*

"This." Jack kissed her. "And this." A deeper kiss with a lingering caress down the center of her body. "And especially this." His hand floated back up to circle her breasts.

The more he kissed her the more difficult the connection was to maintain. Jack flipped her to face him, splashing water up the wall and over the rim of the tub. He straddled her across his lap and wrapped her legs around his waist. Slick skin against slick skin. Mouth on mouth. The kisses were long. Slow. Wet. Endless. And perfect. This man knew just how to touch her. Knew how to read all sides of her.

Jack unclipped her hair and combed his fingers through the strands, letting the ends drift on the water. "Don't ever cut your hair. It's beautiful."

"Same goes." She fingered the wet tips of his hair. "I love that you wear it a little long. It's very bad boy sexy for such a suit and tie wearing professional."

"Then long it stays." His hungry lips slipped down her wet neck as he sipped the water from her skin. "Keely. I need you. I needed you last night, but I..."

"I'd never say no to you, Jack."

"I know that. You don't say no to me even when you should." More sweet kisses. More scorching kisses. More sweeping touches. More urgency. Jack said, "Lift up."

Keely gripped the edges of the tub and raised her body. She lowered onto his shaft bit by bit, dragging out the mutual pleasure until his male hardness filled her. When they were locked together, body to body, soul to soul, breathing the same humid air, everything seemed right.

It was rare for her to gaze into Jack's face from a higher vantage point. She couldn't stop the awed, "Damn, GQ. You are one beautiful man."

His hand shook as he pushed damp tendrils from her cheek. "Not like you, Keely. You undo me. Every time I look at you."

"Show me." She smoothed her hands over his neck and strong shoulders as she moved on him. Held him. Watched him. Wished he felt as...completed with her as she did with him.

Water sloshed everywhere as they rocked together. Came together.

After they'd dried off and slipped between the sheets, Keely understood this really was the end.

Early the next morning, they were subdued as their parting of ways loomed.

Jack helped Keely load her packages and luggage into her truck. Saying goodbye in the parking garage seemed anticlimactic after all they'd been through. Especially since they'd reached for each other twice during the night, not knowing who'd made the first move, not caring, just rejoicing in every touch.

"Come here," Jack said gruffly.

Keely walked straight into his arms without hesitation.

"Drive safe."

"I will."

"Good." Jack kissed the top of her head. "I'll call you after I get to—"

"No."

"What?"

She shook her head and buried her face in his neck, inhaling the dark, familiar scent, wondering if it'd be the last time she'd ever be this close to him. "Don't call me."

"Why not? You don't mean that."

"Yes, I do."

"Keely—"

"I need to wean myself from you, Jack."

A bewildered pause. "Why?"

"I've gotten too used to having you around. In my bed. In my life. We knew this wasn't permanent. Dragging this out will just be harder for both of us."

"I'm just supposed to do what? Walk away from you?"

"Yes."

"Think about what you're saying, buttercup."

"I have. I am. Go back to thinking of me as a client. Better yet, don't think of me at all. Just...go back to hating me."

Jack was silent as his hand stroked the back of her head, over and over, with such gentleness she couldn't stop from melting into him.

Keely whispered, "Be safe. I'll see you on the jobsite in a couple of weeks." She kissed the hollow of his throat and turned away without meeting his gaze.

Or without looking back in her rearview mirror as she headed home to Wyoming where she belonged.

Chapter Twenty

Three weeks later...

"Aunt Keely, how come you're so sad?"

She forced herself to answer Liesl with a half-truth. "I'm not sad. Just tired. And thinking about—"

"Uncle Jack?"

Keely froze. Uncle Jack. Man. That sounded weird. And yet, not weird at all. She managed a smile for her inquisitive niece. "No. I'm thinking about how long it's been since we've had a girl's night. You, Eliza and me. We could paint our fingernails, watch *Hannah Montana* now that I have cable. Eat Oreos and have burping contests. Whaddya say?"

"All right! But I still think you're sad. I think Uncle Jack needs to come home and kiss you because that always makes you happy."

"Liesl. Leave Aunt Keely alone," Domini said. "Take Oxsana outside with you and go play with your brothers."

"But I don't wanna go—"

Domini pointed to the sliding glass door. "Fresh air, girls. Now."

Liesl sighed and grabbed Oxsana's hand. "Mommy said we should make mud pies."

As soon as the door closed, Keely grinned. "She's gonna give you guys fits when she hits her teens."

"I know. Cam is already nervous." Liesl smacked her floured hands into a glob of dough on the counter. "But is my intuitive daughter right? Are you sad because you're missing Jack?"

"I do miss him. What sucks is that's part of his job and he'll always be gone." She scowled. "Or I'll have to go with him, which will be damn near impossible once the clinic is up and running."

Jack had called from wherever the hell he was late last night. She'd fumbled with the phone and cursed at the dead air, until Jack's voice, barely audible, rasped, "Can't believe I missed you swearing at me, cowgirl." Then he'd hung up. Or maybe she'd dreamed the whole damn thing.

Domini's hands stopped kneading. "Are you rethinking your relationship with him?"

"Yes. No. Who knows? I'm just tired. Although I love the work and the people in Cheyenne, the drive is getting old."

"How much longer will you be working at the VA?"

"A month or two. Depending on my cash flow situation with the building." Depending on if Jack kicked her out of the apartment after they officially called it quits.

"I recognize that 'back off' look, as your brother often wears the same one. But if you need to talk, Keely, I'm always here for you."

"Same goes." Keely snatched a cookie. "Speaking of talking...any luck convincing Cam into letting you adopt all the needy children in the world so you two can be nominated for sainthood?"

Domini flicked flour at her. "Smarty. He's considering it."

"That's it?"

"No." Domini sighed. "I get what Cam's saying about us having enough kids."

"But...?"

"But when the woman running the orphanage in Romania called me and emailed me the videos with those two poor darlings..." Domini bit her lip and looked away, struggling to keep her tears from splashing in the bread dough. "Sorry."

"Cam will come around, Domini. He's a softie. You guys are great, loving parents, what difference would two more kiddos make? It's not like you don't have family around to help you out."

"True. I think the fact Markus is only six months old freaks Cam out more than that the poor baby needs eye surgery." She sighed. "Plus, Markus's older sister, Sasha, is eighteen months old and if we do this, we'd have two kids in diapers again..."

"Investing in Huggies for the next three years isn't the issue, is it?" Keely said softly.

"No." Domini slammed her fist into the dough.

A bad feeling surfaced at seeing her normally docile sister in law so angry. "Domini. What's wrong?"

"Nothing is wrong with me, but what is wrong with other people? They can't have children so they decide to adopt and then they only want perfect children? Or just one cute infant?"

"Is there another couple interested in adopting Markus?"

"Yes. But *just* him. Not Sasha. And the director wants to keep the siblings together if possible, but if not, she'll have to split them up. I would never demand to separate siblings and that's what will happen if we don't act on this soon."

"Hey." Keely's eyes filled with tears when she saw the hopelessness in Domini's face. "Talk to Cam tonight. If you need me to watch the kids so you two can have alone time, I will. And when you decide to jet off to Romania to bring home your new additions, I will stay here and crack the whip on your four hooligans for as long as you need me to."

"You would do that for us?"

"Without hesitation. You're my family. It's the least I could do."

"What about Jack?"

Keely frowned. "What about him?"

"Don't you think he might have an issue with you living here for a few weeks?"

I may not have any other place to go. "I don't care if he has an issue with it." She briefly closed her eyes. "I'm afraid it won't be an issue at all, to be real honest, Domini. Please don't tell anyone, especially not Cam, but things aren't going well with me and Jack."

Domini placed a floury hand over hers. "Oh, I'm sorry. I wondered if that wasn't the case."

"Why?"

"Because Liesl is right; you do seem sad since you got back from Denver. And you also seem to be filling all your free time with McKay family activities. While we're grateful, we love you and we all love spending time with you, you deserve happiness of your own, Keely, in your own life. Whether it's here or in Denver, whether it's with Jack or someone else."

Keely looked out the door at the kids playing in the backyard. "I know. I just…" *Love him and he doesn't know it. And none of this was ever real. And even if it was, I don't think I could choose living with him over living around family,* "…wish Jack and I wanted the same things."

"Maybe it'll work out."

Fat chance. "Maybe. Thanks." Keely hopped off the stool. "Have fun hosing off your kids. Liesl and Anton are having a mud fight. Ooh, and look! Now the twins are slinging slop."

"Oh good Lord. What makes me think I can handle two more?"

"You love it and you guys wouldn't have it any other way."

The only thing running through Jack's mind as the outskirts of Sundance shimmered in the distance was, *Thank God.*

Aside from his father's death, the past twenty-three days had been the shittiest of his entire life. The projects had gone all right, although none of them would make him rich. Hell, he'd probably lose money when he added in his travel costs.

Which would fit in with the way his life was going. He'd about lost his fucking mind when forced to say goodbye to Keely in Denver. She'd turned him inside out with her teary, *don't call me* request. Pissed him off too. He'd managed to let her go, but only temporarily. It wasn't over between them. Not by a long shot.

When Jack returned to the hotel room, he noticed the small box of Legos Keely had hidden in his suitcase. With a note,

All work and no play makes Jack a dull boy. Remember to make time for fun. Love, your cowgirl.

He'd stared at the unopened package, blinking back tears. Keely knew him down to the bone, so how could she be so damn oblivious to the fact he'd fallen in love with her?

So during the last three weeks, to take his mind off all the things he missed about Keely, her fiery addictive kisses, her violation of his personal sleeping space, her uninhibited sexual response, her inventive curses, her absolute devotion to her family, her stupid country music, her gas-guzzling dirty-ass truck, her gentle insistence with her clients…he'd worked. But she was never far from his thoughts.

So Jack had broken down and called her. Just wanting to hear her voice. But it hadn't been enough. He'd booked the last flight out of Des Moines. When he'd landed at the Denver airport after midnight, he climbed in his car and had driven straight through.

To her.

The hell if they wouldn't have it out. They seemed to be at their best when they were fighting anyway. Jack just had to convince Keely they were worth fighting for.

Sundance resembled a ghost town at four in the morning. He dragged ass across the alley and fumbled with his keys, only to discover the outside door to the building hadn't been locked.

After he climbed the dark stairwell and reached the landing, he tried the door handle to the apartment. It turned easily. Dammit. Keely hadn't bothered to lock the door. Made him crazy she wasn't vigilant about security measures. Any creepy fucker could've waltzed inside and attacked her.

In Sundance? You've been living in the big city too long.

Jack inched the door open. No squeaking hinges. The apartment was black as pitch. He started toward the bedroom. But the hair on the back of his neck prickled, right before he caught movement in his peripheral vision. He dropped to the ground as air whooshed above him.

Keely shrieked, "Stay down motherfucker. I've got a gun and I will blow your head off!"

"Keely? What the fuck is wrong with you?"

Silence. Then an incredulous, "Jack?"

"Yes, it's Jack. Jesus Christ! You scared the living hell out of me."

"What are you doin' sneakin' into my apartment at four o'clock in the goddamn morning? You could've called."

"You told me not to call you, remember?" He pushed to his feet and squinted at the death grip she had on the item in her hand. "For fuck's sake. You swung a cast iron frying pan at my head? You could've killed me!"

"That was the point, asshole."

He growled. "Where's the goddamn gun?"

"On the kitchen table."

"Is it loaded?"

"Ah. No. I forgot I was out of shells."

"Lucky for me," he muttered. He took another step forward until he could see her face.

If Jack thought his heart was racing from the adrenaline rush of fear, it was flat lined compared to how it pounded being this close to Keely. For the first time in weeks.

The cast iron frying pan hit the floor with a thud and Keely launched herself at him. "Jack, you sneaky bastard."

"Keely, you psycho redneck."

Then her mouth was on his, making a mockery of every passionate kiss they'd shared before that moment. When she twined herself around him, as if trying to climb inside his skin, Jack actually believed she might love him.

"Touch me. Put your hands all over me. It's been so long. God, Jack, I've been dying for you. Please."

He lifted her and she circled her legs around his waist, kissing him like crazy, running her hands through his hair as he carried her into the bedroom.

Keely broke her mouth free and whispered kisses along his jaw, her hands tugging at his throat. "You and these ties, GQ. Makes it hard to get nekkid fast."

Jack laughed softly. "You and these flannel pajamas, cowgirl. Makes it easy to get naked fast. I want the ugly things off you."

"I didn't have you here to keep me warm."

"I'm here now." He flashed her a wolfish grin. "Off."

She stripped. He stripped.

He tackled her to the bed. Pinning her arms above her head, he moved between her thighs.

"Jack. I..."

His body stilled. Keely looked so serious. "What, buttercup?"

"I-I missed you."

He smiled. "I missed you too." He flexed his hips and thrust inside her.

Oh hell yeah. She was hot and wet and perfect. And his. And damn why did he feel like he was finally where he belonged?

"You feel good." She nuzzled his collarbone. "You always feel good on me. In me."

His mouth reconnected with hers. Teasing. Tasting. He fucked her leisurely, but with intent. Wanting to draw it out, but also needing that rush of unparalleled pleasure as he poured himself into her.

Keely met him thrust for thrust. Kiss for kiss. When she writhed beneath him, squeezing his cock with her pussy muscles, he slammed in, giving it to her harder. She arched her neck, gasping his name as she started to come.

Jack couldn't tear his eyes away from her face, so beautiful lost in passion. He rode out the storm with her. His hips pistoning, back straining, balls tight, skating closer to ecstasy with each fast plunge...but it was Keely's openmouthed kiss on his chest that kicked him over the edge.

It was Keely's loving touches that brought him back to reality.

She murmured, "Next time I'll whip out the rolling pin."

He laughed.

They pulled back the covers and crawled between the sheets. Keely wiggled until they were close enough to breathe the same air. A wiggling, hot, naked woman rubbing soft, warm, sexy body parts on him didn't relax him in the least.

Jack brought her on top of his body and whispered, "Again." He took his time licking and sucking and caressing every delectable inch of her body. This climb to pleasure was longer, sweeter, but more intense as they scaled the heights together.

Afterward, spent and wrapped in each other, Jack murmured, "First thing tomorrow we need to have a serious talk, okay?"

"Jack, I need to—"

He kissed her. "Tomorrow."

Jack woke alone. No wonder Keely was gone; the clock read ten a.m. She'd left a note, letting him know she'd gone to Moorcroft.

After he showered and dressed, he checked his phone for messages. Damn. He'd missed a call from Henry. The voice mail merely asked Jack to call Henry at his earliest convenience.

This was it. Jack dialed and paced until the call was picked up. "Henry, Jack Donohue."

"Jack," Henry said flatly.

That didn't bode well. "I received your message. I take it the committee has made a decision?"

"Yes. We've decided to go with BMD, Baxter Ducheyne's company."

Jack slumped forward as if a machete had been driven into his back. "I see. As I spent a considerable amount of time and money pitching this project, I am curious to know why you went with Baxter."

Silence.

"Henry?"

"Well, it came to the attention of the committee you hadn't been forthcoming about a few business things, quite frankly, that disturbed us."

"Such as?"

"I don't really feel it's appropriate—"

"Wrong. If the committee is questioning my business practices, I have a right to know what's being questioned."

"First off, you were aware when you originally bid this project we interviewed morally sound, family type companies to entrust with our project. We reconsidered yours when we learned of your engagement. However, we were not aware of your...living situation with Miss McKay."

"Living situation?"

"Come now, Jack, aren't you and Miss McKay are living together in Sundance?"

Jesus. "You're awarding the contract to Baxter solely because I stay with Keely, the woman I plan to marry, in the building I own, rather than in a hotel, when I travel to Wyoming?"

"No, not solely on that, but it is a fact we can't ignore, nor can we condone. It's also been brought to our attention that there is some...shall we say, nepotism at work?"

"Okay. Henry. You've lost me."

"Are you, or are you not, supervising a remodeling project for Miss McKay?"

"Yes. But what bearing—"

"Come now, Jack, you can't expect us to believe it wouldn't be in your best interest, as well as your fiancée's, for you to automatically sign off on all building changes for her project, regardless if those changes meet the state historical standards?"

Fury shot through him. "Where in the hell did you hear that?"

"Do not curse at me, young man. I am merely relating the facts as they've been presented to me."

"By whom?" Jack asked through clenched teeth.

"That is irrelevant."

"By whom," Jack repeated. "If my professional reputation is being examined, I have a right to know who is attempting to malign it. It is your moral obligation to tell me, is it not?"

Henry sighed. "Baxter Ducheyne's company pitched to us. In the two days Baxter and his lovely wife Martine spent in Milford, she revealed a few disturbing things, including your past relationship with her. Martine questioned whether you'd follow through with your wedding to Miss McKay, given your inability to commit to her during the year you were together in Chicago. She also mentioned you immediately dissolved the partnership with Baxter and moved across the county *before* she married your partner."

Jack seethed. Too angry to speak.

"Baxter brought up the ethics of your company signing off with the Wyoming Historical Society on Miss McKay's building, especially since the two of you are intimately involved."

Unreal. This was a fucking nightmare.

"Imagine our surprise when Mrs. Ducheyne asked if we'd agreed to consider western artwork projects from Miss McKay's brother. I believe you mentioned him to us as a possible sculptor for our city square project, did you not?"

"Yes. But Carter McKay—"

"Will possibly be your brother-in-law, so you can see the committee's point of view about another case of nepotism, Jack. With all of these...incidences staring us in the face, I'm sure you understand why we had concerns."

"I'm sure *you* can understand why I would feel Mrs. Ducheyne's information to you would be biased, based on my past history with her. How she came across information about—"

"I suggest you speak with your fiancée, Mr. Donohue,"

Henry said coolly. "Mrs. Ducheyne stated Miss McKay freely relayed this information to her, during a business conference in Denver a few weeks ago."

Jack froze.

"In addition, your fiancée boldly claimed you had this restoration project wrapped up. Baxter was mightily upset, understandably so, as he hadn't the opportunity to pitch us his ideas yet."

He couldn't think of damn thing to say.

"Rest assured, this information about your company will stay confidential among the committee members. Good-bye Jack and good luck."

Henry hung up.

That big-mouthed cowgirl had fucked him over.

What goes around comes around.

Infuriated, he headed for Moorcroft.

Keely couldn't believe how fast the building was shaping up. In another month, the clinic could open for business.

The door slammed and Jack barreled in.

Speaking of dream fulfillment...Keely intended to tell Jack she loved him, hoping the last piece of the puzzle of her life would fit into place.

But Jack wasn't wearing the soft look of a man in love. Jack was absolutely infuriated. And he got right in her face.

"Did you tell Martine we were living together?"

Weird way to start a conversation. "Yes, but—"

"Did you also tell her I had the Milford restoration project 'wrapped up'?"

"I don't think I said 'wrapped up' but I told her the committee liked your concept—"

"Jesus fucking Christ, Keely, do you have any idea what the fuck you've done to me? You've torpedoed my goddamn career!"

Before Keely defended herself, Jack went off on a tangent.

"I trusted you. And how did you repay that trust? By fucking me over. Big time. Because Martine somehow hurt your poor little feelings, you just had to open your big mouth and one-up her, didn't you? By telling her we were living together. By telling her I had the Milford project in the bag. By taunting her that I offered to marry you, when I hadn't offered to marry her."

"But I didn't—"

"Well, guess what, cowgirl? That offer of marriage is off the fucking table for good."

Keely's stomach roiled.

"Now, not only did I lose the goddamn Milford project, my ethics are in question." Jack jabbed a finger at his chest. "*My* ethics. Do you know how fucking hard I've worked to keep my reputation impeccable? Now I'm being accused of nepotism."

"Nepotism?"

"Don't play stupid. Baxter and Martine are questioning whether I should even be allowed to sign off on this project for you since we're intimately involved. What do you think the odds are the next call they make is to the Wyoming Department of Historic Preservation? I could get my fucking certification pulled! And if I'm pulled in one state, what do you think the odds of me getting pulled in every other state are? Pretty much fucking guaranteed.

"Not only that, you told Martine about Carter? How the fuck do you think that makes me look? Not to mention your brother? Yes, I suggested the Milford committee consider hiring Carter to do a couple of bronzes. Now, I'm being accused of nepotism again, and Carter is going to lose out on a potentially huge fucking commission. Because of you. How do you think he'll react when he finds out you fucked this up for him? You think he'll be so goddamn eager to leap to his baby sister's defense every fucking time I turn around?"

Don't cry. Don't cry. Jesus, Keely, stay Wyoming tough.

"Don't have anything to say for yourself?"

She swallowed hard. Her voice came out softer than usual. "What do you want me to say, Jack? You've got it all figured out. Got all the blame placed. Good for you. Must be nice to be so fucking perfect. So goddamn...smug and self-righteous. But the main thing you're forgetting? Maybe the Milford committee had every right to call your ethics into question."

He bit off, "What. The. Hell. Are. You. Babbling. About."

"You set up a fake engagement with me—a woman you

professed to hate—just to get a crack at their project. And blame me all you want for *your* ex-girlfriend having such a big mouth and blabbing your sordid past personal history so *your* ex-partner could fuck you over in front of a supposed professional organization, but it's bullshit and you know it. The bottom line is this: you'd already lost any chance at the contract *before* you decided to shitcan your ethics and pull one over on the committee. You were so fucking desperate to spit in their eye when they didn't consider you good enough or moral enough to even be considered for their precious fucking project. Did I go along with this charade because I wanted something from you? Yes. Do I feel guilty? No. Because of me and this stupid fake fucking engagement *you* concocted, you actually had a shot at getting that all-important, career-boosting, fucking over Baxter and Martine project. Whereas, before, you didn't. And maybe it's irony or poetic justice or whatever you wanna call it that you're exactly in the same fucking position now as you were two months ago: no chance in hell of getting what you want."

Jack laughed harshly. "Listen up and listen good. I won't be the only one who doesn't get what I want in this fucked up situation, because there's no way in hell I'm ever signing off on this building project, Keely. No. Fucking. Way."

"I expected nothing less of you, Jack-off." In angry, jerking movements, Keely tugged off the engagement ring and whipped at his feet as hard as she could. "You've got ten minutes to get the fuck off my property or I will call the cops."

Keely spun on her bootheel and left without looking back.

Jack picked up the ring and stared at it. He felt none of the vindication he'd expected. In fact, he felt sick to his stomach. Like he'd lost more than a job. He'd lost his dignity. His purpose. His morals. His way.

You lost your way a long time ago, buddy. And now you've lost the best thing that ever happened to you. Happy?

No. Fuck no. What was wrong with him?

Jesus. When had his life become such a fucked-up mess? Just when it'd seemed like everything he'd ever wanted was within reach? What kind of fucking moron slapped it away with both hands and harsh words?

He curled his fingers around the ring, half wishing she'd broken the damn thing and shards of metal would dig into his skin. Maybe then he'd feel something besides the utter desolation weighting him down like an anvil.

You did this to yourself. Everything word she said was true and like usual, you didn't want to hear it. Go to her. Go after her. Make it right. For both of you. Plead your case. Plead insanity. Just don't let this get any more out of hand.

The enormity of Jack's mistake sucked the breath from his lungs. And he'd accused her of having a big mouth? Jesus. Profound shame paralyzed him to the point his damn feet wouldn't move. He knew he needed to chase Keely down right fucking now. Apologize, grovel, cry, beg, crawl. He'd have his mouth surgically sewn shut to stop from ever spewing such vile bullshit again. He'd devote his life to worshipping her as she deserved. He'd show her a hundred times a day he loved her. If only she'd give him one more chance.

"You heard the lady. Get the fuck out."

Jack's head snapped up.

Chet and Remy West were standing side-by-side, fists clenched, postures screaming, *We're gonna kick your ass, dumb fucker.*

"How much did you hear?"

"Enough."

Silence.

"Fucking great."

"By my estimation you've got six minutes left. And trust me, you don't wanna be here when Cam McKay gets wind of this," Chet warned.

"Or Cord," Remy said.

"Don't forget Colby is one mean bastard," Chet added with a sneer.

Remy shrugged. "My money is on Colt."

"Carter's no slouch either. It's them quiet ones ya gotta worry about, huh bro?"

Jack got the warning loud and clear: quiet ones like Chet and Remy, not to mention Keely's father, would be gunning for him. Soon. "Look. If Keely comes back—"

"We'll hand your sorry ass to her on a silver fuckin' platter if you're stupid enough to stick around," Remy snarled.

"Five minutes," Chet snapped.

"I appreciate that you care about her, but don't kid yourselves for a second that I don't care about her too."

They snorted in stereo.

Which just pissed him off. "And honestly, this is between Keely and me, no one else, so I'm gonna say this once, and feel free to pass this on to all the McKays: back the fuck off."

"Four minutes," Remy announced.

Chet leaned forward. "I'll be honest. Part of me wants you to stick around."

Fuck this.

His body heeded the message to scram. He stormed out the door, half-shocked he hadn't felt a crowbar whacking him in the back of the head.

But that wasn't the West boys' style. Nor the McKays'. No, that psycho bunch of cowboys would come for him with a full frontal attack, no backstabbing bullshit like Baxter.

Jack welcomed it. In fact, he had half a mind to make some calls and get the whole fucking thing underway.

He had nothing else to lose.

Chapter Twenty-One

Keely didn't hang around to ensure Jack vacated the premises. Her tires spit gravel as she zoomed off in her truck. The cold, cutting wind from the open window cooled her face, but she couldn't blame the icy air for the numbness inside her.

Tempting, as she whizzed past the Golden Boot, to belly up to the bar and drown her sorrows. Too public. She'd deal with this humiliation in private.

She drove without direction, lost in her misery. She couldn't return to her apartment, which was really Jack's apartment. Neither would she burden her family. Part of her feared her brothers wouldn't let this situation with Jack slide, but an equal part feared her brothers were all male bluster.

Leaning on her parents wasn't happening either. Her mother would talk her ear off and her father wouldn't talk at all, so it was best to split the difference and avoid going home to the ranch.

Truthfully, it'd be best if she disappeared for a day or so to decide the best way to deal with the Jack issue.

Issue? What issue? You weren't in the wrong.

Not about the Milford situation. Jack had lashed out at her because he'd made a mistake and got caught. It sucked Baxter and Martine were so damn vindictive, but Keely figured they'd move on now, after giving Jack the smackdown. Besides, if Baxter called Jack's ethics into question, his might be questioned. From what Keely ascertained from other architects at the conference, Baxter's methods were already under scrutiny.

So despite the stinging accusation, Keely hadn't ruined Jack's professional reputation. But had she ruined any chance of them being together permanently? His claim the marriage offer was "off the table" confused her, now that she thought about it. Had he intended to make the offer for real? Jack had been purposely vague last night when he told her they needed to have a serious talk this morning.

Her grandmother's warning, *Never put off until tomorrow what you can do today,* rang in her ears. Good advice, but Keely feared it was too late.

She loaded up on camping supplies at the grocery store, successfully avoiding anyone she knew. Like any Wyomingite worth her salt, Keely already carried what passed for Wyoming emergency gear—a tarp, a knife, ammo, matches, jerky, a Chris LeDoux CD and a shovel, as well as an old sleeping bag—in her truck.

As she followed the twisty roads leading to the campground at the base of Devil's Tower, Keely realized it'd been months since she'd spent the night under the stars. She had no qualms about camping alone in a remote area. She had food. Water. A pistol. Most importantly, a don't-fuck-with-me attitude.

The campsite she'd chosen was far enough away she could see the entire monument rising up out of the trees like an ancient skyscraper. No wonder the laccolith had been—and still was—worshipped by the Native Americans as a holy place. The quiet power of the rock formation always gave her chills.

Keely set up camp. She had nothing but time on her hands and a whole lot to think about. But bone deep she knew what she wanted. She just needed to gather up the courage to go after it.

The next morning Jack was past crazy, on his way to certifiable. When he'd first pulled up to the apartment after he'd left Moorcroft, he half-expected to see his personal shit strewn in the alley from where Keely had heaved it out the window in a fit of rage.

As hours passed and she didn't come home and she didn't answer her phone, Jack paced to the point he pissed himself off. But he couldn't sit around with his thumb up his ass when he had no fucking clue where Keely had run off to.

Call her family; they'll know where to find her.

True, but the fact her brothers hadn't shown up guns blazing meant her family wasn't aware she'd taken off. Maybe he had a chance to correct the biggest mistake of his life, without any of the crazy-assed male McKays knowing Jack Donohue had done Keely wrong.

So, with nothing else to do but wait, Jack worked out. He did crunches until his stomach hurt. Then he did pushups until his arms wouldn't hold him up. He ran in place until his legs gave out. Covered in sweat, body aching, he fell on the floor and waited until the worst of the muscle cramps passed. Then he started all over again, adding chin ups to the mix. The third go around he added squats to his routine. He planned to add jumping jacks to the fourth set, but he laughed until he cried, knowing Keely would've gotten a big kick out of the play on words. Jack. Doing jumping jacks.

At that point in his delirium last night, he'd considered drinking until he passed out. But he feared Keely would come home and think he was a drunk as well as an asshole, so he'd scratched that idea.

When his stomach rumbled, he realized he hadn't eaten for over twenty-four hours. He shuffled to the kitchen and opened the refrigerator. What he saw on the top shelf almost made him weep.

A meatloaf. Mixed up in a glass baking dish, wrapped in tinfoil, ready to be popped in the oven. She'd gone out of her way to prepare his favorite food. He didn't know why he was so surprised. She was sweet. Funny. Thoughtful. Absolutely perfect for him. Keely McKay was everything he'd never wanted and everything he needed.

The enormity of his mistake increased exponentially with every minute of her absence. He'd do anything to spend his life with her. Move to Wyoming. Become a cowboy. Work on the family ranch. Hell, he'd even listen to that shitty country music she loved. Take her line dancing. Join her dart league. Impregnate her with all the kids she could handle. If she'd just come home.

Jack was so goddamn tired, physically from punishing his body to the point he could barely move. And the emotional beating he'd given himself was way worse.

Man up.

He dialed the only person who could help him. He barely

heard the phone ringing over the thumping of his heart. When the line was picked up, Jack blurted, "I did a dumb, stupid, asinine thing, which is all my fault and I need your help."

Talk about making him sweat. He'd made the phone call three hours ago. When he heard footsteps on the stairs, he forced himself to stay focused on the paper in front of him.

No knocking. The apartment door crashed open.

"It's about fucking time," he snapped, without turning around. "I know you're pissed at me, but Jesus, I'm worried about her—"

"You don't have a fucking clue how pissed we are."

We.

Jack turned around.

Holy fucking shit.

Cord, Colby, Colt, Cam and Carter McKay were spread out like a bunch of goddamn gunslingers.

"What the hell are you guys doing here?"

"What the hell do you think we're doing here?" Cord said.

"Trespassing on private property."

"So call a cop," Cam shot back.

Laughter.

"What's that in your hand, Donohue? Your last will and testament?" Carter asked.

"You're fucking hilarious. Why don't you all trot home to your wives because this doesn't concern you—"

"Wrong fucking answer. If it concerns Keely, it concerns us."

"Back off," Jack warned. "I'm handling it."

"And just how the hell are you 'handling' it?" Colt demanded. "Near as we can tell, she ain't here. She ain't been here all goddamn night, has she?"

"Have you talked to her?" he asked Colt.

"We talked to Chet and Remy. We know what went down."

Jack shook his head. "No, you don't."

"Then why don't you tell us why Keely threw her engagement ring at you and vanished?" Colby demanded.

"What happened is between Keely and me. Period." His

tired eyes sought Cord's. "AJ hasn't heard from Keely?"

"That's between Keely and AJ," Cord said.

"Besides, it ain't like you weren't warned about what we'd do to you if you fucked with her. We're here to make good on our promise."

The room seemed to shrink to the size of a dollhouse. Jack's whole body hurt. If even one of these psycho brothers came after him, he couldn't put up a decent fight, say nothing of taking on five pissed-off cowboys.

You deserve to get your ass handed to you. And it's going to happen either way.

"You know what? You're right. I don't know where the hell Keely is. I've been going crazy waiting for her to show up and yell at me or kick my sorry ass or something." He met each of her brother's gazes, one at a time. "That's why you're here, right? To kick my ass? So go ahead."

Carter stepped forward. "Remember you asked for this, Donohue."

The last thing Jack heard was a cracking sound as Carter's fist connected with his jaw...and then the lights went out.

Dusk started to fall when Keely recognized the crunch of tires on gravel. She kept the pistol within arm's length until she determined whether friend or foe approached. The smoke from the campfire switched direction, making her squint at the vehicle.

A truck. She quelled the disappointment it wasn't a BMW. Her pulse leapt when she realized it was Cord's truck.

AJ had come looking for her.

But all four doors of the quad cab opened. Colby emerged first. Followed by Colt. Cord and Cam came around the front end of the truck. Carter was the last one out.

Keely gaped at her brothers. All five of her brothers.

"You're a hard woman to find," Cord said.

Her gaze moved from face to face. She expected Cam would chew her out for taking off alone. Colby would comment she needed a babysitter. Colt would threaten to whup her butt. They did none of that. She finally looked at Carter, who'd stepped forward. "Hey, little sis. Looks like you need a friend or five."

The tears she'd kept at bay streamed down her cheeks. Keely ran straight into Carter's open arms. He caught her and squeezed. "It's okay. We're here for you."

"I can't believe you guys came." She sniffed when Cam grabbed her from Carter and hugged her tightly.

"I can't believe you thought we'd just let you be when you're hurting." Cam gave her a soft head butt and set her back on the ground. "You'd never let any of us get away with hiding, so what goes around comes around, little sis."

Then Colt scooped her up and swung her in a circle, like he used to do when she was little. "We ain't that easy to get rid of, if you haven't noticed." Colt practically tossed her to Colby.

"We McKays stick together. Although you ain't got a stem, you were born with balls. You're truck tough." Colby kissed her forehead and dropped her in front of Cord.

"Sometimes I think you're the toughest of us all. God knows you're the smartest." Cord hugged her and then smacked her ass. Hard.

"Hey!"

"You're damn lucky we didn't all swat you. You scared the crap out of us, Keely West McKay."

"Sorry. I needed time alone to think. A family trait you're all familiar with." She wandered back to the fire pit.

Her brothers followed and crowded around the fire. Colt and Colby crouched by the fire. Cord perched on a log. Cam and Carter stood, hands in pockets as they stared at the burning embers and the flames licking the pale night sky.

Cord spoke first. "What happened between you and Jack that sent you runnin'?"

"He didn't hurt you, did he?" This from Cam.

"No. We both said some pretty nasty, hurtful things to each other. Sometimes that's worse."

"So is it over?" Colby asked.

Keely stirred the embers, glad the heat in her cheeks could be attributed to the flames. "I don't know."

"Do you *want* it to be over?"

Her gaze connected with Colt's after he voiced that question. "No. God no. I think he probably does."

"We've already established he's a fucking idiot if he walks

away from you," Carter said. "I'm glad we—"

"Carter," Colby warned.

"What? I'm glad we figured out he's just as stubborn as her, that's all I'm saying."

A weird feeling rippled through her. "What are you guys talking about?"

"You. And Jack. Stubborn as all get-out, both of you. Didja ever try talkin' to each other? Instead of throwing insults and stompin' off mad as a wet hornet?"

Keely's mouth dropped open. She stared at Cord, who couldn't be considered chatty on his best day.

"She threw the engagement ring at him this time, not an insult, which tells me it's over for good."

Her gaze whipped to Cam. "How did you know I threw my engagement ring at Jack?"

"Chet and Remy."

And they claimed their word was their bond. She snorted. They'd gone tattling to her brothers fast enough. "When did you find out?"

"When you didn't show up at the building today. Doc Monroe told 'em you weren't at the clinic. You weren't answering your phone. They called everyone... Who'd they call first?"

Cord lifted his hand. "I reckon they started at the top of the birth order and worked their way down."

"They called all of you?"

"Yep."

"When was this?"

"One. Or thereabouts."

Damn. "How'd you find me?"

"AJ," they all said in unison.

"So what have you guys been doin' the last six hours?"

Guilty looks.

Her pulse spiked. "Oh. My. God. What did you do?"

"Now, Keely. You gotta understand. We warned Jack not to mess with you," Cam said amiably.

"He knew the risks and he hurt you anyway, which pissed us off," Colby added.

Colt nodded. "You know we ain't gonna let something like

that slide."

Fear, anger and shock all warred inside her. She forced herself not to scream to get to the bottom of what her crazy brothers had done to Jack. "What did you do to him?"

Carter studied her a minute before he spoke. "Would you care?"

"Yes! How could you think I'd...?" She inhaled, exhaled, amidst awful, bloody, violent scenarios racing through her mind. "Where is he?"

"He's a little tied up at the moment."

Every single one of her brothers started laughing.

Not good. Not good at all. "Tell me where Jack is right fuckin' now or I will call every one of your wives and round up my own McKay posse to track him down. I ain't kiddin'."

More exchanged looks. Something passed between Cam and Carter. They stood, along with Colt, and walked to the back of Cord's truck bed.

The grunting noises were loud in the stillness. Dragging, scraping sounds echoed. Hissed breaths.

Keely couldn't see the action. She gasped when her brothers struggled into her line of sight carrying a bulky form. A six-foot-four, muscular form they dropped on the ground, none too gently. A form that was blindfolded, gagged, with arms and legs tied.

Holy fucking shit. That trussed up form was...Jack.

"Omigod! Please tell me you didn't kill him!"

"Jesus, Keely. Give us some credit. If we woulda killed him, you never would've known," Colby said.

"Yeah, we definitely wouldn't have brought the body here," Cam scoffed.

She glared at him. Before she could move or speak or do anything, another pickup barreled up and skidded to a stop. When the dust cleared she realized it was her father's pickup.

Carson McKay got out of his truck. His impassive gaze swept over his sons and then landed on Jack. His mouth tightened. "What in the hell is wrong with you boys?"

Silence.

"Cut him loose. Now."

Cord crossed his arms over his chest. "Dad, we were just—"

"Jesus Christ. I'll do it." He whipped out a Bowie knife and knelt in the dirt to saw off the binding around Jack's ankles. Then he cut the ties around Jack's wrists. Colt swore and helped her father pull Jack upright when he couldn't move the big man by himself.

When Keely started toward Jack, Carson stepped between them. "You can go to him in a minute, okay?" He threw up his hands as he addressed his sons. "I don't know what kind of shit you boys are pullin', but I raised you better than that. What were you thinkin'?"

"We were thinkin' it was his goddamned fault she was gone," Cam snapped.

"We ain't gonna stand by and let him treat her that way," Colt said stubbornly. "You raised us to protect her."

"If you haven't noticed, Keely ain't exactly six years old anymore. She's old enough to make up her own damn mind about when she needs protection and who she wants it from."

"Are you taking Jack's side?" Carter demanded.

"No, I'm takin' Keely's side."

Keely's head spun. Was she having an out-of-body experience? Or was she just in the throes of a bizarre dream? Had her brothers really kidnapped Jack? And dragged him out here like some kind of trophy for defending her honor? Instead of her father high-fiving them, he was chewing collective ass?

"Don't get me wrong. I understand where you're all comin' from. I thought about flaying the skin offa Jack a piece at a time myself. But the bottom line is Keely chose Jack. He might not be the one you'da picked or I'da picked for her. Jack might be dumb as shit, but we've all been there. Complete and total dumbasses when it comes to the women in our lives. None of us can claim we didn't make a mistake or two. But we've managed to figure out how to fix 'em on our own, and I've gotta give Jack the benefit of the doubt and allow him the same chance with Keely."

She bit her lip, surprised she had the urge to weep within this cloud of testosterone.

"Girlie, tell your brothers goodnight." He turned his back on his sons and crouched by Jack.

Grumbles. Curses. But Carson McKay had said his piece and his word was law.

Cam gave Keely a hug. "If you change your mind and

decide to shoot him, I can get you off on a self-defense charge."

"Thanks, Cam. But that won't be necessary."

Colby pressed a jar into her hand as he kissed her forehead. "This'll help with his sore muscles. Not much good on bruises, though."

"Bruises? What the hell did you guys do—"

"What we thought was right," Colt said, holding her tight. "Can't blame us for looking out for you, Keels, because we love you."

She swallowed the lump in her throat. "You're gonna make me cry."

"As long as they're happy tears, I don't mind. I mostly recognize the difference now." Cord wrapped her in a one-armed hug and mumbled, "Call AJ tomorrow."

"I will." Keely faced a hangdog Carter.

"You deserve the best, K. We'd do anything for you, don't you know that? I feel so damn guilty because Jack is my friend. I brought this on you—"

Keely wrapped her arms around him and whispered, "No, Carter, you brought him *to* me. Thank you."

He pecked her on the cheek. "In that case, you're welcome. And tell him I'm sorry about his jaw."

She didn't even ask what the hell that was about.

Her heroic, but slightly misguided brothers loaded up in Cord's truck and were gone. She didn't move until after the dust settled.

The fire had died down. Keely stoked it, gathering her thoughts before she wandered to where her dad and Jack sat, speaking in low tones.

Jack wouldn't look at her. His elbows rested on his knees. He'd aimed his face at the ground.

"Daddy, how did you know—"

"About your brothers goin' all vigilante? I didn't. 'Cause I sure wouldn't've condoned it. Jack called me earlier this morning and admitted he'd screwed up with you big time. He asked if I'd help him find you. Evidently, before I made it to your apartment, the boys showed up and took matters into their own hands. AJ called me because she knew something was up."

"She also felt guilty because she told Cord where she

thought I might be hiding out, huh?" Keely asked.

"That too." He sighed. "Look. I've given Jack a hard time since you came home wearin' his ring. I stopped questioning how he felt about you after he asked me to see to getting up a teardown party for your building."

She froze. "Jack set that up? Not you?"

"Yep. He didn't want credit. He just wanted it done and wanted you happy. That told me a lot about the kind of man he is."

"I know a little about picking good men, since I've been surrounded by them my whole life."

"I never doubted how you felt about him, punkin, I just never thought he could handle you. Now I see he handles you just fine."

Keely heard Jack snicker.

"And I also realize you ain't a little girl and I oughta butt out of your life."

"Whatever you did, you did out of love, Daddy, not spitefulness, not meanness. I hope the day never comes that you butt completely out of my life."

He smiled. "Never thought I'd hear you say that." He looked over at Jack. "Takes a big man to admit his mistakes and ask for forgiveness, Keely. Remember that. Jack might be dense, but he ain't dumb." He gathered her in a fierce hug and whispered, "Does he make you happy?"

She whispered back, "When he's not making me crazy."

"Then I reckon everything will turn out fine."

Carson McKay climbed in his truck and roared off, leaving her and Jack alone.

Her nerves were strung tight as she erased the distance between them.

Finally, Jack lifted his chin and looked at her.

Keely's heart turned over with love and her belly knotted with pain. She dropped to her knees in the dirt in front of him. "Holy hell, GQ. What did they do to your beautiful face?"

"Carter punched me." Jack ran his fingers across the lump that hurt like a motherfucker. "Hit me hard enough to knock me out so I don't know what the hell else the McKay posse did to me while I was at their mercy. I will say it took all five of them to take me down." His eyes searched hers. "Is it bad?"

Keely's soft fingers traced his stubbled jawline. "No. You're a sight for sore eyes, Jack Donohue."

He circled his hand around her wrist and kissed her palm. He touched her cheek. "Keely. I love you."

She didn't move. She didn't appear to breathe. Neither did she look away.

"I'm sorry. I had no right to yell at you for telling me the truth about my shortcomings, personally and professionally. I had no right to blame you for anything. Or to embarrass you. I don't know if I can ever apologize enough."

"Keep goin'."

Cowgirl speak. She was nervous, which surprised him, because he was nervous as hell too. "You were right about so many things. I never should've gone after the Milford project. I was compromising who I was to make a lousy buck." He smiled and winced when it hurt. "Okay, it was a lot of lousy bucks. But my personal life should have no bearing on whether I measure up in the restoration arena. I've been living in that shadow of bitterness and one-upmanship for years. But you've taught me it doesn't matter as long as I can look at myself in the mirror every morning and be happy with the man I see. At the risk of sounding incredibly fucking sappy, when I look in your eyes, I see the man I've always wanted to be."

Keely didn't bother to hide her tears.

"So, as sorry as I am that we went through all that fake engagement stuff so I could make a deal, I'm not one bit sorry because it led me to you."

"Jack—"

"Let me finish. I love you. I've been happier these last two months than I've ever been in my life. For the first time in my life, my happiness doesn't have a damn thing to do with work. It has everything to do with you. Being with you has changed me. Changed my life. You are my life, cowgirl."

She kissed him in a fiery melding of lips that made his mouth ache. Wait. His mouth really did ache. He pulled back and whispered, "Careful."

"Sorry."

"Just be gentle, okay? I'm a little more fragile right now than I'm used to."

Keely placed tender kisses on his swollen lips. The bump on his jaw. The scrapes on his neck and cheek. She leaned back to look in his eyes. "I oughta kill my brothers for messing up this pretty face I love so much, but I'm glad they brought you to me."

"Is it just my face you love?"

"No. It's all of you I love. Your smart side. Your smartass side. Your sweet side. Your sour side. Your take charge side."

"Good to know."

"And as much as you've had time to reflect, so have I. I want to be with you, Jack, no matter where you are. If that means a move to Denver, then so be it."

"I'd never ask you to move away from your family, Keely. I know how big a of part of your life they are. I love that they're part of your life. They're a very large part of who you are."

"You are my life now, Jack. Remember when I said anywhere you are is my home? I meant it."

Jack was almost more choked up about Keely's willingness to follow him anywhere than he'd been when she'd told him she loved him. "You're finally achieving your dreams here; I won't yank you away from them. We'll figure it out. It'll take lots of compromise, but I admit...I'm finally seeing the appeal of living in Wyoming."

Her eyes lit up. "Really?"

"Yes. But you'll never get me in a pair of cowboy boots. Never."

Keely smoothed her hand up his thigh. "I'd love to see you nekkid except for a pair of fringed chaps, GQ."

"Ditto, cowgirl mine. Come up here." His muscles protested when he lifted her and settled her on his lap. Her legs dangled behind him on the log.

"Did my brothers really beat the shit out of you?"

"No. I beat up on myself. I was frustrated about how I mishandled everything and I worked out to the point of muscle exhaustion. Which is probably why I didn't defend myself when Carter came after me. I couldn't even lift my damn arms."

"Poor baby. I'll give you a deep tissue massage." Keely toyed with his hair. "So since Chet and Remy overheard our fight, does everybody know our engagement wasn't real?"

Jack shook his head. "If they overheard that part of our

conversation they didn't say anything to anyone. Trust me, your brothers would've brought it up when they were grilling me. For hours." He smiled with pure male cockiness. "But I didn't break. I just told them to butt the fuck out and let us work it out ourselves."

"Have we worked it out?"

"Yes, except for one thing." Jack curled his hands around her face. "Will you marry me? For real this time?"

"Did you ask my dad?"

"Yep. He grumbled about being the last to know important shit, which strangely enough reminded me of you, but I think he's okay with it now. Because he did give me his blessing."

"Well...seein's we've already had the engagement party, you bought the ring and everyone already thinks we're in *wuv, twue wuv*, I suppose it's inevitable." She gave him a smacking kiss on the mouth. "Plus, I love you like crazy, Jack-ass."

"Same goes, buttercup, same goes."

Epilogue

Two months later...

Keely suspected she resembled a ghost more than a bride.

She leaned closer to the lighted mirror and scrutinized her reflection. Scratch that. Maybe the *Bride of Frankenstein*. Yikes. Why had they gobbed so much gunk on her face? Especially when her face was completely covered? She batted at the frothy white veil, knocking the headpiece off-center. Again.

"Stop fidgeting," Chassie hissed, smoothing the gossamer fabric back in place.

The door to the bedroom opened. Women scurried forward in case Jack might try to sneak in.

Keely smiled, hoping he *would* attempt to infiltrate the inner sanctum and cart her off.

But a collective sigh echoed as the minister waltzed in and asked, "Has anyone seen the ring bearer?"

"Which one? I have six." Keely had drafted her oldest nephews for the wedding party. They'd drawn straws to decide which unlucky sucker got stuck carrying the "girly" satin pillow.

"I'm looking for the ring bearer with the rings."

"Gib is missing?"

No one answered. Maybe because no one had heard her over the din of giggles and gossip?

Seizing the opportunity to escape, Keely muttered, "I'll find him." She tried to stand; her butt was firmly shoved back down on the tufted velvet chair.

"Nice try, missy, but park it. You're not going anywhere." India jammed more pearl-coated bobby pins in her hair.

"Ouch!"

"Oh, don't be such a baby. You didn't whine this much when I tattooed you."

"Stop gnawing on your lip too, or you'll smudge your gloss," Domini added as she shifted Markus on her hip, directing his grabbing hands away from the veil.

Just wait until the minister pronounced them husband and wife. Keely planned to smear the carefully applied gloss all over Jack's lips. Then she'd rip off the ridiculous headpiece and stomp on it with the equally ridiculous pointy-toed satin shoes.

Temper temper.

Love aside, why did people go through this rigmarole? No wonder couples eloped. She and Jack could've skipped this part and gotten straight to the good stuff: the island honeymoon.

She blew out a frustrated breath, twisting away from the array of beauty products, which ensured she didn't look one bit like herself on the biggest day of her life. Would Jack even recognize her?

A tiny hand tugged on her sequined sleeve. Keely sucked in a surprised breath at the unyielding fit of the wedding gown when she bent at the waist. "Yes, Eliza," she said, squinting at the beribboned flower girl through the gauzy veil.

"I know where Gib is."

At least someone was worried about the missing ring bearer. "Where?"

"He threw up in the bathroom 'bout five minutes ago."

"What?" Panic escalated along with her voice. "Is he sick?"

A sneer wrinkled Eliza's pert nose. "He's not sick, he's stupid. Kyler dared him to drink—" Her eyes widened, she clapped a gloved hand over her mouth and started to back away.

But not fast enough. Keely grabbed her spindly arm. "What did Gib drink?"

"Pickle juice," Eliza blurted.

"Pickle juice?" Keely repeated. "Where on earth did he find pickle juice?"

Eliza debated, then said in a rush, "There's empty pickle jars all over Auntie Caro's kitchen."

"And he couldn't find Kool-Aid or something better?"

"No." Eliza leaned closer and confided, "Know those hot kind with red peppers in the bottom?" Keely nodded warily.

"Kyler bet Gib a dollar he wouldn't take a drink." A grudging sort of admiration lit Eliza's blue eyes. "But Gib showed him. He drank the *whole* jar."

"No wonder he's barfing," she muttered. "Where is he now?"

Eliza shrugged her delicate shoulders, staring with acute fascination at the grass-stained toes of her white Mary Janes. One gloved finger twisted a springy ribbon on her flower basket.

Keely hated to play hardball with Kade and Skylar's stubborn daughter, but if Gib was lost, then so were the wedding rings. She whispered, "You'd better spill it, Eliza Belle, or I'll tell your mom about the plate of mints you stashed in your backpack."

Without hesitation, Eliza rattled off, "He's hiding in the empty closet at the end of the hallway with Thane, Braxton, Kyler, Hayden and Anton."

"Better that than knocking back shots of Wild Turkey in the gazebo with the other groomsmen," Ramona added with a snort.

"What!"

"Ramona!" Jessie McKay gasped.

"I'm not supposed to tell her that her brothers and male cousins are giving Jack very detailed advice on how to handle her?"

India, Jessie and Domini vehemently shook their heads no.

"I'll kick Trevor and Edgard's asses if they're in on it," Chassie assured her.

"Same goes for Carter," Macie promised.

Why had Jack needed a stiff drink? *He* wasn't stuck wearing a feather duster on his head.

"I'll find my oldest wayward son," Channing said, shifting Austin on her hip away from her pregnant belly. "Don't worry. Pickle juice is nothing. Gib has an iron gut." She offered Keely no such promise about Jack's condition. "I hope you and Jack have all girls." She sighed and kissed Austin's dark head. "They've gotta be easier than McKay boys."

"You forgetting Keely took hellraising to a whole 'nother level?" her Aunt Kimi prompted. "What goes around comes around. She's gonna get stuck with a quartet of girls exactly like her, you mark my words."

"Listen to her, Keely," Skylar said. "She predicted Kade and

I would have twin girls."

Her family was already discussing when they were going to have kids? She and Jack weren't even married yet.

Keely froze.

Married. Oh. My. God. She and Jack were really getting married. Today. In front of all these people. In—she gaped at the clock—eighteen minutes.

Keely's stomach pitched like a horse trailer caught in a prairie windstorm. The room was too hot. With too many people. Why did she have so damn many brothers? And cousins? And why had her relatives populated the place with all these noisy kids?

Sweat broke out on her brow. Her skin dried and drew tight over her bones. Muted laughter, the rustle of silky fabrics, the click of high heels on the tile; it was all too loud. The heavy scent of hairspray, perfume and flowers burned her nostrils, stuck in her throat and made it impossible for her to breathe.

Why couldn't anyone see she was suffocating?

Heedless of wrinkling the satin and lace, Keely yanked up the dress, dropped her head between her knees and sucked air deep into her lungs.

The room became momentarily still, then the crowd circled her. Gentle female hands patted her back. The feminine buzzing began again, siphoning every available ounce of oxygen and sanity.

A voice boomed, "Oh for heaven's sake, give her some air." A round of annoyed female whispers and grumbles gave away to eerie quiet as her well-meaning relatives were shooed out.

In a soothing tone, AJ said, "Keely?"

Keely lifted her head. Her BFF-sister-in-law's pregnant belly protruded in her lavender bridesmaid's gown. "You look like an anemic grape."

"Good thing Cord likes grapes. But this isn't about me and my latest McKay baby bump, so cut the crap. Is your dress too tight?"

Maybe the bodice was cutting into her oxygen supply and making her lightheaded. And paranoid.

Nope. The minute Keely sat upright, panic set in again. "I can't breathe. I can't think. I can't do this." She grabbed AJ's hand, pleading, "You've got to get me out of here."

"Where would you go?" AJ asked calmly.

"I don't know!" Keely leapt to her feet and began to pace in the large, sunny bedroom. "None of this is real. These aren't my real clothes. This isn't my real face." Her voice caught on a sob. "What is Jack gonna think when he sees me?"

AJ clasped Keely's hands. "It is you. Maybe a fancier you, but it's still Keely McKay under the layers of chiffon and silk. Jack will think the same thing he always has—you are the woman he loves and wants to spend the rest of his life with."

"Somewhere deep inside I think I know that, I just…" Keely trailed off, her heart threatening to beat right out of the lace-trimmed sweetheart neckline.

She loved Jack. Jack loved her. Simple. When had their simple declaration of that love turned into a three-ring circus, complete with clown makeup and funny shoes?

"We should've made a break for Vegas like you and Cord did."

"It would've hurt your dad not to walk his baby girl down the aisle, K."

"Part of me understands. But I still need…"

"I know exactly what you need, sweetie, and I'll be right back with it." AJ disappeared.

Keely hoped AJ planned to dose her with Wild Turkey. After several minutes passed by, Keely realized she'd been left alone for the first time in hours. She didn't waste time contemplating her options. She needed fresh air. She cracked open the door and peeked out.

The coast was clear.

Grabbing the billowy folds of her ivory wedding dress, she took off, the cushiony carpet muffling her footfalls. At the end of the long hallway stood a narrow set of stairs, which led to the first floor and her temporary freedom.

Hallelujah.

Keely's hand had just connected with the antique brass handrail, when a deep voice behind her inquired, "Going somewhere?"

Jack.

Everything inside her jumped for joy.

Yet, Jack didn't sound particularly overjoyed to see her. In fact, he sounded downright furious.

"Answer me."

She stammered, "Uh, don't you know it's bad luck for the groom to see the bride before the wedding?"

"Yeah? It's even worse luck for the groom to see his bride making a break for it ten minutes before the ceremony is set to start."

Jack was close enough she felt his hot breath teasing her sweat-dampened neck.

"Keely, are you having second thoughts?"

"No!" She spun around so fast the veil whapped him in the face. "I just—" The words died in her mouth at his stunned expression.

Jack stayed absolutely still. Then he smiled the wicked smile that was hers alone. He captured her hand, bringing it to his lips for a gentle kiss. "You'd think by now I'd be used to the way you take my breath away every damn time I look at you, cowgirl."

Speechless didn't begin to explain Keely's emotions. Before she could articulate a single one, voices echoed up the main staircase at the other end of the hall.

Jack read her panic and pulled her into the first available room—which wasn't a room at all, but the closet Gib and his cohorts had hidden in. As soon as they were inside, Jack tugged at the string attached to the light bulb, plunging the space into darkness.

He enfolded her against his hard body and Keely sank into him, inhaling his familiar scent, subtle expensive cologne and warm man. Her man. She sighed. Her heart rate returned to normal. Everything returned to normal.

"Better?" he murmured.

"You have no idea. How did you know?"

"AJ tracked me down. But truthfully, I'd been lurking in the hallway hoping to see you."

"You weren't slamming shots of Wild Turkey with the groomsmen?"

"You heard about that?"

"Did you need liquid courage at the thought of tying yourself to me for the rest of your life, GQ?"

"No, buttercup, I had one to be polite and to keep me from ripping the damn hinges off the door to get to you."

To get to you. "You never follow the rules. Why didn't you just barge in?"

"With all those pregnant women throwing nasty looks my way?" Jack shuddered. "No thanks. Besides, your damn sisters-in-law and assorted crazy female relatives locked the damn door."

"Why?"

"'Tradition' they said."

"I wouldn't think you'd care what they said."

"I didn't. But my immediate response isn't worth repeating." His large hands tightened around her waist. "I was going crazy without you." Jack's warm lips tracked kisses across the slope of her shoulder. "I hardly slept last night, the bed seemed so big and lonely without my bed hog."

Amazing, how quickly they'd melded into one unit. Sharing living space and office space. Sharing their lives, their hopes, their dreams, their fears, their love. The only thing left was to make it legal. Seeing Jack, touching him, knowing he was as anxious as she, set her world right again.

She twisted in his arms to face him. "Just so you know, I wasn't running from you just now, I was running *to* you." The veil fluttered with her every exhalation. "Here it is, my wedding day and I feel like I'm playing dress up." Her voice dropped even lower. "I'm afraid I'll wake up and find it's not real."

Jack's hands slipped up under the veil and tenderly cupped her face. "I'm very real. It is real this time."

"Prove it. Kiss me. Please, Jack."

"No." His hands dropped to her shoulders. "Not until my ring is on your finger and I know you're mine forever."

Forever. She liked the sound of that.

He paused. "Besides, I have no idea what I'm supposed to do with the veil."

Keely laughed at his wariness. "You think the veil is bad, wait until you get a load of the hundred or so buttons on the back of this dress."

Jack groaned.

"But what I've got on underneath will be worth learning how to work a buttonhook."

He actually whimpered.

"Everyone is probably wondering where we are."

"I know. I'd say let them wonder, but I'm ready to do this thing."

"Me too."

Keely stepped out of the comfort of his arms, giddy in the knowledge in a few short minutes, she could take comfort in those strong arms every day for the rest of their lives.

"I love you, Jack. I'll meet you downstairs."

"I'll be waiting."

About the Author

To learn more about *Lorelei James*, please visit *www.loreleijames.com* for a taste of weekly Man Candy, a look at Western Wednesday, a Friday Funny, as well as excerpts, contests and other information. Send an email to lorelei@loreleijames.com or join her Yahoo! group to join in the fun with other wild, crazy and anything goes James Gang members (this group is not for the faint of heart, be warned!) and readers as well as Lorelei who pops in all the time: http://groups.yahoo.com/group/LoreleiJamesGang

When country boys meet a city girl, everyone is in for a wild ride.

Unridden
© *2009 Cat Johnson*
Studs in Spurs, Book 1

Slade Bower and Mustang Jackson are living the high life on the professional bull-riding circuit. The prize money is big, the bulls are rank and the women are willing. But something is missing.

For Slade, waking up in a different city with a different woman each morning is holding less and less appeal. Even Mustang's creative attempts to shake things up don't help. Then along comes a big-city author who's like nothing they've ever encountered. Something about her makes Slade sit up and take notice—and Mustang is always up for anything.

Romance writer Jenna Block has a problem—her agent thinks a cowboy book will jump-start her career. A born New Yorker, Jenna doesn't do cowboys, not on paper, and definitely not in real life. Luckily for her there are two cowboys ready, willing and able to take her out of her comfort zone in every way that counts...and some ways she hadn't counted on.

Warning: This story contains two hot cowboys, one very lucky woman, hot ménage sex and lots of bull.

Available now in ebook and print from Samhain Publishing.

Enjoy the following excerpt from Unridden...

Evaluating that night's possibilities, Mustang's gaze swept the females in the stands until it landed on one woman who made him stop dead in his perusal.

He jumped up onto the rail of the chute and hissed to Slade, "Second section, fourth row back, reddish-brown hair pulled back in a ponytail, black turtleneck."

In the process of tugging the rope that stretched beneath the bull and winding it once around his gloved hand, Slade frowned up at Mustang from the animal's back. "I'm in the middle of taking my wrap and you're pointing out some woman to me? In a turtleneck, no less? Since when are you interested in women whose chest isn't hanging out?"

"This woman's different, Slade. I can tell." The bull hopped once in the chute and Mustang quickly reached over and grabbed the back of Slade's vest, steadying him on the animal's back.

"Dammit, Mustang, quit distracting me." Slade settled himself again and then gave a nod. The cowboy on the ground swung the gate open to release both bull and rider into the arena.

"Talk to you more when you get off," Mustang called after him.

As Mustang watched his friend disappear into a cloud of dust, Chase Reese hopped up onto the rail next to him.

"Slade's amazing. It's like he's glued onto that bull. I wish I could do that. I went two for ten last series." The kid had been favored for Rookie of the Year until he'd hit a dry streak.

"That's because you look at the ground." Mustang followed Slade's progress while the bull spun around to the left without deviation, from one end of the arena to the other.

The eight-second buzzer sounded and Slade released the rope wrapped around his hand. He jumped off the bull, hit the ground with his shoulder and then rolled to avoid a hoof to the ribcage before the bullfighters redirected the charging animal away from him.

"I do what?"

Seeing his friend was safe, Mustang took the time to answer Chase's question. Damn, had he ever been this young? The kid probably didn't even have to shave once a week.

"You're looking down at the ground while you ride. If you look there, you're gonna end up there. It's a fact. Now, 'scuse me. I gotta talk to Slade."

Leaving the kid with an amazed expression on his face, as if he'd just been handed all the secrets of the universe, Mustang jumped down to go meet Slade behind the chutes.

"Hey, man. Good ride. That bull was one hell of a spinner, huh?"

Slade laughed and pulled the tape from around his wrist where it held the glove on his riding hand firmly in place. "Hell yeah. They weren't kidding when they said he came out of the spinner pen. Felt like I was on a ride at the county fair."

"Now we're both done riding for the night, we have to formulate a plan," Mustang began.

"For what?"

"To reel in that woman I told you about."

Slade dismissed that with a wave of his hand. "Just do whatever it is you usually do."

Mustang shook his head. "The usual isn't going to work on her."

Slade sighed. "Where did you say she's sitting?"

Ha! Slade had given in and was actually showing some interest. Smiling, Mustang narrowed his eyes and easily found her again in the stands. She was writing feverishly while trying to watch the rider in the arena at the same time. He tilted his head toward the section directly behind them. "Far end of the fourth row."

"What the hell is she doing?" Slade frowned as he watched her.

"Hell if I know, but I think she's taking notes. See what I mean? This woman is special. She isn't going to just fall into our bed."

Her hair wasn't huge, she wasn't made up like a showgirl and her clothes showed curves but not an inch of skin. She was different, which was what had drawn Mustang's attention to her in the first place.

Since Slade had been in his strange funk lately, Mustang

figured he'd try something unusual. Hell, even the two eighteen-year-olds going at each other in front of them barely got a rise out of his friend. Mustang was running out of ideas, but this woman... She was pretty much the opposite of their usual conquest and that might be exactly what they needed. It was worth a shot to cheer Slade up. Besides, never opposed to trying new things, he could use a bit of a change himself once in a while.

"Mustang, she's probably a damned reporter. That's all I need, to be featured in some exposé. I can see the headline now. 'Slade Bower, third-ranking bull rider in the world, propositions reporter for a threesome with former Rookie of the Year, Mustang Jackson.' That will go over real well with the fans in the Bible Belt." Slade scowled at Mustang. "Pick someone else. How about the one bouncing up and down over there? She's about to pop right out of that top. You might want to keep an eye on her."

Mustang glanced her way. "Yeah, I saw her already. I'm set on the other one."

Laughing, Slade shook his head. "Good luck 'cause I can just about see the stick up her ass from here. That one is wound tight, but you go for it, man, and I'll enjoy watching you get shot down."

Mustang raised a brow. "Is that a challenge, my friend?"

Slade let out a short laugh. "No, it's the truth."

"Well, I think you're wrong. Sometimes it's the quiet ones that are the wildest once you get them naked."

"And you think you can get her naked?"

Mustang nodded. "Yup. I do."

"Well, I'd like to see that."

Grinning, Mustang slapped his friend on the back. "Don't worry. You'll be there too."

Slade shook his head. "*Maybe*, and that is a big maybe, you might be able to get that woman naked, with enough alcohol and bull, but no frigging way will she agree to both of us. Never in a million years."

Feeling cocky and never one to resist a challenge, Mustang crossed his arms and dug in his heels. "We'll see. You willing to make a bet on that?"

GREAT CHEAP FUN

Discover eBooks!

THE FASTEST WAY TO GET THE HOTTEST NAMES

Get your favorite authors on your favorite reader, long before they're out in print! Ebooks from Samhain go wherever you go, and work with whatever you carry—Palm, PDF, Mobi, and more.

SAMHAIN PUBLISHING LTD